THE UNQUIET DEAD

This is a work of fiction. Names, characters, organisations, places, events and incidents are either products of the author's imagination or are used fictitiously. Any resemblance to actual persons, living or dead, or actual events is purely coincidental.

Copyright © 2025 James Harper

All rights reserved

No part of this publication may be reproduced, or stored in a retrieval system, or transmitted, in any form or by any means, electronic, mechanical, photocopying, recording, or otherwise, without express written permission of the publisher.

www.jamesharperbooks.com

ISBN: 9798313920474

PROLOGUE

6 MONTHS AGO

HARRY CALLAGHAN DIDN'T GIVE A DAMN ABOUT WHAT PEOPLE thought of him. They saw a large, middle-aged man running to fat, his body defaced by faded tattoos. Shaved head and mean piggy eyes you didn't want to catch in a bar. They saw the *Dirty Harry* sun strip on the windscreen of his skip loader lorry and laughed to themselves—*who are you kidding?*

Funny how nobody laughed at him to his face. Or if they did, they only ever did it the once.

Harry loved his job. Sitting up high in the lorry's cab, other road users giving him the respect he deserved. What's the point of driving a big vehicle if you can't intimidate hoity-toity pricks in their over-priced BMWs and Bentleys?

It wasn't only the driving Harry enjoyed. It was what people threw in the skips. It was a disgrace. Things that ought to go to a good home, except young people these days don't want hand-me-downs or anything second-hand. *No thank you!* They want it new. And they want it now.

No wonder the country was in such a mess.

Their loss was Harry's gain. Selling the gear he rescued from the skips had provided a nice little earner over the years, paid for many a happy holiday in Benidorm. Him and Babs like a pair of sunburned beached whales swilling cheap Spanish lager on the beach from ten in the morning until six at night.

If he hadn't been so devoted to Babs, there would've been other perks to the job. *Yessir.* Collecting an overflowing skip in the early morning, the lady of the household still in her dressing gown or nightie, overflowing from it herself.

Feel free to help yourself to anything you like, driver.

Happy days.

Despite what sanctimonious, lah-di-dah pricks thought, Harry prided himself on being a responsible driver. He didn't drink on the job. He didn't do drugs. And he didn't drive too many hours without a break. The people who thought he was just another football hooligan with a shaved head and *HATE* tattooed on his knuckles could stick that in their judgemental pipes and smoke it.

He had a full load on the back today. God help any dickhead in a fancy motor who pulled out in front of him thinking Harry could stop on a sixpence.

He scanned the pavements on either side of the road as he drove, always alert for signs of danger, the ever-changing surge and swell of pedestrians registering on a subconscious level. He didn't care if he pranged an impatient prick's car, but if he hit a kid who ran out into the road, he'd never forgive himself.

And the street was busy today.

Movement caught his eye on his left, his pulse quickening. A young mother with a pushchair and another toddler on reins. Looking like she wasn't totally in control of them.

Then two men in a hurry, moving fast as they threaded through the heaving throng.

The one in front jostled the young mother, earned himself a rigid middle finger as he pushed rudely past. The toddler on the reins did the same, laughing as he mimicked his sour-faced mother.

Nice, Harry thought, *teach your kids early.*

The two men were right on the edge of the kerb now. Dangerously close. The man behind more impatient than the one in front. Glancing over his shoulder. Making sure the road was clear before stepping out into the gutter to get past.

Not in front of me, you don't, matey—

A car horn blared. An angry warning from the other side of the road. Harry's head snapped to the right, pulse rocketing. Worried he'd drifted into the oncoming lane as he concentrated on the pedestrians.

He hadn't.

It was nothing. Some idiot too eager to lean on the horn at the slightest provocation.

Harry relaxed.

Looked front—

Jesus Christ!

A man was in the road immediately in front of him. Weaving unsteadily as if he'd stumbled off the kerb, arms flailing uselessly. Eyes wide with terror, mouth open in silent denial. A heartbeat away from Harry's grille turning him from a pedestrian into a statistic.

Into roadkill.

Harry stamped on the brakes. Like he wanted to buckle the pedal, put his foot through the floor. Already feeling the sickening thud of soft flesh and brittle bone meeting hard unyielding metal reverberating in the pit of his stomach, a desperate futile prayer on his lips to a God who'd written him off long ago ...

1

Present day

Detective Constable Lisa Jardine won the toss.

'It's not going to sound right with your stupid bloody accent,' her partner, DC Craig Gulliver, muttered to himself, trailing behind her as she bounded away towards their boss' office.

DI Max Angel looked up at them expectantly when they appeared in the doorway to the broom cupboard-sized office he shared with DS Cat Kincade.

'What is it, Lisa?'

'I was wondering if you feel lucky, sir?' She paused long enough for Angel's brow to crease in confusion. 'Well, do ya, punk?'

Kincade snorted with laughter, an explosive bark she immediately stifled as Angel stared back at Jardine, momentarily at a loss for words. He responded in a similar vein, even if he didn't have the first idea what she was talking about.

'Clint Eastwood with a Geordie accent doesn't really do it for me, Lisa.'

'Told you so,' Gulliver said under his breath from behind her.

Jardine, whose hearing was every bit as sharp as her tongue, hooked her thumb in his direction as he smirked to himself.

'It sounds even worse with a posh Southern twat accent, sir.'

Angel nodded. Not so much agreement, but approval at the return to a more orthodox way of addressing him.

'Is there a reason why anyone should be saying it in any accent at all?' Kincade asked, not unreasonably.

'We've got a man shot to death in the New Forest, Sarge,' Jardine replied, the grin growing wider. 'His name's—'

'Dirty Harry?'

'Close. Harry Callaghan.'

'With a *G*,' Gulliver added.

Jardine gave him a look like she was partnered with an idiot.

'That'd make it *Gallahan*.' The word *dummy* hanging unspoken in the air.

Gulliver returned the look, a sorry head shake accompanying it.

'I meant in the middle.'

Angel was already on his feet, shrugging his coat on, Kincade not far behind. Everybody silent as they trooped out. To the untrained eye, a professional team with their minds already focussed, intent on the task ahead. Anyone who'd worked with them before knew better. Four people wracking their brains to work another classic Dirty Harry line into the conversation.

Angel wasn't sorry when nobody managed it, but he did have a question for Gulliver and Jardine.

'I don't suppose he was shot with a .44 Magnum, was he?'

It took them half an hour to get to the Shephards Gutter car park on Furzley Lane, half a mile west of the village of

Bramshaw on the northern edge of the New Forest National Park.

A uniformed officer on the car park entrance directed them to park on the narrow lane itself, as were the crime scene investigators' vehicles. The first responder's liveried patrol car was the only vehicle in the small car park itself.

'Doesn't look like Dirty Harry drove here himself,' Kincade said, as they picked their way past the rain-filled pot holes that littered the entrance track curving into the seclusion of the trees.

The victim's unofficial moniker had been set in stone from the moment they left Angel and Kincade's office. It was a given that cheesy, movie-related jokes would be rolled out at every opportunity. It could've been worse—a connection to the movie Clint Eastwood made with the orangutan, perhaps, the name of which Angel could never remember.

He made a pistol of his hand, thumb cocked backwards, index finger pointing down at a forty-five-degree angle, as if at a man kneeling on the ground.

'Driven here and executed.'

'It certainly didn't make Callaghan's day.'

Angel groaned, checked his watch.

'Not long before I'm wishing we hadn't been able to identify him.'

The Crime Scene Manager, Christine Hamill, met them at the far side of the car park next to where the first responder's vehicle was parked. Beyond that was an open expanse of rough grassland surrounded on all sides by trees. A crime scene tent was visible through them, the low rumble of the mobile generator the only sound competing with the birdsong.

'Take a look at this first,' Hamill said, leading them to the other side of the car park where crime-scene tape had been used to cordon off an area underneath a large overhanging oak tree. 'The ground's compacted gravel and dirt. The recent rain softened it sufficiently to leave tyre marks. Thanks to this'—indicating the tree's overhanging branches—'they've been protected to a certain degree and not washed away. It was lucky the first responder parked on the other side, then had the sense to preserve the scene. It's a pity more officers don't engage their brains before stomping all over the place.'

Angel ignored Hamill's barbed remark about careless patrol cops and their big feet, asked the obvious question.

'You found something?'

Hamill pointed at the markers.

'A couple of decent tyre marks. Relatively recent. Good enough to get a match off the Treadmate database. From the size of them, I'd say we're looking at a van or a four-by-four.'

'Four-by-fours go with the territory around here,' Kincade said. 'This car park is probably popular with all the dog walkers who drive them.'

Hamill gave her a look like she didn't appreciate Kincade pissing on her parade.

'Apparently not. The first responder told me this car park never gets particularly busy. There's a hotel a quarter mile that way.' Pointing due north as she said it. 'There are no facilities here. I'm guessing a lot of people park at the hotel, take Rover for a walk, then have a coffee or a beer afterwards, use the toilets.'

'It's what I'd do,' Angel agreed. 'If I had a dog.'

Hamill smiled with him as they headed off across the grass towards the activity in the trees.

'Just so you know, the victim didn't have any ID on him, or a phone.'

'They fingerprinted him?'

'Yeah. I authorised it, given he'd been shot with a handgun.' The smile returned fleetingly. 'Not a .44 Magnum.'

'I was wondering.'

'I didn't think you'd want to wait.'

Angel dipped his head, *you got that right*.

'You obviously got a match.'

'Yeah. He was arrested and charged after a road rage incident about a year ago. Threatened another driver with a wheel wrench. Charges were dropped in the end.'

Nobody thought for a moment the victim of the road rage attack dropped the charges planning to take revenge a year later in a secluded clearing in the New Forest. They would interview him in due course, nonetheless.

As they got closer to the trees it became obvious two crime-scene tents had been erected, the second one further into the trees not visible from the car park.

'Let me guess,' Kincade said. 'He was shot there'—indicating the nearest tent—'staggered away and dropped dead over there.' Now pointing at the furthest tent.

Hamill's residual irritation at Kincade's dismissive remark about the ubiquity of four-by-fours evaporated in the face of Kincade's perceptive observation.

'Close. Piecing it together, it looks as if there was a scuffle as the killer was taking the victim from the car park into the trees . . .'

'If you're about to be executed, you might as well take a chance,' Angel said. 'You've got nothing to lose.'

'Exactly. From the disturbance to the ground and surrounding vegetation, it looks like the victim knocked the killer to the ground, then set off running that way.' Pointing towards the second tent. 'The killer shot at him as he was running away and brought him down. He then went and finished him off where he fell.'

'Worth a try,' Kincade said, sounding like she'd lost twenty pounds betting on a horse with the same name as one of her girls. 'Shame Callaghan didn't live up to his namesake, or we'd have a dead wannabe assassin instead.'

Hamill smiled broadly. If Kincade thought it was at her remark, she was very wrong. Hamill was too busy concentrating on Angel as they stopped outside the first tent, the silhouettes of the SOCOs working inside backlit by the arc lamps.

'You used to be a priest, didn't you?' Making the word *priest* sound like *alien*.

Angel hadn't worked with Hamill before, but he wasn't surprised his unorthodox route into the Hampshire Constabulary via the Catholic church was the subject of discussion and gossip.

'I was, for my sins.'

'He was an Army padre in Iraq and Afghanistan, as well,' Kincade cut in, worried Hamill might get the wrong impression. Think of Angel as a mild-mannered parish priest who'd dealt with nothing more serious than absolving parishioners for impure thoughts about their neighbour's wife.

'I heard that, too,' Hamill said. 'It seems God doesn't care you gave him the heave-ho. He still loves you and wants you to be happy.'

Angel had heard it so many times, he knew what Hamill was saying.

'What did you find? Cartridge cases?'

'Yep. Two of them right here. Nine millimetre.' She pointed at the other tent. 'But nothing over there by the body.'

She paused. A challenge to Angel or Kincade to connect the dots. Kincade took her up on it.

'The killer is on his arse on the ground here. He fires twice at the fleeing man. Hits him, brings him down. Gets up and goes over to him, finishes him off. Picks up his brass because it's right there in front of him. But he hasn't got time to come back here and search for the rest of it. He's fired at least three shots—'

'Five in all.'

'—and wants to get the hell out of here. The plan's already gone tits-up when the victim nearly got away. Unless he's a stone-cold killer, he'll be panicking.'

Hamill nodded her approval.

'That's what it looks like to me.'

Angel agreed, voiced the obvious conclusion.

'It suggests a single killer. If there'd been two of them, Callaghan would never have got as far as he did.'

Hamill was shaking her head before the words were out of Angel's mouth. Not disagreement, but managing their expectations.

'Don't hold your breath thinking we'll be able to confirm it from that mess.' She gave an irritated flick of her hand towards the ground at their feet, then took in the whole of the path extending towards the second tent. Hoof prints were evident going in every direction, as well as multiple footprints. 'The hotel I mentioned keeps horses for guests' use. The body was discovered by a couple of residents out for an early-morning ride. One of the horses got a bit skittish at the smell of blood.' She shrugged. *It is what it is.* 'If that's all, I'll leave you to have a word with the forensic pathologist.'

They headed towards the second tent where the morning's main attraction awaited them, keeping to the common approach path set up between the two tents despite Hamill's remarks suggesting there was nothing useful that needed to be protected from contamination.

A white-suited backside greeted them as they stood in the doorway to the second tent.

Angel said, 'Is that you, Isabel?'

Don't pretend you don't recognise that view, Kincade thought, convinced Angel and the pathologist, Isabel Durand, enjoyed a regular game of doctors and nurses.

Durand straightened up, pushed her hands into her lower back as she arched it, her protective Tyvek suit rustling as she did so.

'I don't know who you were expecting, Padre.' She moved to the side to allow them a better look at what they were dealing with.

Harry Callaghan lay face-down on the ground. A large man running to fat dressed in jeans and a red-and-white-striped Southampton F.C. football shirt, his wrists bound behind his back with heavy-duty cable ties. The way his arms were twisted exaggerated his muscular biceps straining the seams of his T-shirt's arms, but the don't-mess-with-me effect was spoiled by the flabby love handles hanging over his belt. A substantial paunch was pressed into the dirt. Angel wasn't paid to be judgemental, but with hair cropped so short as to be almost shaved and tattoos climbing up his neck from his football shirt's collar, Callaghan looked exactly like the sort of man who would threaten another road user with a wheel wrench.

He didn't look so intimidating now.

A cursory glance coupled with Christine Hamill's account suggested he'd been hit once in the right hip as he fled from his killer, then despatched with three shots to the middle of his back while he lay on the ground. It was likely one or both lungs had been penetrated as well as the heart and coronary arteries, and possibly the aorta, resulting in massive haemorrhage and subsequent death.

Somebody had been very determined he wasn't going to walk out of the forest alive.

With the evidence of his own eyes added to the details provided by Hammill, Angel could've skipped asking for Durand's assessment, concentrated on the all-important time of death. Except it never hurt to get a second or third opinion, especially one as well-informed as Durand's. Nor did he want to upset her.

'Talk me through it, Isabel.'

He listened attentively as Durand gave him chapter and verse on what he could see for himself, interlaced with a lot of medical jargon starting with *pneumo* and *haemo*, before finishing with a caveat-laden conclusion in line with his own. Fatal haemorrhage.

The guy bled out, Kincade thought, as she nodded along.

'What about time of death?' Angel asked, when Durand finally paused for breath.

'He's been out here a couple of days, Padre,' Durand confirmed. 'Rigor mortis has been and gone, and livor mortis is well-established. The body has reached ambient temperature. You'll have to wait for the autopsy for details of insect infestation. And the local foxes must be very well fed. There's minimal evidence of predation.'

Kincade had been studying the ground immediately behind Callaghan's feet as Durand talked.

'It looks as if he was hit and then tried to crawl away.' She put her right hand on her left forearm, arched her palm and extended her fingers, then did it again, arching her palm, extending her fingers, moving up her arm. 'Like a giant caterpillar.'

Nobody needed to state the obvious.

He didn't get far.

'I was about to turn him over,' Durand said, moving further out of the way to allow a pair of crime scene technicians access.

'Anyone would think he'd come straight from watching the match a couple of nights ago,' Angel said under his breath once Callaghan was lying on his back, the front of his body a mess of what had been bright arterial red now turned brown, the grass he'd been lying on similarly stained.

Durand pretended she hadn't heard the cynical reference to football violence, stated the obvious.

'It's fair to say he was killed here.' She indicated Callaghan's left shoulder and knee. 'The dirt and grass staining support your hypothesis, Sergeant. He tried pulling his legs up under him, then pushing his upper body forward.'

Angel hadn't paid much attention to the dirt stains, more concerned with Callaghan's forehead.

'What about the blood on his forehead, Isabel?'

Durand hunkered down, took a closer look.

'It's difficult to say without cleaning him up, but I can't see any cuts—'

'It's the killer's blood,' Kincade interrupted, the same certainty in her voice as when telling her girls it was bedtime. 'Callaghan headbutted him. That's how he got away.'

'*Nearly* got away,' Angel corrected.

They left Durand to it, made their way back towards the car park.

'What are you thinking?' Kincade said, interrupting the contemplative silence between them.

'I normally ask you that.' His tone mildly indignant.

'I know. That's why I got in first.'

'And does that outweigh the benefits of rank? *Sergeant*.'

'Absolutely.'

The brief exchange highlighted the unusual dynamic between them. Until not so long ago she'd held the same rank as him, before being demoted from inspector down to sergeant and subsequently shipped out of the Met and down to the south coast. She'd recently confided in him, telling him her promotion to detective chief inspector had been unofficially confirmed before her meteoric fall from grace and resulting new rank of pariah.

It meant she had as much experience as him, if not more. She hadn't wasted ten years of her life as a priest, after all.

The end result was that addressing him as *sir* and any deferral to him on the basis of rank alone felt like a slavish adherence to an artificial difference between them—although that's all rank is a lot of the time.

He still liked to pull rank if he could get away with it, of course.

On this occasion he chose not to, talking his thoughts out loud.

'It's inconsistent. It looks like a well-planned execution, but somehow Callaghan almost got away. Either the killer's incompetent, or Callaghan was more than the aggressive, gone-to-seed bruiser he appears to be.'

'Or maybe the killer was having second thoughts. He hesitated, and Callaghan made his move. One thing's for sure—'

'The fact that he was killed by someone with access to a nine-millimetre pistol suggests he didn't just get caught screwing a neighbour's wife.'

'Exactly.'

They kicked it back and forth as they walked, no further forward by the time they got back. The uniformed officer on the car park entrance told them the first responder had accompanied the couple who found Callaghan's body to the nearby Bramble Hill Hotel where they'd been staying before their short break took an unexpected and unwelcome turn.

Angel and Kincade drove there now, a matter of minutes.

The short interview provided no new information beyond what the CSM Christine Hamill had told them. The couple—Mr and Mrs Gregory from St Ann's in Nottingham—had gone out for a pre-breakfast ride to leave the hustle and bustle of the real world behind as early-morning sunlight slanting through the trees burned off the last of the dawn mist, transforming the ancient forest into an otherworldly paradise.

Finding Harry Callaghan's corpse in the middle of the path brought them back to earth with a bump neither of them were likely to forget for a long while.

The discovery spooked Mr Gregory's horse, destroying crime scene evidence and the Gregorys' peace of mind at the same time. They'd both left their mobiles in their room as part of their early-morning severance from the real world. Mr Gregory remained with the body while his wife walked the horses back to the hotel, where she called 999.

Crucially, the couple had arrived from Nottingham only the previous evening. They were a hundred and forty miles away when Dirty Harry was shot to death the day before. After the disastrous start to their holiday, they made it clear they'd be on their way home again the minute the interview was concluded.

Angel couldn't blame them.

As for Kincade, she couldn't stop herself from analysing everything she said and did through the overly-critical lens of what her sadly-missed predecessor, DS Stuart Beckford—who'd made a recent return to Angel's life—would have done in her position.

2

'WHAT'S WRONG WITH YOUR VOICE?' THE ARROGANT PRICK ON THE other end of the line said.

Callaghan almost broke my nose, dickhead wasn't the right answer in the circumstances.

'I must be coming down with something.'

The Arrogant Prick made an unintelligible noise in his throat that still managed to convey dismissive contempt. As if he'd been told another fifty thousand ordinary people had died from COVID.

'Everything go okay?'

Lots of things he wanted to say.

Define okay.

If you call a flattened nose okay, yeah.

If leaving half your brass at the scene is okay, yeah.

'Like a dream.'

'Good.'

He pictured the smug satisfaction on the Arrogant Prick's face. A click of his soft, manicured fingers that had never known a day's real work, *et voilà*. The problem had gone away. Time to get back to a glass of *Chateau Up Your Own Arse* in the club's dining room with all the other self-important knobheads.

He promised himself he'd put his fist straight through the middle of his conceited face one day. Before that, there was something he needed to get straight.

'That's the end of it. I'm out.'

If silences can be haughty, that's what came down the line at him. Then the voice of a small man carrying a big stick.

'You're out when I say you're out. And not before.'

The unspoken third sentence throbbed in the ether between them.

If you know what's good for you.

'Are you threatening me?'

Now, a mocking laugh. Confirmation that in life some people fuck up, and others are ready waiting to take advantage of it.

'Not at all. Simply reminding you that you are not in a position of strength.'

He closed his eyes, imagined the Arrogant Prick's nose exploding under his fist, much as his own nose had flattened under Callaghan's forehead in real life.

Something about the way he said nothing must have given him away. The arsehole wasn't as stupid as he first appeared. Now, he imagined eyes narrowed, the voice suspicious.

'Are you sure it all went to plan? I hope you're not lying to me.'

He took a deep breath, compounded the lie.

'I'm not lying.'

'Then why do I sense unease? It's not your conscience trying to make itself heard, is it? I can't believe killing a man in cold blood would make you lose any sleep.'

He couldn't tell the truth. But he had to give the prick something. He was like a dog with a bone.

'Callaghan's got a brother. They're pretty close. I don't know how much he might have told him.'

A triumphant bark hit him in the ear, as if the venal parasite on the other end had just split the atom.

'*Ha!* That's why you want out.' His tone took on a finger-wagging quality. '*Uh-uh*. Not with the job only half done. Keep an eye on him. And if he becomes a problem . . .'

The phone went dead in his ear a moment later. He pocketed it, closed his eyes again. Lost himself in the dream. The Arrogant Prick's nose flattened, blood spurting, teeth flying, a dark piss stain growing rapidly from the crotch of his pin-striped trousers, the sickening stink of human excrement all around.

One day . . .

LIAM CALLAGHAN HAMMERED ON HIS BROTHER'S FRONT DOOR WITH his fist like he was trying to break it down. He pushed past his sister-in-law before the door was all the way open. Stood at the bottom of the stairs glaring accusingly up them. Then started up two at a time.

'I'll kill the stupid bastard if he overslept.'

Barbara closed the front door, pulled a pink fluffy dressing gown that shouldn't be held too close to a naked flame tighter around her. Yelled at Liam charging up the stairs.

'He's not here. I haven't seen him since the day before yesterday.'

Liam stopped, turned to look down on her standing at the bottom of the stairs. Wishing she'd pull the dressing gown even tighter around her. Save him from an eyeful of what he imagined his own wife's breasts looked like by now. Thank God she'd buggered off with a man half her age before gravity took its toll.

'He's not answering his phone,' Barbara whined as Liam

came slowly down, the urgency of a minute ago evaporating. 'I thought he was with you.'

It didn't seem possible looking at her now, but Harry had married Barbara for her looks. It sure as hell hadn't been for her brains.

'Then why didn't you call me?'

Now, Barbara did pull the dressing gown tighter around her. A defensive gesture more than modesty.

'I don't like to bother you. I never know what I might interrupt.'

Liam was well aware that his sister-in-law believed he and her husband still went out on a two-day bender as if they were single, got drunk, then picked up a couple of over-the-hill slappers to take back to a seedy hotel—or even the back of Harry's van—and humped them senseless all night long.

The thought of it made Liam feel ill, as well as questioning Barbara's eyesight and grip on reality. He pushed the distraction aside, concentrated on the current problem.

'I thought it was strange when he didn't answer my text.'

'What text?'

Liam gave her a pitying look. As if she'd asked what a text was.

'To confirm we're still on for today.'

Barbara's hand flew to her mouth. Liam wished it was bigger, so that it covered her whole stupid face.

'I forgot all about that.'

Liam gave her another look.

Why am I not surprised?

'I was too busy worrying about him,' Barbara whined in her defence. 'Have you got any idea where he is?'

Liam shook his head. Trying to think. Wanting to slap her to shut her up.

'Did you report him as missing?'

Now, she gave him a look.

And I'm supposed to be the stupid one?

Liam carried on when Barbara didn't bother putting it into words.

'Good. I need to borrow his van.'

'What for?'

Liam looked at his feet. Prayed for the Good Lord to give him strength. Then spoke as if talking to a puppy.

'Because now I've got to go on my own.'

Promising himself that if she said *go where?* with a stupid simpering look on her face, he'd set the pink fluffy dressing gown on fire.

Seemed she read his mind.

'I'll get the keys.'

He checked his watch as she scuttled away towards the kitchen. Yelled after her.

'Get a move on or I'll miss the ferry.'

'Okay, okay,' drifted back over her shoulder. 'You sure you don't want a cup of tea before you go?'

He didn't need to check his watch again.

No, but I could find the time to murder my sister-in-law.

She was back a moment later, keys in one hand, unlit cigarette in the other. He was only surprised she hadn't produced the packet from down the front of her dressing gown.

Snatching the keys out of her hand, he headed for the door. Stopped again halfway there, a harder edge to his voice.

'If the cops turn up for any reason, don't say anything. Not about me or the van or Harry or anything. Okay?'

She sighed wearily, said something stupid.

'I'm not stupid.'

Sometimes he thought his brother deserved a medal for putting up with her all these years.

3

Angel got a surprise when he walked into the Major Incident Room and saw the incident board.

As he would expect, there were a number of photographs of Harry Callaghan. Harry glaring belligerently at the police photographer when he was arrested following the road rage incident. Harry face-down in the dirt in the New Forest not looking so cocky. And a close-up of his face with the blood on his forehead highlighted. There was also a picture of the recovered 9mm shell casings, as well as an aerial view of the crime scene.

But no picture of Clint Eastwood, with or without his .44 Magnum. No Dirty Harry quotes or anything else to lighten the mood in advance of the long slog that lay ahead.

Angel glanced around the room to see if the usual culprits—Gulliver and Jardine—were absent, then saw the reason for the lack of sanity-preserving humour. Detective Superintendent Marcus Horwood was standing at the back of the room, talking quietly into his mobile phone.

Angel wasn't surprised.

A man taken out to the woods to be executed wasn't

something they dealt with on a daily basis. It would grab the media and public's attention more than a drug dealer shot in a crack den by a rival gang—a situation a lot of right-minded people viewed as a slow, but encouraging start. Horwood would be looking for something from Angel to take to his own superiors. Something to demonstrate that the streets of Southampton weren't about to make a housing project in New Orleans look like a safe place to live.

At least Horwood's presence meant Angel could get started without competing with Gulliver's deeply-resonating voice.

Dearly beloved, we are gathered here today...

'Harry Callaghan with a *G*,' he began. 'Same spelling as James Callaghan, Labour prime minister from nineteen seventy-six to seventy-nine for those of you old enough to remember. Aged forty-nine, lived with his wife, Barbara, in Hazeleigh Avenue in Woolston...'

He took the unusually-subdued room through the details of the time and cause of death, also laying out the scenario put forward by Kincade at the scene—the struggle as Callaghan was led to his death, being shot as he tried to escape, then finished off while he attempted to crawl away.

'Sounds like an execution, Max,' Horwood said, when Angel paused for breath.

'It does, sir.'

Everybody in the room nodded to themselves, as if wishing they'd been the one to make the earth-shattering deduction. *No wonder the Super had got to where he was today.*

'I know it's early days...' Horwood carried on.

What Angel heard: *I'm not going to make any allowances for that.*

'But is there anything you can give me to—'

Speed your own progress up the greasy pole?

'—take to the Assistant Chief Constable?'

Angel beamed at him.

'There is, sir.' He indicated the close-up of Callaghan's face. 'There are no cuts on the victim's forehead. He was shot in the hip and then in the back while he was face-down on the ground. It's unlikely his own blood ended up on his face. We're hoping it belongs to the killer.'

'From the struggle.'

'Exactly sir.' Thinking, *do you want it in shorter words for the ACC?*

Angel bit his tongue. It's always better to give a string of positive replies to multiple questions, rather than volunteer all the good news at once. However much you deliver, there will always be another question of the sort Horwood now asked.

'Anything else?'

'Yes, sir.' He indicated the photograph of the 9mm shell casings. 'Two shell casings were recovered from the scene. We're hoping ballistics will get a match.'

He almost felt guilty for emphasising the upside of the forensic evidence without mentioning his own reservations. Although the shell casings would be compared to others on file to determine whether the gun had been used in other crimes, Angel wasn't hopeful. The same applied to the blood on Callaghan's forehead. He'd bet his pension that the killer had made very sure his DNA wasn't on any database.

Angel waited to see if Horwood would repeat his question —*anything else?*—as did everyone in the room, all anxious for Horwood to leave so they could relax.

'That should keep the ACC happy for now,' Horwood said, after a moment's contemplation. He glanced at DCI Olivia Finch sitting perched on a spare desk at the side of the room, a question on her face as she pointed at the door. He shook his head at her, *not now*, then pulled out his phone and left the room.

'You can give us the bad news now, sir,' came from Gulliver's direction, to much amusement—including Finch.

'There isn't any, Craig.'

Standing beside Gulliver, Jardine put her finger at the side of her nose and extended it, as if her nose was growing, Pinocchio-style.

Angel saw her do it before she dropped her hand, waved it off.

'No bad news, but there is an anomaly. Callaghan was killed the day before yesterday. He's married, but he hasn't been reported as missing. Either his wife thought he was away somewhere and doesn't expect him to call, or she doesn't care.'

'Or she's the sort of person who'd poke their own eyes out with a sharp stick before speaking to us,' came from someone Angel couldn't see.

The comment didn't surprise him. With his shaved head and tattoos, added to the undisguised aggression the mugshot on the incident board demonstrated so well, it was difficult not to be judgemental.

Jardine proved the point a moment later.

'If I was married to someone looking like him, I'd be too drunk from celebrating that he'd gone missing to report it.'

A man's voice cut through the laughter from the women in the room.

'If you were married to him, that would explain why he disappeared.'

Angel waited for the jeers and laughter to die down, then did his own bit to fuel the fire.

'He was arrested last year after a road rage incident. He was driving a skip lorry at the time. He pulled out in front of someone who was forced to do an emergency stop to avoid a collision. The other car overtook him and the driver gave Callaghan the finger as he went past. Then he got caught at a red light. Callaghan jumped down from his cab brandishing a wheel wrench. He pulled the guy out of his car, threw him to the ground and sat on his chest. Threatened to beat the shit out of him with the wheel wrench. A pedestrian took Callaghan's registration and called it in.'

'I bet it didn't go anywhere,' Jardine called out, her voice filled with weary cynicism. 'The other driver dropped the charges.'

Angel pointed at her, *got it in one.*

'Intimidation,' came from somewhere to murmurs of agreement.

'I'd drop the charges if somebody looking like Callaghan turned up on my doorstep,' a uniformed PC called Watson joined in.

Angel patted the air with both hands to quiet the indignant chatter that had sprung up about the way lorry drivers and white-van drivers and dickheads in SUVs behave as if they're the only vehicle on the road.

'We will of course be talking to the other driver, but I feel confident we're not looking at road rage retribution here.'

He was very grateful nobody asked out loud the question that was written all over their faces.

What are we looking at?

Because he wasn't paid to stand at the front and tell the room, *fucked if I know.*

He wrapped it up after that, left Kincade to allocate responsibilities. He hadn't got more than two paces towards the door before Finch was on him. Much to his surprise, she picked up on Jardine's earlier gesture.

'A word, please, Inspector Pinocchio.'

'I don't know what you mean, ma'am.'

She gave him a look he knew well—he was not to be an arse his whole life.

'It's all very well giving Horwood the impression you'll have it wrapped up by lunchtime in order to get him out of the room, but I know you, Padre. What is it about the blood on Callaghan's forehead and the shell casings that isn't good enough for you?'

'You're right, you *do* know me.'

She made a rolling gesture with her hand.

'And I'm waiting for you to tell me exactly how I'm right.'

'It's just a feeling . . .'

'In your water?'

'Exactly, ma'am.'

She glowered at him for the repeated use of *ma'am*.

'You've got exactly two seconds to spit it out before you have a different kind of feeling very close to where your water comes from.'

Put like that, Angel could hardly refuse.

'I don't think we'll get a match to the gun or the DNA.'

'You want to talk me through those pessimistic opinions one by one?'

'I think we're dealing with a professional. He drove Callaghan out to the woods to kill him. And when Callaghan knocked him down and ran away, he brought him down with a single shot, then picked himself up and casually—'

'Why casually?'

He opened his hands wide, the gesture reflecting the hazy nature of his thoughts.

'It's the picture I've got in my mind. He strolls over and shoots Callaghan three times in the back as he's crawling away. Callaghan's begging for his life. This guy doesn't care.' Angel slapped his fist into his open palm three times. '*Bang! Bang! Bang!* Then he picks up his brass. The failure to pick up the first two shell casings isn't indicative of a stupid or careless man. It's the opposite. In a perfect world, he'd pick it all up. Except things have already started to unravel. He leaves it, comfortable in the knowledge that he's never left any behind before so it won't help us. And having left casings behind for the first time, it's likely the gun's already in the sea by now.'

She leaned away, as if to get a better look at this perceptive but pessimistic man in front of her.

'That's a lot to deduce from only picking up half his brass.'

He shrugged.

'You asked.'

'I can see why you didn't want to explain all that to the Super. Or the team. What about the blood?'

'Nothing specific. But if he's a professional, he'll have made sure his DNA isn't on file anywhere.'

She shook her head, disappointed at his glass-half-empty attitude.

'At least I know who not to come to when I want somebody to give a motivational pep talk.'

The comment had the feeling of a light-hearted parting remark. Recognition of a brick wall she wasn't about to bang her head against. Angel relaxed. Then Finch cocked her head at him, and he knew the game had changed. They'd both been right earlier—she knew him.

'It's not like you to be so negative, Padre. There's something on your mind.' She paused, scrutinised him even more closely when he didn't volunteer anything. 'It's not your dad, is it?'

He was tempted to tell her to ask Kincade for the latest on that front. She lived with him, after all.

'No, nothing like that.' He hesitated, then came out with it, feeling like a fourteen-year-old schoolboy admitting to smoking behind the bicycle sheds. 'Stuart Beckford got in touch recently.'

Finch gawped at him as if he'd said his dead wife and not their former colleague, currently on long-term sick leave. She glanced around the busy incident room, curled her index finger at him as she headed purposefully towards the door.

'This is not the place for this conversation.'

Nowhere was, as far as Angel was concerned, already regretting telling her. He trailed behind her, nonetheless, feeling like that same schoolboy being led to the headmaster's study for six of the best.

ANGEL AND FINCH HAD WALKED AS THEY TALKED. A SLOW, meandering drift towards the door through the activity around them before his revelation lit a fire under her. True to the way in which the world works, they'd been within earshot of Kincade when Angel dropped the name *Stuart Beckford*. The timing was perfect. Kincade caught the name only, not the context.

She stiffened, a flood of paranoia coursing through her, a single question consuming her.

Why was he telling Finch about Beckford?

She'd been present when Angel and Beckford met for the first time since his wife's funeral. The occasion had been another funeral—that of an ex-Parachute Regiment veteran who'd committed suicide in the course of their last major investigation, and for which Angel held himself partially to blame.

They'd been making their way back from the graveside to where their cars were parked, her arm linked through his as they talked. They'd discussed Beckford briefly. She'd been preoccupied looking at a different type of Angel—a stone, winged variety guarding one of the old graves—when she'd felt him stiffen beside her, his stride faltering. Looking up, she'd seen a man lounging against his car waiting for them. Angel's words were as fresh now as they'd been alarming then.

Speak of the devil and he shall appear, he'd said quietly. *That's Stuart there, waiting for us.*

Now, as then, a chill settled in her stomach. She'd stopped

walking, her arm still through his, forcing him to do the same as Beckford watched them approach.

'You talk to him on your own.'

'He'll want to meet you.'

'He doesn't know who I am.'

He'd given her an incredulous look. That she should be so naive as to think people didn't talk, that Beckford wouldn't already know exactly who she was.

'It's going to be awkward enough between you, as it is,' she'd said. 'You don't need to be saying, and this is Cat Kincade, your stand-in replacement who's shit-scared of you deciding you're ready to come back to work and want your old job back.'

'I wouldn't say all that.'

'You wouldn't need to. It'd be written all over my face. And Beckford would feel even more awkward. Or he might say, pleased to meet you, Cat, make sure you've got your shit off *my* desk by tea time. Either way, it's awkward and embarrassing all round, so let's give it a miss.'

Fate had stuck its oar in at that point. Angel's father had joined them. Having been a warrant officer in the Parachute Regiment himself, he'd insisted on attending the funeral even though he'd never met the deceased.

'Isn't that Stuart Beckford?'

Kincade hadn't missed the pleasure the recognition put on his face. It had increased her resolve. She wasn't going to stand around like a spare prick at a wedding while the three of them had a tearful reunion, *we should never have left it so long* and all that bollocks that was perfectly fine if you were part of it, but excruciating if you were an outsider. And that's what she was. An outsider. Looking in.

Carl Angel had set off towards Beckford before Angel had a chance to confirm it.

'It's not the right time,' she'd said to Angel as he flicked his head, *c'mon let's get it over with* in the direction of Beckford and Carl now shaking hands like long-lost friends.

She'd shaken her head, walked off in the opposite direction. Let them think she was an anti-social, miserable curmudgeon, she didn't care.

Except she did.

And now, Finch and Angel were talking about Beckford right here in the incident room.

She might as well go straight to the office she shared with Angel and clear her desk.

'Help yourself,' Finch said, after Angel had already poured himself a cup of proper coffee from the private machine she kept in her office. Then, when he leaned against the wall, sipping it, 'Aren't you going to pour me one?'

He went back to the machine, got a curt nod—*I should think so, too*—when he put a cup down in front of her.

'What's this about Beckford?' she said.

'I left a message on his answering machine—'

'About bloody time.'

'—and he turned up at Amos Church's funeral.'

She sipped thoughtfully at her coffee as he took her through what had happened at the cemetery, then interrupted before he finished.

'Kincade didn't want to meet him?'

'Not in those circumstances.'

'I suppose she's worried about her position here if he wants his job back?'

'I would be too.'

He raised an eyebrow at her. An invitation for her to shed light on matters above his pay grade.

'We'll cross that bridge when we come to it,' she said, her

tone making it clear the subject was closed. 'So? What about you and Beckford?'

'Lots of tears, that sort of thing. Hugging. You know what it's like.'

'I know what it's like for normal people. The day I see you hug another man, I'll . . . I don't know what I'll do. As for tearful —' She suddenly realised he'd deflected her question. 'You didn't say what happened between you and Beckford.'

'We've arranged to go for a beer.'

She rolled her eyes heavenwards at the predictability of it, weary resignation in her voice.

'A man's answer to all of life's problems.'

'Certainly most of them, ma'am.'

'I'll be interested to see what use it is in solving who killed Harry Callaghan.'

He glanced at his watch as if he had no idea how the time had got on.

'Speaking of which, I better be off to notify the new widow.'

'That's certainly not going to make her day,' she said to his back as he left the room, her attempt at a *Dirty Harry* reference falling on deaf ears.

4

'You're very quiet,' Angel said, and immediately regretted it, after he and Kincade had been driving for five minutes in a less-than-comfortable silence.

Things had been strained between them since Stuart Beckford's unexpected appearance at the cemetery. Angel hadn't volunteered what had transpired after she walked off, wary of bringing up the topic that might one day put her out of a job. And she hadn't asked, believing it wasn't her place. Either that, or a simple case of sticking her head in the sand. He didn't know which, and nor did she.

Instead, they both acted as if there was nothing to talk about, often using humour to stop them from straying into serious conversation. Which is what she did now.

'I was trying to imagine what Mrs Barbara Callaghan will be like.'

Although it was a blatant lie, he played along.

'Physical appearance? Or her attitude towards us?'

'Both.'

'And?'

'I think she'll look exactly like him, but with longer hair.'

'Tattoos?'

'Definitely. Visible, and in places I don't want to think about. And she'll have bigger biceps.'

'In order to keep her husband in line? As all women like to do.'

'Can you blame us?'

Although he'd instigated the change in direction, it wasn't a road he wanted to go down—particularly with her, given her marital situation.

'What about Mrs Callaghan's attitude towards us?'

She became more thoughtful. That in itself proved she hadn't been thinking about it when he accused her of being quiet.

'Hostile. Her husband is the sort of man who believes pulling a person from their car and threatening to beat them to a pulp with a wheel wrench is an appropriate response to somebody he's already wronged giving him the finger. He's also annoyed somebody sufficiently to make them take him out to the woods and execute him. Anyone married to a man like that is going to view us as the enemy.'

'Even when we're trying to find out who killed poor old hubby?'

She nodded firmly.

'Even then, yes.'

'We'll find out soon enough.'

The remainder of the journey passed in silence, although it was a more companionable one with the shared prospect of a potentially difficult conversation ahead uniting them.

When they arrived, a silver Vauxhall Corsa was parked on what used to be the front garden but had long ago been concreted over and subsequently colonised by weeds.

'If that's his car, he must have been snatched off the street,' Kincade said, taking hold of the door handle ready to get out.

He reached over and stopped her with a hand on her arm.

'Get it checked out first.'

'What for?'

He couldn't put it into words, made a joke of it, instead.

'Call it a woman's intuition.'

Her face said *idiot* even if the word never made it past her front teeth. She put in a call to Jardine, waited on the line while Jardine entered the registration into the PNC.

'Liam Callaghan,' Jardine announced a minute later. 'Aged forty-six. Must be the victim's younger brother.'

Kincade ended the call, went to relay the information.

'I heard her,' Angel said, smiling at the idiosyncrasies of his team. 'She doesn't need a phone. So long as she's standing on a chair and pointing in roughly the right direction.'

'It's handy Liam's here. A bit of support for his sister-in-law.'

It wasn't only a question of support for the new widow. It made things easier for them. Someone familiar and trusted on hand to provide physical comfort after they delivered the life-changing news.

It didn't exactly put a spring in their step, but it certainly lightened the load as they got out of the car.

'I wonder if they already know?' she said, waiting for him to come around the front of the car to join her on the pavement.

'Is that wishful thinking? Or is it a serious question?'

She scrunched her face.

'Semi-serious. If he was mixed up with some really nasty people, they might've sent a picture to her.'

'I think the sort of warning you give your girls is called for. You watch too much TV. One other thing . . .'

She was nodding, *I know*, before he got the words out.

'Don't call him Dirty Harry.'

. . .

Barbara Callaghan proved Kincade half-right when she opened the door to them. Her hair was indeed longer than her husband's, scraped off her face into a severe bun on the top of her head. Her left arm was covered with tattoos that looked as if her husband had tried to make copies of his own with a needle and blue ink when he got back from having his done professionally. And her upper arms were flabby more than muscular, the flesh hanging down like bat wings and wobbling when she lifted her arm.

Kincade made a mental note to watch what she ate and never grow old.

Unsurprisingly, Barbara recognised them for what they were and ushered them in.

Despite the initial impression that any sensible person would choose to get into a fight with her husband before they did with her, she looked close to tears. She led them into a gaudily-decorated sitting room with a monstrous TV monopolising one wall that could've provided electricity for the whole street had it been a solar panel.

'It would be best if you asked your brother-in-law to join us,' Angel said, before any of them sat down.

Confusion creased Barbara's brow, pulling hard against the pressure from the hair bun above.

'He's not here.'

'His car's outside,' Kincade said, a stupid thing to say, given its presence proved nothing.

It might not have proved anything, but it told Barbara plenty —they'd checked the registration before knocking.

The attempt to soften the coming blow had just backfired. A well-meaning suggestion had changed into proof that they were on one side of a line and she the other. The decent, everyday folk of the UK were living in a police state where a member of your own family couldn't leave a car on your drive without you being subjected to the third degree.

It wasn't a good start.

And it was only ever going to get worse.

Before it did, Angel did his thing, delivering the blow in words Kincade knew she'd never remember and a voice she couldn't hope to emulate, however much she practiced in the mirror.

Barbara sagged at the knees, nonetheless. It doesn't matter how much you know it's coming, it still hits hard when it lands.

A packet of cigarettes appeared as if by magic before Barbara's substantial backside hit the brown velour sofa. A moment later, she was sucking hard on one of them as if it was the only thing preventing her from joining her dead husband, rather than accelerating the reunion.

Angel fielded all of the usual questions—*how, where, when*—managing to not answer the *why*. He guessed Barbara was more likely to know that than he did.

Halfway through her second cigarette, Barbara made a vague waving gesture towards a drinks cabinet designed to look like an old-fashioned red telephone box.

'Get me something to drink, will you, luv?' she said to Kincade. 'And I don't mean a cup of bloody tea.'

Kincade hopped to it. With her back to Angel and Barbara as she crossed the room, neither of them saw the effect the term of endearment *luv* had on her face. Angel couldn't imagine it put a smile there, although it would've been worse coming from a man.

She poured a generous slug from an already-open bottle of Chardonnay into a glass with *Love ya to bits, babe* and a heart etched on the side, carried it back to Barbara, who accepted it with a blurry-eyed smile.

Angel waited until she'd taken a fortifying slurp, then began.

'When did you last see your husband, Mrs Callaghan?'

She's going to ask you to call her Babs soon, Kincade thought, as Barbara hesitated over what should've been a very easy question.

'Day before yesterday.'

'And where—'

'He's moved out.'

Barbara looked directly at him as she told what he knew was a lie, her eyes challenging him to contradict her. Instead, he played along, his voice reflecting his pleasure at the answers to all of their questions falling into place so neatly.

'That's why you didn't report him as missing?'

The aggression went out of Barbara's stare in a heartbeat, relief on her face that he'd accepted her story.

'That's right.'

'And did he take your car?'

Barbara nodded happily, the conversation going in the direction she wanted it to.

'It's a Ford Mondeo. I can give you the registration.'

Angel said that would be very helpful, thank you, made a note of it when Barbara recited it by heart.

'Don't ask me why I remember it, but I always have,' Barbara said, smiling at her own mental prowess.

Angel didn't. He wasn't interested.

'Did he say where he was going?'

'No.' Still smiling as the easy answers continued to roll out.

Until he asked something she wasn't so happy about.

'Why did he move out?' Congratulating himself on not using the word *allegedly*.

'We had an argument.'

'About what?'

Barbara sat upright on the sofa as if she'd been goosed, lifted her chin.

'You shouldn't be asking me personal questions like that.' She gave a quick sniff. 'I'm a grieving widow.'

If it hadn't been for the sniff and the unnecessary emphasis on her new-found status, Angel wouldn't have thought anything of it. But he saw from her face how pleased she was with the *grieving widow* line, planning to roll it out every time he asked a question she didn't want to answer.

'Sorry, I didn't mean to pry,' he said, making a mental note to pass everything she said through a different filter.

Barbara sniffed again, in case he'd already forgotten she was a grieving widow.

He glanced at Kincade, flicked his eyes at the ceiling when she looked back at him. She immediately jumped to her feet, pointed at Barbara's half-empty glass.

'Let me top that up for you.'

Barbara didn't need to be told twice before holding her glass out. Kincade plucked it out of her fingers, poured another generous slug.

'Do you mind if I use your loo?' she said, already on her way towards the door. 'Just pouring the wine makes me want to go.'

Barbara smiled back, told her to go ahead, it was on the right at the top of the stairs.

Don't worry, Angel thought, *she'll find it when she has a good nose around.*

'She's got two daughters,' he said, an attempt to make Kincade seem more human before she came back down and proved Barbara was a liar. 'Isla and Daisy.' He leaned in conspiratorially. 'Don't tell her, but I can't remember which one's the eldest.'

He was saved from having to continue with the sham conversation, ask Barbara about her own children, by the sound of the toilet flushing upstairs.

'Better?' he asked when Kincade came back into the room, as if he always kept a close eye on his team's toilet habits.

'Much.'

The firm nod she gave to go with it told him he'd been right. He leaned back into his chair, let her take over.

'All of your husband's shaving kit is still in the bathroom, Mrs Callaghan. And his toothbrush. Unless you have a different coloured one for mornings and nights. And unless he's got more clothes than any man I've ever met, all of his clothes are still in the wardrobe. I don't believe he's moved out at all.'

Barbara knocked her wine back in one and pushed herself to her feet instead of answering. Went over to the drinks cabinet and half-filled her glass with neat vodka.

Kincade let her get settled on the sofa again before repeating herself.

'He didn't move out, did he? He went to work the day before yesterday and didn't come home. Or last night. And for some reason you didn't report him as missing.'

Anger flared in Barbara's eyes, the vodka she'd swallowed helping it come through in her words.

'What's the point? You lot don't give a shit. Not unless it's some rich bastard or a stuck-up politician. Then you're all tripping over yourselves.'

Kincade ignored the oft-heard complaint, stuck to the point.

'Your husband didn't move out, did he?'

Barbara gripped her wineglass like she was thinking of throwing the contents in Kincade's face.

'No, he didn't bloody move out. Happy now?'

'Why did you lie? It's as if you don't want us to find out who murdered him. You might not believe we take every missing person report seriously, but we sit up and pay attention when somebody gets murdered, whoever they are.'

'Yeah, right.'

Kincade gave Angel an exasperated headshake as Barbara took an exaggerated interest in the carpet pattern—which, if anyone had asked Kincade, was truly horrible.

He took over before Kincade grabbed Barbara by the shoulders and shook her.

'Did somebody tell you to lie, Mrs Callaghan?' A mental image of the silver Vauxhall Corsa on the drive outside came to him as he asked the question. 'Was it your brother-in-law, Liam?'

The weight of her grief added to the rapidly-ingested alcohol added to their questions hit her all at once. Angel guessed there was bitter resentment in there, too. Liam Callahan had turned up at her house, left his car there while he went to do God knows what, leaving her to field awkward bloody questions they might turn up and ask.

'Yes, it was bloody Liam. He wanted to borrow Harry's van. He said if you lot turned up, play dumb. Everybody thinks that's what I do best, anyway.' All of this had been addressed to the stomach-churning carpet. Now, she raised her eyes, although not to glare sullenly at them. She looked past them in the direction of the front door. Raised her middle finger towards it.

'*Fuck you*, Liam.'

Angel waited for her to drop her finger before continuing.

'Why did he want to borrow the van?'

Despite the outburst aimed at her brother-in-law, an animal cunning came over Barbara. You might fight amongst yourselves, but the enemy is still the enemy.

'He didn't say.'

'He didn't need to. You already know. Was it something he was supposed to do with your husband?'

Barbara took a deep breath, let it out. She looked close to tears again.

'Leave me alone.' She swallowed thickly, grief mixing with self-pity as the first tears rolled down her cheeks.

I'm a grieving widow, Angel mouthed to himself as Barbara said it out loud.

'THAT CARPET AND THE TELEPHONE BOX DRINKS CABINET WOULD make me move out,' Kincade said, once they were back in the car. 'And as for that wine glass ... and anyone who called me babe ...'

'I did think you were going to spit in her wine after she called you *luv*.'

A spasm of disgust twisted her lips as he used the word. She held her hand up, index finger and thumb pinched a millimetre apart.

'I was this close.'

'But she's a grieving widow.'

'Exactly.'

They shared a small, unprofessional smile, then Angel took them in a serious direction.

'Why didn't she report him as missing?'

Kincade looked out the window at the Vauxhall Corsa on the drive, talked her thoughts through out loud.

'His main job is driving a skip lorry. But he's got a sideline. Something with his brother, Liam. Something that involves the van. And when Callaghan went missing, his wife and brother immediately assumed it was to do with the sideline.'

'And whatever they're up to is something they don't want us anywhere near.'

Working in the UK's second-biggest container port with Portsmouth only fifteen miles to the east and a number of smaller ports and harbours within an hour's drive, all of which offered an easy route to mainland Europe, it wasn't difficult to make a stab at what the Callaghan brothers might have been doing with Harry's van.

The only question was *what* they were smuggling.

Harry Callaghan shot to death in a lonely forest suggested they'd moved on from booze and fags.

'You think we'll find Callaghan's van booked on a cross-channel ferry?' Kincade said.

'I think there's more chance we'll find it burned out in a field to destroy any evidence of what they brought back on previous trips.'

'If he's got any sense, Liam Callaghan will have gone to ground by now.'

They shared another knowing smile, words unnecessary.

If petty criminals had any sense, they would've lost the fight against crime years ago.

5

'Would you like to carry a gun?' Jardine asked, the question coming out of the blue, as did a lot of what she said.

Gulliver glanced at her to see if it was a serious question. He guessed the victim's unofficial moniker, Dirty Harry, had prompted the question, rather than a secret desire to take policing to a different level.

'Not sure. One thing's for certain—'

'I know, I know. I shouldn't be allowed one.' She put her hand over her mouth, yawned loudly and unrealistically. 'That's *sooo* boring. Here I am trying to have a sensible conversation, and you start talking out of your arse. As usual.'

Gulliver was speechless. Torn between asking her to define *sensible conversation* and countering the habitual-arse-talking accusation. In the end, he did neither, throwing it back at her.

'Would you?'

'I think so, yeah.'

He gave her a quick glance up and down, as if appraising her.

'Actually, I think I can see it. You, swaggering around like Johnny Big Bollocks with a gun on your hip—'

'It'd be in a shoulder holster.'

He shook his head firmly at the interruption.

'You wouldn't be happy wearing a shoulder holster. You complain enough about your bra strap being too tight, as it is.'

'I do not.' Adjusting herself as she denied it. 'Shows how much you know about bras and shoulder holsters.'

'Knowing you, you'd forget to put the safety on and the gun would go off while you're fiddling with yourself...'

The conversation continued in a similar surreal vein all the way to where Piotr Adamczyk, the victim of Callaghan's road rage attack, lived. The contentious issue of whether police officers should be armed or not hadn't been resolved by the time they arrived, but it passed the time.

They were expecting Adamczyk to be a scrawny, bespectacled weasel of a man standing five-foot-nothing in his stockinged feet. A caricature victim. They were wrong. The man who opened the door to them was about the same size as Callaghan, and younger with it.

'Call me Pete,' he said, inviting them in. 'English people have a problem with Piotr.'

Thank God you're not a pompous stick-in-the-mud who insists we call you Mr Adamczyk, Jardine thought, bringing up the rear as Pete led them into the house.

The account Pete gave of the incident added nothing they didn't already know, apart from his pride-fuelled explanation of how he'd come off second best.

'He's an old man. A fat slob who thinks he's still tough. He would never beat me. But my seatbelt got stuck. I was trying to undo it to get out and punch his ass. Or kick it. I got it unstuck but he pulled me out while I was still busy. I banged my head on the ground. The fat pig sat on me while I was dizzy so I couldn't breathe—'

'Sounds like he had a lucky escape,' Gulliver said, cutting short the bullshit bravado.

'Very lucky,' Jardine agreed, managing to keep a straight face.

Pete grew an inch in his chair, his pride restored. Nodding in agreement with them.

'Never beat my ass.'

'Is that why you dropped the charges?' Gulliver asked. 'You didn't want him to get away with a fine or maybe a few weeks in prison. You wanted to get even properly. Kick his arse to show him who he was messing with.'

A light came into Pete's eyes as if wishing he'd thought of it himself.

'Because somebody got even with him,' Gulliver continued, before Pete took them through what he'd like to do, blow by blow. 'He was shot to death two days ago.'

Pete showed very little reaction to the news. Certainly, no surprise. A man who pulls people from their car and threatens them should expect his actions to catch up with him one day. And if he picks on a small man, that man might decide he needs a gun to even the odds.

'Wasn't me. I wouldn't need gun if I wanted to get even.' He smacked a large fist into his open palm. 'Anyway, I was back home visiting my family in Krakow. That's in Poland. I got back yesterday.' He shrugged apologetically. 'Sorry. Wasn't me.'

Jardine smiled like she was relieved to hear it.

'We didn't think it was. But we have to ask. We're more interested in why you dropped the charges.'

'They ask me to.'

'Who's they?'

'Callaghan and another man. I think maybe his brother.'

'Where was this?'

Pete pointed at the floor.

'Here. They came to the house.' The pointed finger came up

until it was directed at Jardine. 'Maybe you gave them my address?'

'We'd never do that, sir.'

Had they been interviewing John Smith or Dave Brown, they might have been worried. Asking themselves whether Callaghan had access to the PNC through a bent cop. Since they were talking to Piotr Adamczyk, the answer was likely to be less sinister.

'Are you in the phone book?' Jardine asked.

Pete's face compacted as he realised his mistake. He might not care about being plagued by double-glazing sales calls and payment protection insurance shysters, but it had never crossed his mind there might be more serious consequences to having his name and address available to anyone with an internet connection.

'Yeah. But I never answer landline. Only mobile.'

'What happened when they came here?' Gulliver said, moving them on. 'Did they threaten you?'

For a brief moment it looked as if Pete was about to blow his own trumpet again. Tell them Callaghan would've needed more than one brother with him. He decided against it, satisfied he'd established his credentials sufficiently already.

'No. Callaghan said his boss would sack him if he got a criminal record. He said he was very sorry for attacking me. He was having a bad day. He made up a lot of excuses.' Pete waved his hand dismissively. 'I did not believe him. But what should I do? Make him lose his job?' He dropped his eyes briefly. 'Sometimes I get angry in the car, too. I know what it is like. Dickhead car drivers. Head up ass or on mobile phone. Stupid women talking and not paying attention or shouting at kids in back seat. If you drive all day, it must make you angry.'

Gulliver and Jardine knew exactly what he was saying.

Except he was making a meal of it, labouring the point way beyond what was necessary.

Jardine had a good idea why.

'Did he offer you money to drop the charges?'

Pete shook his head, horrified at the suggestion.

'That would be illegal.'

'You agreed out of the goodness of your own heart, did you?'

'Yeah. I forgave him.'

Jardine ignored Pete's facetious tone, glanced around the room. It needed a lot more than decorating. An all-encompassing fire before starting from scratch would do it. The windows needed replacing. It smelled damp. There was a good chance it was a repossession after being used as a crack den or pop-up brothel.

'What do you do for a living, Pete?'

'Carpenter.'

She swept her hand in the air, took in the whole room.

'You're doing this place up?'

'Yeah. I started with the kitchen. What a shithole!' He looked around the room they were in, as if he hadn't appreciated the size of the task ahead until now. 'It takes time. And money.'

'Did Callaghan offer you free skip hire if you dropped the charges? What does a big one of those cost these days? Five hundred quid?'

Pete's face told them she'd hit the nail on the head, even if his words didn't.

'No. That would be as bad.'

You're lucky we've got bigger fish to fry, Jardine thought, as they got up to leave.

'SOMETIMES I WISH I LIVED SOMEWHERE CORRUPT,' JARDINE announced as they headed back to the car.

Gulliver, unsure how to respond, chose the cynical route.

'And you don't?'

'I don't mean only at the top. The politicians and rich people.' She kicked the tarmac immediately outside Pete's house with her toe, damage evident from a skip being dropped carelessly. 'I'd get Pete out here now, show him that damage, then get him to come to my house, fix everything that needs doing in return for turning a blind eye.'

Gulliver dipped his head in admiration as if he wished he'd thought of it himself.

'Today's turning into a real eye-opener. First, you want a gun. Now, you want to move somewhere you can call in favours for not doing your job. Any idea where you want to go?'

'I quite like America . . .'

Gulliver chose not to pass comment. Jardine had already moved on, asking a sensible question for once.

'Are we any further forward?'

He took a moment to think about it as they got into the car.

'It's obvious Callaghan was worried he might have jeopardised his day job. That might imply his sideline was small beer, making it less likely it was related to his death.'

'Unless whoever killed him was thinking ahead. Got rid of him before he became big enough to be a serious problem.'

'It's possible. One thing's for sure . . . he was very close to his brother.'

His mind caught up with his mouth as he talked. He could've been talking about the woman sitting beside him. Jardine had recently accessed the PNC for personal reasons in an attempt to help her own brother, Frankie, who was in trouble with their Northumbria Police counterparts back home in the North East. If it came to light, it could potentially end her career.

She didn't appear to have noticed, picking up on what he'd

said about the bond between the Callaghan brothers from a different perspective.

'But how close? Do we need to tell the gravediggers to leave room for another one in Harry Callaghan's grave in case Little Bro starts thinking about revenge?'

Liam Callahan had lied to his sister-in-law.

He didn't go to France without Harry. He chivvied Barbara along, told her he'd miss the ferry if she didn't get her finger out, anything to get out of the house as quickly as possible. Give him a chance to think without her fussing around him, her dressing gown that should be permanently sewn up gaping, giving him an unwelcome eyeful—at any time of the day, forget about first thing in the morning.

Liam had no intention of going without Harry by his side. Because Harry really did act like he was Dirty Harry—he had it on the sun strip on his skip lorry, for Christ's sake—and the sort of people they were dealing with respected that.

My bollocks are bigger than your bollocks. Or cojones, or whatever they called them in French.

Without Harry, it would be just him against God knows how many of the greasy little foreigners.

He didn't care if he pissed them off, jeopardised the relationship Harry had worked tirelessly to develop after he lost his job. Better safe than sorry. The relationship could always be patched up, trust re-established. At the end of the day, they were a very small cog in a very large wheel—however much Harry liked to kid himself.

He'd driven Harry's van home, parked it in the alley at the bottom of his garden, then changed into his cycling gear and gone for a ride in an attempt to work some of the restlessness out of his system. He'd settled on one of his favourite routes—a twenty-mile loop out to Romsey and back that skirted the edge of Earl Mountbatten's Broadlands Estate. At the halfway point, in Romsey, he'd sat on a bench on the banks of the River Test, thinking. Wondering if Harry's disappearance was linked to those greedy greasy little foreigners.

That's when Babs called him and dropped the bombshell.

Harry was dead.

Shot to death.

Like an execution.

No, not *like* an execution. An execution.

Suddenly Liam's palms were sweaty, the smell of his own fear in his nose. He hadn't made many good decisions in his life, but not getting on that ferry, not meeting with the murdering greedy greasy little foreigners had more than made up for all the bad ones.

And some.

He sat on the bench for a long while afterwards.

Not thinking, because thought was beyond him at the moment. Vacant he could manage.

And not cycling home. Because pushing those pedals round and round for the ten miles home suddenly felt like it was more than his leg muscles had in them. That's if the synapses made it through from his addled brain in the first place.

So, he sat. Doing nothing.

He could get accustomed to it. Might have been able to afford to, had things not suddenly gone so disastrously tits-up.

His phone rang a second time while he was sitting there. He didn't recognise the number. It looked foreign to him. The sort of number murdering greedy greasy little foreigners would have. He ignored it. They didn't leave a message.

Ha, ha, we killed your brother. You're next.

Despite the brain-numbing shock and the debilitating fear —he was able to admit that to himself, even if he'd never let anyone else see it—something was scratching away at the back of his subconscious. A memory trying to make itself heard. Something that explained exactly why Harry died.

And when the creeping realisation finally crystallised, he wished to God it hadn't.

6

'I wish I was coming in with you,' Catherine Beckford said for the hundredth time, pulling to the kerb outside the Jolly Sailor in Bursledon.

You're the only one who does, Stuart Beckford thought, and had the good sense to keep to himself. It was a long walk home if he pissed her off.

'Tell me again how that would be a good thing,' he said, instead. 'The three of us sitting there. You, me and Max. *Oh!* And there's an empty chair at the table, of course.'

'Okay.'

'And we're all making damn sure we don't look at it. Then maybe when it gets so excruciatingly uncomfortable—'

'I said *okay*.'

'—one of us isn't thinking and puts their mouth on autopilot. *When was the last time we were all out like this?*'

'For Christ's sake, Stuart. You made your point.'

They sat in silence for a long moment. He didn't want to get out, leave things on a sour note. And it wasn't only a question of needing her to come and pick him up later.

Ever since it happened, since Angel's wife Claire died while he was driving, while *he was in charge*, Beckford had been acutely aware of fatal road accidents. How final they are. How abrupt. No time to say goodbye. *Bang!* Here today, gone tomorrow. Except forget days—it's here this minute, gone the next.

So, he made very sure he didn't leave things on a sour note with Catherine.

Not ever.

She took hold of her wrist as they sat without talking, massaged it distractedly.

'It still hurts.'

He touched his clavicle.

'Yeah, me too.'

Neither of them needed to say any more.

Claire was beyond the reach of pain.

And her widowed husband lived in a sea of it, even if he'd been a goody-two-shoes and adopted the brace position, walked away with nothing worse than a stiff neck. On the outside, that is.

Catherine looked at the pub as if it was possible to see Angel through its walls.

'Do you think he wishes he'd died instead of her?'

'I'll ask him, shall I?'

She shook her head at him, anger and frustration in the gesture. Her voice sharper than she intended as the approaching reconciliation by which they'd measured the passage of their lives these past months finally arrived.

'I don't know what's wrong with you, Stuart. To tell you the truth, I'm glad I'm not coming in. Or was that the whole idea?'

'I'm flattered you attribute scheming on such a high level to me.'

He saw what went through her mind.

You call that scheming?

It wasn't an argument he wanted to get into. Not with her or any woman, every one of them a past master in the art of deviousness in his experience.

'What time do you want picking up?' she said, finding relief in the safety of logistics and arrangements. She waited while her husband made a difficult mental calculation, multiplying the number of pints he wanted or needed to drink by the average time it takes to consume one, after allowing for slowing down as he filled up with beer and unhealthy snacks. In the end, she gave up waiting for him. 'Stupid question. And I don't know what you're doing trying to work it out to the minute. The answer is when you're too drunk to remember to call me. I'll be back at ten-thirty, okay?'

He leaned over and gave her a peck on the cheek, opened the door.

'Why do you think he picked this pub?' Catherine said when he was halfway out.

Beckford shrugged.

'It's only a short taxi ride home for him?'

'It wasn't their favourite was it?'

'Don't think so. I'll ask him.'

This time, she didn't jump down his throat, as she had when he'd joked about asking Angel if he wished he'd died instead of Claire.

She might have done so—or, better still, driven them both home—had she known where tonight might lead them, a place where petty bickering would be a fond distant memory.

'JESUS CHRIST! WHAT ARE YOU DOING OUT HERE?' BECKFORD SAID, when he came out of the pub, a pint of Fursty Ferret bitter in each hand, and found Angel sitting at a table outside, overlooking the river at the rear of the building. He glanced suspiciously at the table top. 'Normal people start smoking when they're fourteen, not forty-something.'

'Sounds like you've gone soft since I last saw you.'

'Says the man sitting there shivering with his collar turned up. C'mon, let's sit inside.'

Angel couldn't blame Beckford for complaining. It was unseasonably cold, a chill wind blowing off the water that felt as if it was coming from the North Sea, not the English Channel.

'No, there's a reason.' He pointed at the beers Beckford still hadn't put down. 'Get a few of those down your neck and you won't even notice.'

Beckford grudgingly acquiesced, putting one glass beside Angel's first, almost-finished pint and taking a long swallow of the other.

'Shift along,' he said, squeezing in behind the table to sit with his back against the wall, get some protection. Then, when he was settled, 'I could've let Catherine come in, after all. She wouldn't have sat out here.'

'Best you didn't.'

Beckford turned to look at him, concern clouding his features.

'There's a reason we're sitting here freezing our nuts off *and* it's best Catherine isn't here. Should I be getting worried?'

'Probably.'

'You seem to have forgotten I've got an Angel-to-English dictionary permanently installed in—'

'Up where?'

'—my brain. You say *probably*, I hear *definitely*.'

'Only when it's something bad, surely?'

Beckford raised his glass solemnly in acknowledgement of one of life's greatest truths, then changed tack, an unspoken agreement between them that there were other topics to speak about first. Let alcohol break down the initial reticence their months apart had resulted in before the conversation turned serious.

'That was your new DS with you at the cemetery, was it?'

'Yep. Catalina Kincade. Down from the Met to show us how it's done.'

'Her choice?'

'But at least she's a damn sight better looking than you are.'

Beckford grinned at him, counting off the words Angel had spoken on his fingers.

'Fuck me—'

'Not while there's dogs on the street.'

'—that's twelve words to say *no*. That's gotta be some kind of a record. Don't worry, if you're that determined not to answer a simple question, I'm not going to ask what she did. Is she any good?'

Angel pretended to give it serious thought. Beckford didn't wait for him to deliver the line that was visible rowing down the river from a mile away.

'Better than me.'

'Definitely.'

'And you?'

'Probably.' He held his hand up before Beckford jumped in. 'That's the exception where probably doesn't mean definitely.'

Now it was Beckford's turn to pretend to think deeply, except the curl to his lips gave him away.

'Good looking and bright? She hasn't got a hope. You've got to be stupid and ugly to make it all the way up the greasy pole.'

The remark reminded Angel of the last time he'd been sitting at the table they were currently occupying. It had been with Kincade. And she'd told him she'd already had her promotion to DCI unofficially confirmed—until her fall from grace put an abrupt end to her accelerated rise up that greasy pole.

'Why didn't she want to meet me?' Beckford asked, when Angel didn't share his thoughts.

'Can you blame her? *I* wouldn't want to meet you.'

'Is she worried about her job?'

'Of course, she is. Wouldn't you be?'

'Not if I'm the competition.'

Angel didn't let his concern show, but this was not the Stuart Beckford he knew of old. Self-doubt was not a weakness Beckford had suffered from. Seemed Claire's death had changed all that. Angel got the first inkling of why his friend might not feel ready to come back to work. In his mind, if he screwed up, people got hurt. It didn't matter if the error was beyond anybody's control. So long as Beckford believed he was to blame, facts were irrelevant. It was an insidious vicious circle. Self-doubt and remorse fed off one another, resulting in a paralysing refusal to accept responsibility.

'Tell her not to worry,' Beckford said under his breath, losing the words in the beer glass he lifted to his lips as he said it.

Angel pretended he hadn't heard. Changed the subject.

'Guess where she lives.'

As anyone would, Beckford immediately jumped to the wrong conclusion, surprise mixing with horror on his face.

'Not with you?'

'Uh-uh'

Given the affirmative response he was expecting, plus Angel failing to enunciate properly, Beckford heard *uh-huh* instead of *uh-uh.*

'Really? How's that working out?'

Angel was halfway to putting him straight when he changed his mind, had some fun.

'Not bad. She brings me a cup of tea in bed every morning. Has my breakfast ready on the table by the time I get downstairs.'

He tried to form a mental picture of it as he spoke. Kincade in her apron putting a plate of eggs and bacon down in front of him, but it wouldn't come. Something must've showed on his face. Beckford narrowed his eyes at him.

'You're winding me up.'

'Yep. But it's close. Who's the last person you'd expect to take in a lodger?'

Beckford took a sip of beer, gave it some thought.

The back door to the pub opened as he was doing so. A young couple stepped outside, drinks in hand. Shook heads at each other and went back inside.

'Good decision,' Beckford called after them. 'Sitting out here is the pub equivalent of wearing a hair shirt.' He glared at Angel. 'You'll be trying to get me to go to confession next.' The remark, with its associated ideas of penance and punishment, worked in a mysterious way in Beckford's subconscious, brought to mind another institution steeped in ancient traditions—the military. 'Are you telling me your DS is living with your dad?'

'Yep. And they're getting on like a house on fire.'

Beckford shook his head in amazement. This beat anything he'd heard across an interview-room table. He was sufficiently aware of Angel's family dynamic for a grin to break out on his face.

'How's Grace taking it?'

'Do you need to ask?'

Angel's younger sister was a criminal defence lawyer. As such, she viewed all police officers as agents of the devil. Enthusiastic guardians of a fascist regime hell-bent on persecuting innocent citizens on the basis of colour and creed, satisfying their own power-crazed agendas at the same time. In her mind, her father had invited the enemy into his house.

'Stupid question,' Beckford admitted.

'That's not all.'

Beckford shook his head again, refusal this time.

'I'm not even going to try to guess.'

Angel pointed in a vaguely southerly direction down the river towards the village of Hamble-le-Rice.

'Guess who's waiting for me at home?'

'Not your mother?'

'Got it in one.'

Beckford immediately jumped to his feet.

'I don't know about you, but I need another beer just thinking about the prospect of what that's like.'

And I don't know about you, Angel thought as Beckford disappeared inside the pub, *but I don't feel as if it's five minutes since we last saw each other.*

He wasn't surprised. In fact, he'd been expecting it. They shouldn't have left it so long, but they'd been caught in a circular loop. The belief that they would pick up from where they left off allowed the procrastination to endure without feeling any pressure to end it.

Nor would they perform an emotional autopsy on the situation. The *F*-word would have no place at their table. *How does that make you feel?* It never ceased to amaze him that women didn't understand how asking a man that question achieved nothing, beyond making him want to run for the hills. Let's get that scalpel out and start cutting. The deeper, the better. And bring that interrogation light closer while you're at it . . .

'Nice and warm in there,' Beckford said, when he came back outside. He waited hopefully for a moment, the beers still in his hands, then accepted the inevitable when Angel wagged his finger at him. He raised his glass towards Angel in a toast. 'Commiserations. Here's to your mother going home soon.'

Angel clinked glasses.

'Don't hold your breath.'

'She's come over because of your dad?'

'That was meant to be the idea.'

According to Angel's sister—a hypochondriac who actively looked for symptoms of insidious diseases in everyone she met—their father was suffering from late onset Huntington's disease. Carl the old warhorse refused to take her or the suggestion seriously, a pig-headed stance that surprised nobody.

It was a different story with their mother. Grace talked to her regularly on the phone, and the more Carl pooh-poohed the idea, the more Grace chewed her mother's ear about it. The inevitable consequence was that Siobhan Angel came to believe it, herself.

That conviction prompted her to visit the mainland for the first time in fifteen years after returning home to Belfast following the split with her husband.

As Carl Angel unkindly put it, she'd come to watch him die.

To do so, they would have to meet. So far, that hadn't happened.

'And the old man's still refusing to take a blood test, is he?' Beckford said.

Angel gave him a look. Beckford nodded.

'Another stupid question.'

'I went for one, myself.'

The glass in Beckford's hand stalled halfway to his mouth at Angel's admission. He was well aware that Huntington's is one of nature's great gambles. There's a fifty-fifty chance of the faulty gene being passed from parent to child. A lot of children born to parents suffering from the disease choose not to take a test, preferring to live each day as it comes in ignorance, rather than risk having it confirmed and spend their life watching for symptoms.

'And?'

'I'm clear.'

Beckford clinked glasses again, more genuine feeling behind

it than when they'd jokingly toasted Angel's mother going home.

'Thank God for that. I don't suppose Grace has taken one?'

Not for the first time, it struck Angel that Beckford knew him and his family as well as he did. It was like going for a beer with a mirror.

'It's not a topic I choose to raise.'

'Sensible man.' Leaning away, he looked Angel up and down, then summed up his friend's life in four words. 'Never a dull moment.'

And we haven't even got onto talking about Inspector Virgil Balan's offer, Angel thought.

So far, the conversation had centred on him exclusively. He suspected that was exactly how Beckford liked it. The last thing he wanted was for Angel to ask him what he'd been doing these past months. Ask if his broken clavicle gave him any bother. Enquire after Catherine's wrist. And by the way, when's your mind going to heal?

Beckford continued to steer the conversation away from himself, asking about work, what Angel and the team he used to be a part of had going on.

Angel could've told him about Harry Callaghan, and they would've had a laugh about Dirty Harry. Instead, he told him about the previous investigation, which would lead seamlessly into what they needed to talk about.

'You probably saw it in the paper. The murdered people trafficker?'

'Yeah. I remember the word *butchered* being used.' Said with a spiteful gleam in his eye that he'd been safely on sick leave and not in the firing line for the top floor's ire.

'*People trafficker butchered at the side of the road*,' Angel quoted.

'I bet that went down like a turd in the punch bowl on the top floor.'

Angel agreed some things would never change, however long Beckford was away from the job.

'The thing is, the victim was Romanian.'

Beckford took a deep breath as he digested the information, the potential complications not lost on him.

'Is it too much to ask that it was Florescu?'

Being men, they both acted as if he'd asked if it was the Pope or the Prime Minister, not the name that haunted them, the name of the man who was the root cause of their long separation.

Bogdan Florescu was the Romanian lorry driver who fell asleep at the wheel and ploughed into Beckford's car when they were out in a foursome. The man responsible for the head-on collision in which Angel's wife Claire was killed. Being men, or maybe simply being human, they both blamed themselves. Angel for playing the fool in the back seat. Threatening to play his harmonica to the point where Claire unclipped her seat belt to reach around and confiscate the irritating instrument. And Beckford for ignoring or forgetting about—it made no difference now—the airbag warning light he'd seen a couple of days previously.

'I'm afraid so,' Angel replied. 'The people trafficker's name was Constantin.'

Beckford flicked his head heavenwards, disappointment colouring his voice.

'After you gave him upstairs the best ten years of your life, it would've been the least he could do.' Then, when Angel chose not to respond, 'Was Horwood okay with you taking the lead, given the Romanian connection?'

Angel rocked his hand.

'Reluctantly. But they didn't trust me to take the press conference.'

'Makes sense. Doesn't look good for the Super if the man he puts in charge loses his rag and yells, *I hate all Romanians* on TV.'

Angel smiled with him. It was a ridiculous thing to say, even in jest. As if he would be so unprofessional. He felt his pulse pick up as they approached the point where he would tell Beckford about something equally outrageous—and most definitely unprofessional should they go ahead.

'The victim's half-brother approached me,' he started. 'Virgil Balan. He's an inspector with the Poliția Română.'

It took a moment for the words to register with Beckford, being so far removed from what he was expecting.

'What? Officially?'

'Uh-uh. *Un*officially.'

'What did you do?'

'Kept him at arm's length. Treated him like any other grieving relative.'

Beckford had been sitting leaning forward with his forearms on the table. Now, he sat back. Crossed his arms as he studied his friend and ex-colleague.

'There's something you're not saying.'

'I didn't know whose side he was on. The Poliția Română who pay his salary, or the people trafficking gang his half-brother worked for. I still don't know. Even after I received a couple of severed fingers from two of the gang's thugs hand-delivered to my house.'

'Are you serious?'

'Yep. With a note suggesting I don't waste my time looking for the rest of the bodies.'

Beckford grinned at him.

'That's the sort of unofficial assistance we could use more of.'

It was obvious from the remark and Beckford's demeanour that he thought the story was over. The surprise package containing two severed fingers had been the point of telling it.

A sudden gust of wind made him shiver—and think otherwise.

'Hang on. Why are we sitting out here freezing our bollocks off? I get the feeling this is all connected.'

Angel tapped the table top with his middle finger a couple of times.

'This is where I was sitting when Balan called me after he'd gone back to Romania. He wanted to thank me for everything I'd done—'

'You were only doing your job.'

'I know that. But he wanted to do something for me in return.'

'As well as the two fingers he sent you? Taking a couple of people traffickers off the streets.'

'Something for me personally.'

Beckford rubbed his thumb over his first two fingers in the universal sign for money. Ran his eyes up and down Angel in a quick once-over.

'Doesn't look like you spent any of it on new clothes.'

Angel suddenly felt guilty for stringing Beckford along, allowing him to jump to the wrong conclusions—even if it did give him the opportunity to joke about Angel accepting a bribe.

'Not money. He's offered to find Florescu.'

Beckford stared back at him as if Angel had turned into Florescu in front of his eyes. When he finally coaxed his vocal chords into action, it was to ask the exact same question as before.

'What? Officially?'

'I don't know. He said, find him *for you*.'

'Not just find him.'

'Exactly.'

Angel's mind was immediately filled with the same image as when Balan made the offer. Florescu shirtless and tied to a wooden chair in a dimly-lit basement, his face blood-smeared, lips swollen and eyes semi-closed, a black gap where teeth used to be. And Balan standing beside him, his jacket off and shirtsleeves rolled up, extending his hand towards the frightened man stinking of piss and shit.

Your turn now. Enjoy.

'What did you tell him?' Beckford said eventually.

'He wasn't looking for an answer right away. He said I should ask you.'

'*Me?* How does he even know who I am?'

'Because he's good at his job. He does the research.'

'And now he's waiting for you to call him to let him know what we want to do.'

'Yep.'

'Fuck.'

'Yep.'

'I'm bloody glad I didn't let Catherine come in.'

'Yep.'

'Should we tell him to go ahead?'

Angel wagged a finger at him rather than fall into Beckford's trap, say *yep* again.

A shiver went through Beckford, made him snuggle down into his jacket. Whether it was the wind or Angel's news was anybody's guess.

'Can we at least go inside now?'

'You really want to sit with a bunch of other people discussing whether we authorise a man who might well be a corrupt cop to find somebody for us, so we can work our guilt out on him?'

Beckford couldn't argue when Angel put it like that. He got to his feet, nonetheless.

'My round,' Angel said, starting to rise himself.

Beckford put a hand on his shoulder, pushed him firmly back down.

'I don't give a monkey's whose round it is. I'm going to get all the warmth I can. Something tells me we're going to be out here a long time.'

Something told Angel he was right.

7
———

'Bloody hell,' Kincade said, when Angel walked in the next morning. 'You look like you died, were buried and then somebody dug you up again. *Sir*.'

'Good morning to you, too, Sergeant. And there's no need to look so pleased about it.'

'One too many glasses of children's blood with Doctor Death . . . I mean Durand, last night?'

Angel didn't have the strength to get annoyed about her continued attempt to bait him over his supposed relationship with the pathologist.

'What *did* you get up to last night?' she said, when he refused to bite. She didn't give him a chance to reply, her subconscious supplying the answer even as she asked the question. 'You went for a beer with Stuart Beckford?'

If only it was a beer, singular, he thought, and not however many they'd consumed.

'And?' she said, when he grunted in confirmation.

He knew exactly what she was asking. He'd told her about Balan's offer a while back in an attempt to mend bridges after he met Balan without her.

'We agreed six or seven pints wasn't the best preparation for making a decision like that.'

'Potentially more serious repercussions than sleeping with someone you regret in the morning, you mean? Not that I think that's the sort of thing you'd do, of course.'

He ignored the remark, dropped into his chair. Started to prepare himself for the day. What he needed to do was invent a reason to talk to DCI Finch in order to snaffle some of her proper coffee. He was thinking about ways to engineer it when his phone pinged in his pocket as a text arrived. He dug it out. Stuart Beckford. They'd been friends long enough to know it would be unrelated to what they'd discussed the previous evening.

How's your head? I'm having a relaxing lie-in, then a leisurely breakfast in half an hour or so. Speak soon.

He tapped out a quick reply that summed up his feelings perfectly.

Up yours.

Kincade saw the smile on his face as he pocketed the phone again.

'Who's that?'

'Stuart Beckford.'

'If it's a decision about Balan's offer, I don't want to think what the smile on your face implies.'

'It isn't. He's reminding me there are advantages to not having a job to get up for in the morning.'

He attempted to go back to work, but was aware of her still looking at him. After what he'd just said, it was obvious what she wanted to discuss. He stopped what he was doing, did his best to work a look onto his face that didn't tell anyone with eyes in their head that all he wanted to do was to be left alone.

'We didn't discuss whether he wants his old job—'

'*My* job.'

'—back, but if you want my opinion—'

'Formed before you'd drunk six or seven pints?'

'Formed before then, yes. In my opinion, he's not ready to come back. Will he ever be? I don't know.'

She shrugged, *can't say fairer than that.*

'Would you like him to?'

'What kind of a question is that?'

'A difficult one that puts you on the spot.'

'I'd worked that much out for myself.'

'And?'

And I need a cup of strong coffee more than ever.

'I think you've been spending too much time with my old man. Enrolled yourself in the Carl Angel school of diplomacy.'

'Then you should be used to it. *Sir.*'

It was obvious that if he wanted to get any work done—and for her to do any—he was going to have to pull rank or answer.

'It was good to see him . . .'

'Like it was only last week?'

'Exactly like that, yes. But I'm not sure he'll ever get over what happened. And if that's the case, I don't want him sitting in that chair.' Pointing at the chair she was sitting in.

'Do you think taking Balan up on his offer will get him over it?'

He held up both hands, palms towards her.

'I think you're forgetting I've got a hangover.'

'*Aw*. Want Mummy to rub it better?'

He couldn't help laughing, a wheezy, spluttery sound that leaked out of him as he imagined her saying the same to one of her daughters.

'Don't you have any work to do? Weren't you going to give your mate DS Ian Wright a call?'

It did the trick in terms of taking the spotlight off him.

She pursed her lips.

It wasn't really her style. If she didn't like what somebody said to her, she was more likely to give them a slap. She wasn't old and dried-up enough to purse her lips—despite what her current tone of voice suggested.

'He is *not* my mate. As you well know.'

He did. But it never hurt to have some fun—especially after the grilling she'd been giving him.

Wright was a detective with the South East Regional Organised Crime Unit. Based out of Thames Valley Police's headquarters in Kidlington, Oxfordshire, SEROCU worked with the Hampshire Constabulary, as well as other police forces and law enforcement agencies, to combat cross-border organised crime. At least that was the theory. Angel's experience suggested the flow of information was a one-way street—and there were no prizes for guessing which way it went.

At first glance, it might have appeared that one man and his van would be too small to be of interest to SEROCU. Except Angel was aware that roll-on, roll-off traffic via the Eurotunnel and ferry services from ports across mainland Europe was the most common method organised crime groups used to smuggle illicit goods and people into the UK. Employing a *little and often* approach spreads the risk of their goods being seized and minimises the loss when they are.

As for DS Wright himself, he was more than one of their detectives. He was Kincade's bête noire. One of them. He'd known her from her days working undercover in the Met Police. And he'd been privy to the fiasco that led to her fall from grace and subsequent banishment from that great force.

He'd also been stupid enough to make an inappropriate remark implying that any information Kincade gleaned whilst undercover had been obtained whilst on her back. Shortly after, he was on his own back, flat on the floor, and Kincade was nursing a sore but satisfied right fist.

On balance, it was best if Angel made the call himself.

Kincade got up from her desk as he picked up the phone to do so.

'I'll find somewhere else to be. Let the two of you talk about me without feeling uncomfortable.'

'I thought you liked making Wright feel as uncomfortable as possible.'

She showed him her eye teeth.

'Yes, but in person, not over the phone.' Screwing her fist into her palm as if using a mortar and pestle as she left the room.

Angel's most recent discussion with Wright had been very different to all those that preceded it. The early discussions had highlighted exactly how one-sided the flow of information between them was. Angel had also been made aware that he was a very small fish in a very big sea. As such, his investigation into the death of a single people trafficker was insignificant in terms of the bigger picture. He'd been warned off the most promising avenues so as not to jeopardise what the grown-ups were doing. Naturally, he'd taken no notice whatsoever. Hence the antagonistic flavour to their meetings and discussions.

The final conversation after they arrested and charged two suspects with the people trafficker's murder had been very different. As a result of Angel's investigation, the man at the top of the people trafficking gang had been taken off the board by his own people back in Romania. Angel suspected Virgil Balan had been involved. He also guessed DS Wright knew for sure whether Balan was involved or not—and he was sitting on that information. If nothing else, it meant the relations between them improved.

As a result, Angel was determined to adopt a positive attitude towards the upcoming call until proven wrong. Naive was a word some people might use—Angel himself, if anyone asked him. Certainly Kincade.

As expected, a flood of effusive bonhomie came gushing down the line from Wright's end, as if Angel had been out for a long-overdue reunion with Wright and not Beckford the previous evening.

'We've got a man taken out to the New Forest and executed,' Angel said, when the gushing died down. 'Shot three times with a nine-mil pistol.'

'Not exactly your garden-variety, street-corner thug's style,' Wright agreed.

'He also owned a van his brother and wife are very concerned we don't get a look at until the brother has had a chance to clean it or torch it. We'll be checking ferry crossings and expect to see it making regular trips to mainland Europe. The way he was killed suggests he'd progressed from smuggling booze and fags.'

'What's the victim's name?'

Angel found himself smiling even before the words were out.

'Harry Callaghan.'

There was a slight delay as if Angel had called the original Dirty Harry in San Francisco.

'Are you serious?'

'Uh-huh.'

'Dirty Harry.'

'You're not the first one to say that.'

'I don't suppose I am. And you're calling me in the hope that I go ahead and make your day?'

'I was actually hoping you'd use a line I haven't heard a hundred times already since yesterday.'

'Sorry to disappoint. On both fronts. Ignoring the movie character, the name doesn't mean anything to me.'

Already Angel felt the potential conflict of interest looming.

Wright wouldn't want his, Angel's, investigation into one potential low-level drug smuggler Wright had never heard of jeopardising bigger operations that might be going on.

'I'd remember somebody with that name,' Wright added, as if it was necessary for him to justify his inability to help. Except his next words proved what a slippery fish he was, the purpose of the remark to prepare Angel for a lack of help going forward. 'I'm sure everyone will be the same, but I'll ask around anyway.' He didn't bother to say the last part out loud—*don't hold your breath*.

Despite his determination to be positive, Angel hadn't expected anything different. At least this time Wright didn't follow up with a warning for Angel not to go off half-cocked—a phrase that had irritated the hell out of Angel with its implications that he was the sort of copper who jumped in feet first without a regard for the wider implications of his actions.

It was clear Wright believed the conversation was over. Angel knew it was—in terms of getting useful information. He had to try, nonetheless.

He did his best to work a similar, *we're all fighting crime together* bonhomie into his voice, knowing it sounded as false to Wright as it did inside his own head.

'Did you get to the bottom of who the people traffickers in Bucharest sent to clean up the mess this end?'

He held his breath as Wright processed the question. Angel guessed Wright was considering two options. Saying no, which might or might not be true. Or telling Angel that it was above his pay grade—which was definitely true.

A third option—Wright mentioning the name Virgil Balan, thereby confirming Balan was corrupt and as a result his offer of assistance was unofficial—was never on the cards.

'We gained some useful insights as a result of your investigation,' Wright said, a response that failed to answer the question but indicated that he was destined for greater things. 'And for which we are very grateful to you and your team.'

You can shove your thanks, Angel thought as they ended the call. *Just tell me if it was Balan.*

Five minutes later, Kincade's return was heralded by the aroma of proper coffee. She followed it in carrying two cups filled with something that most certainly hadn't been dispensed by the machine next to the lifts.

'I bumped into Finch in the corridor,' she explained, placing a cup on his desk. 'She mentioned that she'd seen you getting out of your car looking like death warmed up...'

'And you told her I'd been out on a bender with Stuart Beckford?'

She bristled at the accusation, her voice defensive.

'*No.* I said you'd had a heavy night, that's all. It's not my fault if she works it out.' She indicated the cup of coffee she'd put on his desk. 'She said you probably needed something to perk you up.'

Angel couldn't disagree, sipping appreciatively at the coffee. But there would be a price to pay, as well as difficult decisions ahead.

'So, how is the wanker?' Kincade said, changing the subject in no uncertain terms.

'If you mean DS Wright, he asked me to pass on his best wishes to you, too.'

'Yeah, right. And what did the useless prick have to say for himself?' She stopped him with a raised hand before he answered. 'Let me rephrase that. What exact words did he use to tell you to piss off?'

'He said he hadn't heard of Callaghan, but he'd ask around—'

'Then have a meeting with his superiors to assess whether

it's in their best interests or not to pass anything he might learn on to us.'

'I didn't realise you'd been listening in.'

They shared a knowing look. They could joke about it all they liked, but Wright would have the last laugh—despite what Kincade now said.

'Let's hope we accidentally tread on somebody's toes.'

They didn't know it then, but they would find themselves deep inside somebody else's territory soon enough.

8

Pacing the floor in his kitchen, Liam Callaghan was still fuming. He'd pulled down the window blind so that he didn't have to look at Harry's van sitting in the alley at the bottom of the garden with four slashed tyres. He knew it was still there, obviously. That didn't mean he wanted to look at it.

If Transit vans can laugh at people, that's what it was doing.

And if Transit vans owned mobile phones, it would be texting the police.

Come and search me.

Liam was convinced they were on their way at this very moment, nightsticks and handcuffs at the ready.

His rage had known no bounds when he discovered the damage the previous night. When it finally subsided to a seething desire to punch and kick everything and anything in sight, he sat in the van in the dark, eyes closed, trying to think. Local kids going too far having a laugh? He didn't think so. One tyre, maybe, but not all four. A message? *We killed your brother, but we're giving you one last chance.* No van, no shipments. Take the hint and sell the shitty van for scrap. That didn't feel right, either. He knew Harry had been threatened recently, but the pig-headed bastard refused to say who by, or what it had been about.

Now, Liam wished he'd pushed him harder.

He'd contemplated torching the van where it sat, parked in the alley. The cops would know he'd done it, but what was worse? Torch it and make them look at him twice as hard? Or take his chances? Trust that Harry had cleaned it thoroughly. Or the sniffer dogs had canine flu and blocked noses.

Then the doorbell rang.

Of course, it did. It was in cahoots with the bloody van.

He trudged down the hall, a single thought in his mind.

Dead man walking.

Angel wasn't one hundred per cent comfortable with the upcoming interview with Liam Callaghan. The man had recently lost his brother in a shocking, violent way. The natural instinct was to go easy on him. Except Liam ignored what should've been his own instinctive reaction when his brother went missing. To sit with his sister-in-law and comfort her. Reassure her that Harry would walk through the front door any minute, a guilty smile on his face and an innocent explanation about where he'd been on his lips. Instead, he'd taken Harry's van and told her to keep her big mouth shut if anybody came asking.

That still didn't make it any easier to lay into him.

Except Liam looked as if somebody had been doing exactly that for the past hour when he opened the door to them. The unhealthy pallor of his skin, the dark bags under his eyes, suggested he hadn't slept a wink. Angel suspected it was less to do with lying awake thinking about poor old Harry, and more to do with a two a.m. drive out to somewhere secluded to torch the van and then a long walk home.

Liam stepped to the side when he saw them on his doorstep, ushered them in with as much good grace as if they'd been carrying the Black Death.

'Barbara called me and told me about Harry,' he said, indicating the open doorway into the front sitting room.

'Please accept our condolences,' Angel replied, determined as ever to avoid the over-used and insincere *sorry for your loss* as if the bereaved had made a poor investment decision or broken a favourite vase.

He paused in the doorway as Kincade went into the sitting room ahead of him, looked to his right. The kitchen was at the end of the hall, a window overlooking the back garden directly facing him. The blind was down. He made a mental note to take a closer look later, then allowed Liam to herd him after Kincade into the front room.

'Did your sister-in-law give you the details?' he said, once they were all settled.

Liam nodded slowly, eyes out of focus as if imagining being led into the trees by a man with a gun himself.

'We don't come across many people killed like that,' Angel went on. 'Sorry to be so blunt, but it was an execution. Do you have any idea why, or who would do that?'

Liam had taken the armchair facing the sofa Angel and Kincade were sharing. He sat perched on the edge of the seat, leaning forward with his forearms resting on his thighs. The picture of a man paying attention, desperate to help catch his brother's killer in any way he could.

It couldn't have been further from the truth.

He dropped his head, shook it. As if overcome by the enormity of it all.

'No idea.'

Angel leaned back in his seat as if he could now relax, the

most difficult question behind them. He even tried a smile. It never hurts.

'I have to ask. And I wouldn't normally expect any other answer. I am not my brother's keeper and all that. Except this is different.'

He glanced at Kincade—*you're on.*

'When exactly did your sister-in-law tell you about Harry's death?' she said.

'Yesterday morning. Right after you told her. Like you'd expect. He was my brother.'

Kincade gave a firm nod, *glad to hear it.*

'But your brother was killed approximately forty-eight hours before that. He'd gone missing. Then, early yesterday morning before we called on your sister-in-law and she phoned you, you went to her house, left your car there and drove Harry's van away. You also told her to keep her mouth shut if we turned up. That all suggests you already suspected something bad had happened to Harry.' She gave him a self-deprecating smile, an acknowledgement of their role as bearers of bad tidings. 'Because we don't turn up when good things happen.'

Liam didn't smile with her.

'What made you think something bad had happened to Harry?' she went on, crossing her arms over her chest as she waited for an answer.

'Like you said, he'd gone missing. He wasn't answering texts.'

'What did you think had happened to him? Did you think he'd had an accident?'

'Maybe.'

'But you didn't phone round the local hospitals? Or did you?'

Liam kept his eyes on the carpet between his feet, grunted an indistinct negative response. His palpable discomfort and evasiveness encouraged Kincade to increase the pressure.

'Is that because you don't care?'

Liam's head shot up, giving Kincade the evil eye as if she'd just admitted to pulling the trigger.

'Of course, I bloody cared. What sort of a person do you think I am? He was my brother.'

'So you keep saying. The only reason I can think why you didn't do what normal people would do is because you knew it wasn't something as ordinary as a car accident. He wasn't in a hospital somewhere. You knew Harry was into something that could potentially turn very nasty. Something you were into with him. Something that made you think, *Christ knows what's happened to Harry, but I better get rid of the bloody van asap before plod turn up*.'

Angel smiled to himself as Kincade pushed Liam further into a corner, relieved he didn't have to face her across an interview table.

'Why did you take the van?' he said, taking the lead once more. 'And where is it now? We didn't see it parked on the street. I hope you're not going to tell us it was stolen last night and then we find it burned out somewhere.'

Liam didn't say anything.

Angel couldn't understand why he was having such difficulty answering. He'd collected the van because he expected them to turn up at Harry's house. He knew they'd find their way back to him sooner or later. He'd had twenty-four hours. Why didn't he have a list of plausible answers ready for the questions he knew they'd ask? Something had rattled him. And Angel had an idea it was connected to the closed window blind in the kitchen. He pushed himself to his feet.

'I'm going to get myself a glass of water while you think about answering.'

Liam was on his feet before the words were all the way out of Angel's mouth.

'I'll get it.' Already moving towards the door.

Angel blocked his way.

'You sit down and tell my colleague why you took Harry's van.'

For a brief moment Liam looked as if he was going to argue. Then he slumped visibly, dropped into the armchair Angel was pointing at.

'I'm all ears,' Kincade said, as Angel left the room.

Bit dark in here, drifted in from the kitchen a moment later. *I think I'll open the blind.*

Liam lurched forwards, realised the pointlessness of it. Threw himself back into the chair.

I've found the van, came from the kitchen, a happy twang to Angel's voice.

Kincade extended her hand towards the door as she got to her feet.

'Shall we?'

She was already in the kitchen by the time Liam stood up. Angel was standing at the sink in front of the window, looking down the garden to where a knackered old Transit van was parked in the alley at the bottom.

'Where's the back-door key?' he said to Liam when he joined them, then saw it on a hook at the side of the door before Liam answered.

A minute later, they were all trooping down the garden, Angel in the lead, the van keys in his hand. Not long after that, two of them were having trouble keeping the smiles off their faces as they contemplated the van sitting on four flat tyres.

'Nice neighbours you've got around here,' Angel said.

Kincade disagreed.

'It can't be because he's parked in somebody else's space.'

'Did you puncture the local kids' football when they kicked it in your garden?' Angel asked. 'We had a neighbour used to do that.'

Liam glared back at them, saying nothing—not even to ask if Angel slashed the neighbour's tyres.

'Do you believe in coincidence, Mr Callaghan?' Kincade said. Then, when he didn't reply, 'That's an actual question.'

'No, I don't believe in fucking coincidence.'

'Nor us.' She kicked the nearest slashed tyre. 'And it's no coincidence that forty-eight hours after your brother was shot to death, somebody slashed all the tyres on his van while it was parked behind your house. What do you think they're trying to say to you, Mr Callaghan?'

Angel joined in when Liam didn't answer.

'That's another actual question.' Then, when he still didn't answer, 'I don't know if you're stupid or being deliberately awkward, but if you ask me, it's in your best interests to work out what the message is. And to take notice of it. And if you don't want to spend the rest of your life looking over your shoulder, you should think about cooperating with us to help us find who killed your brother before they get to you, too.'

Liam gave him a tight smile.

'And what if the message is, *don't talk to nosy coppers?*'

'Then you're caught between a rock and a hard place, Mr Callaghan. Only you can decide. In the meantime, we'll get a recovery truck to collect the van. I'm sure our sniffer dogs are going to have a field day. In case you were thinking of blaming whatever we find on Harry, we'll be checking the last time this vehicle made a cross-channel day trip, and who was travelling. It might all be a waste of time, of course, because you might be dead by then.'

'You don't have much time,' Kincade added, turning the screw. 'You need to ask yourself how the person who slashed the tyres knew the van was here. Were they watching Harry's house? Your house? Either way, they know where you live now. They might even have seen us turn up. I don't know about you, but that'd keep me awake at night.'

They'd given Liam a lot to think—and worry—about. They were hoping it would help loosen his tongue. Before they arrived, Angel planned to accuse Liam of helping his brother intimidate the road-rage victim Piotr Adamczyk. Suggest they might conveniently forget about it again if Liam played ball. With this latest development, Angel dropped the idea. He wanted all of Liam's worrying focussed on the tyre-slashing killer stalking him. They sent him back inside the house, let his own imagination do their job for them while they waited in the alley until a uniformed officer arrived to stand guard over the vehicle.

'Why does one brother get a warning and the other one gets three bullets in the back?' Angel said, when they were back in the car.

'Because Harry was the organ-grinder and Liam's only the monkey?'

'Could be. Or because Harry already had his warning and ignored it. He really did think he was Dirty Harry.'

Both suggestions were plausible, both impossible to determine at this juncture. What Kincade suggested next after they'd both mulled it over for a minute or two only confused matters.

'Or it's not a warning at all.'

'You want to talk me through that?'

'Somebody wants Liam Callaghan out of the way. Maybe they did threaten Harry and he ignored it. They're thinking Liam will be the same. They're not ready for a scorched-earth campaign yet, and decide dropping him in the shit with us will keep him occupied. They immobilise the van in a way that stops him from moving it, but doesn't destroy anything incriminating that might be inside.'

'Okay.' Stretching the word out to double its normal length as he thought the idea through. 'We're back to the question of how did they know the van was here?'

'Like I said to Liam, they were watching his or Harry's house.'

Maybe it was because it was the second time she'd said it, but her words triggered a vague memory, a random thought that crossed his mind when they arrived. A vehicle that looked out of place on the street of small, terraced houses. Something big and black and expensive. A Range Rover, perhaps? He'd paid no attention at the time, thankful Kincade hadn't spotted it, made a disparaging remark about local drug dealers made good visiting dear old mum on the streets where they grew up.

Still parked at the kerb, he glanced in his mirror. There was an empty space where the vehicle had been parked, squeezed in between a faded-red ex-Royal Mail van and a twenty-year-old Toyota Hilux pickup truck.

And he thought about what Christine Hamill, the Crime Scene Manager at Harry Callaghan's murder scene, had said as she indicated tyre tracks in the mud.

I'd say we're looking at a van or a four-by-four.

9

If either Gulliver or Jardine had been short-sighted they might have thought Harry Callaghan had risen from the dead when they saw the man who opened the widow Callaghan's front door to them. Aged about thirty, he had a little more hair cut equally short, a little less doughy flab around the middle. Roughly the same number of tattoos, the colours not so faded. Neither of them had met Callaghan while he was still breathing, but the man in front of them gave them a good feel for the amount of attitude they could've expected if they had.

'You must be Harry Callaghan's son,' Gulliver said, ignoring the way the man looked them up and down, his nose wrinkled like he had something unpleasant on his top lip.

'Yeah.'

His hands remained firmly thrust into his jeans pockets as he said it. An insolent *you don't scare me* pose. A close call between that or arms folded aggressively over his chest, which would've had the added benefit of showcasing his pumped-up and tattooed biceps.

'Do you want to tell us your name?' Jardine said.

The answer was clearly *no*. Despite that, Junior grunted a grudging reply.

'Sonny.'

'And are you going to invite us in, Sonny?'

'Mum's asleep.'

'We don't need to bother her. We're here to search the house.'

Sonny smiled like he'd been itching to use the line he now rolled out.

'Got a warrant?'

Jardine smiled right back like a shark that's just caught a baby seal.

'We don't need one. We're authorised to search premises without one if we believe a delay in obtaining a warrant is likely to result in evidence being destroyed or removed. Your uncle, Liam, already removed your dad's van with the intention of destroying evidence. He also told your mum to lie to us.'

Sonny crossed his arms over his chest, as if the aggressive pose would make his inevitable unwilling agreement less of a climbdown.

Jardine got fed up with the posturing.

'Just go and wake up your mother and ask her, will you?'

'I'm already bloody awake,' came from the top of the stairs, followed by the rest of Barbara Callaghan, once again dressed in her inflammable pink fluffy dressing gown. 'Thanks to you.' Then, to her son. 'Let them in, Sonny. We've got nothing to hide.'

Nothing left to hide, Jardine thought sourly as Sonny stood aside.

They started with the upstairs rooms. Nobody hides anything in the sitting room or the kitchen, rooms where a visitor might innocently stumble across something. People hide things in bedrooms and other private rooms where guests rarely go.

Jardine took the master bedroom, Gulliver the box room that had been converted into a small home office. An Ikea desk sat under the window overlooking the back garden, a computer monitor sitting on it. The CPU was in a cradle suspended from the pale wood desktop. Gulliver moved the mouse and the screen came alive, no password required. He closed a partially finished game of Solitaire, then stifled a laugh at the desktop image. A Ferrari or an Aston Martin he could've understood. Maybe with Harry at the wheel on a track day Babs bought him for his birthday.

But a skip lorry with a bright yellow skip on the back?

Different strokes for different folks, he thought, opening the web browser and calling up the history. From the short list of websites visited all dated that day, it was clear the browser was configured to delete all history on shutdown—that, or the Callaghans were paranoid about clearing the cache. It wasn't a problem. The ISP would provide a full history if necessary. He ran his eyes down the list, nonetheless—not that Harry Callaghan had been doing the browsing. The first item was a Google search for local funeral directors, the second for florists. Gulliver felt confident Harry would get a good send-off, even if the answer to why he needed one would not be revealed.

The email system was equally uninformative. Both Callaghans had a separate email address, and both inboxes were filled almost exclusively with spam. Barbara's was all high-street clothes shops and supermarkets, the subject lines filled with words like *Hurry!* and *Don't Miss Out!* There were a lot of exclamation marks. Harry's was filled with messages from online gambling sites urging him to waste his hard-earned cash on a momentary lapse in judgement, and special offers from

DIY retailers for when the gambling sites left him too strapped for cash to pay the professionals.

It was all very mundane. Gulliver felt the will to live deserting him.

He got up from the desk, went to see if Jardine's efforts had proved more fruitful in the master bedroom.

'Nothing,' she said, then, apropos of nothing, 'Did you know you can't call it a master bedroom anymore? I mean, *really*. Who can be bothered to get upset about something like that when people are getting shot to death and all the other shit that goes on?'

Gulliver left her to it, very relieved they were working separate rooms. Back in the box room, he started on the desk drawers. The top two contained nothing of interest. Dried-up ballpoint pens and Post-it sticky notes that were no longer sticky, multi-coloured paperclips and boxes of staples that no normal person would get through in two lifetimes.

What he found in the bottom drawer was a different matter —if only because it was the last thing he'd expect to find in the drawer of a man who had a skip lorry on his desktop.

Jardine appeared in the doorway as he lifted it out.

'What have you got?'

He held it towards her.

'I know you wouldn't recognise it coming from the North East, but it's what we call a book.'

She snatched it out of his hand, read the title out loud.

'*Pass The Buck: A history of political scandal in post-war Britain*. By Robert Brinkley, whoever he is. It sounds like the reading equivalent of watching paint dry.'

'Not enough pictures for you?'

She hefted the thick paperback in her hand, looking at his head at the same time.

'It's a good weight. It might be useful for something. Knock some sense out of you.'

There'll still be plenty left, he thought and kept to himself, given the implied challenge in the thought.

She was busy flicking through the pages, the sudden annoyance in her voice surprising him.

'I hate it when people do that.'

'Do what?'

'Turn over the corners of the pages. Don't you have bookmarks down here in the South if you're so great?'

She handed the book back to him, the discussion over as far as she was concerned.

'He didn't get far,' Gulliver said, opening the book at the furthest folded-over corner. 'Page thirty-two.'

'Unless he read the rest of it in one go.'

They both looked at the thickness of it, shook heads at each other.

'I'm surprised someone like Callaghan bought it in the first place,' he said.

She suddenly grinned at him.

'Most men keep their porn hidden in the bottom drawer. In this household, he needs to hide his boring, high-brow books. I bet we find a secret subscription to *The Guardian* when we check his bank account.'

They were interrupted by the sound of a person climbing the stairs, then Barbara Callaghan's voice tinged with impatience behind the wheezing breathlessness.

'Are you nearly done up here?'

'Shouldn't be long now,' Gulliver said, when she appeared behind Jardine in the doorway. He showed the book to her. 'Have you ever seen that before?'

She stuck out her hand, *gimme here*, then shook her head slowly as she studied the front cover.

'Nah. Where was it?'

'In the bottom desk drawer.'

She looked at the front cover again, her face compacting in concentration.

'Did your husband have an interest in political scandal, Mrs Callaghan?' Gulliver asked.

Barbara scowled at him as if she'd heard *paedophilia*, not *political*.

'Are you having a laugh?' She waved the book in his face. 'Even if he did, he wouldn't need to waste his money buying a book to know all politicians are scumbags who're only interested in themselves and think they're above the laws they make.' She flicked through the pages as he had, made the same observation. 'He didn't get far, did he? That's all it took for him to realise there was nothing he didn't already know inside.'

She handed the book back to him in disgust, as if its centre pages had been removed and hard-core porn inserted in their place.

'And he never mentioned it to you?' Gulliver persevered. 'He didn't read a few pages, then say to you, can you believe what this toerag did, fiddling his expenses or screwing his secretary or whatever?'

Barbara rested her hands on her substantial hips.

'Do I look like the sort of person who'd be interested?'

'I'm done in the master bedroom,' Jardine said, to save Gulliver from having to reply. 'You can get back to bed, if you like.'

'Find any clues?' Barbara said sarcastically, not waiting for the negative reply from Jardine. 'I could've told you that. I hope you haven't made a mess.'

Jardine smiled at her disappearing back, whispered to Gulliver as Barbara closed the bedroom door firmly and pointedly behind her.

'Hard to tell, given what it was like to begin with.'

She left him to finish up in the box room, went to give the sparsely-furnished second bedroom the once over. Finding nothing further of interest in the desk drawers, Gulliver got down on his hands and knees, crawled under the desk.

It was a tight fit with the drawers on one side, the computer CPU in its cradle on the other. The floor was free of junk, no shoe boxes filled with dead mice and broken headsets, no half-empty packs of copy paper. The CPU was humming away beside him, flashing blue lights from terminals at the back reflected off the wall. The cradle it sat in was adjustable, a three-inch gap between the top of the CPU and the underside of the desk. He slid his hand in and knocked an ancient clam-shell phone to the floor.

He opened it, the battery life still at sixty-eight per cent. Without the obsession with slim design constraining it, and not filled with battery-draining apps reporting the user's every move back to giant faceless corporations, it was good for weeks. Despite its dinosaur-era design, it still required a pass code. It wouldn't be a problem for the tech nerds. He bagged the phone, slipped it in his pocket.

He considered the book on the desk for a long moment. Ordinarily, they wouldn't be interested in a victim's book collection. Except this book was so out of character with the man it belonged to. It was the only book in the house as far as Gulliver remembered seeing. And something about Barbara's reaction was off. He bagged it, *better safe than sorry*.

'LOOKS LIKE I FOUND THE CRUCIAL PIECE OF EVIDENCE,' HE SAID, showing Jardine the phone once they were back in the car. 'As usual.'

'That's only because you couldn't be trusted in the bedroom

not to waste your whole time going through her underwear drawer.'

'I think a more appropriate response would be, *good work, Craig, well done.*'

'Don't worry, you'll get a pat on the head from the boss when we get back.' She stuck out her hand for him to pass the phone across, fond reminiscence entering her voice. 'This takes me back. I bet you can't even get on the internet with it. Is it locked?'

'Yeah.'

'What do you reckon will be on it?'

'If his computer desktop image is anything to go by, numbers for phone sex with lady skip lorry drivers.'

'Do they even exist?' She stuck a rigid digit in his face before he could answer. '*Careful!* You've already had your one smartarse crack about the North East for today.'

Long experience had taught him such warnings were not to be ignored. He moved on, showed her the paperback book in its evidence bag.

'I bagged this, too.'

Ordinarily, he'd have expected a remark about the pointlessness of wasting time over the book cancelling the positive effect of finding the phone. Instead, she turned pensive.

'I thought you gave her a hard time over it. What was that about?'

He blew the air from his cheeks, tried to put the vague impression of something not quite right into words.

'Not sure. I believed her when she said she'd never seen it. And I don't think they discussed it—'

'It'd be a two-second conversation if they did. *All politicians are wankers. Yeah, I agree.*'

'—but there was something about it she recognised. She tried to hide it, but I saw something register.'

'The author's name? Robert Brinkley?' She took the book out

of his hand, hefted it—although not looking at his head this time. 'But if you think I'm going to wade through this to find out what it might be, think again.'

'You wouldn't even get as far as Callaghan did.'

'Too bloody right, I wouldn't.' Throwing the book on the back seat as she said it. 'I'd be asleep by page three.'

'Like I said, not enough pretty pictures...'

The conversation continued in the same unprofessional vein all the way back to the station.

That didn't mean Gulliver's gut instinct was wrong.

10

'Are you thinking of staying for the whole show today?' Kincade asked, as she and Angel made their way through the bowels of Southampton General Hospital on the way to watching Isabel Durand carve up Harry Callaghan's considerable remains.

'Not today, no.'

Generally, he chose to leave after the external examination. Before the Y-incision was made and the pathologist started desecrating the body in the name of the truth. It wasn't squeamishness. He'd seen more than his fair share of blood and gore in his time as an Army chaplain in Afghanistan and Iraq. He'd held the hands of too many young men who'd lost the fight against death, the pointless waste of a young life staying with him long after the blood had stopped pumping and writhing limbs were still. The clinical dissection of an already-dead body held no horrors for him. A lot of the time, when dealing with death by violent trauma, it gave no additional insight.

Any man with eyes in his head could see that Harry Callaghan had died from gunshot wounds. Durand's report would tell him exactly what damage the bullets had caused as they made their merry way through his internal organs. It was fascinating stuff if your mind was wired a certain way, but it wouldn't tell him who or why Callaghan's killer had pulled the trigger. Nor would attending the procedure tell him whether drugs or alcohol had played a part. He'd have to wait for the toxicology report for that.

At times, he wondered why they attended at all.

'I hope that's not because you're still feeling rough from too many beers last night,' Kincade carried on. 'Don't want to get a preview of what your own insides look like.'

She was right in one respect—it was the first time he'd attended an autopsy with a hangover. Even so, there was no chance of him losing his lunch.

'Of course not.'

'Word of advice, sir. Keep moving while we're in there. You're so pale Doctor Death might start carving you up if you stand still for too long.'

'I'll try to remember that, Sergeant, thank you.'

Seemed Kincade wasn't alone in her thinking. Durand looked up as they entered, did a small double-take.

'You look nearly as bad as him, Padre.' Pointing at Callaghan's corpse on the stainless-steel table in front of them.

Angel gave her a half-hearted smile.

'You say the nicest things, Isabel.' Then, to get her off the subject of him, 'Bet you wish it was the real Dirty Harry lying there.'

'I'm not sure how to take that, Padre. The implication that I'd like to have cut up Clint Eastwood in his prime. Sounds like a terrible waste to me, wouldn't you agree, Sergeant?'

Kincade startled as Durand drew her unexpectedly into the conversation.

Was that an attempt to bond? To mend bridges that had never been intact in the first place?

'Absolutely, Doctor. Stick to the fat and ugly ones. No loss to us girls there.'

Even behind the mask, Durand's face suggested it would be the last time she deviated from anything other than a professional conversation with Kincade.

Callaghan's corpse was currently on its side, his wrists secured behind his back making it impractical to lie him flat. Durand left him in situ as she began talking into a microphone clipped to her lapel. She noted that rigor mortis had been and gone, which, when coupled with the degree and positioning of livor mortis that was no longer blanchable, confirmed her estimate at the scene. He'd been dead, face-down on the ground where he'd been found, for approximately forty-eight hours before his body was discovered.

She then cut the cable ties securing his wrists and inspected them briefly before passing them to the waiting exhibits officer when she saw nothing of interest.

Everything changed when she examined the deceased's hands—and it wasn't the word *HATE* tattooed across his knuckles.

'What is it, Isabel?' Angel said, picking up on Durand's increased interest when she lifted Callaghan's left hand and examined the little finger.

She put a blue-gloved finger against the edge of Callaghan's fingernail and wiggled it before answering.

'This nail is about to come off. There is also a large subungual haematoma as evidenced by the purplish-black discolouration.' She glanced at Kincade and Angel knew retaliation for Kincade's earlier put-down was on its way. 'Blood in the space between the nail bed and the fingernail, Sergeant. It results from direct injury to the fingernail. It could have been caused by something as innocent as shutting his finger in the door. Given that we're dealing with a man who has been shot three times, a more sinister explanation seems more likely.'

'Someone hit his finger with a hammer,' Kincade said, a statement more than a suggestion.

'Very probably. I'll take x-rays. From the amount of damage, I wouldn't be surprised to see that the distal phalanx of the little finger has suffered multiple fractures.'

Someone beat the shit out of his pinky with a hammer, Kincade corrected to herself.

As for Angel, he was immediately back in the alley behind Liam Callaghan's house. Speculating with Kincade about why Liam received a warning when his brother had been shot to death. Were they looking at Harry's own, earlier warning? One he'd ignored, prompting the one-way ride out to the New Forest in the killer's van or SUV?

He tuned the proceedings out as Durand continued with her examination. The evidence of Callaghan's finger being cold-bloodedly maimed as a warning brought Virgil Balan's offer to find Bogdan Florescu to mind, the dilemma it might pose if he was successful. As before, he formed a vivid mental image of Florescu tied to a chair, his face already cut and bloodied. This time, Balan was offering him a hammer as a lackey untied one of Florescu's hands, held it firmly down on a wooden table top, the fingers splayed. Ready for Angel to take his pick. Take out his anger and grief on delicate finger bones—

'Are you still with us, Padre?' Durand asked, dragging Angel from his reverie before he saw himself take the hammer from Balan's outstretched hand, feel its weight, its ability to cause pain and irreparable damage, in his palm.

'Absolutely, Isabel. Thinking about the implications of Callaghan's injured finger.'

'I've taken samples of the blood on the deceased's forehead,' she said, well aware that he'd been miles away. 'Having had the opportunity to clean the area, I can confirm what I said at the scene. There are no cuts or grazes on his forehead.'

It wasn't necessary for her to spell out the implications. Being shot in the back while he was face-down on the ground could not have resulted in his own blood ending up on his forehead. He might have touched the hip wound and subsequently touched his forehead with bloody fingers, but that seemed unlikely.

'Let's hope it's the killer's,' Angel said. 'Callaghan obviously incapacitated him sufficiently for him to almost get away. A head butt would do that.' He put his fingers beneath his nostrils, pulled his hands down and apart in an imitation of blood gushing from his nose. The demonstration immediately highlighted a flaw. 'How does the blood get on Callaghan's forehead? He butts the killer, a short sharp blow to the nose, pulls his head back. The killer's blood might get on Callaghan's T-shirt, but I don't see how it gets on his forehead.'

'He butts him twice,' Kincade said, her tone questioning why anyone wouldn't use a double headbutt to be on the safe side. 'He butts him once, the killer's nose explodes and his head is thrown back.' She angled her own head towards the ceiling as she said it. 'Then Callaghan butts him a second time while his head is tipped back. On his nose or his mouth, both of which are covered with blood from the first blow.'

Angel was impressed, even if he put it in a different way.

'Remind me not to get into a fight with you in a pub.'

Kincade smiled like he'd paid her a compliment, the words *and don't you forget it* all the louder for not being spoken.

The remainder of the external examination provided nothing of value beyond what they already knew. A bullet entry wound in the rear of Callaghan's right hip supported the hypothesis that he'd been brought down as he tried to flee. Dirt and grass stains on his clothes and exposed flesh was consistent with crawling away as his killer stalked after him. And after cutting away his red-and-white-striped football shirt that looked as if it had been used to clean an abattoir floor, Durand confirmed the three entry wounds in his back were also consistent with nine-millimetre rounds.

Angel nudged Kincade and flicked his head towards the door as the pathologist prepared to start the Y-incision.

Durand looked up as they started to slip away.

'A wise choice, Padre. Even if you're not sick, you don't want to risk seeing what your own liver looks like.' She prodded Callahan's distended stomach that she'd soon be slitting open. 'Or anything else that might encourage you to live a healthier lifestyle.'

'Exactly, Isabel. Where's the fun in that?' He took one last look at Callaghan's flabby corpse. 'At least he didn't spend his whole life eating rabbit food and drinking fruit juice only for someone to put three bullets in him.'

Durand smiled back, and Kincade couldn't decide whether she'd been privy to a coded message between them. An arrangement to meet for a juicy, cholesterol-rich steak and a bottle of red wine, follow it with salty saturated-fat cheese and a crusty old port, share a big fat carcinogenic cigar to finish.

She'd have given him a hard time over it as the autopsy room door closed silently and reverently behind them and they made their way down the corridor towards sunlight and the world of the living, their shoes squeaking on the polished floor, had her mind not been occupied by something more pressing.

'Something doesn't make sense. Callaghan almost getting away suggests there was only one killer. We don't know what happened that gave Callaghan the chance to headbutt him, but whatever it was, it wouldn't have happened if there'd been two of them...'

Angel saw where she was going with it.

'Given the size of Callaghan—'

'And the fact that he could obviously look after himself.'

'—how did one man manage to smash his finger with a hammer?'

'Exactly.'

'Maybe he forced Callaghan to do it to himself at gunpoint.'

She pulled her head back to get a better look at him, see if he was serious.

'Where does an idea like that come from?' she said, when it looked as if he was.

'Beats me.' Spoken with a noncommittal shrug, before making a more constructive suggestion. 'Or it could be a falling out between the killers. There were two of them involved in smashing his finger. But when he ignored the warning, only one of them was prepared to escalate things to the point of killing him.'

She stopped walking abruptly, forcing him to do the same.

'Isn't the point of attending an autopsy supposed to be to provide answers, not more questions?'

Shows how many autopsies you've been to, he thought as they resumed their journey towards daylight, if not enlightenment.

11

'That's the skip lorry Callaghan used for his desktop image,' Gulliver said, pointing at one of the vehicles in Hall-It-Away Skip Hire's yard, all of them lined-up in a perfectly-spaced row as if they were about to take promotional shots for their website.

Jardine gave him a look of incredulous horror.

'How on earth can you tell? They all look the same.'

He tut-tutted, disappointed that his partner was so unobservant.

'Look closer.'

He made a point of driving slowly as they passed the lorries on the way to a brick-built, single-storey admin block with all the charm of a public urinal. She groaned out loud when she saw what he was talking about.

'I don't believe it! Who wants to drive around with a *Dirty Harry* sun strip across their windscreen?'

'Someone called Harry Callaghan?'

'Someone who wants to hear the same cheesy jokes everywhere he goes, more like. You'd think he'd have got bored with it.'

Gulliver wasn't so sure. Everything they'd learned about Callaghan suggested he enjoyed swaggering around like a badass cop in a 1970s movie, assaulting other drivers for giving him the finger, then turning up on their doorstep with his brother to intimidate them.

'Stops people complaining if he spills rubbish on their new driveway.'

'The way he looked was enough to ensure that. It still doesn't explain why the new driver wouldn't take it off.'

Callaghan's entry on the PNC showed that he'd worked for Hall-It-Away Skip Hire at the time of the road rage incident involving Piotr Adamczyk. It wasn't clear whether the company name was a play on the name of the owner—Reg Hall—or ignorance about how to spell *haul*. Jardine didn't bother asking when she called the company's offices to arrange to meet with Hall, and was informed Callaghan had been *let go*. The woman Jardine spoke to claimed she was new and didn't know why. The weight of evasiveness coming down the line only made Jardine twice as determined to book an appointment.

The combined smells of bacon and coffee hit them when they entered, as if they'd walked into a greasy spoon café. Gulliver's mouth immediately watered and his stomach grumbled, but it was a lot better than the smells the building's public-urinal appearance might prepare visitors for. A large man who looked very similar to Harry Callaghan was leaning on the front counter eating a bacon sandwich while he chatted to the woman working behind it. She was complaining about him dripping grease on the counter. He was telling her she could lick it clean any time she liked. The chewable aura of sexual innuendo could've filled another sandwich.

They both fell silent as Gulliver and Jardine entered, apart from the unspoken shout—*watch out, the old bill's about!*

'He's in his office,' the woman said, before either of them

opened their mouth. She pointed down a corridor behind her with a tattooed arm that would come in handy unloading the skips if the hydraulic winches broke down. 'Last door on the left.'

'There's only one door on the left,' Jardine muttered, as they made their way down the short corridor.

Reg Hall and his office were a pleasant surprise. Hall himself was the first person they'd come across who didn't look exactly like Harry Callaghan. His office was plain and utilitarian, but at least it didn't smell of bacon sandwich. Raising your voice to make yourself heard over the sounds of a growling stomach isn't the most professional way to conduct an interview.

Things went downhill as soon as Hall opened his mouth.

'I thought Vicky told you he doesn't work for us anymore.'

'She did,' Jardine replied. 'But what I didn't want to say over the phone is that Harry Callaghan was murdered a couple of days ago.'

'What's that got to do—'

He'd been so desperate to distance himself from anything they might want to talk about, he hadn't paid attention to the word *murdered*. Now, it registered, the colour draining from his face.

They saw him about to say all of the usual, stupid things that pop out—*you can't be serious* or turning the word *murdered* into a question—before composing himself.

'That's awful. But I still don't see what it's got to do with us.'

Had Hall spent a little more time saying how dreadful it was or what a great guy good ol' Harry had been, and not been so keen to get back to trying to get rid of them as quickly as possible, Jardine might not have said what she did next, borrowing a line Gulliver used when they were in the car.

'Maybe he dropped the skip on somebody's new driveway

while he was working for you. Knocked the head off one of their stone lions.'

If Hall was aware of her ridiculing his clients, he didn't show it. Instead, he took the suggestion seriously.

'Nobody would murder somebody because of that.'

'It's been done for a lot less, sir. However, we're aware of a serious incident that might have caused somebody to hold a grudge. He attacked another motorist—'

'The bloke shouldn't have given him the finger.' Raising his own middle finger as he said it.

Jardine stared pointedly at the offending digit until Hall realised what he was doing and dropped his hand. Given the implications of what Hall had just said—that it was perfectly acceptable to physically attack a person for nothing more than giving an offensive hand gesture—Jardine felt her next question was a little pointless.

'Was the road rage incident the reason you got rid of Mr Callaghan?'

Hall looked at her as if she'd asked whether he fired Callaghan for not having his work boots polished and a crease ironed in his jeans.

'I wouldn't have many drivers left if I was worried about that. Car drivers think we don't give a shit about other road users—'

'We're not here to go into that, sir. Can you tell us why you did get rid of him? I'm assuming he didn't resign.'

Hall looked momentarily indignant at being talked over in his own office, but when he answered, his voice was filled with more regret than either Gulliver or Jardine would have expected, given his attitude so far.

'No. Harry loved working here.' He smiled suddenly. 'Did you see the sun strip on his lorry? Dirty Harry.'

'We saw it,' Jardine confirmed and got an accusing look from Gulliver. 'But you had to let him go?'

'Yeah. He killed somebody.'

If Hall had been able to rewind the conversation, he might have phrased it differently, more accurately. As it was, the blunt statement left Gulliver and Jardine speechless. Hall saw the effect his revelation had on them, immediately explained.

'I mean he knocked down a pedestrian.'

It wasn't necessary to point out that when a skip lorry knocks you down, you don't get up again.

Hall's demeanour changed, a seriousness coming over him that hadn't been evident before. He sat forward in his chair, elbows resting on his desk, his tone earnest.

'It wasn't Harry's fault. The bloke just walked out in front of him. Wasn't looking. Nothing Harry could do. He had a full load. It's not like he could stop on a sixpence.' He tapped the desktop with the same middle finger he'd raised before. 'He was stone cold sober. Hadn't been drinking. I won't tolerate that.' He hooked his thumb towards the window. 'I catch a driver doing that, they're out. Bollocks to your disciplinaries and all that shit. *Out!* Same goes if they're caught on their phone.' He scissored his hands above the desk. 'On yer bike.'

He leaned back in his chair, his stock of hand gestures exhausted.

'Glad to hear it, Mr Hall,' Gulliver said, then stroked Hall's ego a bit more. 'We could do with more people taking such a responsible attitude. So, what happened to Callaghan? Was he prosecuted?'

Hall shook his head firmly.

'Nah. There was an inquest and all that bollocks. The judge . . . is it a judge?'

'Coroner,' Gulliver said.

'The coroner said it wasn't Harry's fault. It was an accident.' He coughed a short laugh devoid of humour. 'You wouldn't have thought so from the fuss some woman at the inquest made. Stupid cow.'

'What kind of a fuss?'

'Yelling and screaming at Harry. The judge had to tell her to shut up. The coroner, I mean.'

'What exactly was she saying?'

'I wasn't close enough to hear properly. Half of it was in French and what was in English was hysterical.'

Gulliver and Jardine shared a look given the Callaghan brothers' likely connection to France and their own shared scepticism towards coincidence.

'She was French?' Gulliver said.

Hall gave a dismissive shrug, the detail clearly not important to him.

'Sounded like it. I know she wasn't Spanish. We've got a villa in Spain—'

'Do you know who she was?'

Again, Hall looked mildly indignant at being talked over, or it might have been disappointment that they weren't interested in whether his villa had a private pool or not.

'The dead bloke's girlfriend?'

The way his intonation turned it into a question made it clear he didn't know. She was a stupid hysterical cow and that's all Reg Hall needed to know.

Gulliver phrased his next question very carefully. He didn't want it to sound as if Hall had kicked Callaghan when he was down, already distraught for killing a pedestrian. The passive tense came to the rescue.

'But it still became necessary to let him go?'

Hall looked away, didn't meet their eyes.

'Twenty years he worked for me. Longer than anyone else. Never took the piss, never let me down. But he became unreliable after the accident. Didn't turn up for work and didn't even call to say he wasn't going to be in. Stress, I suppose. You wouldn't think it looking at him, but it obviously affected him. I would've understood. I told him to take time off, but it was all *no, no, no, there's nothing wrong with me*. I suppose that's pride. No bloke wants his mates to think he's lying on his bed sobbing into his pillow.'

He took a deep breath, let it out in a rush. Now he did meet their eyes. Looking from one to the other of them as if trying to determine who would be the most accepting of what he now said. He settled on Gulliver.

'I ignored it for as long as I could. But when he let me down, I let my customers down. It wasn't only about losing money. I worked hard building up my reputation. I didn't want people saying, *call Hall-It-Away if you don't want anybody to turn up*.' He shook his head sadly. 'Worst day of my life when I let him go.'

Gulliver allowed Hall a moment to reflect on it before asking the obvious question.

'How did he take it?'

'He called me a—' His mouth snapped shut, looking at Jardine. 'The *C*-word.'

'Did you have any contact with him afterwards?'

Hall smiled again, not so much wistful reminiscence in it.

'He was very bitter. A couple of weeks after I let him go, somebody vandalised my car. Did a proper job on it, too. Slashed the tyres, keyed it, paint stripper on the bonnet and roof, the works. I don't know for sure that it was Harry . . .' He shrugged, the gesture easy to interpret—*and I don't really want to*.

'Did you report it?' Gulliver asked.

'Nah. I sucked it up. If it was Harry, I didn't want him getting into trouble with you lot on top of everything else.' He grinned suddenly. 'I'd have done the same in his position. Or worse.' He suddenly realised what he was saying, and who to, a note of alarm entering his voice. 'I don't hold it against him. I didn't kill him because he trashed my car. I got a good pay-out on the insurance. Do you need my alibi?'

Gulliver told him they'd get back to him if they did, asked a question that might potentially lead somewhere.

'Do you remember who he killed?'

Hall made a show of trying to remember, removing his glasses and chewing on the end of one arm. Mercifully, he didn't drag it out for too long.

'Sorry. It was a bloke. It's not like he knocked down a mother and her kid. But I couldn't tell you the first thing about him.'

'Was he French, as well?'

'Don't think so. I would've remembered if Harry killed a foreigner.'

The emphasis he put on *foreigner*, the way it cried out for the addition of *bloody*, made it unnecessary to ask whether that would have been more or less serious than killing a decent English person in Hall's personal scale of the value of a human life.

They could have wasted time asking whether Hall knew what Callaghan had been doing since he'd been let go. Except a man like Reg Hall would sell his own grandmother into a life of sexual slavery before he dropped anyone in the shit with the police.

They were the enemy. Even when they were trying to catch the man who'd cold-bloodedly murdered Hall's longest-serving employee, a salt-of-the-earth geezer who never took the piss, never let him down.

BACK IN THE CAR, JARDINE'S OPENING OBSERVATION SURPRISED Gulliver, in the same way as when she admitted she'd like to carry a gun and wished she worked somewhere corrupt.

'I can understand why Callaghan got into smuggling.'

Gulliver had the good sense not to ask if her insight was based on where and how she was brought up.

'How's that?'

'He's worked for twenty years for the same company. Model employee by the sound of it. Loves his job. Then he kills somebody in an accident that wasn't his fault. And because he's only human and his boss is only trying to run a business, he ends up losing his job. I can see how he's going to ask himself, what's the point of playing by the rules if fate can blindside you like that?'

'Everybody could say the same thing. I could. You could . . .'

'And if I ever get sacked, maybe I'll get into smuggling.'

It wasn't a road Gulliver wanted to go down. With her brother in trouble with their counterparts in the North East, the conversation would require more mental agility than he could spare when driving—Oxford Bloody University education or not. He took them back to the safety of what they'd just learned.

'I wonder who Callaghan killed?'

'No idea. We'll be able to find out soon enough when we get back.'

They didn't know it, but they'd already held the answer in their hands.

Reg Hall felt very unsettled after Gulliver and Jardine's visit.

It wasn't so much the woman, taking the piss in her stupid Geordie accent. What was wrong with having a pair of stone lions guarding your driveway, anyway? Reg didn't particularly like lions himself. He was more of a horses' heads man. He knew it made people think he was a pikey, but he was okay with that.

It meant the genuine pikeys were less likely to break into his house when he was away in Spain.

No, it was the posh copper who triggered unwelcome memories. Gulliver. He reminded Reg of the geezer who'd turned up after the accident. The one with the lah-di-dah accent in a suit Reg reckoned cost more than one of his lorries. His words were in Reg's mind now—they'd never bloody gone away —the same anger rising up inside him remembering the finger pointed at the middle of his face like he was a disobedient dog.

Persuade your driver to keep his big mouth shut. Or else you and your tin-pot company will have a bigger problem than bad publicity because he killed a pedestrian.

After the visit today, it seemed Harry had been the one with the bigger problem.

Despite that, Reg didn't feel guilty about the way the interview had gone.

It wasn't his fault if they'd assumed the *C*-word meant the four-letter variety women hated. Reg couldn't give a toss about that. He'd been called it more times than he cared to remember. The guys in the yard used it as a term of endearment, for Christ's sake.

No, it was the other *C*-word. The one no man wants to be called.

Coward.

That had really hurt. It hadn't helped that Harry had stuck the word *yellow* in front of it. In case Reg was a thick coward who didn't even know what a coward was.

Yellow and a coward and alive, or balls like a prize bull and dead? he thought. *Who's having the last laugh now, Harry?*

He pulled out his phone, made a call.

'It's me, Babe,' he said, when his wife picked up.

'I know that, Reg. Your name is on the screen. What I don't

know is why you're calling. You *never* call me when you're at work. Is something wrong?'

He shook his head even though she couldn't see him.

'Nah. I was thinking, that's all. Why don't you give the travel agent a call, book a flight to Spain? We'll spend a couple of weeks at the villa.'

'When?'

'How about tomorrow?'

A suspicious silence came down the line before she tried to make a joke of it.

'I think I should call the doctor, not a travel agent. And anyway, I do it all online.'

'Whatever.'

'What's brought this on? You're not in trouble, are you?'

'Nah, nothing like that. I had some bad news about an old friend, that's all.'

'Who?'

Reg removed his glasses, pinched the flesh between his eyebrows. Closed his eyes. Immediately, he had a picture in his mind. Harry and Barbara sitting round his table the last time they'd been over for dinner. The gold-plated cutlery they saved for special occasions on display, the gold-leaf plates, the works.

'Nobody you know. But it made me think. Life's too short.'

'If you're sure.'

'Never been more sure of anything in my life, Babe.' He worked a smile onto his face because he'd heard the person on the other end can feel it. '*Love ya!*'

He knew she'd give him a hard time over it sooner rather than later. She'd been nagging him for years to slow down, enjoy life a bit more instead of work, work, work. Already, he heard her asking him—what if I'd dropped dead instead of an old friend? Then it'd be too late.

But you didn't, wouldn't be the right answer when it

happened. He'd cross that bridge when he came to it. He'd be on a beach in Spain by then. And his biggest problem would be a sore head after drinking too many San Miguels toasting Harry's memory.

Happy days!

12

'What's that you're reading?' Kincade said. 'How to get rid of guests who outstay their welcome?'

Angel smiled half-heartedly with her, even if the reference to his mother staying with him was too close to the bone to be funny. He didn't believe what his father claimed, that she'd come to watch him die, but at times it felt to him as if she planned to stay until he did.

'*Welcome* implies they were invited in the first place.'

She took the book when he offered it to her, read the title.

'*Pass The Buck: A history of political scandal in post-war Britain*. Are you having trouble sleeping at night?'

'You're as bad as Jardine. At least you've got the excuse of reading too many picture books to your girls.'

'You can't *read* a *picture* book.'

He gave her a look—*pedant*.

'I'd have thought it would be a lot thicker, given the subject matter,' she said, assessing the thickness of the spine.

'Small type.'

'Too small to read sounds the perfect size to me. What's the relevance?'

'Gulliver found it in Callaghan's desk drawer.'

She looked up at him as if he'd said one of the team had found a book on advanced algebra in her girls' bedroom.

'Really? I'd have thought *The Big Book of Skip Lorries* was more his style. Or *Classic Headbutts*.'

'You and everyone else. Gulliver bagged it because it's so out of character. Accepting that we're all being judgemental based on what he looked like, of course.'

'Was that my name I heard being taken in vain?' came from the doorway as Gulliver himself appeared.

'Craig wants to know if he can keep the book after the investigation is over,' Jardine said from right behind him.

He gave her a withering look, his tone equally scathing.

'I would say you can have it after you've finished all the Winnie-the-Pooh books, but I don't suppose you'll live until you're a hundred.'

'There's not going to be any competition from me,' Kincade joined in. Then, more constructively, 'What's up, Craig?'

'I pulled the file on the pedestrian Callaghan ran over and killed, Sarge. He was a freelance investigative journalist called—'

'Russell Baldwin,' Angel cut in.

Everybody looked at him. They were impressed. There was also a suspicion he'd cheated somehow.

'How did you know?' Gulliver said.

Angel turned his computer screen so that they could all see it rather than reply. It showed the Amazon sales page for the book Gulliver had found in Callaghan's drawer.

'Are you buying your own copy, sir?' Jardine said, trying hard to keep a straight face.

'Don't bother ordering one for me,' Kincade added.

Angel let them finish, then scrolled down the page as he explained.

'Robert Brinkley, the man who wrote—'

'The dullest book in the world.' Jardine, of course.

'—is the pen name of the investigative journalist Russell Baldwin. The man Callaghan ran over and killed.' He picked the book up off the desk, waved it at them, Jardine in particular. 'Not so boring after all, eh?'

Jardine came right back at him.

'The *implications* are very interesting, sir. The book's still boring as hell.'

'I think *well done, Craig, for recognising its significance* is appropriate,' Gulliver said, and was ignored by everybody.

'Talk me through those implications, Lisa,' Angel said to Jardine, continuing to tap away at his keyboard.

'I'll wait until you've finished ordering your copy, sir.'

He couldn't help laughing with her and everybody else, didn't bother spoiling the moment by saying that wasn't what he was doing.

'Callaghan was obviously interested to learn about the man he killed,' Jardine started, when they were all paying attention. 'That might be innocent interest—'

'I'd call it morbid.' This from Gulliver.

'—or there could be more to it. Especially if the book was controversial or offensive. The world's full of people who actively look to be offended.' She flicked her finger at the book on Angel's desk. 'A book about political scandal is bound to offend a lot of people.'

Despite his earlier dismissive remarks towards Jardine, Gulliver picked up the thread.

'You don't smash somebody's finger and then kill them for buying a controversial book. But Callaghan had time on his hands. Maybe he started digging a bit deeper into something he read in the book.'

Jardine gave a self-satisfied nod—*got there at last.*

Angel immediately shot her down, holding up the book as he did so.

'How did Callaghan know about this in the first place?'

'He looked it up like you did, sir,' Jardine said, not happy he'd found a crack in her theory. Everyone in the room knew that if he thought he saw a flaw in a theory, it was because there was one. Unlike some people in the room, he wasn't in the habit of opening his mouth until he was confident about what was going to come out.

'I already had this,' he said, continuing to brandish the book. 'I looked it up on Amazon, scrolled down to the author bio. That's where it said Brinkley is the pen name of the journalist Russell Baldwin. But Callaghan only had the name Russell Baldwin, the name of the man he killed. And if you put Russell Baldwin into Google, you get lots of results about him and what he's done as a journalist, but nothing that says he wrote a book under the pen name of Robert Brinkley. Things don't always work both ways. Unless there's a reference hidden away on page five hundred of Google, Callaghan must have found out about Brinkley and the book he wrote some other way.'

'More proof he was digging into Russell Baldwin's life,' Kincade said.

'Exactly.'

'Why?'

'Good question. And how? Who did he talk to? Presumably he researched Baldwin on the internet. Is that why his browsing history was deleted? We'll have a better idea when we get into the burner phone Craig found in his office and get his browsing history from the ISP.'

'Unless he had a laptop as well,' Jardine said. 'And he hid it somewhere.'

'Or asked somebody to hold onto it,' Gulliver added.

Angel summed up the general consensus in the room.

'Everybody knows more than they're saying. His brother, his wife . . .'

'She wasn't nearly upset enough when we notified her,' Kincade agreed. 'She knew what he was up to. She saw what happened to his finger. When he didn't come home one night, she knew in her heart what had happened. All we did was confirm it. That *leave me alone, I'm a grieving widow* crap was an act. And she was happy to allow us to perform a rudimentary search because she knew there was nothing there.'

'What about the burner phone I found hidden?' Gulliver objected.

A small, knowing smile curled Kincade's lips as she answered.

'You're not married, are you, Craig?'

'You know I'm not, Sarge.'

'Who'd have him?' Jardine muttered under her breath.

'Why?' Gulliver said, ignoring her and concentrating on Kincade.

'If you were, you'd know there are always secrets.'

'It's just a question of how many,' Angel said quietly. 'And how serious.'

Jardine paused in the doorway as she and Gulliver headed back to their desks, pointed somewhat insubordinately at both Angel and Kincade.

'Don't ever think about applying for a job as a marriage guidance counsellor, okay? Either of you.'

Liam Callaghan wasn't as badly spooked by his interview with the police as Reg Hall had been, but he was still far from happy. A number of phrases the detectives used kept going through his head, the casual way they'd dropped them into the conversation making his anxiety ten times worse.

You might be dead by then.
You don't have much time.
They know where you live now.
They might even have seen us turn up.

He was convinced they weren't allowed to say things like that, trying to scare him into doing their job for them. They hadn't even played good cop, bad cop, for Christ's sake. They'd both rubbed it in, stressing how vulnerable he was, what danger he was in. Enjoyed it, too, the bastards.

Despite that, Liam didn't book an immediate flight to Spain as Reg Hall told his wife to do. Instead, he changed into his cycling gear, hoping the catharsis of physical exertion would clear his head, allow him to think straight.

He'd only gone half a mile when he turned around and headed home again. It was pointless. It wasn't going to blow his mind clear. The exact opposite. He'd spend the whole twenty miles thinking about nothing else. Desperate to get back home, do what he had to do. Worse, he'd be so preoccupied he'd forget to concentrate on the road, end up getting wiped out by a dickhead in a car on his phone.

He didn't bother to change out of his cycling gear when he got home. It wasn't as if he'd broken sweat. The tight knot in his stomach told him he'd be sweating like a pig soon enough, but from fear, not exertion. He might as well be wearing his moisture-wicking cycling gear when it happened.

He went up into the loft, retrieved Harry's laptop from where he'd hidden it behind the cold-water tank and carried it down again.

He'd thought Harry was going soft in the head when he turned up with the laptop and asked him to hold onto it, say nothing about it to anyone. With Harry in the morgue, it looked like his paranoia hadn't been misplaced.

Liam and Harry had gotten into plenty of bar fights together over the years, the Callaghan brothers taking on all comers. But when Liam saw what was left of Harry's little finger, his stomach had turned over. The discussion about it had been short and not at all sweet.

What happened to your finger?
Shut it in the door.
Like fuck you did.

Harry hadn't said another word about it. And for once in his life, Liam had the sense not to poke the bear that was his big brother.

That didn't mean Liam couldn't work it out for himself. Harry turned up with a finger that looked as if he'd dropped one of his own skips on it and made up an excuse about it. Then he asked Liam to hide a laptop for him. The two things were connected. It made Liam's own fingers tingle just thinking about the implications, a shiver running across the back of his neck.

The laptop was a cheap, refurbished model that looked as if Harry rescued it from a skip. Liam got himself settled at the kitchen table, powered it up, another short conversation with his brother in his mind.

What's the password?
You don't need to know.

With the benefit of hindsight, Liam would've objected.

You're asking me to hold onto something that probably got you killed and you won't even let me get into it?

Except it wasn't a problem.

He loved his brother. Harry had a natural affinity for all things mechanical. He should've been a mechanic. And Liam couldn't think of anyone he'd rather have covering his back when things turned nasty. But he had no problem admitting Harry wasn't the sharpest knife in the drawer.

It made him smile as he began the process of working out Harry's password. Made him feel closer to him. Because all he had to do was work through all the classic Dirty Harry quotes, try upper and lower case, maybe add the year the film was released, and he'd have it in no time.

As it turned out, it took him longer than he expected. He quickly became confused and couldn't remember what passwords he'd already tried, especially when he started playing around with upper- and lower-case letters. He found a scrap of paper and a pencil in one of the kitchen drawers and started again, writing down each password as he entered it, then drawing a line through it when it didn't work.

He'd also forgotten what a soft, sentimental fool Harry had been when it came to Barbara. When he added 1975—Barbara's birth year—onto the end of *makemyday*, he was in.

And it wasn't long after that before he wished he wasn't.

ANGEL FELT AS IF HE WAS TAKING THE FIRST STEP DOWN A SLIPPERY slope when he made the call to Stuart Beckford. He went down to the men's toilets on the ground floor to do it, safely out of Kincade's hearing, even if Sergeant Jack Bevan on the front desk gave him a strange look.

'I hope you're not still in bed,' Angel said, when Beckford picked up.

A self-indulgent chuckle came down the line at him.

'Not me! I was up at the crack of nine-thirty.' There was a brief pause while Beckford's brain got into gear, realising Angel wouldn't call him simply to joke about lounging around the house doing nothing all day. 'You're not calling about Balan's offer already, are you? I need more time to think it through.'

'Nothing to do with that. I want you to have a word with Ricky Shorter for me.'

The pause that came down the line was a lot longer than the previous one.

Shorter was what used to be known as an informant. Whether he was aware of it or not, he was now a *Covert Human Intelligence Source*, after the powers that be decided there wasn't enough bureaucratic bullshit and jargon in policing and came up with The Regulation of Investigatory Powers Act 2000 to do something about it.

The Act did more than invent pretentious, corporate-style terms, and the acronym *CHIS* also covers undercover police officers as well as civilian informants. Despite that, to ordinary coppers like Angel and Beckford, they were still informants.

As an aspect of policing, the use of informants occupies its own social milieu. The potential for moral and emotional tension is huge, both for the police officer and the informant. The relationship is all about power, inequality, and conflict. It's extremely personal. And it's about trust.

Ricky Shorter was Beckford's informant. Angel couldn't simply call Shorter himself in Beckford's absence.

Except it was more than that. The days of one-to-one relationships were long gone. The covert use of civilian informants leaves law enforcement agencies open to accusations of unethical conduct. As a result, interviews with informants now have to be conducted by two officers.

Angel tried not to think too hard about the implications of what he was asking Beckford to do.

'Okay,' Beckford said, the way he stretched it out suggesting it wasn't okay at all.

As with a lot of informants, Ricky Shorter spent his life hopping back and forth between honest employment and criminal activity. He'd tried his hand at most things illegal, but felt happiest if drugs were involved in some way, due to a lifelong commitment to personal consumption. If Angel wanted a handle on the Callaghan brothers' position in the drug-dealing food chain, a chat with Shorter was likely to be a lot more rewarding than waiting for the left-over crumbs SEROCU's DS Wright might throw his way.

Beckford summed it up as soon as Angel finished giving him the background.

'You don't think Callaghan's death is related to the low-level smuggling he might have got up to with his brother?'

'I'm starting to feel that way.'

'Shall I waste my breath asking what you think it *is* related to?'

'You can ask, seeing as you've got nothing better to do with your time...'

'But it won't get me anywhere. Some things never change. One last thing...'

'No, nobody else knows about this call.'

'Why am I not surprised?'

Angel smiled to himself as they ended the call, encouraged that they were both still on the same page despite the months apart. That pleasure was short-lived, offset by guilt about making the call and the request behind Kincade's back.

He tried telling himself he wasn't keeping her in the dark so much as protecting her, except he didn't believe it any more than she would. She'd been different since he'd re-established contact with Stuart Beckford.

And different is rarely a good thing, either in itself or as a harbinger of things to come.

13

Carl Angel was in the back garden mowing the lawn when Kincade got home. She heard the drone of the petrol mower as soon as she got out of the car, the smell of freshly-cut grass in the air. Growing up, it would've been enough to trigger a debilitating attack of hay fever. Luckily, she'd left that affliction behind long ago, along with the other scourges adolescence inflicts on the young as hormones run amok.

She went directly up to her room to change out of her work clothes, then went into the small, unused third bedroom. From there, she watched Carl through the window, dressed as always in a check shirt and threadbare raspberry-coloured cords, as the mower pulled him along, up and down the lawn in perfect, alternating stripes.

She almost felt as if she was spying on the old warhorse. As if Angel—or, worse, his sister Grace—had set her the task of watching for the insidious symptoms of Huntington's disease. God knows, there were enough of them, from difficulty concentrating and memory lapses to involuntary jerking and fidgety movements in the limbs and body.

She hoped she never saw any—not only because she didn't

want Carl to suffer them, but also to make her own life easier. The thought of walking into the office one day and telling Angel she'd seen his father stumble for no reason at all, or that she'd noticed violent mood changes, made her blood run cold. The choice between betraying Carl's trust, acting like a two-legged nanny cam, or leaving his children ignorant of the state of their father's health, was not a decision she looked forward to.

Despite that, she knew that one day, should Grace's hypochondria prove to be based on fact, it would be hers to make.

'I was watching you from the back bedroom,' she said, after joining him in the garden, her voice suddenly too loud in the quiet of the evening after he shut the mower's engine off. 'Good job I was, too.' She pointed to a random spot in the lawn. 'There's a nasty kink in that stripe over there.'

'Is that so?' He fixed her with a steely-eyed stare the raw recruits on the parade ground would've recognised. 'That sort of thing might fool Max, but you'll have to up your game to fool me.'

She sat on the weathered bench against the back wall of the house and watched him as he made the last half dozen passes up and down the garden. When he'd finished, he carried the collection bag out to the wheelie bin at the front and emptied it, then joined her on the bench, the last of the evening sun warming them.

'Good day at work?' he said, after they'd sat a while in a companionable silence broken only by the sound of birdsong, her eyes closed, if not his.

'Better than your son's.'

'Why's that?'

'He had a hangover, poor thing.'

'I bet I know who he didn't get any sympathy from.'

'You got that right.' She nudged him with her elbow. 'It must be living with you.'

He didn't respond, on the face of it too busy watching a robin that had settled on the handle of the lawnmower, head cocked as it surveyed the cut grass below for displaced insects.

'Any particular reason he was drinking last night?' he said, after the robin had flown away, its wriggling reward clamped in its pointy beak. 'Although I suppose having his mother living with him would drive a saint to drink.'

It wasn't a road she planned to go down. Not now, or ever, if she had anything to do with it. Trouble was, the truth was no less contentious.

'He went for a few beers with Stuart Beckford.'

'About bloody time! I don't know what the pair of them have been playing at. Should've sorted it out months ago. It can't be doing Beckford any good sitting at home on his arse all day long. *Stress!* God help us.' He shook his head, the gesture easy to interpret—*you young people don't know what stress is.* In Carl Angel's world, a tour of duty in some godforsaken hell-hole on the other side of the planet getting shot at by angry natives might give you stress. Nothing less could. There wouldn't be any such thing as long-term sick leave, that's for sure.

And where would that leave me? she thought.

Carl might have been uncompromising in his attitudes, but that didn't mean he was blind to the effect the things he thought were of no consequence had on other, more sensitive souls.

'Are you worried Beckford will want his old job back?'

'Of course, I am.' She went to say more, thought better of it.

Carl wasn't having any of it. He barked at her.

'Spit it out.'

She sat forward on the bench, held her hand at her brow as if shielding her eyes from the sun as she stared down the garden.

'I could've sworn that was the lawn. Must've changed into a parade ground while I wasn't looking.'

He put his hand on her arm, worked a sickly-sweet note into his voice.

'What's on your mind, dear? Is that better?'

She couldn't help laughing as he held the simpering look on his face.

'I think I prefer the parade-ground bark.'

He let his hand slide off her arm, nodded his approval.

'Good. I wouldn't be able to keep that insincere sympathy lark up for long. So? You were about to say something else, other than of course you're worried.'

'Max was different today. He had a hangover, but it was like he had more of a spring in his step at the same time.'

Carl pushed himself to his feet, made the obligatory old-person noises as he did so. Back when she first met him, she might have thought he was ignoring her remark, the subject either out of bounds or of no interest to him. Having shared a house with him, she knew better.

She also knew what was coming next, beat him to it.

'Thirsty work, mowing the lawn?'

'You took the words right out of my mouth.'

She patted the still-warm bench where he'd been sitting.

'Sit yourself down and relax. I'll get you a nice glass of water from the tap.'

A frown creased his weathered brow, as if he'd heard of water but had no intention of ever trying it.

'As I said, you need to up your game.'

With that, he disappeared into the house. It struck her that there are some new tricks you can't teach an old dog. She'd got home and immediately changed into more comfortable casual clothes. He'd just gone upstairs to change out of his comfortable clothes into something more formal to wear to the pub. Admittedly, her work clothes hadn't smelled of grass cuttings.

He was back down five minutes later. Smart trousers perfectly pressed and a different check shirt, this one freshly laundered and ironed. Brown brogues polished to a high shine, his silver hair neatly combed.

'No tie or medals?' she said.

He gave her a look that would've taken Angel back thirty years.

'There'll be no supper for you, let alone beer, if you keep that tone up.'

'Aren't you meant to finish a sentence like that with *young lady*? Threaten to tan my hide?'

He smiled with her, but something passed behind his eyes. It wasn't that he'd taken offence. His own hide was far too thick for that. It was as if he'd asked himself a question.

Are you surprised Max misses Stuart Beckford, if you give him as much backchat all day long?

She knew it was only paranoia at her predecessor's sudden presence in all their lives, but try telling that to the old enemy, your own subconscious.

What Carl said was very different, of course. The glint in his eye made it clear he was ready for as much impertinence as she could throw his way.

'I don't suppose you'll be going upstairs to smarten yourself up.'

'You don't suppose right. I can always walk ten paces behind you, if you're ashamed of me.'

'Make it five. That's what I used to do with Max's mother. So? Are we going or not?'

She fell into step beside him as he headed for the side gate, the familiar refrain in her head.

Quick march! Left, right, left right.

'You shouldn't be surprised Max is different,' he said, as she kept pace beside him. 'But you shouldn't make the mistake of thinking it's because he's excited at the prospect of Stuart Beckford returning to work. That's all in your head, not his.'

Not for the first time, it struck her that he was able to understand her and talk to her like nobody else did. Certainly better than her estranged husband, Elliot, ever could. It wasn't a surrogate father sort of thing. It just was.

She also knew she should accept it, not analyse it. Being a woman, that was hard. Men didn't realise how hard. Despite that, she had the sense to recognise that the day she understood it would be the day it no longer applied. Back when he still wore a dog collar, Angel would've told her that was the essence of having faith in something. Belief based on conviction rather than proof.

'It's understandable,' Carl carried on, saving her from disappearing up her own backside with her existential thoughts. 'A man who's been out of his life for a long time is suddenly back in it. Who wouldn't be different?'

For reasons she couldn't identify, something in his voice told her she would learn something about the man she worked for tonight. Why Stuart Beckford coming back into his life would have more of an impact than another man's return would.

Before they got into that, there was beer to be drunk, already being pulled by the barman, Declan, as they walked through the door. Because men who visit the same pub every night and sit at the same table every night drink the same beer, come rain or shine.

Except, this evening, there was one small deviation. Carl's regular drinking buddies were already settled at the big table in the window—Kincade assumed they had smaller lawns or set their mowers to a faster speed. Carl acknowledged them with a wave, but didn't join them, leading the way outside to the same table where they'd sat when she bared her soul and told him about her fall from grace.

'This is ominous,' she said.

He wagged a finger at her while he took a well-earned slurp, then sucked the foam out of his moustache. The gesture was easy to interpret.

This isn't about you.

'Max was in a very bad place when he came out of the Army and turned his back on the priesthood,' Carl said, when his thirst was suitably slaked.

She knew those twenty words were both the beginning and the end of what Carl would say on the matter. Proving her right, he moved on.

'Max and Stuart Beckford joined the police at the same time. They formed an immediate bond. Max was all over the place mentally. He'd failed as a priest. He couldn't hack it in the Army.' Carl held up a liver-spotted hand before she objected to the harsh way he'd described the major trauma in his son's life. 'His words, not mine. I realise how easily they flow from my own mouth, of course. Anyway, entering the police had the feel of third-time-lucky, and if that doesn't work out . . .'

Kincade wished she had a hood over her head, or was wearing dark glasses. That way, he wouldn't have seen what went through her mind reflected in her eyes.

Would he have taken the way out his younger brother had?

Except even if she'd been hooded, Carl would've seen the question. It was a permanent fixture in his own mind, despite what he now said.

'Max would never do what Cormac did. He's not wired that way.'

None of us ever know until push comes to shove, she thought and hid her face behind her glass.

'Stuart Beckford helped Max get past the blackness that

consumed him,' Carl went on. 'That allowed Max to put his heart and soul into the new job. He didn't view it as a third failure waiting to happen, the only question being how long it took.'

'And he progressed faster than Beckford as a result.'

Carl rocked his hand.

'It was a combination of factors. Yes, Max applied himself. But Beckford was never interested in promotion beyond sergeant.'

Great, she groaned to herself. The much-loved and sadly-missed DS Beckford really was the archetypal copper's copper. At the opposite end of the scale to fast-track graduate recruits whose accelerated promotion is resented by the rank and file, Beckford had chosen to remain at the coal face, his experience and efforts channelled into the job and not his own promotion prospects. Loved by all and sundry, unlike her, the incomer down from London under a cloud.

She had no idea whether Carl saw the impact his words had on her. His next words suggested that maybe he did.

'I'm not telling you this so you can give yourself a hard time comparing yourself to him. You should never compare yourself to others. That only ever results in one of two outcomes. You feel cocky and superior, or you feel you're a failure. Neither of them is good. Do you know Rudyard Kipling's poem *If*?'

'Vaguely. I get the feeling I might find a framed copy on my bedroom wall when I get home tomorrow night.'

'Whether you do or not, read it.'

'Memorise it?'

'You could do a lot worse than try to live your life by it. There are a couple of lines I think you—'

'Should have tattooed on my forehead?'

'I was going to suggest somewhere more intimate where only you will see it. *If you can trust yourself when all men doubt you, but make allowance for their doubting too.'* He pointed a finger at her when he saw her lips twitch. 'If you were about to ask me how well I've done trying to live up to it, don't.'

There was no sharpness in his tone. There didn't need to be. The subject was not up for discussion. With a son who'd committed suicide in part due to his father pushing him too hard, as well as a wife who'd left him as a result of it, she guessed Carl Angel had long ago accepted he'd fallen short of Kipling's unrealistic ideal.

He drained his glass and jumped to his feet, his agility never ceasing to surprise her. Pointed unnecessarily at her glass, the words *when have I ever said no?* unspoken.

She waited until he'd disappeared inside the pub, pulled out her phone and found Kipling's poem on the web.

Yeah right, she thought, after she'd read it. She'd be interested to meet anyone who'd come anywhere close.

If he hadn't been carrying two pint glasses, he would've wagged his finger at her again when he returned. The knowing look in his eye made up for it.

'I saw you on your phone. Looking up Kipling's poem, were you?'

'If I'm going to memorise it, I might as well make a start now.'

He grinned at her as he put the glasses down.

'It'll be easier when I put a copy on the wall.' He waved his hand, *move on*. 'Enough about that. I want to explain about the bond between Max and Beckford. It helps explain why they left it so long, why it's hit Max so hard now they've taken the first step.'

'Let me guess. Something beginning with *G*?'

The look on his face was a mix of admiration and a question —*isn't everything?*

'Guilt, yes. About Claire's death, of course.' He interlaced his fingers, twisted both hands so that his fingers writhed against each other. 'But not ordinary, straightforward guilt . . .'

'Max Angel style guilt.'

'The worst kind. Not only does he blame himself for what he did, he blames himself for Stuart Beckford blaming himself. If Max hadn't been playing his harmonica in the back, Claire wouldn't have unclipped her seat belt. Then it wouldn't have mattered so much that Beckford forgot about the airbag warning light. She'd have been badly injured, but she'd still be alive.'

'Are you saying he blames himself for Stuart Beckford's stress and inability to work?'

'That's exactly what I'm saying. And he would've been very relieved Beckford was happy to meet and go for a beer. Beckford's father had a serious drink problem. Max was worried Stuart would follow in his footsteps. Sitting at home, wallowing in self-pity and hitting the bottle all day long. That worry has now been lifted. That's what you're seeing when you say he had a spring in his step despite the hangover. It's basic human nature. People go to greater lengths and get more benefit from avoiding or removing something negative than they do achieving something positive. It's the survival instinct.' He glanced behind him at the pub, specifically at the window where his cronies were sitting, watching them intently. 'Shall we go inside?'

They both got to their feet, but she remained standing at the table and drained her glass rather than follow him as he set off. He stopped again when he became aware of her not following behind.

'You go,' she said, shooing him with her hand. 'I'm heading home. I've got to memorise that poem, remember?'

He raised his glass in a salute. *Attagirl.*

'I might test you on it when I get back. If I remember.'

'Say *hi* to the old farts for me.'

He nodded, *will do.*

'You realise we'll talk about you?'

She gave him a thumbs-up—*be my guest*—rather than reply, or the exchange might have gone on all night. The comforting sound of laughter and conversation as he opened the pub door accompanied her down the road. She felt a lot better for talking to him, his words and two pints of beer taking the raw edge off her paranoia.

She wouldn't have felt so sanguine had she known about the call Angel made to Beckford asking for assistance.

What you don't know can't hurt you.

Allegedly.

14

The horror Liam Callaghan felt when he got into his brother's laptop didn't start immediately. At first, the laptop's contents made him smile. The desktop was clear apart from the default icons down the left-hand side and a single folder smack bang in the middle. It was the folder's name that made him smile.

Open me first.

There aren't any others, you stupid arse, Liam thought as he double-clicked it. The contents were displayed as a list of file names, the file extensions indicating a combination of text files and images.

The name of the top text file—*Liam*—also made him smile, even if it started an uneasy churning in his gut at the implications. Harry had known he would try to get into the laptop and persevere until he succeeded.

Liam was hoping it would be a rude message. All in capital letters, telling him to keep his nose out of his brother's business unless he wanted a slap, and ending with an appropriate four-letter word.

If only.

With Harry in a refrigerated drawer in the morgue, Liam knew it wouldn't be so simple. He felt no satisfaction to be proved right when he opened it.

Congrats, Bro! You worked out the password. I made it nice and easy for you, ha, ha!

Don't pat yourself on the back too hard. Things go downhill from here. If you're reading this, either I'm in a coma with tubes sticking out of me and a nurse wiping my arse, or I'm dead. I'm not sure which is worse.

I've got some advice for you. Take this laptop and chuck it in the sea, forget you ever saw it. I know you've never listened to a word I've said before, but for once in your life, do what I'm telling you. Get rid of it.

Still here?

What a fucking surprise, I don't think.

You always were an awkward, stubborn bastard. I just hope you don't pay the same price I did for sticking my nose in where it wasn't welcome. And if you think those greasy little foreigners we did business with were scary, wait until you see these evil fuckers.

When you read this, you're going to think I've been sticking too much of our own product up my nose. I would if I was you. But it's all God's truth. Remember what my finger looked like? Shit doesn't come any more real than that. Fuck me, did it hurt!!

Anyway, here goes, you stupid bastard...

Liam's mind was spinning by the time he finished reading. There was only one thing he knew for sure. The option to throw the laptop in the sea and walk away had passed its sell-by date. Because there was no way the four slashed tyres on Harry's van was a coincidence. He was already involved. The question was, how deeply?

Were the slashed tyres a final warning?

We know where you live. We know you were close to your brother. Don't make the same mistake he did.

Or was it already too late? They were playing with him. Having a bit of spiteful fun before sending him to join Harry on the other side.

The words of the detective who'd interviewed him, Angel, were in his mind. Like a prophecy, as if he'd known Liam would get into the laptop.

If you don't want to spend the rest of your life looking over your shoulder, you should think about cooperating with us to help us find who killed your brother before they get to you, too.

Liam put the kettle on and did exactly that. Thought about it. He'd finished thinking about it long before the kettle boiled.

Harry hadn't taken what he'd found out to the police.

Why should he?

The answer was pretty bloody obvious when he thought about it.

Because Harry was now dead. And he might not be if he'd gone to the police instead of trying to live up to his namesake, Dirty Harry.

Did Dirty Harry have a brother or a sidekick in the movies called Stupid Liam?

Didn't matter. Cooperating with the police was not in the Callaghan brothers' DNA. That aside, Liam wasn't interested in handing it over, seeing the man who killed his brother sent to prison for less time than he'd get if the sniffer dogs found anything in Harry's van. That's if the useless wankers got to the bottom of who killed his brother in the first place.

No, Liam was more of an eye-for-an-eye man. You killed my big brother, you're gonna eat the big dirt sandwich yourself. *Jesus*, listen to him. He was turning into a cheesy movie character himself.

He finished making the tea, grabbed a pack of biscuits from the cupboard and went back to Harry's laptop feeling more energised than he had since Barbara called him with the news.

The file called *Police Statement* was self-explanatory, as was the one called *Contact Details*. Liam opened it, saw phone numbers and addresses and places of work for a number of the people involved.

Russell Baldwin, the investigative journalist Harry knocked down and killed.

Fiona Baldwin, the stiff's ex-wife, also a journalist.

Véronique Dubois, his girlfriend at the time of his death—

Liam did a small double-take when he saw the name Véronique Dubois, surprised to see it anywhere in Harry's notes. He remembered seeing her at the inquest into Baldwin's death when he attended with Harry, providing moral support after Barbara said she didn't want to go, the whole process too reminiscent of a criminal trial.

Liam remembered Véronique for a couple of reasons. She was a good-looking woman, and stylish with it. On account of being French, he supposed. He'd joked with Harry that it was a pity the people they dealt with when they made their cross-channel sorties didn't look like she did, instead of looking like they belonged on the back of a camel in the desert.

Except it had all gone sideways when she lost it. Started yelling and screaming at Harry in a hysterical mixture of French and English like he'd deliberately run her boyfriend over. The fuss she'd made, anyone would think Harry climbed the kerb and chased the bloke down the pavement in his lorry until he flattened him, then jumped down from the cab and pissed all over his still-twitching body.

Despite that, Harry had met with her. The details were right there in black and white in front of Liam's eyes. What wasn't so clear was who contacted who. Much as he believed his brother had possessed good qualities other people didn't immediately see, he couldn't picture Harry seeking out Véronique to apologise.

That wasn't all.

Something about the date they'd met was bothering him. It seemed familiar. Then it came to him, one of those random *aha* moments that take your breath away. It was the day before Harry turned up with the laptop and his finger mashed to a pulp.

The more Liam thought about it, the more confused he became, the questions multiplying in his head until he felt like he was on bloody Mastermind.

Why hadn't Harry said any of the stuff Liam had just read at the inquest? Did he think they wouldn't believe him? Did his boss, Reg Hall, ask him to keep schtum, scared of bad publicity and the effect it might have on his business?

The thought of Hall put a sour scowl on Liam's face. He'd never liked the bloke, even though he was Harry's best mate. Harry couldn't see it, but it was all *me, me, me*. It took an outsider to see it. Liam firmly believed the secret to running a successful business was taking advantage of the staff without them realising it—and Reg Hall excelled at that.

He'd never believed the reason Hall gave for sacking Harry. That he was unreliable. What a load of bollocks. Liam knew for a fact Harry was one hundred per cent dependable right up until the day he was sacked. Liam had always suspected there was another reason. One that Harry hadn't told him. He'd guessed at the time that they'd had a falling out. Now, Liam was getting the feeling he knew what it was about.

That was all water under the bridge.

What mattered now was what he was going to do about it going forward. He had a sudden, vivid image of Véronique Dubois in his mind. At the inquest. Right after she'd finished yelling, her cheeks flushed, eyes flashing, lips parted as she panted for breath. Liam hadn't said anything to Harry looking a little shell-shocked, but he'd thought to himself, *you can yell at me any time you like, luv.*

It was clear to him now that he would have to re-trace Harry's footsteps. And he couldn't think of a better place to start than with the fiery Ms Dubois.

Voulez-vous coucher avec moi, ce soir? he sang to himself as he made himself another cup of tea.

Things were looking up already.

15

'Have I grown an extra nose?' Angel asked, when he finished the call.

'Depends,' Kincade replied. 'How many did you start with?'

'I only noticed one when I was shaving this morning.'

'Then the answer's *no*. Why do you ask?'

'Because you were staring at me as if a new one was growing out of the top of my head the whole time I was on the phone.'

She smiled, shook her head at his confusion.

'No, I wasn't. I was concentrating on what you were saying.'

Angel didn't believe it for a minute. It hadn't only been when he was on the call he'd just taken. He'd caught her throwing sly glances his way all morning, as if she was a shy teenager and he the best-looking boy in the class. He had a good idea what it was —something she'd discussed with his father the night before. Something about him. And she'd been secretly observing him, wondering if it was true.

'And there was something your dad said last night,' she admitted, proving him partially right. 'He mentioned a poem—'

'*If* by Rudyard Kipling. *If you can keep your head when all about you are losing theirs and blaming it on you . . .*'

'That's the one.'

'I knew it wasn't *The Owl and the Pussycat*. I'm only surprised it's taken this long for him to mention it to you. And you were staring at me wondering how well I manage to live up to it?'

'It crossed my mind.' Then, when he didn't volunteer anything, 'So? What about the phone call?'

'The van's clean.'

The call had been from one of the forensic technicians examining Harry Callaghan's van. The sniffer dogs had been over it and found nothing to indicate it had ever been used to transport drugs in greater quantities than the Callaghan brothers sharing a joint in the front seats.

'Callaghan must've cleaned it with a pressure washer,' she said.

He wasn't so sure. As he'd admitted to Stuart Beckford on the phone the previous day, he was expecting Beckford's informant to confirm that Callaghan hadn't been a player in the local drug market, and if he'd dabbled at all, it certainly hadn't been enough to get him killed.

That wasn't something he could currently share with her. It was going to cause a problem when it came out, and the further he pushed that eventuality away, the better.

'It's an ill wind that blows nobody any good,' he said instead. 'It makes it easier to talk to Callaghan's widow again if she's not scared we're about to arrest her whole family for drug smuggling.' He got to his feet, shrugged himself into his jacket. 'Coming?'

'Why not? I want to see if she's had *grieving widow* tattooed across her forehead.'

'I MIGHT AS WELL MAKE UP THE SPARE BED FOR YOU LOT,' BARBARA Callaghan said when she answered the door. 'First you, then the other two turning the house upside down, now you two again. Who's it going to be tomorrow?'

'One day soon I hope it'll be somebody who tells you we've caught your husband's killer,' Angel responded, smiling politely.

Barbara gave him a look she usually reserved for Jehovah's Witnesses and carol singers.

'Pardon me if I don't hold my breath.' She turned away and headed down the hall towards the kitchen, her voice floating back to them over her shoulder. 'Close the door behind you.'

They joined Barbara in the kitchen, her broad back turned towards them as she busied herself at the sink filling the kettle. Today, she was decked out in a pale peach velour leisure suit that showcased what can be achieved with polyester and very little imagination or design skills. Kincade promised herself that she would disown her mother if she ever caught her wearing something similar. And she'd put her head in the gas oven before she wore one herself.

They waited patiently while Barbara made herself—and very pointedly not them—something to drink. A person's back gives very little away when they've been asked a question they don't want to answer. Eventually, Barbara turned to face them, a long-suffering expression on her face. Added to the large glasses she hadn't been wearing when they last interviewed her, she made Angel think of a stoic pale-peach owl being pestered by smaller birds. Her voice was filled with weary resignation, the voice of a person ready to shoulder today's burden.

'What is it now?'

'Some good news,' Angel said brightly. 'Harry's van is clean.'

Barbara let out a breath that sounded as if she'd been holding it since they first knocked on the door.

'Told you. When can I have it back?'

'As soon as you've bought four new tyres.'

Confusion creased Barbara's face, quickly followed by anger

as she jumped to the wrong conclusion. Angel cut her off before she demanded the Hampshire Constabulary pay for them.

'Nothing to do with us, Mrs Callaghan. Somebody slashed them while the van was parked in the alley behind Liam's house.'

'What? All four of them?'

'I'm afraid so.'

'Who?'

'That's something we thought you might be able to tell us.'

'If I knew that, I'd do a damn sight more than tell you about it.' She put her hand over her mouth in mock horror. 'I shouldn't say that to you, should I? You might arrest me.'

We wouldn't do that, Kincade wanted to say. *You're a grieving widow*.

What she did say was hardly any better.

'You can pretend you don't know what's going on until you're blue in the face, Mrs Callaghan. Claim Harry played his cards close to his chest, never told you what he was up to. And who knows, if you catch us on a good day, we might even believe you. But what you can't do is pretend you didn't see what was done to his little finger. And *please*'—emphasising the word—'don't insult our intelligence. Don't say he shut it in the door or hit it with the hammer when he was doing repairs around the house. And don't say he kept his hand in his pocket the whole time so you didn't see it, either.'

Barbara looked as if she was trying hard to think ahead of Kincade, come up with an excuse before Kincade ruled it out. In the end, she chose to say nothing.

'Did you ask your husband what happened to his finger?' Angel said, his tone softer than Kincade's had been.

It didn't make a blind bit of difference to the sharpness in Barbara's reply.

'Of course I bloody did.'

'And what did he say?'

'He said it was nothing. Don't worry about it. Typical bloody Harry. And the whole time I can see him thinking, *just shut up and let me get some paracetamol down my throat*. So, that's what I did. We've been married long enough for me to know when it's time to keep my mouth shut.' She turned her glare Kincade's way, identifying her as the most cynically suspicious of them. 'Before you say it, no, he didn't used to hit me. For all his faults, he was a good man.'

They left a respectful silence to allow Barbara's posthumous praise the acknowledgement it deserved, even if they both wanted to shake her, scream at her.

If he was such a saint, help us find who killed him.

After a minute, Angel nudged the conversation gently in that direction.

'It looks as if he was investigating the man he knocked down and killed. Do you know why?'

Barbara showed no surprise that they knew about the accident, a major incident in her husband's life she'd said nothing about.

'It's obvious. He felt bad about it.'

There was nothing obvious about it at all. If Angel had wanted to provoke an angry reaction from Barbara, he might have asked her how investigating the life of the man he'd killed would help him get over feeling bad about it. Was he hoping to discover that Baldwin had been a bad person? A rapist or paedophile? Instead, he nodded as if she'd just made most of the case fall neatly into place and he only had one or two little questions left before the killer was as good as behind bars.

'Do you know what he was doing specifically?'

'Like you said, investigating.'

Angel nodded again, as if he could hear the judge passing sentence already.

'Do you know if he met with anyone recently, or talked to them on the phone? Around the time he had the accident with his finger?'

They both saw the mention of talking on the phone register in Barbara's eyes. Angel couldn't be bothered with pussy-footing around her, let Kincade deal with it. She went straight for the jugular.

'What about the phone, Mrs Callaghan? Our colleagues found a phone hidden in your husband's office upstairs. It's what's called a burner—'

'I know what a burner phone is. I'm not stupid.'

'Did you know about the one your husband hid?'

Barbara dropped her eyes to the floor, repeated herself.

'I'm not stupid. Of course I knew about it. Are you married?' It was an accusation, more than a question. She waited until Kincade said that she was, the easiest option. 'Then you'll know what men are like. Think they can hide things from us. But they can't. I found the phone. I didn't have a problem getting into it. Harry always uses the year I was born as his PIN or passcode. Nineteen seventy-five.' She paused briefly, giving them the opportunity to say she didn't look her age, then resumed when neither of them obliged. 'At first, I thought he was having an affair.' She looked pointedly at Kincade again, more conspiratorially this time—*what man doesn't?*

Angel didn't even try to understand how Barbara's thought process worked. How she reconciled the idea of her husband keeping a secret phone filled with other women's phone numbers, but used her own birth year as the means of keeping her out.

'Harry was a good-looking man,' Barbara went on, then took hold of a substantial roll of flab around her midriff, her red-tipped fingers disappearing out of sight into the doughy, velour-covered flesh. 'He could've done with losing a pound or two, same as me, but even so, it didn't surprise me if other women were interested in him.'

Angel and Kincade kept their expressions as impassive as possible—no easy task in the face of Barbara's delusions. They made very sure they didn't meet one another's eyes.

'There were only two numbers in it,' Barbara said, disappointment in her voice that her cuddly hunk of a husband didn't have dozens of desperate women's names and numbers. 'I challenged him about it.'

I bet you did, Angel thought. He would've loved to ask how much, on a scale of one to ten, her husband had enjoyed that challenge. Whether he'd happily have offered his other little finger as a sacrifice to avoid it.

'What did he say?' he asked, instead.

'One number was to do with work...'

Angel chose to say nothing, given their interest was in solving Barbara's husband's murder, and he was now more convinced than ever that Harry Callaghan's so-called work, aka criminal enterprises, did not result in his death.

'Did you believe him?'

A glint appeared in Barbara's eye as if she was re-living squeezing her husband's shattered little finger in the jaws of a pair of pliers.

'*Oh yes!* I always knew when my Harry was lying—'

'What was the other number?'

'Some French bint.'

It was too much of a coincidence for it not to be the same woman Reg Hall told Gulliver and Jardine about, the one who'd become hysterical when the coroner ruled Russell Baldwin's death an accident. Barbara saw the way the word *French* registered with them, misunderstood it for ignorance about what a *bint* was. 'A French woman. Harry said she was the girlfriend of the bloke he killed.'

'How did he get hold of her number?' Kincade asked.

'He didn't. She got in touch with him at work. Harry didn't tell me what she wanted.'

It wasn't to recommend her dead lover's book on political scandal, Angel thought.

'Did he say anything at all about her, or what she wanted?'

Barbara shook her head, clearly growing as bored with their questions as she had with Harry's secret phone once she'd satisfied herself he wasn't screwing every housewife whose property he delivered a skip to. Her next words confirmed it.

'Nah. I wasn't interested. He promised me he wasn't shagging her, and I believed him. Harry didn't like French birds, anyway. They don't shave their armpits.'

At times, Angel wished he was a psychiatrist. Then someone would actually employ him and pay him good money to ask the questions that went through his mind. *Would it have made a difference if they did? If she'd been German or Italian, with or without shaved armpits?* But he wasn't, he was a detective. And the less he knew about what passed for a thought process inside Barbara Callaghan's vacant head, the better.

'I suppose you want to inspect my armpits,' Kincade said, once they were back in the car.

He made a strange noise in his throat. It was a mix of a snort and a giggle and a whimper. It summed up how he felt perfectly. It also matched the way his body slumped listlessly behind the steering wheel.

'Only if you're implicated in Callaghan's murder in any way.'

She shrugged, *only trying to help.*

'I thought I'd offer.'

He dipped his head appreciatively.

'It's very kind. But if I want any insights along those lines, which I doubt, I'll ask my father.'

'What? You think we share a bathroom?'

'You do.'

'I meant at the same time.'

'Then, no. But I know for a fact he drilled a spy-hole in the wall when he knew you were moving in.'

'Is that so? And he streams the footage live to the internet?'

He rolled his eyes, *what a stupid thing to say*.

'You're crediting him with too much tech savvy. I do that for him.'

He expected her to come right back at him, continue with the ludicrous conversation she'd started. Instead, she peered at him as if worried about his mental health.

'Talking to Barbara Callaghan has really got to you, hasn't it?'

He turned his head to the side, touched his neck immediately below his ear.

'If you see any wetness there, it's my brains leaking out of my ear.' He shifted in his seat, sat upright. Started the car. 'At least we got something useful from it.'

'Yep. All we have to do now is find the French bint.'

16

If Angel had been in charge of the way the universe was designed, he wasn't sure women would exist at all. If they did, he would've needed to come up with an alternative means of getting food into their bodies, because they sure as hell wouldn't have a mouth that opened.

At times, it seemed their sole purpose was to make him feel as if someone had opened the top of his head and given his brain a good stir with a wooden spoon.

First, delusional Barbara Callaghan.

Then Kincade in the car, eager to demonstrate her depilatory credentials.

And now, DCI Olivia Finch, who'd just collared him in the corridor.

'Feeling better today, Padre?'

His immediate reaction was to come out with a quick, *much better, thank you, ma'am*. Keep it as brief as possible. Unfortunately, he couldn't help himself.

'Why do I get the feeling that whatever I say, you're going to do your best to ensure that I'm not?'

'Because you're a cynic who can't get to grips with one

person asking after another's wellbeing?'

'In a police station?'

'We're all people first and foremost, Padre.'

He took hold of his little finger, preparing to count off the many individuals he saw on a daily basis who clearly weren't. She cut him off before he got started.

'What would you say if I told you Stuart Beckford wants his old job back?'

Get me outta here, I don't want to deal with this, went through his mind and stayed there.

'I'd say you're playing Devil's advocate, ma'am.'

She pursed her lips briefly at the use of *ma'am*, a term which always conjured up old ladies with blue rinses.

'And if I told you I wasn't?'

He was suddenly aware of his heart thumping in his chest. *Was this for real?* He carried on as if it wasn't.

'I'd say that since moving behind a desk—'

'Into a more administrative role is how I'd put it.'

'—you've lost those interview-room skills that allow you to lie your face off without being caught out.'

She shrugged the shrug of a person who has indeed been caught out.

'Fair enough. But hearing Stuart Beckford's name, and you going for a beer with him, reminds me that the possibility of his return still exists. And I'd be interested to know what you'd say if you had to make a choice between him and Kincade.'

So would I was not the answer she was looking for, however true it might be.

He spent a few moments saying nothing, hoping the question was rhetorical. The way she crossed her arms over her chest suggested it wasn't. She immediately dropped them again, started walking.

'Let's do this in my office.'

How long an answer do you want? he thought, falling into step beside her.

'You might as well raid my coffee as usual,' she said, grudgingly, once they were in her office and he'd closed the door after she flicked her fingers at it.

He didn't need to be told twice, even remembered to pour a cup for her. Then proceeded to waste time, saying things that conveyed no information whatsoever.

'It would be a difficult one—'

'Which is why I'm asking you.'

'—and I'd need more time to think it through—'

'Bollocks. I'm asking for a gut feel.'

'—rather than make snap judgements I might later regret.'

She immediately swivelled her chair to face the wall.

'I'm now going to ask the wall the same question. See if I get anything more useful out of it.'

'And I'll cross that bridge when I get to it,' he said, throwing in a cliché to round things off.

She swivelled back to face him, mainly because she'd left her coffee on her desk. He didn't like the mischief he saw in her eyes as she picked up her cup.

'I've just had an idea—'

'Be sure to let the Super know.' Pointing at the ceiling as he said it.

'How about we promote Kincade into your role? Then Beckford can have his job back . . .' She took a sip of coffee, her eyes on his over the rim. 'Still want me to mention my bright idea to the Super?'

Definitely, if I have to interview Barbara Callaghan again, he thought.

Then her phone rang, saving him from having to answer. He stayed where he was when she didn't shoo him towards the door, enjoying his coffee and the short hiatus in being put on the spot.

Sadly, it wasn't a long call. He raised an eyebrow at her when it ended.

'Stuart Beckford calling about his old job, ma'am?'

'Actually, no.' Now it was her turn to point at the ceiling. 'The Super wants an update.'

'What? On Stuart Beckford's return?'

'*No*, Padre. On Dirty Harry's murder. You better bring me up to speed.'

He glanced at his watch, the purpose of the gesture not lost on her.

We'd have a lot more time for it if you hadn't wasted the last ten minutes giving me a hard time over Stuart Beckford.

'The preliminary forensics are back, and support what we already knew or suspected. The blood on his forehead wasn't his, supporting the view that he'd headbutted his killer in an attempt to get away.'

'No DNA match?'

He smiled sadly, raised his eyes to the ceiling.

'I know how much you'd have liked to take that to the Super, but I'm afraid not.'

'It's not on the national database at all?'

His face told her the bad news for him.

The DNA sample taken hadn't matched an identified individual on the database, nor had it been matched to an unidentified sample found at a previous crime scene. The sample collected from Callaghan's forehead would be invaluable when they had a suspect to match it to, but until then it was just blood.

He moved on.

'As you know, a number of nine-millimetre shell casings were found at the scene. Ballistics have confirmed that the gun was a Glock seventeen.'

Angel felt his eyes drooping just remembering the call he'd

taken from a gun nerd in the ballistics lab who'd chewed his ear for ten minutes. Talking about the distinctive rifling on Glock 17s as if Angel was as anally retentive about it as he was. How Glock barrels are made by a hammer-forged process that uses a mandrel which, itself, is made to extremely accurate tolerances and polished smooth. As a result, although it's possible to identify the gun as a Glock, it's not possible to identify the specific weapon. Not like it was in the old days, yadda, yadda, yadda...

Despite that, the fact that it was a Glock said something about the sort of person who might have used it. The Glock 17 might be the most common handgun in the world, but not on the streets of Britain. It is, however, the most commonly issued pistol among all UK police forces and other law enforcement agencies.

Finch knew this as well as Angel did, but without having to suffer the lecture. Angel had a feeling the identification of the gun and its implications wouldn't be passed to Superintendent Horwood at this stage.

'We've also got details of his internet browsing history from the ISP...'

'Your tone of voice suggests it was a waste of time asking for them.'

'It was.' He raised a finger. *Not so fast.* 'But I can let you have the details of where Mrs Callaghan bought the horrendous velour leisure suit she was wearing, if you're interested.'

She stared hard at him until he gave a single nod, *as you wish*.

'What about the pink fluffy dressing gown she was wearing the other day?'

The stare intensified. He nodded again.

'Maybe not. Apart from that, nothing of interest.'

'Making it likely he had a laptop hidden somewhere. His brother is the most likely candidate.'

'Agreed. Same goes for his phone records. Nothing jumped out at us. That fits with him having the burner phone we found.'

'Have we got into it?'

'We have now . . .'

He took her through what Barbara Callaghan had told them, and how they'd confirmed it for themselves when they unlocked the phone. The number she'd described as work-related was a French mobile number, easily identified by the first two digits, 06. Although it felt as if it would lead nowhere, a start had already been made on identifying its owner.

'The other number belonged to Véronique Dubois, the girlfriend of Russell Baldwin, the man Callaghan knocked down and killed.'

'Sounds like she's French, too.'

Angel bit his tongue to stop himself from smiling at the memory of the conversation Ms Dubois' nationality had led to.

'I'm pretty sure it's a coincidence.'

'Only pretty sure? What if Baldwin's latest investigation was drugs related—'

'He specialised in political scandal.'

'What? A politician can't be involved in drugs?'

'Fair enough.'

'Callaghan's contact is in France. Baldwin starts investigating with the help of his French girlfriend. The French gang get in touch with Callaghan. *Zis Anglais journalist is becoming un problème. Deal with heem.*'

'Very good French accent, ma'am.'

'Thank you. Callaghan then runs him over.' She scissored her hands. 'Problème . . .'

'Terminé?'

She smiled gratefully.

'Exactly, Padre. Ms Dubois is distraught—'

'On account of her fiery Gallic temperament.'

'—and kills Callaghan in revenge.' Then, when he didn't respond, 'So? What do you think?'

'I was wrong about the accent. It needs more work.'

'Why do I get the impression you're not taking my suggestion seriously?'

'I'll give it some serious thought, ma'am.'

She let out a heavy sigh. *Why do I even bother?*

'I would've thought this was right up your street, Padre. Callaghan getting shot for stepping on someone's toes in a drug-related turf war is too dull for you.' She flicked her fingers dismissively. 'It's so *passé*.'

He assumed what he called *Kincade position #1*. Left arm across his body, right elbow resting on it, forefinger pressed into his top lip. It was a great pose to adopt when you wanted to give the impression that someone had made you think deeply. His response suggested the opposite.

'Why don't you run it past the Super, ma'am? Cheer him up after you give him the bad news about the DNA.'

Finch gave him a look he knew well. He was only surprised it had taken so long coming.

He was not to be an arse his whole life.

'What do you think's going on?' she said, the second half of the sentence left unsaid—*if you're so bloody clever.*

'Not sure. Baldwin has got a nose for unearthing political scandal. He's been sued for libel a couple of times, and he's won both times. That suggests he makes sure he gets his facts straight before he commits himself. It's not as if he can only persuade the more rabid anti-establishment publications to print his stuff, either. He's worked for all the big national papers. He's not interested in going after the small fry, either.'

They both knew he could've saved a lot of breath and words.

When the shit hits the fan, it could get seriously messy.

She glanced at the time in the bottom corner of her computer monitor, a flash of irritation passing over her face at the way the time had disappeared.

'I'm late for the Super.' He rose with her as she got to her feet, the annoyance replaced by a relieved smile as a silver lining came into sight. 'I'll only have time to give him the edited highlights of what we've discussed.'

'Feel free to blame me, ma'am.'

'Thank you, Padre, I plan to.'

At the door, she paused as if she wanted to kill more time, keep her meeting with Superintendent Horwood shorter still. Except it wasn't to speculate further about how Baldwin's death might be connected to Callaghan's. She'd come full circle, back to how their discussion first started in the corridor.

'How's Kincade taking Stuart Beckford's reappearance on the scene?'

'As well as can be expected. She's worried about how it might impact on her, and doing everything in her power to not let it show.'

'But she can't fool you, eh?'

'She can't, ma'am.'

'Everybody thinks they can keep things hidden, but they can't.'

He didn't like the way she leaned in towards him as she said it, unsure whether she was delivering a veiled warning about the things he did his best to keep from her.

I know about Virgil Balan's offer.
I know you've asked for Stuart Beckford's help.
I can only turn a blind eye for so long . . .

He knew it was only his own guilty conscience, but he shot out his arm nonetheless, made a big deal of checking his watch.

'*Uh-oh*. Better not keep the Super waiting any longer, ma'am. There's only so much blame I can shoulder.'

'Anyone would think you're trying to get rid of me, Padre.'

She took a step away, then stopped again.

What now? he thought, and kept off his face.

'If Beckford ends up coming back and Kincade moves on, she'll have to throw a leaving party in that penthouse apartment she lives in over at Ocean Village marina. I've always wanted to see what they're like.'

He kept the smile plastered on his face, despite it doing its best to slide off. An unspoken pact had been made between Kincade and himself when she was forced to move out of the apartment and moved in with his father. The arrangement would stay between them for as long as it was humanly possible for them to keep it that way.

Yet another lie to live, he thought as Finch finally strode away. *Where will it end?*

Angel came away from the meeting feeling dejected. Not about the discussion regarding the Callaghan investigation, but about Kincade's worsening situation.

His father quoting Kipling's poem *If* to her told him they'd had a serious conversation about something. Carl Angel had always taken great comfort from it. For eleven years he'd kept a copy of it pinned to the wall of his cell in HMP Whitemoor. Angel had heard him sum it up in his own words many times. *When life shits all over you—and it's when, not if—get over it, move on*. Carl loved to quote lines from it, believing it would provide other people with the comfort he'd found in it himself.

Against that backdrop, Finch's parting remarks had brought everything into sharp and bleak focus.

He'd told her Kincade was *worried* about the Beckford situation. It was a damn sight worse than that.

Finch's remark about the Ocean Village apartment highlighted Kincade's equally-unstable domestic arrangements. She liked living with his father, and Carl liked having her live with him. It was good for both of them. But Angel's sister, Grace, was as determined as ever to see Kincade kicked out of their father's house.

All of that was as nothing compared to her biggest heartache. He'd worked with her long enough to know she'd let Beckford have his job back in a heartbeat and happily live in a cardboard box on the street if it meant resolving the situation with her estranged husband and her girls, have them come to live with her—although not in a cardboard box.

She hid it well.

Because the majority of her colleagues saw only what she projected. An over-confident outsider down from the Big Smoke with the hide of a rhinoceros and the empathy of a scorpion.

At times, he worried they saw a lot of the same traits in him.

17

Angel had made two very basic mistakes. He hadn't taken account of how bored Stuart Beckford might have become sitting at home watching daytime TV. And he'd forgotten that fate never sleeps, never misses an opportunity to stick its finger in your eye.

Had he not made those mistakes, he'd have kept his phone switched to silent. Then Kincade wouldn't have been aware of it when it went off in his pocket, not long after he'd got back to their office after briefing Finch.

It was the default ringtone, not a custom ringtone like the sound of seagulls fighting over fish heads he'd assigned to Grace. Despite that, he knew it was Beckford calling.

How? He just *did*.

A number of thoughts flashed through his mind while it rang happily in his pocket. Should he ignore it and let it ring out? Glance at it and kill the call with a muttered *I haven't got time*, as if to himself, but for Kincade's benefit? Stand up and answer it as he left the room?

Doing none of the above only drew Kincade's attention to the sound. She got up, headed for the door herself.

'For God's sake, if you think that's Stuart Beckford, just bloody answer it.'

The ringing stopped abruptly. She didn't. Kept on going, out the door without looking back.

He let his head pivot backwards as if it was hinged at the neck, eyes on the ceiling.

What am I supposed to do?

There were no answers up there.

He called Beckford back, feeling as if he'd signed off on a recommendation that Kincade be dismissed by the end of business that day.

'That was quick.'

Beckford half-snorted, half-laughed, his voice incredulous.

'Are you surprised? When was the last time you watched daytime TV?'

'At a rough guess . . . before I went to primary school.'

'Precisely. And that's exactly the audience the programmes are aimed at. If we wanted to make a real difference to the quality of people's lives in this country, forget about taking drug dealers and rapists off the streets, we should be taking game-show hosts off the board altogether.'

It struck Angel that if he ignored the voice, it could be Kincade on the other end of the line.

'Talking to Ricky Shorter must have been like a breath of fresh air.'

'Not sure about that. I think I'm still high from the smell of weed coming off him.'

'And?'

'And nothing, as far as Callaghan being a drug king-pin is concerned. Ricky knew of Callaghan, and he knew he was dead, although the exact details are a bit slow filtering down to the street. He called Callaghan a joke. As far as his impact on the local drug market's concerned, it'll be hard to tell the difference between when he's dead and when he was alive. He used to get the occasional job when somebody needed a fat moron to stand in the background looking tough. But they wouldn't have trusted him to collect the sandwich order from the café next door.'

'Meaning nobody killed him for trying to muscle-in on their territory.'

'Definitely not. That's what you were expecting to hear, wasn't it?'

Angel confirmed that it was, getting up from his desk and crossing to the door as he did so. From there, he had a straight line of sight into the incident room where Kincade was talking to Lisa Jardine. The conversation looked intense. Angel got a feeling he couldn't justify that they were discussing something personal, not work-related. They enjoyed a good relationship, but surely Kincade knew better than to share any misgivings she had about Stuart Beckford with Jardine? It would be all round the station by tea time. Except it was Jardine doing the talking. Something she said made Kincade shake her head, then run her fingers through her hair. She looked up as he was standing there watching her with his phone at his ear. Raised her chin at him in a question—*do you need me?*

He shook his head at her, went back to his desk, preparing to end the call.

Except the way Beckford cleared his throat told Angel he hadn't finished. He was expecting another fishing trip along the lines of the previous day. Quizzing him about what was really going on now that he'd confirmed Callaghan's tin-pot smuggling activities weren't the cause of his death.

Angel was wrong.

'Ricky said something else . . .' Beckford started.

Angel immediately picked up on the change in his voice, now filled with the excitement of a man who's saved the best to last.

'He said he heard Callaghan ran down and killed a man in his skip lorry.'

'He did. A journalist called Russell Baldwin.'

Angel felt Beckford nodding on the other end of the line, then an edge of caution crept into his voice.

'This is all third or fourth hand, but Ricky heard a rumour that it wasn't an accident. He knows a man who knows a man whose sister-in-law was there when it happened. Trouble is, Ricky claims he doesn't remember any details.'

'Did he say how much it would cost to restore his memory? Or is it your memory that needs lubricating?'

Beckford laughed with him, a sound that made Angel think of all the times they'd shared a laugh in the past, how long it had been since he'd last heard it.

'I should be offended,' Beckford said.

'But you're not.'

'Nah. Anyway, I told Ricky I wasn't authorised to agree to that. Told him I'd ask and get back to him.' The words rolled out on the back of a chuckle. Angel assumed it was because Beckford would blame him if he had to go back to Ricky and tell him he could go whistle for his money. Again, he was wrong, as Beckford made clear. 'Ricky doesn't miss a trick. He threw in a morsel to tempt you. He said he knew the guy Callaghan killed was a journalist. And the reason his death wasn't an accident was because he was sticking his nose into the business of the sort of person sensible people cross the street to avoid. Someone involved in the supply of narcotics at a level Callaghan couldn't even have dreamed about.' He chuckled again. 'That might be complete bollocks, of course, something to get you to bite. But on the other hand . . .'

'How much did you say your cut of what we might pay Ricky was?'

Angel tuned him out as Beckford prattled on in the

background. Saying that whatever his cut was, he was worth every penny, identifying the break that cracked the case within twenty-four hours of Angel first contacting him.

Angel was busy thinking about coincidence. As a default position, he didn't believe in it. But he had Finch's suggestion bouncing around in his mind. In particular, what she'd said when he pointed out that Baldwin specialised in investigating political scandal.

What? A politician can't be involved in drugs?

'You still there?' Beckford said. 'Some things don't change. I think I've got your attention, and suddenly I realise you're off in your own little world, communing with the man upstairs or dreaming of choir boys.'

Yeah, and there are some things I don't miss about you, Angel thought. *Not one jot*.

'Tell Ricky I want the details of the woman who was there when Callaghan flattened Baldwin. And if you're having difficulty calculating your cut of Ricky's fee, fifty per cent of jack shit is still jack shit.'

Kincade came back into the room in time to catch the last dozen words. It made her wonder what she'd missed as Angel ended the call.

'I'm assuming Stuart Beckford was the lucky recipient of that impromptu maths lesson? From the sound of it, I'm not sure I want to know what it was about.'

Trouble was, he needed to tell her.

If Beckford had ended the call after confirming Callaghan was a nobody as far as drug-dealing was concerned, that would have been the end of it. The subsequent revelation about Baldwin's death not being an accident meant saying nothing was no longer an option.

'I asked Stu to have a word with one of his informants.'

She looked at him as if she'd heard something different.

I've written out your resignation letter for you. All you have to do is sign it.

'Okay.'

Now he heard something different.

Not okay at all.

'You know what it's like. I wouldn't get half of what Stu could get out of his informant.'

'I can't disagree with that. But let's pretend for a minute that I'm the SIO on the case, and I have this *aha* moment about Beckford's informant.' She jabbed her breastbone with her middle finger. 'There's an extra step I'd insert before calling him and asking for help. I'd tell my number two about it. Not go behind their back.'

'I didn't exactly go behind your back—'

'Really? That's what it feels like from where I'm standing. You want to know what else it feels like? *Sir.*'

'I think you're going to tell me whether I do or not.'

'Bloody right, I am. It feels as if you're easing him back into things. Give him a simple task so you can assess his performance. Then, when Finch or Horwood take you to one side, *let's have a little chat about Stuart Beckford, God how I miss him*, you've got something to say on the matter beyond, *yeah, I miss him, too*. I caught Finch looking at me like I was a leper the other day, so maybe the process has already started.'

She'd remained on her feet since she came back into the room, standing in front of his desk as she talked at him. Now, she dropped heavily into her chair, then immediately bounced out of it again, as if even it had rejected and ejected her, waiting for its rightful owner's long-overdue return.

'I need a cup of coffee. You want one?'

No thanks, I had one in Finch's office while we were talking about you wasn't going to help.

'Please.'

'Aren't you worried I'll spit in it?'

'Couldn't make it taste any worse.'

'Is that a challenge?'

He extended his hand towards her, *be my guest*. Thinking, *I'd happily drink it if it meant we could've avoided the last five minutes.*

'Whatever you put in it has sunk to the bottom,' he said, when Kincade put a cup of brown sludge on his desk a couple of minutes later.

'I've heard lead does that.' She raised her cup towards him. '*Cheers!*'

He took a sip, worked an exaggerated grimace onto his face, then took another. Not because he wanted to continue with the joke, get them past the atmosphere in the room as thick as in the old days when people smoked at their desks. To give him time to think of a way to convince her it really was all about Ricky Shorter's particular expertise, and nothing to do with easing Beckford back into the job and her out of it.

Except it wouldn't make a blind bit of difference whatever he said. Kincade felt threatened. At the mercy of forces outside her control. It would take more than a few carefully-chosen words from him to loosen her fear's grip.

He'd left it too long, anyway.

'So?' she said. 'Did Beckford's informant come up with anything worthwhile?'

What he heard: *anything worth the damage to our working relationship.*

'Actually, yes...'

He took her through it, relieved as he watched her anger slip away, pushed aside by professional interest when he told her about Ricky Shorter's claim that Baldwin's death was more than an accident.

'At least something came out of it. Something that feels as if it's got potential to lead somewhere.' She assumed *Kincade position #1*, her voice turning thoughtful. 'I'm not sure what I feel about that. As a cop, I should be excited about it. As a person, I wish it was anyone other than the person who wants my job who came up with it. What does that say about me?'

'That you're honest.'

'Maybe. I don't suppose Rudyard Kipling's still alive, is he?'

The abrupt change in direction threw him momentarily.

'I think he died in the nineteen thirties. Why?'

'I'd email him if he was. Suggest a new line. *If you can watch your arch rival come up with the best lead, and still be happy for the investigation* . . . how does the poem end?'

'Then you'll be a man, my son.'

She shook her head.

'Forget that. *Then you'll be an idiot, my son.* I'd like to see Rudyard Kipling try to live up to his own bloody poem.'

18

Lisa Jardine startled when Angel arrived unexpectedly at her desk.

'You shouldn't creep up on people like that, sir. You could've given me a heart attack.' She dropped her eyes to his feet, a smile appearing on her face. 'Even though you're not wearing Jesus Creepers.'

The way you were lost in your thoughts, I could've been wearing hob-nailed boots and you wouldn't have heard me, he thought, and softened it.

'It's only monks who wear sandals, Lisa, not priests. You looked miles away. Is everything okay?'

He saw what went through her mind—*why shouldn't it be?*—his rank obliging her to put it a different way.

'I was thinking.'

'I've made a note of it with the date and time,' Gulliver said from the next desk. 'I log them all. I'll let you know when I need a second sheet of paper.'

Jardine wagged her finger at him, except she got the gesture wrong, using her middle finger and pointing it straight up.

'It's the quality that counts Craig, not the quantity.'

'That's rich coming from Ms Gob-on-a-stick.'

Angel had never worked as a primary school teacher, but he knew what they must feel like. He'd have to separate them soon before they started pulling each other's hair.

'You like a good rumour, Lisa—'

'She starts most of them.' This from Gulliver.

Jardine came right back at him.

'I'm going to start one soon about a posh Southern twat—'

'*Enough!*' Angel yelled. 'Anyone want to hear one about Dirty Harry?'

'I'm all ears,' Jardine said, the glare she gave Gulliver challenging him to refute the ridiculous claim.

Angel took them through the details of Ricky Shorter's rumour, praying that neither of them asked for its source.

'Where did this come from?' Jardine said, as soon as he'd finished.

'A source.'

I could've worked that out for myself was hanging in the air before Gulliver came to Angel's rescue.

'If he told you who it was, it wouldn't be confidential anymore, would it?'

Jardine ignored him, her brow furrowed.

'What's that stupid name we're supposed to call them now?'

Gulliver looked at her as if she was an old dog he was fond of that he couldn't teach new tricks, his voice patient.

'A Covert Human Intelligence Source. *CHIS*.'

She looked at him as if he'd said it was pronounced *FART*.

'I'm going to call them CHIPs.'

Angel and Gulliver stared at her, not sure what to say. Trying hard not to think about what the letter *P* stood for, the possibilities endless—*prick, pillock, prat, plonker*...

'I have curry sauce on my chips,' she explained, as if she was dealing with a pair of idiots. 'That'll help me remember.'

Gulliver was looking as if he wanted to pull his hair out. Or hers.

'I think you're confusing *sauce* with *source*.'

'Whatever.' She gave Angel her best attentive look. 'You were saying, sir, until Craig got us off track.'

Angel felt confident that whatever the intense conversation he'd witnessed between Jardine and Kincade had been about, Jardine was back to her usual self. For the time being. A bit like the pin being reinserted into a grenade.

'If Baldwin was killed deliberately, it was either payback for something he'd already written, or to stop him from disclosing something new. We need to look into both of those possibilities.'

'I'll take what he's already written,' Gulliver said. 'Lisa can take what he hadn't.'

If he was expecting an indignant reaction from Jardine—*how am I supposed to investigate what hasn't yet happened?*—he was disappointed. The enthusiasm in her voice suggested she'd have allocated the work on the same basis herself.

'Okay by me. Baldwin sounds like a bit of a muck-stirrer. Somebody like him probably had a blog as well as the published articles and the book he wrote. That's where he's likely to post the stuff the papers won't touch. The sort of stuff that might get him killed.'

Angel came away feeling sorry for Gulliver having to spend all day with Jardine, his mind bouncing back and forth like a tennis ball between the absurd and the insightful.

Angel was pleased when he saw DS Ellis Hudson had been in charge of the investigation ordered by the coroner into Russell Baldwin's death. He'd never worked directly with Hudson, but their paths had crossed many times. Their relationship was good enough for him to pick Hudson's brains, which is what he planned to do after leaving Gulliver and Jardine, taking the stairs down to the floor below.

Hudson raised his eyes to the ceiling as Angel approached, a rapturous smile on his lips as if witnessing the second coming of the Son of Man.

'I'm honoured to receive a visit from heaven above, Padre.'

Heaven? Angel thought. *You try having a conversation with Jardine and tell me if that feels like heaven to you.*

'Keep saying your prayers, Ellis, and we might let you in one day.'

Hudson gave him a sceptical look, pointed at the floor.

'I've heard it's more fun downstairs. So? What can I do for you?'

I'm here to ruin your day, Angel thought, and put a name to the sentiment.

'Russell Baldwin.'

Hudson let out an exaggerated sigh. *Here we go again*. Resigned acceptance that a visit from Angel or one of his team only ever meant one thing—somebody had missed something. Something that led to worse things.

'You're here to tell me it wasn't accidental death, after all?'

'There's a rumour to that effect.'

'At least it's not a proven fact. *Yet*. How long have I got? A minute? Two minutes to prove I couldn't possibly have known at the time?'

Angel consulted his watch.

'I'm feeling generous. I'll give you two. *Go!*'

'There was no alcohol or drugs in Callaghan's bloodstream. He wasn't on his phone at the time. He wasn't speeding. I suppose the sun could've been blinding him the way it was flickering through the stupid *Dirty Harry* sun strip he had on his windscreen. Or he might have had his head up his arse daydreaming or watching some woman with no bra letting it all hang out . . .'

'What about Baldwin?'

'He did have alcohol in his bloodstream. He'd drunk a couple of glasses of wine with lunch, but he was a regular drinker. It wouldn't have been sufficient to make him incapable of walking in a straight line or cause him to stumble into the road.' He raised a finger, anticipating Angel's next question. 'I know what you lot are like upstairs, and, no, there was no evidence of drugs, date rape or otherwise.'

'Who did he have lunch with?'

'I'll have to get back to you on that. According to Callaghan, one second the road was empty, he glanced away and back again, and there he was, right in front of him. Callaghan slammed on the anchors, but he had a full load and kept on going for thirty yards with Baldwin spread-eagled on his grille. There was nothing he could do. Despite looking like the sort of thug who bites the heads off live chickens as a party piece, he was really shaken up by it. We checked the pavement adjacent to where Baldwin was hit, but there were no broken paving slabs or anything else obvious that might have made him trip. What does your rumour say happened?'

'Nothing specific. Only that it wasn't an accident. The implication is he was pushed.'

'Yeah, well, there was nobody saying anything like that at the time.'

A defensive edge had entered Hudson's voice. It was understandable. Turning up with the benefit of hindsight, Angel expected it. Even so, the level of resentment in Hudson's voice registered with him.

'Any witnesses?'

'Dozens while Baldwin was lying in the road impersonating roadkill. All pushing and shoving to get a better look. Trying to see some blood. Maybe, if they're really lucky, see him actually die in front of their eyes. When it came to asking for witnesses who actually saw it happen, he might as well have been hit in the middle of a desert.' He lifted his hands towards the ceiling, palms down, fingers fluttering like Baldwin's soul departing his body on its way up to heaven. 'It's incredible how rubberneckers simply fade away into the ether.'

There would've been more bitterness in his voice at people's selfishness, had long experience not left him resigned to man's indifference towards his fellow man, his expectations precisely zero as a result.

Angel smiled to himself, remembering Kincade's suggestion to add a new line to Rudyard Kipling's poem. A further one came to him now.

If you can listen to a thousand selfish excuses, and not think badly of the self-centred bastards...

'Actually, that's unfair,' Hudson said, backtracking. 'All the ghouls who'd been crowding around disappeared, but a witness came forward the next day. He was in his car on the other side of the road, driving towards Callaghan's lorry when it hit Baldwin. He told us he didn't see anything suspicious. The reason he didn't stop—'

'Was because he didn't see the point in telling you what he didn't see?'

'Exactly. And he was already late for an important meeting . . . you get the gist. But when he got home and told his wife, she insisted he come in and make a statement. If a hundred witnesses say they didn't see anyone push someone, it's likely nobody did, sort of thing.'

'Sensible woman.'

'Yeah. Shame there aren't more of them around.'

If Stuart Beckford hadn't told Angel about the rumour, he might not have thought any more about the witness. But since the witness was saying the exact opposite to what the rumour implied, it was worth following up.

'I'll talk to him, seeing as he's the only person who admits to even being there.'

'Up to you. I'll email you his details. To tell you the truth, I thought he was a crank. It wouldn't surprise me if he made up the story about his wife telling him to come in just to give himself an excuse.'

And it wouldn't surprise me if you're saying that to explain why you didn't pay him more attention, Angel thought, and said something more constructive.

'Anything else I need to know? Anything that set your antennae twitching?'

Hudson leaned back in his chair, looking through Angel as he thought back.

'He still had his wallet on him, so at least the rubberneckers didn't steal that. And his phone. I know how you lot upstairs get hot under the collar about a stiff's mobile phone. But he didn't have any keys on him.' He raised a hand, some of the earlier defensiveness in the gesture. 'And yes, we visited his property. It hadn't been ransacked, and his car was still parked outside. He spent half his time at his girlfriend's place, the other half with her at his place. She was away visiting friends when he died, so he would've needed to take keys with him when he went out. We thought he might have had them in his hand when he was hit and they ended up falling down a drain. Seeing as it was looking like an accident, pure and simple, we didn't search the drains for keys that might have never existed.'

Hudson lapsed into silence. Angel was happy to let him, allow his mind to make connections after the initial prod into life.

'There was one other thing. The medics said somebody told them a man had already checked the victim to determine whether he was still alive. He'd disappeared by the time the medics arrived. It sounded a bit suspect, but not many people have got the balls to frisk a still-twitching body in front of a crowd of onlookers. When it turned out the victim still had his wallet and phone on him, we didn't give it another thought. The only reason it's crossed my mind now is because you've turned up with the benefit of hindsight wanting to look at everything from a different point of view.'

Again, Angel was surprised by Hudson's irritability. The tone of their conversation had completely changed from how it started out, with Hudson joking about Angel's previous calling. Hudson had grown progressively more defensive. It wasn't the best note to end on. Nor would it help matters going forward, should Angel need to come back to him—on this or subsequent investigations. He was trying to think of a way to end on a positive note when Hudson coughed out a laugh.

'Something funny happened at the inquest. Funny if you weren't Callaghan, that is. Baldwin's girlfriend kicked up a fuss after the accidental death verdict.'

'Véronique Dubois?'

'Yeah. Have you spoken to her?'

'Not yet.'

'Good luck when you do, although she'll have calmed down by now.'

'What was she saying?'

Hudson gave an exaggerated shrug, arms extended forward from the elbow, palms up.

'Nothing coherent. She was nearly hysterical. A lot of it was in French. That's what happens when you're upset, I suppose. You revert to your native language. The coroner told her to shut up and she stormed out. And no, we didn't go after her, ask her to say it all again calmly and in English.' He smiled to himself. 'I thought about it. Not because I thought it was important, but she's a good-looking woman. I could interview women like her all day long. And that French accent...'

The remark was like a lifeline thrown to Angel. An opportunity to rescue the tone of their conversation as he thought back to the discussion with Barbara Callaghan about her finding Véronique's number in her husband's secret burner phone.

'You remember what Harry Callaghan looked like?'

Hudson thrust his stomach out and jutted his jaw aggressively at Angel.

'He's not the sort of person you forget. Why?'

'His wife was worried he was doing his bit for Anglo-French relations, slipping Véronique the old garlic sausage.'

It took a moment for Angel's colourful euphemism to register, then a snort of incredulous laughter erupted out of Hudson's mouth.

'Sounds like Baldwin wasn't the only person Callaghan hit with his lorry. He must've driven right over his wife's head a couple of times. *Splat!* Squeezed her brains out of her ears like toothpaste.'

Angel smiled with him at the somewhat gross mental image, his reply riding out on the back of it.

'Shame we couldn't have squeezed the truth out of her the same way.'

'You know what it's like, Padre. There's always a bit left stuck in the bottom.'

Ain't that the truth, Angel thought to himself as he came away.

19

Liam Callaghan had a sneaking suspicion he was trying to be too clever by half. He hadn't wanted to tell Véronique Dubois that Harry was dead over the phone. She'd been suspicious enough taking the call from him. Telling her Harry had been murdered would have spooked her. She'd have refused to meet with him at all.

Instead, he told her Harry asked him to get in touch with her. It was true in a way. The note Harry left him on his laptop had encouraged him to follow in his brother's footsteps. Admittedly, he'd omitted the most important detail, the one Véronique would have based her decision on, had she known it.

They agreed to meet in Mayflower Park, right next to the City Cruise Terminal on the River Test. That's when Liam had a bright idea. Véronique was already nervous. She might be even more anxious if he turned up in his crappy old Vauxhall Corsa that looked exactly like the sort of nondescript vehicle someone would steal if they were planning on abducting a young woman. He decided to cycle to the rendezvous, instead.

Now, as he cycled through the car park to where she waited,

leaning against the metal railings with a monstrous multi-storey cruise ship towering above her, he felt a bit of a twat. She'd approached Harry for help. That had got Harry killed. And now here he was, Harry's replacement reporting for duty, a man on a pushbike dressed in brightly-coloured Spandex with a cycling helmet on his head—not exactly the perfect protection for when things turned nasty with the sort of men who put three nine-millimetre rounds into his brother's back.

The surprise wasn't all one-way. She might have been horrified to see a dickhead on a bike turn up, but he wasn't expecting to see her heavily pregnant. The size of what Inspector Clouseau would call her *bermp* sticking out in front of her made Liam worry he might have to perform an open-air delivery while the seagulls shrieked encouragement from their perches on the railings.

At least he didn't make a complete fool of himself as he dismounted with an idiotic, *you're pregnant!*

'Yes, the baby is Russell's,' she said, when she caught him staring, her matter-of-fact tone of voice giving him some reassurance she wasn't about to break down and sob her heart out on his shoulder. He'd still have preferred it if she hadn't been pregnant, feeling the added pressure the unborn child represented. This wasn't only for Harry now, or even Harry and Véronique. It was for Russell Jnr, too. Again, he managed not to make a prat of himself, ask if she was going to name it after its dead father, if it was a boy of course.

He was saved from his own thoughts when Véronique cut to the chase.

'Where is Harry?'

It immediately became clear he was going to have to put his helmet on the wrong way around so that it covered his face if he didn't want her reading all the answers on it before he opened his mouth.

Her hand went to her bump as she answered her own question with another.

'Is he dead?'

He nodded rather than say the words, conflicting emotions pulling at him as he talked to the woman indirectly responsible for that death. He understood that she wanted to get to the bottom of who killed the father of her child, but Harry died because she'd approached him. Liam knew his brother well enough to know that seeing Véronique pregnant would have swayed Harry's mind, made him determined to stick his nose in where it wasn't wanted.

'How?' Véronique said, making it sound like *I don't want to know*.

'He was murdered.' He thought about leaving it there, but she would only ask more questions. 'Somebody took him out to the New Forest and shot him. *Executed* him.'

He dropped his eyes, settling on her belly, convinced she could read his mind, see the accusation behind every thought in his head. He went to the railings, leaned against them looking out over the water so that she didn't see it written all over his face, the taste of salt on his lips. He realised he was still wearing his helmet. He pulled it off, gave his scalp a good scratch, enjoying the coolness of the sea breeze on his skin. She turned to lean and look across the water with him, even if the view was nothing to write home about. They stayed like that for a minute or two, adrift with their own thoughts of what each of them had lost, but finding no comfort in one another's company or pain.

Liam knew there was accusation in his voice when he spoke, but there was nothing he could do about it. Besides, she was looking to hear it, whatever he said.

'Did you notice Harry's little finger when you met him?'

'No. Why?'

'Did it look as if somebody hit it with a hammer?'

'I don't think so. I don't understand why you are asking.'

'Trying to get things clear in my mind, that's all. I think they gave Harry a warning after he talked to you.' He raised his arm, brought the side of his fist down hard onto the railings, a hopeful gull perched ten feet away taking to the air with a raucous squawk. 'Harry ignored the warning. I think he tried to talk to your boyfriend's ex-wife next. That's what made them decide to kill him.'

She turned away from the water, brushed her hair out of her eyes as she smiled at him.

'Thank you for saying that.'

He hadn't realised what he'd done, lessening the blame attached to her. It wasn't her fault for approaching Harry. It was Harry's own fault for ignoring the warning that followed. The relief on her face made him feel comfortable bringing up what started the whole chain of events.

'I don't understand why you got in touch with him. I was at the inquest.' He grinned suddenly, an involuntary nervous gesture. 'I heard you kick off when they said it was accidental.'

She smiled with him, resting her hands on her belly, eyes on the ground now.

'I was very emotional, yes.'

Liam nearly told her to blame it on the hormones, caught himself in time.

'I didn't understand a word of it, but it sounded like you wanted to kill him. What changed?'

The question wiped the last traces of the smile at her own outburst off her face.

'Somebody broke into my apartment.'

'Are you sure it wasn't a burglar?'

She shook her head, an ambiguous gesture, but there was no room for doubt in her voice.

'Very sure. My cat was outside in the hall. It can't get out on its own. It must have run out and hid when they opened the door. It was waiting for me in the hallway when I got home. Otherwise I wouldn't have known. There was no damage. Nothing was missing. It is the only explanation. The people who killed Russell thought he might have left details of what he was working on with me.' She gave a very Gallic shrug. 'They are wrong. I do not even know what he was working on.'

'No idea at all?'

She waved her hand dismissively.

'Political scandal. I was not interested in the details. It's so boring. They are politicians. What do you expect? I used to say to Russell, you will never change anything. Dig some dirt on one of them and maybe he resigns. Then another one pops up who is even worse.' She smiled softly to herself, her hands moving slowly and rhythmically over her belly. 'I used to say to him, do you want the first one back now? It made no difference. He was obsessed. He used to shout at the television until the neighbours banged on the wall.'

Liam couldn't help the thought that went through his mind.
Not so boring now.

He thought she'd said everything she had to say on the subject. It was boring. End of. But he was wrong.

'All I know is that he met with a woman,' she said. 'I asked him who she was. He put his hand on my stomach and asked me if I was jealous. It was his way of telling me to mind my own business. I think maybe he was protecting me.'

If Liam had thought things through in advance, he might have jotted down the questions he wanted to ask, maybe even put them in a logical order. As it was, Véronique's mention of protection and its implication of danger to her prompted the next one.

'If you were suspicious about his death, weren't you worried that Harry was involved when you contacted him?'

She looked at him as if the breeze blowing off the water had loosened his brain from its moorings.

'Your brother drove a skip lorry, yes? It is the stupidest name. *Skip* means to move with a light, bouncing step . . .' Demonstrating the movement with her fingers.

Liam was about to point out that the term referred to what the lorry carried on the back, not how it moved down the street, but thought better of it.

'A skip lorry does not skip,' Véronique stated firmly. 'If somebody pays you to run a man over, you do not choose a skip lorry to do it. You choose a fast car that can take him by surprise, hit him and then escape.' She waved her hand as if he'd been about to object. 'I wasn't thinking properly at the inquest. Later, I thought about it and realised your brother did not do it deliberately. Somebody must have pushed Russell. That is what I wanted to ask your brother.'

'What did he say?'

Véronique looked at him for a long while, as if assessing him, this man on a bicycle in his tight-fitting Spandex gear and his plastic helmet with ventilation slots.

'He said he did not see anybody push Russell. He was very careful about the words he used. He answered my question, but that did not mean there wasn't more to say. I think he wanted to say more, but he was scared.'

Liam's mouth was halfway open to protest, say that his brother hadn't been scared of a thing in his whole life, when Véronique corrected herself.

'Maybe scared is too strong. I got the impression he felt guilty because he wasn't completely truthful at the inquest, didn't say everything he knew.'

'Why would he do that?'

It was a stupid question, out before Liam could stop it. Despite that, Véronique didn't give him the brain-floating-free look again, her tone deadly serious.

'It is obvious. Because somebody told him not to.'

Liam guessed that if you were in a relationship with a man obsessed with political scandal, you became prone to conspiracy theories yourself. He suddenly felt as if they were rubbing off on him. There were parts of Véronique he'd like her to rub against him, but her paranoia wasn't one of them. He glanced around the car park, the realisation taking hold that he might have inadvertently made a target out of both of them. It was only a quick glance—not nearly thorough enough to notice the black Range Rover on the far side of the car park—or else he'd have felt more anxious still.

'What are you going to do now?' Véronique said.

'I don't know.'

'Have you told the police any of this?'

He was still angry at the way the detectives who interviewed him had tried to scare him into doing their jobs for them. *You might be dead by then. You don't have much time.* A lot of that residual anger came through in his reply.

'Of course not.'

If she heard the sharpness at all, she took it for grim determination.

'Good. Make sure you don't. I think they're the ones who told your brother to keep his mouth shut.'

Liam glanced around the car park again, then pulled his helmet on as if it might give him protection from the unseen dangers he now sensed lurking around every corner.

'What are you going to do?'

She looked behind her at the cruise ship towering over them as if it were a cross-channel ferry, her hands gravitating protectively to her belly once more.

'After what you've told me, I'm going home. Back to France. I don't think I want my baby to be born in this country.' She put her hand on Liam's arm, sent a shiver through him at the depth of concern in her voice. 'If you've got any sense, drop this now. You can't avenge your brother if you are dead, too.'

He stayed by the railings for five minutes after she'd walked away, her coat wrapped tightly around her as if the breeze off the water had stiffened and chilled.

When he did leave, he cycled right past the front of the black Range Rover without knowing it.

At least it didn't surge forward with an angry roar of its engine and turn him into just another cycling mortality statistic.

They were in a busy car park, after all.

EVIE ST. JAMES LIKED TALKING TO HER SISTER. SHE DIDN'T CARE that Orla was dead. It meant she got to do a lot more of the talking, that was for sure. And in terms of the sense she got out of her, it didn't make a lot of difference either way, if she was honest. Orla had been a real live wire. The sort of woman who turned heads in the street, the men's tongues lolling out, happy to suffer a kick in the shin or a tongue-lashing from their jealous, frumpy wives for the chance of a smile. As for Orla's own head, blessed with the face that caused all that marital strife, well, that had been pretty empty on the inside. It didn't seem to bother the men any.

Evie would've traded her brains for Orla's looks in the blink of an eye. Orla looked prettier lying in the casket in the funeral home after they'd fetched her out of the freezer cabinet than Evie ever did on a night out on the town, for Christ's sake.

Evie liked the peace and quiet of the cemetery as much as the sense of closeness to her sister it gave her. The sense of gentle melancholy. Of being a part of a wider universe that was unfolding around her as it should, however much recent events made her believe otherwise. A reminder of her own place in the world, as fleeting and insignificant as the yellowing leaves that littered the ground. And a reminder that she was not alone, neither the first nor the only one to feel the keen edge of loss.

These days, it was also the only place she was able to get her head straight and think. Talking her thoughts through with ever-patient Orla without passers-by giving her uneasy looks or crossing the street to avoid her. Everybody talks to the dead in a cemetery.

Not everybody talks about the same things, of course.

Evie was very glad she didn't believe in any of the religious claptrap spouted by pious hypocrites. A fork of righteous lightning from on high would've speared her for the thoughts that went through her mind, the whispered promises she made to her dead sister each time she visited. And as for the warm rush she felt in her belly, an eternity in the fires of hell awaited her for that wicked pleasure.

Down on one knee as she placed a fresh spray of flowers on the still-raised mound of Orla's grave, with its simple wooden cross awaiting a proper headstone, Evie watched an old man dressed in a threadbare black suit at a nearby grave. She'd seen him every time she'd come, all her visits on different days. It was either the mother of all coincidences or he came every day.

Was it guilt that forced him out in all weathers?

Because he'd taken his wife for granted while she was alive, and now he was over-compensating when it was too late?

Join the club, mate.

Except it wasn't not spending enough time with her sister that bothered Evie. That had been Orla's choice. She was the one who'd always been too busy to spare an hour or two for her dowdy sister, not the other way around.

No, it was what Evie had done after her sister died that plagued her, kept her awake at night.

Because Evie St. James had the death of an innocent man weighing on her conscience. A black mark on her soul that would be with her until she was every bit as dead as her sister.

Some days that prospect felt a lot closer than others.

20

Angel was acutely aware of Kincade thinking he was going behind her back. As if he was running a parallel mini-investigation with Stuart Beckford's help. Even so, it wasn't worth both of them meeting Ralph Stone, the witness who'd come forward to say that he saw nothing untoward when Russell Baldwin was run over and killed.

He could've sent Kincade alone, of course. Except he'd been intrigued when Ellis Hudson said he thought Stone was a crank. There are different varieties of crank. Confused well-intentioned cranks, malicious cranks, just-plain-nuts cranks. Angel wanted to talk to Stone himself to get a feel for what flavour Stone was, if he was one at all.

Unfortunately, the feeling of excluding Kincade was reinforced when he agreed to meet Stone at the Holiday Inn, half a mile from the station. The proximity did at least mean Angel could walk there in under ten minutes, striding out down West Quay Road.

Stone was already there when Angel arrived, a broad-shouldered man in a suit that had seen better days and hair that looked suspiciously like a toupée. He waved at Angel as he stepped into the foyer, made him feel as if he had a neon sign on his head flashing *police officer*. He would've approached Stone even if Stone hadn't waved first, his name fitting perfectly with the solidly-built man who looked as if you'd break your fist on his jaw. Did people think something similar about him, he wondered, expecting a pair of folded wings under his jacket?

Stone had a half-full cup of coffee on the table in front of him. Angel waved the offer of a cup for himself away, got down to business. The whole situation was too similar to when he'd met with Virgil Balan without Kincade being aware of it, and he was keen to keep the interview as brief as possible.

'DS Hudson told me you witnessed Russell Baldwin actually being hit by the skip lorry.'

A shudder of revulsion passed over Stone's face at the memory.

'That's right. Although it's not much of an exaggeration to say that I *felt* it. It was horrible. Seeing him in front of the lorry a second before it hit. Knowing it was inevitable and not being able to do a thing about it.' He passed his hand quickly over his face. 'I keep getting flashbacks. My wife says they'll fade with time, but I'm not so sure, myself.'

Despite being conscious of the time, Angel let him talk. Until now, at least. He tried to get things moving when Stone paused for breath.

'Can you tell me exactly what you saw leading up to the impact. Anything and everything you can remember about the scene. Baldwin himself. Other people on the pavement, other cars. Anything at all. Let me be the judge of what's important.'

A spasm of irritation passed over Stone's face at effectively being told his interpretation of what he saw was of no interest to Angel. Stick to the facts. As if he was nothing more than a CCTV camera on legs. The irritation manifested itself in his voice—not anger, but the nasal whine of petulance. Nor did he answer the question.

'The fact that we're having this discussion after the coroner came back with a verdict of accidental death tells me you suspect it was more than that. The most obvious alternative is that he was pushed.'

He pumped his arm out like a hydraulic piston as he said it, his hand flat, fingers splayed. It would've been an appropriate gesture if he'd used an obscure technical term and not an everyday word like *push*. It was all Angel could do not to recoil as if he'd been pushed himself—physically pushed, that is, not just into areas he didn't plan to discuss with Stone.

'We have to consider all possibilities.'

Stone nodded his understanding and acceptance that Angel couldn't commit himself to a member of the public.

'I can tell you that I definitely didn't see anyone push him.'

'That sounds very definite. Almost too definite.'

'That's because it is.' He realised what he'd said, corrected himself. 'Not *too* definite, of course.'

'I can see from your face there's a reason why you're so convinced.'

Stone immediately dropped his eyes to the floor. The gesture felt a little staged to Angel, but Stone seemed to be a demonstrative man, his hands and eyes and head always on the move.

He took a deep breath, let it out in a rush.

'I didn't tell DS Hudson what I'm about to tell you.'

'Why not?'

'Bear with me. It'll become clear in a minute.'

Angel forced himself to ignore the annoyance that surged inside him. He liked witnesses to answer questions when they were asked, not build them into their story. Against that, he recognised that people have to be given the leeway to tell it their way, or things will slip through the cracks.

'The reason I'm so definite is because I was watching the pavement on Baldwin's side of the street. I'd noticed a mother with a pushchair and another toddler on reins. The toddler got away from her and was running towards the road. I thought he was going to run out in front of the lorry. It's bad enough watching a grown man being run down, but a child?' He took another deep breath, blew it out again. Then held his hand three foot above the floor, palm downwards. 'The thing is, the toddler was this tall, so I can't be sure with all the other people around, but I think he ran into Baldwin's legs. Baldwin stumbled into the road. That's when the lorry hit him.' He smacked his fist into his open palm, another unnecessary gesture as far as Angel was concerned. 'It was still an accident, but I didn't want that child growing up knowing he'd been responsible for a man's death. And the mother, for losing control of him.' He held up his hand. 'I know you're going to say it wasn't my decision to make, but there it is. And don't worry, it's been preying on my mind ever since. But until you called me out of the blue, I saw no reason to complicate matters by volunteering things which make no difference to the verdict.'

Angel guessed Stone had done a lot of this, having the same conversation with himself, justifying himself. He didn't want to make him feel worse, but he still had to say what he said next.

'You said it yourself. You couldn't be sure because of the child's size and all the other people around. That alone should have prompted you to say what you've just told me.'

Stone coughed out a sour laugh, devoid of humour. Nor was there any remorse after Angel's reprimand.

'I'll know for next time, if I'm unlucky enough to ever witness something like that again.' He downed the last of his coffee, now cold, looking like he wanted to spit it out again. 'You don't look very relieved, Inspector. I would've thought what I've told you would reassure you that it really was an accident, after all.'

'I'm a naturally suspicious person, Mr Stone, that's all. I don't take anything I'm told at face value. Don't take it personally.'

'Well, if you find the mother and her child, they'll back up what I've told you. Unless the mother denies it because she feels guilty for losing control of her kid, of course.'

Angel was hoping he'd have a better idea about that as soon as Stuart Beckford's informant came up with a name for the witness who claimed Baldwin's death wasn't an accident. There was no point worrying about the inconsistency between that claim and what Ralph Stone had told him before he'd heard both sides.

As far as DS Ellis Hudson's assessment that Stone was a crank was concerned, Angel was in two minds. Stone didn't come across as an interfering busybody, desperate to feel that he was a vital part of a real, live police investigation to compensate for the ordinariness and tedium of his own life.

Despite that, Angel couldn't shake the feeling that the guy hadn't been completely straight with him.

ANGEL KNEW SOMETHING WAS UP AS SOON AS HE GOT BACK. JACK Bevan, the desk sergeant, looked him up and down as he walked in, then shook his head at him.

'I'm not sure it's working, Padre.'

Bevan was an escapee-cum-refugee from a small town in Wales with an unpronounceable name, although that didn't narrow it down much. As such, his thought processes weren't always the same as those of other men, in this case Angel, who had no idea what he was talking about—apart from knowing he was about to be the butt of something.

'You mean me praying for your soul every night, Jack?' He pointed at the floor. 'You still feel the irresistible pull of downstairs?'

Bevan shook his head again and rubbed his stomach.

'No. I mean you'll have to do more than go for a quick afternoon walk to work off all the food your mother's feeding you.'

Angel glanced at his stomach, a fraction of the size of Bevan's own. He didn't need to speak the words.

Pot. Kettle. Black.

So far, the conversation had followed the same lines as it always did between them. Good-natured abuse about Bevan's heritage and Angel's previous calling. It was harmless and filled Bevan's day, even if Angel was anxious to get back upstairs.

Now, it turned less harmless.

Bevan leaned over the counter, lowered his voice.

'I know you haven't been for a walk, Padre. I assume you were meeting Stuart Beckford.'

Angel's heart sank.

The meeting that hadn't taken place became a fact the minute the words left Bevan's mouth. It couldn't have been more set in stone if Angel had pulled out his phone and showed Bevan a selfie of him and Beckford having a cup of coffee together.

It was an inescapable fact of station life that even in the modern era of instantaneous digital communication, the fastest way to disseminate information was to tell something to Jack Bevan. That applied as much to things Bevan had made up himself as it did to actual facts.

Angel felt obliged to waste his breath, nonetheless.

'I was meeting a witness at the Holiday Inn. They were

understandably wary about coming into the station because they'd heard the horror stories about the desk sergeant.'

Bevan winked at him.

'Your secret's safe with me, Padre. Give Stu my best wishes next time you see him.'

Angel gave up.

21

'I feel like I'm a character in a book,' Jardine announced.

The remark puzzled Gulliver, coming out of the blue as it did. He didn't let that stop him from taking advantage of it.

'It's not one I'd want to read. Although that's not the right word, seeing as it would only contain cartoons.'

'Better than a book about a posh Southern twat with so many long words readers would be asleep by the end of page one.'

The exchange—it didn't qualify as a conversation—had the feeling of something that could deteriorate rapidly. Luckily, Gulliver's curiosity got the better of him before it did.

'You want to tell me why you feel like a character in a book?'

They were on their way to interview Lacy Cooper, the young woman who'd witnessed Harry Callaghan turning Russell Baldwin into roadkill. They'd both been glad of the opportunity to get away from their desks, take a break from wading through the mass of Baldwin's vitriolic writings, trying to identify which of the many people who'd been a victim of his merciless exposés might be sufficiently enraged or their careers destroyed to want to kill him.

It was the way it had come about that prompted Jardine's remark.

'The way the boss turned up at our desks and said, *go and interview Lacy Cooper* like he'd pulled her out of a hat and didn't say where the information came from.'

'Got you. *Deus ex machina*.'

Jardine narrowed her eyes at him, not sure whether he'd just insulted her.

'It's hard enough understanding you when you speak English, so you can drop all that foreign bollocks right now.'

'It's when a problem is magically solved out of the blue by an unexpected, unlikely event.'

'That's what I said, wasn't it? The boss turned up with a witness like she fell out of a horse's arse.'

Gulliver was ready to give up at that point, except the way Jardine turned thoughtful piqued his curiosity again.

'What?'

She swivelled in her seat to face him properly, the look on her face telling him he was about to witness the full power of the Lisa Jardine gossip machine gearing up and going into action, a process as impressive as any military invasion.

'I heard a rumour—'

'*Started* a rumour.'

'—that the boss went out and got shit-faced with Stuart Beckford the other night.'

'So what? They used to be mates until . . .'

'Yeah, yeah, I know all that. But what if he's using him on the sly, and that's why he won't say where the information came from. Doesn't want it getting back to Kincade.'

'Too late now.'

She did her best to look indignant. She needed to work on it.

'I don't know what you're talking about.'

'I might as well call Beckford now, tell him to dust off his work clothes. He'll be back by the end of the week.'

With that, he went back to concentrating on driving. Except Jardine still hadn't finished.

'Who would you vote for if you had to choose between Kincade and Beckford?'

It was a difficult question, and not one he wanted to think about. One thing was for sure. He wouldn't be giving anything away to the woman sitting beside him, waiting expectantly for him to nail his colours to the mast. If he did, the rumour mill would churn out a new one, that he either did or did not support Stuart Beckford reclaiming his job from Kincade.

'Whichever one promised to fix me up with a new partner the quickest.'

'I'm trying to be serious here.'

'In that case, you need to give me advance warning of a once-in-a-lifetime occurrence.'

'You're impossible, you know that?'

'Are you surprised? I learned from the best.'

She fell silent, gazing out of the side window. He was congratulating himself on successfully deflecting the Beckford-Kincade question, when she spoke again.

'You'll miss me when I'm gone.'

It wasn't only the seriousness of her tone that registered. It was the words, the tense she used. Not you *would* miss me. You *will* miss me.

And suddenly he didn't want to ask what lay behind it.

Lacy Cooper lived in a council flat on the tenth floor of Castle House, a brutalist thirteen-storey tower block located a little over half a mile from the station as the crow flies.

'It would've been quicker to walk,' Jardine complained,

when Gulliver finally found a parking space, and they had to walk almost as far back.

'We can take the stairs if you're so desperate to get some exercise.'

'What floor did you say she's on?'

'Tenth.' Feeling very pleased about it.

Except he'd misjudged his partner's mood, her response surprising and dismaying him.

'Fine by me.'

Pride then kicked in, preventing Gulliver from backing down.

Five minutes later, they took a breather on the tenth-floor landing, both of them doing their utmost to look as if they were breathing normally.

'Quick question,' he said, keeping the words to a minimum.

'Fire away.'

'Would you have still wanted to walk if she lived on the eleventh floor?'

'Of course. One more floor won't kill you.'

'The twelfth?'

'Yep.'

'Thirteenth?'

'Uh-huh.'

'Then why did you ask what floor she lives on?'

She tapped her temple with her middle finger.

'It's all about expectations. If you told me the second floor and it was the tenth, I'd be pissed off. If you told me the top floor and it was the tenth, I'd be happy about it.'

'And how did you feel when I told you it was the tenth and it was?'

'Normal.'

He gave an emphatic headshake.

'I'll accept halfway between happy and pissed off, but you, normal? No way.'

She showed him her eye teeth as they started down the open walkway ten floors above the pavement.

'I'd keep away from the edge if I was you.'

With the uncharacteristic melancholy of her remark—*you'll miss me when I'm gone*—still fresh in his mind he made sure he put himself between her and it.

'NATURAL CONTRACEPTION,' GULLIVER SAID, WHEN THEY ARRIVED at Lacy Cooper's door, the sound of more than one child crying behind it. 'If that doesn't make you keep your thumb over the end, nothing will.'

He hammered on the door, heavy knocks loud enough to be heard over the bedlam inside. Lacy opened the door two minutes later, a wall of noise hitting them like a freight train blowing past as it swung open.

A boy of two or three immediately made a dash for freedom from behind Lacy's legs. Her arm snaked out, a practised, reflex action, grabbing him by the back of his Southampton F.C. football shirt before he collided with Gulliver's legs. Holding the child to her body, she stepped backwards against the wall to let them pass after Gulliver and Jardine showed their warrant cards.

'Come in,' she said, through the gum she was chewing.

They didn't need to look at each other to share a single thought.

Can't you come out?

'Room on the left,' Lacy called, after they'd squeezed past her and the struggling child, then negotiated the double pushchair being used as an impromptu clothes dryer blocking the hallway.

They could have described the room they'd been directed to any number of alternative ways.

The room with the TV on the loudest.

The room with the most crying children in it.

The room where the dog is going to start barking the minute you step in.

Or, the most accurate description—the worst room in the whole place to attempt to have an important conversation.

'Your favourite, Craig,' Jardine said, as they entered the room and were met with a TV the size of a dining-room table. '*Peppa Pig*. We better ask her to switch it off or you'll never be able to concentrate.'

Gulliver was ahead of her, spotting the TV remote on a side table. A girl sitting cross-legged on the floor who looked to be the same age as the wannabe escapee was steadily feeding chocolate into her mouth, not all of it hitting target. She watched him as he grabbed the remote and muted the TV, then pocketed the remote.

Lacy came in a moment later, towing the boy behind her as he tried to kick her. She gave the TV a curious glance, as if she hadn't realised it was possible to dispense with the sound, didn't say anything about it. She waved her hand, took in the room-cum-bombsite littered with toys.

'Sit, if you can find somewhere.'

Gulliver perched on the arm of a sofa, the girl immediately coming to stand at the end of his knees, a colouring book and a crayon in her hands. Looking up at him as if it was the first time she'd been taken to the zoo.

Jardine remained standing, a suspicious stain on the only free seat making the decision for her. Gulliver, who'd just been offered the book and crayon, let her begin in a very out-of-character manner.

'I realise this was an extremely traumatic incident to witness—'

'*Bianca! Stop that!*' Lacy snapped, as the girl continued to thrust the book and crayon towards Gulliver. 'He doesn't want to colour the pictures.'

Bianca ignored her, dumped the book and crayon in Gulliver's lap. Crossed her chubby arms over her chest, a gesture she'd clearly picked up from her mother.

'It's not a problem,' he said, picking them up from his lap as Lacy glared at her daughter.

Jardine tried again as Gulliver started to colour, skipping the niceties given that time and Bianca were working against a long conversation.

'Can you tell us exactly what you saw immediately before the skip lorry hit Russell Baldwin?'

'I didn't really see very much at all. *Tyler! Come here!*' She made a sudden lunge at the boy who'd wriggled out of her grasp while his mother tried to avoid the question. She missed him, and he was at Gulliver's knee faster than any small child should be able to move. He snatched the colouring book out of Gulliver's hand, threw it on the floor, then went for the crayon. Gulliver let him have it.

Everybody started to cry. At least that's what it sounded like. Jardine felt like it wouldn't take much more before she joined in. That, or threw at least one of the bawling brats off the balcony.

'Tell us what you did see.'

Gulliver heard something very different behind the carefully-controlled tone of voice.

I'm not leaving this madhouse without getting some useful information.

'The street was really crowded. The twins were in the pushchair, and I had Quinn, he's my oldest, with me. He's four. He's at nursery school today.'

Jardine shuddered inwardly as she listened, not wanting to think about the environment they were currently in plus an added four-year-old who no doubt lived on a diet rich in sugar and chemicals.

'I was watching the bloke who got run over because he pushed past me when I stopped to light a fag. I'm sure he called me a stupid cow, but it was noisy so I can't be sure, or else I'd have given him a piece of my mind.'

Careful! Jardine thought. *I don't think there's enough to go around.*

'Anyway, I was staring at him and then I saw this other bloke right behind him. And I thought, yeah, I bet you pushed past him and called him a wanker and now he's gonna punch your lights out. Serve you right, arsehole.' Her mouth froze half-open as she realised how they might take her remark. 'I wasn't hoping he hit him and knocked him in front of the lorry.'

'Of course not,' Jardine agreed, hoping it sounded more sincere out loud than it did in her head.

'Then the twins started playing up in the pushchair. Tyler grabbed Barbie and threw her on the ground . . .'

Gulliver made very sure he didn't catch Jardine's eye. Even so, he knew exactly what went through her mind.

Is Barbie another of your children, Ms Cooper? And where is she today?

'So, I had my phone in one hand and my fag in the hand that was holding Quinn's reins. They're only ordinary reins. I can't afford ones with a Velcro wrist strap. So, I've got the fag and the phone and the reins and I've gotta pick Barbie up because Bianca's wailing and somehow I lost my grip on Quinn's reins.'

Again, Gulliver read Jardine's mind.

Thank God it wasn't the fag or your phone!

'Quinn took off like shit off a shiny shovel. He can really move when he wants to. I remember one time—'

'Could we finish talking about the accident?' Jardine cut in.

Lacy smiled apologetically.

'Sorry. Anyway, Quinn took off and he's heading straight for the road. I went after him and I'm trying to grab the reins and I'd dropped the fag by this time and the bloke who was killed and the other one behind him were right in front of Quinn. And I'm looking down at Quinn and the reins trailing on the ground so I didn't really see properly, but I got this funny sort of feeling the bloke behind pushed the other one.' She took a deep breath, glanced around the room as if searching for her cigarettes to ease the palpitations recounting her story had brought on. 'He looked behind him like he was going to step into the road to get past, and then suddenly there's a screech of brakes and this horrible sound as the lorry hit the bloke who called me a stupid cow. But it was all in the background, like. I'd caught hold of Quinn and that's all I was thinking about—'

Definitely only one thought at a time, Jardine confirmed to herself.

'—and it might be because I was worried about Quinn getting knocked into the road that I imagined seeing the bloke push the other one. That's why I didn't hang around and say anything.' She looked from Jardine to Gulliver and back again, her voice earnest. 'I know how busy you lot are. You haven't got time to listen to every busybody who thinks they might have seen something. And of course the kids were *really* playing up by now. I'd forgotten all about Barbie and some bloke trod on her so Bianca's really kicking off. And then Tyler joins in. And Quinn's bawling too because maybe I was a bit sharp with him when I caught him. I didn't smack him, of course. I'd never do that. Not in public. There's always some dried-up nosy old bitch who's never had kids waiting to give you a lecture. Anyway, I thought to myself, no way the filth ... I mean the cops ... are gonna want to listen to all that racket when there's other people who got a better view. And I was already late for my appointment at the benefits office.'

Despite the outward appearance of Gulliver and Jardine's relationship—that they were always at each other's throats, bickering like an old married couple—and their very different backgrounds, they were invariably in tune regarding their assessment of people and situations.

Jardine believed, and was confident Gulliver would agree, that there was no point in mentioning what Ralph Stone had said to Angel—that he believed one of Lacy's children had run into Baldwin's legs and knocked him off balance and into the road in front of Harry Callaghan's lorry.

Five minutes closeted with Lacy and her children was all anybody needed to be convinced she would deny it to her own dying day. Simple denial would be the best outcome. Indignant outrage was a distinct possibility.

How dare they suggest her little monsters would do such a thing!

Worse, the suggestion—what she would see as an accusation —would make her defensive and alienate her. It would make her unwilling to help going forward—a difficult enough trick to pull off as it was.

Jardine responded accordingly.

'That sounds like it was a very stressful situation all round. Did you get a look at the man's face? The one who might have pushed Mr Baldwin.'

'Yeah, I saw it when he looked behind him.'

'Would you recognise him again?'

Lacy's face compacted as if Jardine had asked for the man's name and address.

'It was only a quick look. And I was concentrating on the kids.'

'You'd be surprised how much goes in without you realising it.' Thinking, *especially when there's a lot of empty space inside.*

'Would you be prepared to come into the station to help us produce an e-fit image of him?'

Lacy shrugged, then glanced at her children as if assessing whether to use them as an excuse to refuse.

'If you think it would help.'

Jardine and Gulliver both nodded enthusiastically.

'Definitely,' Jardine said, then tapped her temple. 'Like I say, there's more in there than you think.'

Or anyone talking to you would ever think.

'What do you reckon?' Gulliver said, once they'd left the madhouse behind and were taking the stairs down to the street. 'Will the e-fit guys be able to squeeze a memory out of her stunted mind?'

'God knows. But I hope I'm right, that there's more in there than anyone thinks. Forget about the implications for the case, it makes me despair for the future of the human race if I'm wrong.'

'You do realise you missed a trick there?'

Jardine blew the air from her cheeks like she didn't care what she'd missed, so long as it allowed them to get out faster.

'Yeah? What did I miss?'

'You should've asked to see her phone. I bet as soon as Quasimodo or whatever his name is made a dash for freedom she got it out to video him. Post it on TikTok. There'll be a hundred million people who've seen who pushed Russell Baldwin by now.'

She shook her head like he'd never met a member of the public, her mouth turning down.

'People in the street don't video things like that. They're only interested in police brutality when we arrest a little gobshite and all we're doing is trying to do our jobs.'

The sudden cynicism of the remark brought to mind what

she'd said earlier, that he'd miss her when she was gone. He knew what was behind it, but she snapped herself out of it before he broached the subject.

'You looked as if you were enjoying yourself with the colouring book. At least that's your Christmas present sorted.'

'And a chastity belt for you?'

She glanced up at the tower block above them, shuddered.

'After the last half hour, you buy it, I'll wear it.'

Sensibly, he decided it wasn't the time to ask if he could be in charge of fitting it.

22

'Did you tell Jardine and Gulliver where the name Lacy Cooper came from?' Kincade said.

Angel took his eyes off the road to give her a long-suffering look. It came through in his voice, too.

'What do you think?'

'Before you asked Beckford for help, I'd have said absolutely not. Now, I'm not so sure.'

'Well, I didn't.'

'At least that's something. Weren't they interested?'

'Of course they were. But they recognised that when they, as detective constables, ask me, a detective inspector, something I don't want to answer, they have to live with it.'

'The source of a witness' name doesn't normally fall into the *above your pay grade* category. You do realise it's not wise to give Lisa Jardine something to speculate about? You have to be prepared to accept the consequences.'

The *above your pay grade* reference reinforced his decision to say nothing about the rumour Beckford's informant Ricky Shorter had alluded to—that Baldwin was sticking his nose into the business of some nasty people in the local drug market.

Angel didn't know what Beckford said to Ricky after their first conversation, but Ricky supplied the name Lacy Cooper without any further mention of a cash payment in exchange. Ricky also admitted he'd invented the rumour—as Beckford had guessed—in order to tempt Angel. Drugs played a major part in Ricky's life and so, when he needed to invent something quickly, his mind automatically worked along those lines.

None of that changed the possibility that Russell Baldwin had been killed for looking into *something*. Hence their trip today to interview his girlfriend, Véronique Dubois, in the hope of finding out what.

What Angel didn't need as they drove there was for Kincade to continue bringing up Stuart Beckford every two minutes. The mention of Jardine gave him the perfect opportunity to change the subject.

'It looked like you were in a very intense conversation with her yesterday. What was that all about?'

She waved her hand dismissively, then looked out of the side window so he couldn't see her face.

'It was nothing.'

That you're prepared to share with me, he completed in his head, and had the sense to not push it.

He was no further forward as far as knowing what the problem with Jardine was, but at least it had moved the conversation away from Stuart Beckford, the remainder of the journey passing in a less-than-comfortable silence.

A MAN WITH A WHITE, FLUFFY, HANDBAG DOG ON A BRIGHT PINK leash was coming out of Véronique Dubois' apartment block as they approached. He made a point of closing the door firmly before they got to it. Kincade flashed her warrant card at him and asked him—none too politely and accompanied by a cold-eyed glare—to open it again.

Count yourself lucky, Angel thought as they went in. After the atmosphere in the car, he wouldn't have been surprised if she'd put the dog walker's arm up behind his back and used his face to batter the door down—and then used the handbag dog to clean the blood off.

Things didn't get any better when they got to Véronique's apartment and hammered on the door to no avail. Already Angel was getting a bad feeling. Not a *dead body in the living room* bad feeling, more a speed bump in the investigation.

He tried the nearest neighbour's door when there was no answer after a full five minutes.

'Who is it?' came from inside, a woman's voice sounding as if she'd heard about packs of roaming serial killers in the neighbourhood.

Angel introduced himself through the door, which then cracked open an inch, a fiftyish woman peering out from behind the security chain. Angel smiled reassuringly and showed her his warrant card. The door closed briefly and opened again fully. A tabby cat immediately shot out and went to sit in front of Véronique's door, looking up expectantly at it.

The speed bump grew in Angel's mind.

'He belongs to Véronique,' the neighbour said, as if they hadn't worked it out. 'I'm looking after him for her.' Her tone of voice said she wasn't happy about it, either. The cat's position in front of its owner's door said the feeling was mutual. 'She normally puts him in the cattery, but she left in such a hurry, she didn't have time. I could hardly say no, could I?'

'When did she leave, Ms ...?'

'Doyle. Irene Doyle.' She glanced at her watch. 'She only left a couple of hours ago.' Glaring at the cat as if it already felt like a couple of weeks. 'I caught him scratching the sofa a minute ago.'

'Get his claws clipped,' Kincade said from behind Angel.

Irene looked at her like she'd said cats don't scratch much after you've drowned them in the bath.

'Can we talk inside?' Angel said, before Irene put words to the indignant look on her face. He bent and scooped the cat up, carried it in with him as they all trooped inside, then set it down once Irene had shut the door. It immediately wound itself around his legs.

'He obviously likes you,' Irene said. 'He doesn't like me.'

Nobody chose to pass comment.

'Did Ms Dubois say where she was going and for how long?' Angel asked, when it became clear they weren't about to be invited further in.

'Back to France. Paris, I think. And no, she didn't say for how long. She said she'd call me as soon as she knew.'

'Did she say why she had to go back? And so urgently?'

'She said her mother has been taken ill.' All the emphasis was on the word *said*. 'But I've never heard her talk about her mother before. If you were that close that you drop everything, you'd talk about her. I think she said it because it puts me on the spot more than if she'd said she fancied a week on the beach.'

'How has she been recently?'

'How am I supposed to know that? The woman lives in Paris.'

'I meant Ms Dubois,' Angel said, working hard at keeping a straight face. 'Not her mother.'

'*Oh!* Yes, of course you did. Silly me. She hasn't been herself since her boyfriend was killed. And obviously the prospect of having to bring the baby up on her own was weighing on her mind.'

The unexpected detail gave Angel pause for thought, before asking the obvious question.

'She's got a baby, or she's pregnant?'

'Pregnant. She's out here.' Irene extended her arms and held her hands fingertips to fingertips as if cradling a swollen belly. 'It must be due any minute. And to think the poor little thing will never know its father . . .' It was as if the clouds parted above her, the *aha* moment lighting up her face. 'Is that what this is about? Her boyfriend's death?'

'It's connected, yes. Is there anything in particular that makes you say she wasn't herself?'

'It certainly didn't help when she was burgled.' She glanced past them at the front door, as if in two minds about whether to put the security chain on again, two police officers in the hallway or not. 'Whoever it was, they were very good. There was no damage. That's why I was so nervous when you knocked.'

Angel might have pointed out that your average burglar does not knock on the front door before breaking in to steal all your valuables. Instead, he moved on.

'Did she say what was stolen?'

Irene narrowed her eyes at him. As if he'd just put his insurance claims investigator hat on. Even though her neighbour might have fed her a pack of lies about her supposedly-ill mother, she wasn't about to drop her in it for making a fraudulent insurance claim.

'She didn't say. But she was very shaken up. Who wouldn't be? A strange man going through your drawers, if you know what I mean.'

Angel did, which is precisely why he moved on so quickly.

'What about more recently? In the past day or two?'

Irene thought about it, staring at the cat that had grown bored with winding itself around Angel's legs and was now waiting patiently by the front door. As if by concentrating on her neighbour's unwelcome pet she might get a better insight into its owner's life.

'She was fine this morning before she went out. It was when

she got back that it was panic stations. I assumed she took the call about her mother'—making it sound like *excuse*—'while she was out.'

'Do you know what she did this morning?'

'She was meeting someone. I bumped into her in the hallway and we had a quick chat.'

Angel and Kincade had no problem translating *bumped into*.

I was standing with my ear to the front door waiting to pounce as soon as I heard anyone's door open.

'Did she say who?' Angel tried, on the face of it a total waste of perfectly good breath.

'No. But it was a man. She definitely said *him*.' Her face compacted as if she was considering saying more, then she shook her head at herself.

Kincade made a lightning-fast assessment. Irene Doyle's hobby, if not raison d'être, was chewing the ear of anybody who stood still long enough. She'd already shared her cynical assessment of the reason Véronique gave for leaving so abruptly. A couple of minutes listening to what she'd almost said about the man Véronique met with that morning would be time well spent.

'What were you about to say?'

'It's just a feeling ...'

'Tell us anyway. Better than regretting not telling us later.'

Irene hesitated, took a deep breath, then lowered her voice as if about to reveal a terrible secret.

'She was excited, and worried at the same time. As if she didn't want to go, but didn't have any choice. I think it was about what happened to her boyfriend. Somebody with new information and she wasn't sure she wanted to hear it.' She shrugged. *That's it, make of it what you will.*

They did, the reason for Véronique's abrupt departure now clear in their minds.

They wrapped it up after that. Kincade took a mobile number for Véronique for all the good it would do them, then they made a move to leave, a distance of about two paces since they hadn't been allowed further in. The cat got to its feet as soon as Kincade opened the door, arched its back and stretched. Angel scooped it up as they left, nipped out of the door after Kincade, then dumped it back in Irene's hall just before the door closed.

Sorry, puss, but I think you're stuck there for a while yet.

'Are you thinking what I'm thinking?' Kincade said.

'If you're thinking you're really pissed off with Liam Callaghan for spooking Véronique Dubois, then yes. Sounds like getting the tyres slashed on his van after his brother was shot to death wasn't enough of a warning for him. He's trying to find out who killed his brother. I'm guessing he told Véronique about Harry being shot to death.'

'That'd make me do a runner back to France.'

'Definitely. But taking her dead boyfriend's secrets with her or not? It's obvious her apartment was searched, not burgled. The question is, was there anything there to find?'

Kincade already had her phone out, tapping in the number Irene Doyle had given them. They both heard the automated response when it kicked in. Kincade repeated it, nonetheless.

'*Currently unavailable.* Let's hope for her sake it doesn't turn into as permanently unavailable as the baby's father is.'

23

'*Bollocks!*' Angel said, pulling to the kerb outside Liam Callaghan's house. 'I forgot to call in at a paint shop on the way here.'

Kincade shook her head as they climbed out of the car.

'He doesn't need any help from us painting a target on his back.'

She was expecting him to continue with a remark about limited gene pools, how the sum total of human intelligence on the planet wouldn't be diminished by Liam Callaghan's passing, should he succeed in bringing that event about. Instead, he dropped his voice to a whisper as they faced each other over the car roof.

'Don't look behind you, but there's a black Range Rover parked on the other side of the street. It was here the last time we came.'

If it hadn't been for the urgency in his whisper, she'd have thought, *so what? Maybe the owner lives here?* Except the urgency *was* there. And after joking about Liam Callaghan making a target of himself, it wasn't difficult to work out why.

It was only a matter of seconds as they held each other's eyes over the car roof, deciding whether to approach the vehicle immediately. It was too long, nonetheless. They might as well have turned up in a liveried patrol car. If Angel had seen the Range Rover twice, the driver had seen him twice. That was one time too many.

Kincade started moving at the same time as the Range Rover's engine growled into life and it pulled out into the road.

Angel yelled at her, as pointless as if he'd ordered the car to stop.

'Don't be bloody stupid!'

She was fumbling for her phone when the driver gunned it, heading directly at her standing in the middle of the road. She threw herself sideways as the big car hurtled past with a throaty roar from the engine that wasn't how it sounded when it left the showroom, the side-draught spinning her, bouncing her off Angel's car, righting herself again, phone in her hand now, legs pumping, tearing down the middle of the road, phone hand steady as she got into her stride, less frantic, videoing the rapidly disappearing vehicle, then slowing, slowing, until coming to a stop, resting a hand on the nearest car's wing as she heaved oxygen deep into her lungs.

She hit *play*, watched the video as she walked back, saw the road, the nearby cars, a glimpse of the Range Rover's rear end, the road again, then steadying, settling on the disappearing car, triumph mixing with breathlessness in her voice.

'*Gotcha!*'

He was on his phone by the time she got back to him, calling it in, waiting for the registration from her.

Nobody was holding their breath.

The owner of a similar Range Rover with the exact same registration was likely to get a confusing call from one of the team in the next half hour.

'Gotta get back to running on a regular basis,' she said,

resting her rump on the wing of his car as she recovered her breath, eyeing up his stomach as she did so. 'You too, with your mother fattening you up.'

It hadn't been a lot of exercise, but the effect was cathartic, nonetheless, flushing away the oppressive air of aggrieved resentment she'd carried around with her ever since learning Angel had asked for Stuart Beckford's help.

'I'm touched that you yelled at me to not do anything stupid,' she said, the sly grin that had been missing from her face for the past days making a reappearance. 'Me being dead or retired on a disability pension would've been the perfect solution to your Stuart Beckford problem.'

He scrunched his face as if he wished he'd kept his mouth shut.

'I know, but the paperwork would be a nightmare. My dad would kill me, too. Not taking proper care of his favourite lodger.'

She pushed off the wing of his car, fell into step beside him as they resumed their interrupted journey to interview Liam Callaghan.

Liam wasn't surprised to see them on his doorstep. This time, he led them into the kitchen, given that he didn't have to worry about them spotting his brother's van parked in the alley at the bottom of the garden.

Angel stuck his head into the living room as he went past all the same. In case the kitchen was a deliberate choice to stop them from seeing anything incriminating—Harry Callaghan's laptop, for example—on the coffee table. There was nothing.

'I've got a difficult decision to make, Mr Callaghan,' he started. 'I feel like I want to arrest you. But I don't know whether the charge should be perverting the course of justice, or just plain stupidity. Except, if that was a crime, you'd be arrested every time you stepped outside your house.' He pointed at Kincade's phone. 'Show him, Sergeant.'

She hit *play*, thrust her phone towards Liam at arm's length.

'I just chased that vehicle down the street. It was parked a couple of doors down watching this house. It was here the last time we came, too. Why do you think that is, Mr Callaghan? Apart from the fact that it's a public road and he can park wherever he likes?'

'More importantly,' Angel cut in, 'why do you think he took off in such a hurry when he recognised us? I'm pretty sure it wasn't because he was parked in a resident's bay without a permit.'

Kincade hit *play* again when the video ended, thrust it back in Liam's face.

'You're looking a bit green around the gills, Mr Callaghan. Have you seen that vehicle yourself?' She looked at Angel who nodded back at her, *go ahead*. 'We shouldn't be telling you this, but we're going to make an exception in the hope that it keeps you alive for a little bit longer. We found tyre tracks at the scene where your brother was killed. Guess what vehicle is supplied with the tyres the forensic lab matched the tracks to?'

They both stared hard at Liam, saying nothing, forcing a grudging answer out of him.

'A Range Rover.'

Kincade worked an approving note into her voice she normally reserved for her children.

'*Well done*. The tyres were identified as Pirelli Scorpion Verde all seasons. They're one of the tyres supplied with the Range Rover Sport.' She waved her phone at him. 'The video I took won't be good enough to identify the tyres on the vehicle that was watching your house, but I'm willing to bet they're Pirelli Scorpion Verdes. I wouldn't bet my life on it, of course.' She pointed at him. 'That'd be you who's doing that.'

'Stupidity,' Angel said without any preamble. 'That's definitely the most appropriate charge. To be honest, Mr Callaghan, if you're so determined to meet up with your brother in the very near future, there's not a lot I can do to stop you—'

'It won't even increase our workload,' Kincade added, 'seeing as we'll be looking for the same man who killed both Callaghan brothers.'

'—but what really pisses me off is when you make it more difficult for us to catch the person who killed either of you. Where do you think Véronique Dubois is at this moment, after you met her this morning? It's not the morgue. At least I'm hoping it's not. I might be wrong, after you painted a target on her back as well as your own. If I am, they'll have her in a double-height drawer they normally save for fat people, on account of her bump. That makes three targets you've painted on people's backs. You're going to run out of bloody paint soon at this rate.'

Liam looked a little shell-shocked at the outburst. It surprised Kincade, too, but then she remembered Angel hadn't sprinted down the road after an accelerating vehicle to get rid of his angst.

'You didn't tell Mr Callaghan where Véronique Dubois is, if she's not in the morgue, sir.'

Angel nodded his thanks for the reminder.

'She's on her way to Paris where the people who most likely killed her boyfriend, as well as your brother, can't get to her. Problem is, nor can we, seeing as you put the fear of God into her. She's got her phone permanently switched off. I know I asked you this question the last time we were here, but don't you want us to find out who killed your brother?'

He took a deep breath, as if he'd been the one who chased the Range Rover. Kincade immediately took over.

'In case it hasn't crossed your mind, if you continue to try to find your brother's killer before we do, and in the unlikely circumstance that he doesn't kill you without a second thought and you manage to avenge Harry, guess who we'll be looking at for his murder? Or were you thinking you might join Ms Dubois in Paris? Then you can help her raise the child of the man your brother flattened with his lorry? It's got a nice circular feel to it. If it was a film, I'd be sobbing my heart out by the end.'

Liam looked back and forth between them. It was hard to say which one of them put the bigger scowl on his face.

'You two are like a bloody double act, you know that? Okay, I admit I met her and told her what happened to Harry. You ask me, I've done her a favour if I scared her all the way back to France. Better than her wandering around thinking everything's great with the world while the bastard who killed Harry is stalking her.'

It would've been easy to go around and around in circles. Angel pointing out that Véronique wasn't being stalked until Liam approached her, Liam saying forewarned was forearmed, especially given that the police were about as much use as a chocolate teapot.

It would achieve nothing. They weren't about to arrest him for his completely natural, but even stupider, desire to avenge his brother.

Angel moved on.

'What did she say to you?'

'Not a lot. She thinks her boyfriend was pushed. She thinks it was to do with what he was investigating, but she said she didn't know what it was. Said it was boring and they never talked about it.'

'Did you believe her?'

Liam wasn't prepared for the question. In his experience, the police weren't interested in his opinion. They were primarily interested in issuing fines for some offence or the other every time he got in his car, or putting him in prison for breaking laws that had no relevance in the twenty-first century—the supply of recreational drugs being a prime example.

'What does it matter what I think?'

'Because you've deprived us of the opportunity of talking to her ourselves,' Kincade said. 'And much as it pains me to say it, you're the best alternative we've got.'

Liam looked mildly complimented, expecting them to value a New Forest pony's opinion above his own. It took some of the aggression out of his tone and body language.

'I believed her. All she's interested in now is the baby. She wants to be left alone.'

They didn't have to say anything. The words were humming in the air.

And how's that working out for her after you stuck your nose in?

'Did she say anything useful at all?' Angel persevered, after leaving an appropriate time for Liam's guilt to sink in.

Liam hesitated. A split-second at most. Kincade was right on him, like an attack dog going for the throat.

'Don't even think about holding something back to give yourself a head start over us, Mr Callaghan. We really will arrest you for perverting the course of justice if you do.'

He looked at her like he wanted to spit in her face for reading him so easily.

'She said he met a woman. That was all she said. She didn't know who or why. You two can do your double act all over again, try to scare me, telling me how I'll be shot by a sniper from the house across the street the next time I open the front door, but it won't change anything.'

His assessment of their approach was spot on, even if they'd object to the double-act reference. It also served to remind Angel that more of the same was overdue.

'I shouldn't have to say this, but do *not* continue with this crusade. At best, you'll continue to make our jobs more difficult. At worst—'

'I'll be dead. You said that already.'

'And so might Véronique Dubois and her unborn baby,' Kincade added in response to Liam's dismissive tone. 'The sort of people who can put three nine-millimetre bullets in your brother's back can manage to buy themselves a Eurostar ticket to Paris if they decide it's time to clear the decks once and for all.'

Liam held up his hands, looking and sounding thoroughly beaten down.

'*Okay, okay*. Lecture received and understood. *Jesus!* I bet you've got your husband well-trained, the poor bastard.'

Angel had a hard time keeping the smile off his face as Kincade gave Liam a glare that would lift paint off the woodwork.

'I'm assuming you have a laptop or something similar that belonged to your brother that you've been using to follow in his footsteps,' he said, before Kincade used her tongue to lift the skin from Liam's face.

Liam headed for the door, giving Kincade a wide berth.

'I'll get it.'

He ran up the stairs two at a time, the sound of a loft ladder being lowered coming to them a minute later. He didn't waste time raising it again after clomping around in the loft and was back in the kitchen so fast anyone would think he couldn't wait to get shot of his brother's toxic legacy. He took a sheet of paper from one of the kitchen drawers, handed it to Angel.

'I worked out the password for you.'

Angel glanced at it, smiled with him when he saw *makemyday1975*.

'What would your next move have been? If you hadn't seen sense, that is.'

Liam threw Kincade a dirty look that was easy to read—*had it lectured into me, you mean.*

'Talk to the journalist's ex-wife...'

He trailed off as something occurred to him. It wasn't necessary to repeat Kincade's threat about keeping things to himself. He volunteered the information.

'The French bird—'

'Véronique,' Kincade corrected, a reprimand in her tone.

'—told me Harry's finger wasn't broken when she talked to him. They did it after he spoke to her, but before he talked to the ex-wife.' He pointed at the laptop Angel had placed on the kitchen table. 'There's nothing on that about him actually meeting with the ex-wife.'

Earlier, Kincade had accused Liam of looking green around the gills. Now, his face was the colour of fish bellies as he put together the timeline of his brother's final days, the sequence he'd tried to replicate.

Interview Véronique.

Finger hammered to a pulp as a warning.

Warning ignored.

Attempted contact with ex-wife.

Execution.

He took a deep breath, blew it out again with an evil glance at the laptop.

You're welcome to it.

Angel and Kincade headed for the door, Liam trailing behind. Angel was confident they'd made their point. Liam would drop his crusade—temporarily. He wasn't sure how long it would last if they failed to produce a result quickly enough themselves. What neither of them were expecting was the spiteful sneer that appeared on Liam's face, the schadenfreude in his voice, as he held the front door open for them.

'There's a file on the laptop you're going to love. You'll know the one I mean as soon as you see its name.'

'I'VE NEVER SEEN YOUR GIRLS ON CHRISTMAS MORNING,' ANGEL said, when they were back in the car and Kincade was busy entering the password into Harry Callaghan's laptop. 'But I know exactly what they look like. It's quite cute to see a grown woman look so excited.'

She ignored the remark, knowing he was every bit as intrigued to know what had put the malicious grin on Liam's face as she was. The fact that he hadn't driven off and was watching her every move made that very clear. She double-clicked the folder called *Read me first*, then they both ran their eyes down the short list of files.

'I'm getting a bad feeling about that one,' she said, hovering over the file called *Police Statement*.

Angel knew exactly what she meant, his gut tightening as she opened it.

She beat him to their shared reaction by a split-second.

'*Shit!*'

THE MAN EVERYBODY CALLED MAGGOT HELD THE PHONE AWAY from his ear, the sound of the Arrogant Prick screaming down the line at him reduced to a grating whine.

'*Jesus Christ!* I suppose you had the engine running and three plastic bottles of piss lined up on the car roof from drinking too much bloody coffee.'

Maggot bit his tongue and closed his eyes. Pictured himself looking down on the prick strapped to a board inclined over a bath, the satisfying weight of a full water bucket heavy in his hands.

'It doesn't matter how it happened. What matters is they saw the car. One of them chased me down the road videoing it.'

'Don't tell me you forgot to switch plates beforehand.'

Maggot tipped the imaginary bucket at a greater angle, increased the flow of water down the prick's airways as he writhed and choked on the board.

'Of course I switched the plates—'

'*Hallelujah!*'

'—but they'll be looking for the vehicle now.'

'Then get another one, you moron. Is that so difficult? Steal one, borrow one, I don't care. Just stop calling me with excuses.'

Maggot increased the imaginary angle a second time, the water coursing down the prick's throat, bubbling out of his mouth and flooding across his face.

'I don't think the brother's going to be a problem now.'

He held the phone away from his ear again even before the ranting began.

'I don't give a flying shit what you do or don't think. The police have talked to him twice. He's met with the bloody French girlfriend. What else does he need to do before you think it's time to put an end to his nosiness for good? Speak to that interfering bitch Evie St. James? Except even you should be able to work out it'll be too late by then. No wonder they call you Maggot. You've got about as much sense as one.'

Maggot ran his hand over the shiny dome of his head, an involuntary reaction to the prick using his nickname. Ordinarily, he didn't care. A training instructor landed him with the moniker on day one. Said he reminded him of Archer J. Maggot, the obnoxious character played by Telly Savalas in the movie *The Dirty Dozen*. There were worse nicknames, worse associations. But to hear it come out of the prick's mouth . . . that made him want to choke the life out of him with his bare hands.

On the other end of the line that same prick was still mouthing off.

'I don't need to remind you—'

'No, you don't,' Maggot interrupted, making a rolling motion with his hand. '*If you go down, I go down.* You've said it a thousand times already.'

'Then it should've got through that thick skull of yours by now. Don't call me again until it's done.'

Maggot pocketed the phone after it went dead in his ear. Promised himself that if and when the job was done, and if he wasn't in jail, he'd be doing a damn sight more than calling the prick. Calling *on* him, yes, with a ski mask over his head. One last job before he retired for good.

After he'd finished waterboarding him, that is.

The thought sustained him as he headed out to steal a car. Something with a bit of weight behind it. A pickup truck, perhaps? One with shiny bull bars on the front, perfect for sending an unwary cyclist to the big peloton in the sky...

24

'A BAD NEWS MEETING ISN'T VERY CATCHY OR EXCITING,' KINCADE said, as she and Angel made their way towards DCI Finch's office for just such a meeting, Gulliver and Jardine filtering in from the side to join them like a gathering posse. 'We need to think of something better.'

'Shitstorm symposium?' Gulliver offered, throwing his hat into the ring.

The suggestion got a nod of approval from Angel, a rocked hand from Kincade and a roll of the eyes from Jardine.

'*Symposium?* I prefer clusterfuck conference.'

'You would,' Gulliver grumbled.

Or business as usual, Angel thought but didn't spoil the mood by saying out loud as they all piled into Finch's office.

'Who's in charge of coffee?' Kincade asked with a pointed glance towards the DCI's personal machine once they were all squeezed in.

Finch gave her the smile of a woman who knows her coffee supply is safe.

'Whoever is the first with some good news.' She looked

around at the four of them. 'Funny how I don't see anyone taking a step towards the machine. So? Who wants to go first?'

Gulliver took the lead, a very safe gamble that the mood in the room would deteriorate with each added piece of bad news.

'The Range Rover's plates are cloned. Unless Ms Joyce Gastrell aged fifty-three came down from Swindon to sit outside Liam Callaghan's house, that is.'

'It was definitely a man driving,' Kincade confirmed.

Finch's response was not what anybody was expecting.

'Every time someone says Liam Callaghan, I hear Liam Gallagher.'

'You learn something new every day,' Angel said, surprise colouring his voice. 'I'd never have taken you for an Oasis fan, ma'am.'

'More Perry Como?' Jardine chipped in, her face deadpan.

Finch glared at her.

'I'm not that old, Lisa.'

'Getting back to the Range Rover,' Gulliver interrupted, 'not only are the plates cloned, but, despite being such a large vehicle, it's disappeared into thin air.'

'Or it's in a garage,' Jardine said, as if talking to a puppy or a small child. 'You do have garages down here in the South, don't you?'

Kincade went next before a fight broke out.

'On the subject of Liam Gallagher—'

'*See!* You're doing it,' Finch crowed triumphantly.

Kincade smiled with her, having made the slip in her mind more than once before.

'On the subject of Liam *Callaghan*, he told Véronique Dubois about his brother being shot. She's subsequently done a bunk back to Paris and isn't answering her phone.'

Finch cocked her head at her.

'Is that an underhand way of requesting a visit to Paris yourself to interview her?'

'It wasn't, but it is now. She might even have headed down to St. Tropez.' She glanced at each of her colleagues. 'Although I'm not sure who I'd want to take with me.'

'Do you think she knows anything?'.

Angel jumped in before Kincade had a chance to answer.

'I don't think so.'

'Based on what, Padre?'

That was the question. Angel didn't have a proper answer beyond gut feel. Something in the way Liam Callaghan had said Véronique was only interested in her baby had rung true.

'Even if she does, and we managed to find her in Paris or wherever else in the rest of France she might be hiding, I don't think she'd talk to us. She wants to be left alone.'

Finch shrugged, gave Kincade a sad smile.

'Sorry, Cat. The decision's out of my hands. While we're on the subject of Liam Callaghan, is he going to continue to be a problem?'

Kincade went to speak, but Angel held up a hand to override her a second time.

'If Harry Callaghan ignored having his finger broken, will a verbal warning from me and Cat persuade his brother to stop?' He glanced at Kincade briefly. 'I know Cat's scary, but even so, I think there's a chance that once he's done a lap of the goldfish bowl, he'll have forgotten all about our warnings. His pride and macho desire to avenge his brother will still be driving him.'

'I hope you're wrong, Padre.'

He kept the most appropriate response to himself. *You can wish in one hand and shit in the other, see which one fills up the fastest.* Instead, he concentrated on the positive.

'Véronique told Liam Callaghan she believed Russell Baldwin was pushed in front of Harry Callaghan's skip lorry.

That's why she approached him. To see what he had to say about it.'

He was aware of Kincade's eyes on him as he spoke, what they'd read on Harry Callaghan's laptop in both their minds. That bombshell was coming soon. In the meantime, Finch picked up on the implications of what he'd said.

'Véronique didn't believe what she heard at the inquest?'

'Apparently not. We already know she went berserk when the coroner ruled the death as accidental.'

Finch stared hard at him as she processed the implications. She'd known him long enough to know there was something he wasn't saying. She also knew not to rush him.

'Lacy Cooper's witness statement backs up Véronique's suspicions,' Gulliver said. 'That Baldwin was pushed.'

Finch gave him a look as if he'd farted.

'*Lacy*? Who gives their kids a name like that? I'm not sure I can give any weight to what somebody called Lacy says. What's your assessment of her?'

Gulliver and Jardine shared a look, as well as the memory of the bedlam inside the flat in Castle House. He let Jardine answer even though Finch had addressed the question to him.

'Somebody needs to sit her down and talk to her about birth control, but apart from that, she's a canny lass.'

Finch stared at her as if she hadn't thought things could get any worse than having to deal with a witness called Lacy.

'Let me get this straight. *Lacy is a canny lass*. Can I have that in English?'

'Me, too,' Gulliver said under his breath.

Jardine ignored him, couldn't do much about Finch's ridicule.

'It means I believe her, despite all the evidence to the contrary, ma'am. She might be giving her kids lung cancer from passive smoking and spend all day long on her phone while she plonks them in front of the TV, but I don't think she misses much if she thinks there's something in it for her. Baldwin called her a silly cow as he barged past. She was hoping the man she saw push him was going to punch his lights out for doing the same to him.' She smiled, acceptance of the likely outcome reflected in the gesture. 'That's not the same thing as the e-fit image being anything remotely useful, of course.'

Finch shrugged her agreement, then summed up everybody's thoughts.

'Baldwin was a muck-raking journalist. There's a good chance he was pushed to silence him. Harry Callaghan was then killed when he started to investigate the man who'd been pushed in front of his lorry. I know drug dealers like a Range Rover with tinted windows, but so do other people. The sort of people who have legitimate access to a nine-millimetre pistol.'

Just say spooks, Kincade thought, knowing she wasn't alone.

'The question is,' Finch went on, 'is this something official, or a maverick on the loose?'

She looked at them all as the question hung in the air. Caught sight of the look passing between Angel and Kincade and groaned.

'No, Padre. *Don't!*'

'You make me feel like a disobedient dog, ma'am.'

Finch gave him a look that said she wished digging up her flowerbeds was the worst thing he ever did, flicked her fingers at him to continue, get it over with.

'I talked to Ellis Hudson, the SIO on the Russell Baldwin case, earlier today. He told me Harry Callaghan's statement was short and to the point. *I was driving along and suddenly he was right there in the middle of the road in front of me*, sort of thing. I took a look for myself. What Hudson said was about right'—he held up his index finger—'except for one additional line. *I was momentarily distracted by a woman chasing a young child on the pavement.'*

'Obviously the Cooper woman,' Finch said, unable to get the name Lacy out. 'What's the problem?'

'First of all, I quoted that line verbatim.'

'So?'

'I never met Harry Callaghan while he was alive, but I've met his brother twice. It's fair to say talking to Liam gives you a good feel for what it would be like talking to Harry. And men like that do not use the phrase *momentarily distracted.*'

It was obvious Finch wanted to say *so?* again. Point out that the officer taking the statement had suggested appropriate words after Callaghan said, *I woz watchin' this bird chase her kid.* Except she knew it was pointless, that he'd shoot whatever objections she raised down in flames.

'Spit it out, Padre.'

'There's a file on Callaghan's laptop called *Police statement.* It contains a much longer statement than the one in our files.'

'It should be re-named *buried statement*,' Kincade said under her breath.

'Let me read you the relevant paragraph,' Angel carried on, unfolding a sheet of paper he'd pulled from his pocket.

Finch stuck out her hand impatiently.

'I'll read it myself.'

'The highlighted paragraph,' he said, as he handed it over.

'Thank you, Padre. I could probably have worked that out for myself.'

She found her reading glasses where they were hidden under one of the many piles of paper on her desk, perched them on her nose and started to read.

I saw two men hurrying down the street pushing past other pedestrians. The one in front was the man I hit, Russell Baldwin. The man behind him looked around. I thought he was checking to see if the road was clear so that he could step off the pavement to get past the people in his way. He looked straight at me as I was approaching in my lorry. I heard a car horn beep on the other side of the road and looked away from him and at the oncoming traffic. I thought maybe I had drifted into the oncoming lane while I was concentrating on the pedestrians. I only looked away for a split-second. When I looked back, Russell Baldwin was in the middle of the road right in front of me. I braked hard but I couldn't stop in time.

Finch finished reading and passed the sheet of paper to Jardine, then considered Angel over the top of her glasses.

'That puts a different slant on things.'

Angel was forced to correct her.

'*Two* different slants.'

Finch threw her eyes heavenwards, which also happened to be the direction of where she would soon have to take the bad news.

'Silly me.'

'First, it opens up the possibility that the man behind Baldwin wasn't looking to make sure the road was clear. He was making sure something sufficiently large was coming to push Baldwin in front of. Presumably, he heard the skip lorry approaching.'

'That's the minor different slant,' Kincade said, almost sounding pleased about what was to come.

'Second,' Angel said, 'is that somebody made Callaghan change his statement, omitting the most important paragraph. Or it was switched altogether.'

'And his signature forged,' Kincade finished.

Nobody needed to say what it appeared they now had on their plates.

A vehicle of the sort favoured by the less-transparent government agencies. Access to a 9mm handgun. And the wherewithal to influence or switch a police statement.

It certainly wasn't necessary to voice the word *spook*.

Finch had already summed up the situation on at least one occasion during the meeting. She did it again, now, but a lot more succinctly.

'Shit!'

Everybody nodded. *Well put, ma'am.*

Encouraged by the reaction, she did it again.

'Fuck!'

More nods—and it wasn't everyday brown-nosing.

They never did get to find out if she'd make it a hat-trick and how she would've continued with the expletive escalation. A tentative knock on the door broke the tension, then the forensic pathologist, Isabel Durand, stuck her head around the door.

'That's where you all are. I thought you were all hiding from me.' She'd spoken before the atmosphere in the room hit her. She recoiled slightly when it did. 'I feel like I've interrupted something important.'

Finch waved her in, the more, the merrier.

'Only if *important* is one of those incomprehensible medical terms that actually means *bad*. Don't tell me . . . the body you carved up the other day isn't Harry Callaghan after all? It's Superintendent Horwood's long-lost brother.'

'Got any sedatives on you, Isabel?' Angel said out of the side of his mouth.

'No need to whisper, Padre,' Finch said. 'The way I feel, I'd volunteer for a frontal lobotomy.'

'I'd rather have a bottle in front of me than a frontal lobotomy,' Jardine said, apropos of nothing at all.

'I can always come back later,' Durand said, edging towards the door.

Finch waved her back in again.

'Nope. Let's hear it.'

'It's nothing bad,' Durand reassured her. 'I was thinking

about how a big, strong man like Callaghan came to have his finger beaten to a pulp, and how he was forced into the vehicle that took him out to the murder scene. Obviously one answer is that there was more than one person involved. The toxicology results showed that he wasn't under the influence of drugs, and it crossed my mind that he might have been subdued or incapacitated another way. Tasered, for example. So, I took a closer look.'

'Difficult to see at first glance on account of all the tattoos,' Angel said.

'Exactly, Padre. Taser barbs typically leave two small puncture wounds with minor burns similar to sunburn surrounding them. They generally heal within a few days, but can remain swollen if there is a local infection. When I went back and specifically looked for puncture wounds, that's what I found.' She touched the side of her neck. 'Here. Partially covered by one of the tattoos.'

'Tasering somebody in the neck's pretty hard-core.'

'Not a problem if you don't have to worry about a misconduct hearing,' Jardine said under her breath, a remark Finch either didn't hear or chose to ignore.

The information would have been expository rather than earth-moving, had it not been for Finch's earlier question about whether they were looking at an official clandestine operation or the work of a single maverick. The evidence of a Taser being used to subdue Callaghan made a one-man mission entirely feasible.

'Thank you, Isabel,' Finch said, sounding like she meant it. 'You can come into my office more often. Although I don't think you'd ever be able to outweigh all the shit this lot like to dump on me even if you moved your desk in.'

Durand gave an almost-shy smile. It made Angel think it was a shame she spent most of her time with a face mask on. He made very sure he didn't let Kincade see that particular thought reflected on his own face, although the way she was staring at him suggested he wasn't doing a great job.

Durand hesitated at the door, as if in two minds about something, then fuelled Kincade's fire.

'Can I have a quick word, Padre, when you're finished?'

'They're finished *right now*,' Finch as good as yelled, looking at them all, challenging them to spoil her day further. 'If there's any more bad news, it can wait until the morning.' She shot her arm out as if trying to grab the nearest available throat, but it was only to consult her watch. 'If anyone's interested in trying to drown bad news, I'm buying.'

Angel raised an eyebrow at Durand, got a small headshake back just as Finch was looking at them to see if they were interested.

'Watch out, Padre, looks like your presence is required on the dissection table.'

Dissection table, kitchen table, bedside table, Kincade thought, as everybody filed out. *You name it, he's up for it with Doctor Death.*

25

Angel wasn't stupid, even if at times his career choices might have suggested it. Durand could have easily called him or Finch with her latest findings, or emailed them. The fact that she'd made a special journey to deliver the information personally wasn't because she wanted a physical pat on the head. It hadn't been the main reason for the trip.

Whatever was coming next was.

'Should I be nervous, Isabel?'

'I'm the one who's nervous.'

He suddenly realised that she was. He wasn't sure he'd ever seen her suffer from such a human weakness before. It was lucky for the pathologist that Kincade wasn't present to capitalise on the opportunity it provided.

Although they were headed that way, his office didn't seem the appropriate place. It would be empty, Kincade having joined the others with Finch in The Wellington Arms, but Angel got the impression he was about to be taken back to his days as a priest—not exactly the confessional, more pastoral care. At times, he'd wished he'd secreted a bottle of something fortifying in the confessional as he listened to guilt-wracked parishioners on the other side of the grille bare their blackened souls to him. Now, more convivial surroundings seemed appropriate.

They went to The Pig in the Wall, a small boutique hotel built into the old city walls at the bottom of the Western Esplanade, the old-world charm of its carefully-antiqued leather armchairs and weathered wooden tables taking the edge off whatever might be coming.

Nervous or not, the choice of location put a mischievous glint in Durand's eye.

'You better hope your sergeant doesn't find out where we've come for a drink. You'll never hear the end of it. I suppose we best order a couple of glasses of children's blood so as not to disappoint the acerbic Sergeant Kincade.'

Angel wasn't exactly sure how Durand was privy to the remarks Kincade made about her and the supposed relationship between them. He couldn't be worrying about it now. Nor did they order children's blood. Durand opted for a Campari and soda—suitably bitter, Kincade would say—and he, a Margarita, not exactly the sweetest of drinks, either.

He took a small sip making sure to get plenty of salt, and waited for her to start.

'You know Oliver is in his final year now . . .'

Angel didn't. He knew Durand's son was currently following in his mother's footsteps studying medicine at Imperial College London, but he was unaware of the stage he'd reached.

'His final year? Already?'

Durand sighed, a soft smile on her lips at how quickly time flies past without you realising it.

'I know. It makes you question what you've done with your own life. Brings home how short a time we have on this earth. And how do I spend mine? Stuck in an antiseptic basement carving up dead bodies day-in, day-out.'

The unexpected melancholy took Angel by surprise. It

wasn't a good start to the conversation, or the evening. He made a valiant attempt to lighten the mood.

'You get to go to crime scenes as well. Plenty of fresh air there.'

'Unless they've been dead in a closed room for a month with the central heating on full blast.'

He couldn't argue with that, made another attempt to raise her spirits.

'I'd expect you to be more excited if you're about to suggest the two of us say *bollocks to it all* and take off for a year.'

If he'd thought her earlier smile had been tinged with regret, the one she gave him now was groaning under the weight of it.

'If only, Padre, if only.'

The heartfelt emotion behind her words made him regret the remark. He couldn't say whether it was the prospect of leaving all of life's drudgery behind, or leaving it behind with him on her arm. Too late he realised the remark might be misconstrued as teasing.

Was this how affairs started? he wondered—not that *affair* was the right word with her divorced and him a widower. An innocent decision to go to a quiet, comfortable bar in the middle of town. A conversation that grew more intense and emotional, too much alcohol consumed without realising it as the moment claimed them. And comfortable—but expensive—rooms above their heads making a shared room a sensible choice...

He was suddenly aware of the heavy beat of his heart—and if he were to put his hand on it, he couldn't swear that such a situation could never occur between them.

'Anyway,' she said, working a brightness into her voice he knew she didn't feel, 'this isn't about me. It's about Oliver. As I said, his final year. Time to think about what comes next after he qualifies.'

Angel couldn't have said how the epiphany came to him,

beyond the fact that Durand had changed into a mother in front of him, driven by emotion, no longer a forensic pathologist concerned only with dry clinical facts. His own background also contributed to the insight.

'He wants to become an Army surgeon?'

'He does.'

'And you don't want him to.'

'I do not.'

He didn't say what came immediately to mind. What he now knew was the purpose of Durand seeking him out. That she wanted him to try to dissuade her son. It would be coming soon enough.

'How determined is he?'

He couldn't have interpreted the look on her face to save his life, there was so much going on behind it—worry, anger, bitterness, self-loathing, they were all there, jostling for pride of place.

'I could blow my own trumpet, Padre, say that he is his mother's son.'

He almost pushed himself to his feet to leave, a joking acknowledgement that he'd be wasting his time trying to change Oliver's mind. He stopped himself in time when he remembered she hadn't asked him yet.

'Minimal scope for flexibility?' he said, instead.

She smiled properly at that.

'That's a very kind way of describing me and my son.' The smile disappeared as quickly as it had come, bitterness pushing it aside. 'Oliver is not so kind in the things he says. Certainly not to his mother. I blame his father—'

'Me too, and I've never met him.'

'Oliver said that if I thought he wanted to spend seven years training as a doctor just so that he could lock himself away in a basement cutting up already-dead bodies, rather than trying to stop people from dying in the first place, then I had less sense than the bodies I'd already removed the brains from.'

Angel nodded, big long strokes, the cause of Durand's earlier melancholy and references to her own life now clear.

'Feel free to laugh, Padre,' Durand went on, a nervous twitch on her own lips. 'I would, if it wasn't my son.'

He didn't laugh, but he did let the smile come.

'A forensic pathologist isn't the only option available to a newly-qualified doctor.'

'Very true. But by concentrating on that example, he was accusing me of arrogance. That I would naturally assume he wanted to emulate me. It was also Oliver's way of saying that my own choice to be a pathologist proves beyond doubt that my opinion regarding what he should do with his life is worthless, at best.'

'Or, as he would say, worth less than that of the corpses you spend all day desecrating.'

'Exactly. Although I'm not sure he'd use the word *desecrating*. I think that's a personal thing with you, given your God-bothering background.'

'Have you ever considered there might actually be a God, and now you're being punished for your irreverent remarks?'

'The punishment part sounds about right. We're getting off-track...'

'You'd like me to have a word with him?'

She stretched out her hand, gave his arm a grateful squeeze. Not only for the offer, but for saving her from having to say the words.

'I hate to ask, but nothing I say will make a blind bit of difference.'

'What about his father?'

Her face said, *what about him?*

'Oliver is also his father's son—'

'Particularly when it comes to the choice of unkind words?'

'I didn't realise you'd met him, Padre. All Jeremy had to say on the matter was—'

'Better than a bloody forensic pathologist?'

'Exactly. Except he didn't use anything so quaint as *bloody*.'

The way he'd pre-empted everything she was about to say was testament to how long they'd known each other, how similar they were in many ways. The downside was that it highlighted the stark contrast in their hopes and expectations given what he now said.

'I'm happy to talk to him. But what approach should I use? Stress how dangerous it is? The more I talk about the horrors of war, the dreadful casualties he'll have to deal with, the sickening disappointments that will make him question his own value in the world when young men die in front of him, the more determined he'll become to do it, to rise up to the challenge.' Now, he gave her hand a squeeze. 'If he really is his mother's son, that is.'

She swallowed hard at his words, a wet sheen in her eyes. Then sniffed, angry at herself for letting the emotion leak out, before tipping the last of her drink down her throat.

He followed his cue, swivelled in his seat to get somebody's attention, then ordered them the same again.

Durand's temporary lapse was over by the time it was done, more thoughtful than anything else now.

'You're right. I know what he's like. Stressing what a challenge it would be would only make him more determined.'

She sagged a little at what appeared to be the end of the matter, the despondency of earlier threatening to make a reappearance. He did his best to head it off.

'Or did you ask me specifically because you thought I'd be a graphic example of what a basket case a support role in the Army can turn you into.'

She smiled with him.

'That's a more compelling argument. Except only you can do that to yourself. With your parents' help, of course.'

Somehow, she'd found a way to blame herself again. He wasn't about to bang his head against the brick wall of her determination. All he could do was be positive in the face of her negativity, let time work on that.

'I'll have a word with him.' He pointed at her, trying to work a harder, cautionary edge into his voice. 'But you have to prepare yourself for the possibility of him dropping medicine altogether, deciding he wants to be a priest.'

She gave him a disbelieving look, her voice an incredulous squeak.

'That's the last thing I have to worry about after he's talked to *you*.'

They sat for a while in an easy silence, the low hum of conversation around them. All of them comfortably-off people enjoying good food and drink with friends or family in a safe country that hadn't felt the touch of a foreign oppressor for eighty years. It highlighted what her son was contemplating. What he would give up. And what he risked never returning home to.

Against that was the eternal truth—you get out of life what you put in.

'Why don't you want him to join the Army, Isabel?'

'I would've thought it was obvious. I'm worried for his safety. I know he's not a child any longer, but nothing will ever change the fact that I'm his mother.'

'That's all about you.' He tapped his pocket where his phone sat. 'You want me to call my father, arrange for the two of you to meet?' He swept his arm wide, took in the whole room. 'Somewhere comfortable like this, then he can lecture you until the cows come home about the dangers of trying to live your children's lives for them.'

She knew his family history well enough for him not to have to spell it out for her. The damage Carl Angel had done with his blind determination that his sons should do the exact opposite of what Durand wanted for her son, bullying them into joining the British Army.

How the pressure on Cormac as the youngest became impossible to resist after he, the eldest, the chosen one, disgraced himself and his father with him by joining the priesthood—*a waste of a life if Carl Angel had ever heard of one*—and how Cormac's incompatibility with the rules and codes of the Army ultimately pushed him into taking his own life.

'Think about that overnight. Then let me know if you still want me to talk to Oliver.'

They chatted for a while longer, but her heart wasn't in it. She was keen to get away and do as he'd suggested. Take herself out of the equation, see if that helped her find peace and accept what she couldn't control. Besides, they both had to drive home, a useful throttle on excess alcohol consumption and the potential consequences he'd idly considered earlier that they would both regret in the morning.

He wasn't sure he'd been of any use to her, even if he understood why she'd come to him. He'd joked about her presenting him to her son as a living, breathing example of how badly things can go wrong when you make an ill-advised decision early in life—and she knew exactly how much truth lay behind that remark.

Because, of all the people he worked with, she was the only one who knew the reason he'd walked away from the Army himself and, with it, the priesthood and any belief in God, whether loving, jealous or any other kind.

26

'Hit me with it,' Angel said, entering his office the next morning, Kincade already at her desk.

'That's a *very* tempting offer. Do I get to choose the implement?'

'What? Bored with your favourite one? Jokes about drinking children's blood, going back to Durand's coffin with her...'

'I think you're suffering from the sin of pride, sir. What makes you think we were talking about you and Doctor Death in the pub last night?'

'Because it's your hobby?'

She turned suddenly thoughtful.

'Where did you go for your little tête-à-tête? I know it wasn't in here. There was no smell of formaldehyde when I got in this morning.'

If only you knew, he thought, tapping the side of his nose with his index finger, the memory of his thoughts the previous evening about how easily the situation could have progressed from a comforting chat into something more physical still in his mind.

'Ready to do some work now?' he said, instead of answering.

She slid out from behind her desk, already pulling on her jacket.

'Just waiting for you, sir.' A long pause. 'Wherever you might have been coming in from.'

Better this than the sour-faced cow sulking about Stuart Beckford, he thought, as they headed out to interview Russell Baldwin's ex-wife.

Fiona, who still used her married name, also worked as a journalist. Unlike her freelance and now-deceased ex-husband, she was employed by one of the national daily papers, working four days a week from home and only having to commute into London once a week.

She'd shown no surprise when she took the call to arrange the meeting, her attitude summed up in one sentence—*given what an irritating pain in the arse Russell could be, it was only a matter of time before somebody showed up claiming his death wasn't an accident.*

They arranged to meet at her apartment in Vantage Tower on trendy Centenary Quay on the east bank of the River Itchen —directly across the river from the equally-trendy and upmarket Ocean Village marina where Kincade had lived briefly.

She was dressed as if they'd caught her about to go for a job interview when she opened the door to them. Tailored dark grey trousers and a crisp white blouse, black shoes with sensible heels. She noticed them noticing.

'I need the discipline.' Running her hand down her body as she said it. 'It's hard enough working from home. What a lot of people rightly call *shirking* from home. I need to make a clear distinction between my time and work time.'

'I might ask you to come in and give my team a pep talk,' Angel said. 'Some of them look as if they've just rolled out of bed.'

'Why are you both looking at me?' Kincade said indignantly,

before Fiona led them through into the living room with its view over the river.

The door leading onto the balcony was open. Kincade went over to it and stepped outside, Fiona joining her at the railing. Kincade pointed across the river.

'I used to live over there for a while.'

Fiona dipped her head approvingly.

'Nice.'

'A penthouse apartment, too.'

'Even nicer.'

'Yeah. Except it wasn't mine. A friend of a friend.' Feeling somewhat slimy for describing her estranged husband as a friend.

They moved back inside and Fiona closed the door, the outside sounds cut off as if flicking a switch. She offered them the white leather sofa and took the matching armchair, a folding table with a laptop on it in front of her.

'Personally, I never thought Russell's death was an accident,' she said, before they had a chance to start. 'Although that's only based on knowing how irritatingly persistent he was.'

Angel made sure there was no accusation or criticism in his tone when he asked the obvious question.

'You never thought to voice your concerns?'

Fiona grinned at him as if he'd cracked a joke.

'Who to? You can't live with Russell for as long as I did without at least some of his paranoia rubbing off on you. If Russell got a chance to take a final breath, he'd have used it to croak that one of the establishment's many clandestine agencies was behind his death. We were divorced by then with no children, and I'm not ashamed to admit I was thinking about myself.' She made a point of looking between the two of them to see if they planned to criticise her for what she'd said so far. Satisfied by their non-committal expressions, she carried on. 'If I do something, I do it properly. I wouldn't have come to you, said I thought it was more than an accident, and then gone away, my duty discharged. If you hadn't taken me seriously, I would've started digging. Even though I don't suffer from the sort of paranoia Russell did, it was easy to envisage a situation where I made a nuisance of myself. Whoever was behind Russell's death might have decided to punish or warn me. Make a few calls and I'd lose my job, for example. Or worse. All for the sake of something I could never hope to prove.'

It all made sense to Angel. Despite that, he got the impression she'd spent a lot of time and thought satisfying her harshest critic—her own conscience.

'Tell me a little bit about your relationship with your ex-husband,' Angel said, rather than pass comment on Fiona's excuses, which she appeared to be waiting for him to do.

'The divorce was all very amicable. To be honest, we should never really have got married in the first place, and we both recognised that fact. It was a professional relationship that strayed into the romantic, and it never should have.'

Angel was very aware of Kincade's eyes on him. He made sure he didn't look at her, in effect proving there was something to stare at him about.

'The relationship continued on a reduced professional basis afterwards,' Fiona went on. 'We'd bump into each other while networking, that sort of thing. I ran the blog with him when we were married. I've contributed the occasional guest post since.' She smiled, the sort of thing she no doubt kept permanently pasted on her face at those professional networking gatherings. 'So, you can cross me off your list of potential suspects for who pushed him. Or do you need an alibi?'

Angel told her that wouldn't be necessary, moved on.

'It sounds like you might still have had an idea about what he was working on ...'

'I *might*. But I *didn't*.'

On the face of it, they'd run into a brick wall. Angel wasn't overly discouraged. He was happy for witnesses to start out with an adamant flat denial. It often led to backtracking—a lot of the time in the very next sentence—as the subconscious considered a question more fully while the conscious mind rejected it out of hand.

Sometimes, it needed an additional prompt, which is what he did now—almost anything would do, so long as it got the grey cells moving.

'We heard a rumour Russell might have been sticking his nose into the business of some nasty people in the drug trade.'

Fiona gave a firm headshake.

'Absolutely not. For one, he wouldn't be interested. Political scandal was his thing. And secondly, he would avoid anything potentially dangerous like the plague.'

Angel didn't point out that everything was *potentially* dangerous. What she meant was *obviously* dangerous. And that was often misleading, the caricature thugs less deadly than the threat from well-spoken men from good schools wearing expensive suits.

'Sorry, I didn't explain that properly,' he said, then borrowed what Olivia Finch had suggested. 'What I meant was a politician involved with drug dealers.'

Again, Fiona shook her head, a parental-style gesture that suggested he could argue until he was blue in the face but she wouldn't be swayed.

'Okay, he'd be more interested. But it's still a fail on the danger issue. Overall, it's too risky. Drug barons don't resign and disappear to their country estate if they're outed. They make sure the person who outed them disappears altogether.'

Angel was hoping the *aha* moment might have happened by now. He gave things another nudge when it didn't.

'Why was he so obsessed with corrupt politicians?'

She gave a dismissive wave as if she was about to explain how Stalin had started by pulling the legs off spiders, and look how that turned out.

'It was when he got his first job as a journalist. He wrote an exposé on some arsehole I can't even remember now. It was like water off a duck's back to them, but the vindictive prick went after Russell with a vengeance. Got him sacked. Just because they could. Russell never forgot it. He's been on a crusade ever since.' She did something with her mouth that might have been a smile but was more likely a sneer. 'And with all the sleaze, he'd never go hungry. Not much of a career awaits the man who wants to write about honest, honourable politicians and their public-spirited business partners.'

She paused, and he held his breath, hoping the *aha* moment had finally arrived.

It hadn't.

She was adrift in her memories, the soft half-smile on her lips suggesting they weren't all bad.

'He was *so* paranoid. It's ironic he had to die to prove himself right. That's what I call commitment to the job.'

Angel smiled with her, then probed a little deeper.

'Paranoid how?'

'Big Brother sort of paranoid. He was convinced we're being watched twenty-four hours a day. He's right in some ways. Look how many CCTV cameras we have in this country. A damn sight more than somewhere like Russia.' She pointed at her laptop as if it had been planted in her house to spy on her. 'And as for computers . . . he was convinced everything is monitored and recorded by shady government agencies that make MI5 look like the local Women's Institute.'

'He didn't use a computer himself?'

'He did. He had to. But he didn't store anything important on it. That all went on a USB thumb drive he kept on his keyring. It's not much of an exaggeration to say that he slept with it under his pillow.'

Angel smiled, an automatic reaction to her smile, not really hearing the last sentence. His head was too full of DS Ellis Hudson's words when describing the scene of Russell Baldwin's death.

He didn't have any keys on him.

In itself it had meant nothing. What Hudson said subsequently about a man supposedly checking Baldwin for signs of life changed all that.

Not many people have got the balls to frisk a still-twitching body in front of a crowd of onlookers.

He glanced at Kincade, saw the same realisation on her face.

Fiona hadn't noticed, too caught up in her own thoughts and memories. Then she shook her head as if to clear it.

'It's bloody contagious, this paranoia. I was convinced I was being stalked a while ago. I kept seeing a man who looked a lot like the driver of the lorry that hit Russell.'

'Did he approach you?' Kincade said.

'No. I was always with other people.' She couldn't fail to see the effect her words had on them. 'Was it him?'

'Probably,' Kincade said. 'He was taking an interest in your ex-husband.'

Fiona's *aha* moment hit her hard in that moment, but it wasn't the one Angel had been hoping for.

'I thought this was some kind of cold case investigation. But it isn't, is it? The driver's been killed, hasn't he? Because he was starting to suspect Russell was pushed.'

There was no point denying it.

'That's what it looks like,' Angel admitted.

Fiona barely heard him, the chain of events already irrefutable fact in her mind.

'*Jesus!* What had Russell raked up?' She looked at them as if surprised to see them there. 'No wonder you wanted to pick my brains.'

No wonder we're so pissed off there was nothing in them, Angel thought, and moved on.

'There's a chance his brother might try to do the same. You'll recognise him. They look very similar facially, although he's not as fat. We recommend you don't talk to him.'

Fiona was ahead of him, the horror creeping across her face.

'Turn myself into a target, too, you mean? If it's not already too late.' She glanced towards the front door as if she'd heard someone interfering with the lock. 'How do you convince someone that you don't know anything, and have no intention of trying to find out?'

They didn't have an answer for her, but Kincade had a final question.

'We identified your ex-husband's blog called *brinkmanship.com* and we're going through it. Do you know if he had another one he kept his name away from? Somewhere he might have posted his most contentious material.'

'It would've been a good idea, but as far as I know, *brinkmanship.com* is the only one. He was so proud of that name. A play on his nom-de-plume, Robert Brinkley, with the connotations of the word itself—'

'Pursuing a dangerous policy to the limits of safety before stopping,' Kincade said, as if she felt the need to prove herself to a woman whose whole career was based on her skill with words.

'Precisely. And a reminder that he was there to catch the ones who didn't stop. You're on the right track. You should definitely speak to Lucas.'

Angel made a mental note that they should pencil in some time for a training session for when witnesses blindsided them. Practice not letting their jaws go slack, that sort of thing.

Even without the training, Kincade recovered quickly.

'Who is Lucas?'

Fiona looked at her as if she really was worrying for her safety now. Not only had Harry Callaghan potentially made a target of her, this was the calibre of the official protection from the psychopath on a killing spree.

'Lucas McIntyre. He runs the blog with Russell. He took over when I left.'

'There is absolutely no mention of anybody called Lucas McIntyre anywhere on that blog.'

'There won't be.'

Fiona seemed unaware of the contradiction in her statements. She'd been incredulous that they hadn't heard of Lucas McIntyre. And now she was adamant his name wouldn't appear anywhere.

'Why not?' Kincade said, her tone suggesting her patience was wearing thin, that it wouldn't take much before daylight would be visible through it.

'Hard as it is to believe, he's even more paranoid than Russell was. Have you seen the movie *Enemy of the State* with Gene Hackman? That's Lucas.'

'It sounds like we might have a problem getting hold of him. Unless . . .' She raised an eyebrow at Fiona, who nodded back.

'I've got a number for him, but I've got no idea whether it's still current. Given what he's like, he probably changes it every week. If it is still in use and you speak to him, please—'

'Don't worry, we won't tell him we got it from you. We'll let him think the dossiers he believes we keep on every honest citizen led us to him.'

They wrapped it up after that, left Fiona to dwell on the truth in her earlier remark—that she and Russell should never have got married in the first place.

For better, for worse only goes so far.

. . .

'That's some balls,' Kincade said, sounding impressed, once they were back on the street. 'Pushing Baldwin in front of a lorry, then frisking him and stealing his keys as he lies dying on the ground. What the hell was Baldwin investigating that's worth killing two people over? Three, if that idiot Liam Callaghan ignores our warning.'

Angel disagreed.

'It doesn't necessarily have to be anything big.'

They were almost back at his car, walking side-by-side. She turned to look at the side of his head, as if checking whether she could see all the way through it and out the other side, her line of sight not impeded by functioning brain matter.

'I'd hate to think how many bodies we'd have piling up if it was what you *would* call big.'

'It's a question of how much the killer has got to lose if he's exposed, not what the crime is.'

'Like if the Prime Minister goosed a secretary at the Christmas party, you mean?'

'Exactly.'

'Word of advice, sir. I wouldn't float that theory past the Super just yet.'

They were in the car by now, windows up, radio off, the sounds of the outside world somewhat muted. In the silence that followed her joking remark, neither of them missed the *ping* from the phone in his pocket as a text message came in.

He should've opened it.

But he didn't.

Because he knew it was Stuart Beckford. He didn't know how he knew, but he did. He knew what it was about, too—and it wasn't to update him with anything as trivial as the latest word on the street from the informant Ricky Shorter.

It was only because he didn't look at it that Kincade knew who'd sent the text a split-second later. She tried to make a joke of it, but the damage was already done.

'That must be Beckford wanting to know what to do with my stuff that's on *his* desk.'

If only, he thought, as he pulled away, feeling as if the axe was hanging over him, not her.

27

Angel made a point of not going to the toilet when they got back. More specifically, of not diverting to the men's toilets on the ground floor. After Kincade's remark in the car when the text came in, he was surprised she didn't point at the toilet door as they went past. Say she'd see him upstairs after he'd read the text and responded in private—although she'd have used the word *secret*.

Her self-control wasn't sufficient to last the whole of the journey up in the lift, however.

'Aren't you going to read the text? It might be something important.'

'You sound more concerned about it than me.'

'And you sound like you're deliberately trying to pretend you're not interested. And you're—'

'Not doing a very good job?'

She gave him an incredulous look.

'*Not very good?* Bloody awful is what I'd call it.'

He shrugged like she'd caught him out.

'Men aren't as good as women at being devious. We don't get as much practice.'

The ping of the lift as they arrived at their floor stopped the conversation from deteriorating further.

If the text hadn't arrived when it did, and he wasn't so concerned about Kincade thinking he was running around behind her back, he would've got off at the floor below. Gone directly to DS Ellis Hudson to have a word about the discrepancy in Harry Callaghan's witness statement. It would wait. Unfortunately, that situation wasn't about to go away.

Back at his desk, he pulled out his phone, composed himself. Worked an expressionless mask onto his face of the sort he used every day of the week in the interview room. As he'd known it would be, the text was from Stuart Beckford. His heart was thumping as he opened it and began to read.

I've made up my mind about Balan's offer to find Florescu . . .

Angel was aware of Kincade watching him, even though he could hear her tapping away at her keyboard. For all he knew, she was typing gibberish in an attempt to fool him. If so, she'd failed. He made sure he kept his face free of emotion, no relief or horror at what he read.

The majority of the message comprised Beckford making excuses. Explaining why he'd sent a text instead of calling, realising that Angel would've thought the importance of the matter and Beckford's decision warranted at least a telephone conversation if not a face-to-face meeting.

The text finished with a brief line that Beckford would call him later, give Angel time to digest the contents.

He slipped the phone back into his pocket, found Kincade looking directly at him, no attempt to look away, pretend she hadn't been observing him.

He was expecting her to say, *so?*

He was wrong—about that, and about her typing random gibberish while she surreptitiously studied him.

'Lucas McIntyre is on the PNC. He was convicted of hacking

when he was in his early twenties. He got away with a thousand pound fine so it can't have been anything too serious.'

'Probably a script kiddie, given his age.'

Typically young and immature, script kiddies employ tried-and-trusted techniques utilising ready-made illegal programs and scripts to find and exploit weaknesses. The attacks are often random, motivated by personal rather than financial reasons—to create chaos, impress their peers or because they're having a bad day and don't see why they should suffer alone.

'That would explain his paranoia,' Kincade agreed. 'If it's that easy for him to get people's details, imagine what the countless hordes of serious hackers working twenty-four-seven in secret government bunkers get up to.'

'You sound like you've been talking to Grace.'

The remark put an immediate scowl on Kincade's face.

Angel's sister was a criminal defence lawyer. She believed her brother and his goose-stepping fascist colleagues—including Kincade—were willing and enthusiastic instruments of a government hell-bent on persecuting innocent citizens, particularly on the basis of colour or creed. It was the reason she was determined to convince her and Angel's father to kick Kincade out of his house.

'Just so long as you don't accuse me of turning into her,' she said, then went back to the PNC.

They were both hoping the identification of Lucas McIntyre was a major step forward, perhaps the pivot point in the investigation. Sadly, the feeling of moving forward was short-lived.

It was time for Angel to head downstairs to discuss the fluid nature of Harry Callaghan's witness statement with DS Ellis Hudson. The last time they'd spoken, Angel managed to salvage the relationship between them. This time, it would be more difficult.

He printed off a copy of the original statement they'd found on Callaghan's laptop, waved it at Kincade.

'How do you fancy discussing this with Ellis Hudson?'

He wasn't serious, and she knew it.

'I don't. But thank you for offering, sir. Besides, it wouldn't be a good idea on account of his name.'

It took a moment for the remark to click.

'I'm with you,' he said, heading for the door. '*Ellis* is a bit too close to *Elliot*.'

Even though she'd brought it up, the mention of her estranged husband's name put as much of a sour scowl on her face as Grace's name had a minute earlier.

'Yep. I hope for your sake you don't end up feeling how I feel after speaking to Elliot when you're finished with him.' Pointing at the floor as she said it.

The line about wishing in one hand and shitting in the other carried Angel all the way to the stairs and down.

Hudson looked resigned more than anything as Angel approached his desk. From the minute Angel came down on the previous occasion he would've known the upcoming conversation was a question of *when* and not *if*. Angel guessed it had given him time to adjust to what was coming, work out any anger or resentment in advance. Hudson went so far as to begin in his usual manner, hanging his head as he did so.

'Bless me, Father, for I have sinned . . .'

'I'm not sure about that, Ellis.' He waved the printed witness statement without having to say what it was. 'A sin has been committed. I get the feeling it might have been foisted on you.'

Hudson glanced at the closed door to DCI Steve Lane's office, a subconscious gesture blaming his boss, then pulled out his phone. Angel continued with his attempt to lessen the blame attaching to Hudson.

'Even better. A photo of the man who did the foisting.'

Hudson shook his head sadly.

'Afraid not, Padre. You know how vampires aren't reflected in mirrors? Same thing with this guy. Even if I'd taken a picture of him, there'd be nothing there.'

'Apart from the bad smell?'

'You got it.' He raised his phone towards Angel. 'I'm logging into my personal cloud storage. I've got a file there that's probably identical to what you've got in your hand.'

'Named *insurance*?'

'Close. *Arse-covering*.'

'Must be a hell of a big file.'

'Tell me about it.'

They both knew perfectly well they weren't about to compare the two statements line-by-line. It was Hudson's way of admitting he'd done as he was told, but hadn't been happy about it, saving a copy of the original as insurance against future accusations of incompetence or worse.

It would have been very easy for Angel to make accusations of his own now. Point out to Hudson that if they hadn't persuaded Liam Callaghan to give up his brother's laptop, they'd still be flailing around in the dark, unaware of the original statement. Except it would achieve nothing beyond souring the relationship between them to the point of no return.

'What happened?'

Again, Hudson glanced towards DCI Lane's door, a deliberate gesture this time.

'I got called into the boss' office. A guy in a suit was in there with him. Arrogant prick in a regimental tie acting like he owned the place. Douglas—'

'Farebrother.'

'You know him?'

Angel nodded, *oh yes*, then pinched his finger and thumb together.

'I was this close to hitting him.'

'Until thoughts about your career stopped you?'

'No. Kincade was holding my arm.'

Hudson laughed with him, but it had been no laughing matter at the time. Not only had Farebrother hijacked one of Angel's investigations, he'd made disparaging and insulting remarks about Angel and his father.

'I thought priests were meant to rise above that sort of thing,' Hudson said.

'*Ex*-priests.'

'Then it all comes pouring out, eh?'

Doesn't it just, Angel thought, and got Hudson back on track.

'So Farebrother took over the investigation?'

Hudson worked a disapproving look onto his face as if Angel had maligned one of his closest friends.

'Of course not. He provided guidance to help me get over my own bad habits.'

'Like a mentor.'

'Exactly.'

'And what were these sinful habits?'

Hudson hung his head in mock shame, his voice penitent.

'I have no regard for the environment. I'm personally responsible for half of the deforestation in the Amazon basin, given how much paper I want to waste on long-winded witness statements. Farebrother pointed out that the path to a better life—'

'And continued employment as a police officer.'

'—lay in learning how to be more succinct. Cut out all the unnecessary—'

'Hard facts?'

'—distractions, and concentrate on—'

'Producing a sanitised version.'

'—not wasting everybody's time in arriving at a verdict—'

'That had already been decided in advance.'

'Precisely. It was then my job to share the benefit of what I'd learned with Harry Callaghan.' He worked a big smile onto his face as if he'd just shaken hands with one of the biggest philanthropists on the planet. 'What a great guy Farebrother was. He didn't care how many times I got it wrong, he stayed patient, sent it back again until I'd got it right. He even found time to have a nice long chat about pensions. How good police pensions are, how it would be a shame if mine was to go up in smoke, that sort of thing. I can't imagine why you wanted to punch a nice guy like that.' He made a show of peering all around his desk. 'I used to have a framed picture of him on my desk...'

'Some bastard stole it?'

'Can't blame them.' He narrowed his eyes at Angel. 'It wasn't you, was it? Another one of those repressed sins bubbling up to the surface after you threw out the dog collar.'

Angel smiled with him, *you'll never know*. He didn't want to spoil things by stressing the importance of what Hudson had been compelled to bury, but he thought it was only fair to bring him up to date. He explained the significance of Russell Baldwin having no keys on him, then asked the question he was most interested in—trying not to make it sound as if he was prefixing it with, *now that you're telling the truth...*

'Is there any information on the man who frisked him while supposedly checking for signs of life?'

'None. He was long gone by the time we got there. It was just something one of the medics said.'

'Did the medic see him?'

'No. He was told by one of the morbid onlookers standing around gawping. Good luck trying to trace them.'

We don't need to, we've already got Lacy Cooper, Angel thought, and ended the discussion another way.

'Check in the toilets for the photo of Farebrother. Somebody probably used it to wipe their arse.'

Kincade looked up as Angel came back into their shared office, a question on her face.

'How'd it go?'

'Better than anticipated with Hudson himself. It was out of his control.'

'And he's got his job and pension to think of.'

'Exactly.' He grinned at her, eye teeth on show, a hard glint in his eye. 'Now tell me the last name you want to hear.'

It was a no-brainer for her, given the way the investigation was headed.

'Not Fareprick?' Using Angel's nickname for him and making it sound like *Lucifer* at the same time.

'The one and only.'

It was the third time that day he'd put a scowl on her face, this one the worst by far.

'*Shit!* I really wish I hadn't stopped you from hitting the jumped-up prick.'

'Don't forget you almost hit him, too.'

She looked at her right hand, gave her fingers a flex.

'Yeah. Why'd you stop me?' She held her arm out straight, hand curled into a fist. 'Let's have a pact. I won't stop you next time, and you don't stop me.'

He bumped fists with her, even though the gesture made him feel like one of her girls trying to emulate the older children in the playground.

'What makes you think there will be a next time?'

'Because we both want there to be.'

Have we grown alike, he thought, *or were we always the same?*

28

'These twats need to get a life,' Lisa Jardine announced, catching a massive yawn in her fist.

Gulliver went to say something, then yawned himself after almost being swallowed up by Jardine's gaping maw.

'What are you looking at?'

'Baldwin's blog. *Brinkmanship.com*. A right riveting read, it isn't.'

'Too many long words?'

She gave him a tight smile and a raised middle finger, *up yours*.

'The articles he writes are okay, as far as boring shite goes. Although there was one I read yesterday about politicians' expenses that was interesting in a depressing sort of way. Hang on. Let me find it . . .' He waited patiently, knowing it was pointless going back to his own work. Luckily, he didn't have to wait long before she found what she was looking for, her voice a blend of taxpayer's indignation and world-weary resignation as she quoted from it. 'Did you know that between August twenty-nineteen and July twenty-twenty-two, MPs spent ninety million on expenses. *Ninety million!* All the old farts in the House of

Lords spent the same again. And if that's not bad enough, there's another three hundred and ten million claimed by MPs' staff. Together that's—'

'Four hundred and ninety million. Just short of half a billion in three years. But it's not exactly ground-breaking news. No wonder you're falling asleep.'

She shook her head, yawned again.

'It's the dickheads leaving comments I was talking about. They're the ones who need to get out more instead of bleating on about it online.'

He gave her a disapproving glare at her harsh choice of words.

'*Bleating on?* Did it cross your mind they might have genuine grievances? What if someone's mother died because they couldn't do the operation she needed in time because there aren't enough hospital beds? And at the same time, greedy MPs are claiming half a billion in expenses for fancy hotels and expensive meals. I think I'd *bleat on*, too.'

She waved the objection away as if he'd yawned again, not given a reasoned argument.

'Yeah, there's plenty of stuff like that. But really? Who can be arsed to take the time to leave a comment when half the time nobody ever sees it? Even if they do, they're just more whingeing losers. It's not going to bring their dead mother back. It's one big bragging competition. *My situation's more tragic than yours, oh no it's not, oh yes, it is . . .*' She shook her head in dismay. 'People don't even stick to the point. They just say what they want to say. They don't give a toss if it's relevant or not.'

'Must be a lot of women commenting,' he said under his breath, then tried to tune her out.

Except she had the bit between her teeth by now, determined to postpone going back to trawling through the comments for as long as possible.

'There are some real nutters out there. One silly bint called Evie—'

'I'm surprised you remember her name if it's all so boring.'

She picked up a notepad off her desk, waved it in his face.

'I don't have to. I wrote it down.'

'What for?'

'She left the same cryptic comment on a lot of articles. I thought she might be worth looking into if I don't find anything more promising. I wrote the comment down, as well.'

He took the notepad she was holding towards him, read what she'd written.

Wherever you look, you See More Evil.

'I suppose it fits with the paranoid tone of Baldwin's blog.' He read it again, a frown on his face. 'Why did you capitalise see more evil?'

'Because she did.'

'Probably a typo.'

'What? At the beginning of each of those words and nowhere else? Besides, she did it every time.' His face reflected his scepticism, made her more determined to prove her point. 'I'll see if I can find an example.'

Gulliver was happy to let her try if it kept her quiet. He went back to what he was doing, fully expecting the rambling diatribe to continue in the background, calling a man a twat here, a woman a silly cow there, as she worked through the comments again.

It didn't happen, her voice an irritated squawk a few minutes later.

'What the . . .?'

'What now?'

The addition of the word *now* was a mistake, the long-suffering impression it gave, the fact that *for Christ's sake* would've fitted perfectly on the end. She turned her screen towards him, accusation in her voice as if he was responsible.

'It's gone.'

Any chance of getting some work done myself definitely has, he thought, and said something different.

'What's gone?'

'The comment by Evie, what do you think?' She curled her finger at him. 'Come over here and see if you can find anything by her.'

A list of inadvisable things to say flashed through his mind.
I'm busy.
Are you looking at the correct articles?
Who cares what a nutter called Evie thinks?

He kept them all to himself as she pushed back in her chair, made room for him to slide across in front of her desk. Sat with her arms folded over her chest, smugness mixing with irritation as she watched him scroll up and down the page.

'There's nothing by somebody called Evie,' he confirmed a minute later. 'Are you—'

A rigid digit was half an inch off the end of his nose before he got what would've been a very unwise question out.

'Don't even think about saying it. It was definitely there. I didn't imagine it.'

Despite all the evidence to the contrary, he trusted her instincts, and her memory. If she said she'd seen it, she'd seen it.

'Somebody must've been working on the back end deleting her comments overnight. If they're that worried, it would've been easier to take the whole site down.' Clicking on the site logo to be taken back to the homepage as he said it. '*Ha!* They must have heard me.'

She looked over his shoulder to see what had produced the sudden outburst, saw a blank page with a message in the middle of the screen.

Site temporarily unavailable for scheduled maintenance.

'They didn't hear you,' she said, 'but I reckon Fiona Baldwin phoned Lucas McIntyre. Told him about the boss and Kincade's visit and how they were planning on talking to him, too. He panicked and started deleting comments—'

'Then took the site down when it was taking too long.'

'And now he'll have disappeared down a rabbit hole himself.'

Gulliver looked in the direction of Angel and Kincade's office, far too much relief in his voice for Jardine's liking.

'I'm glad it's not my job to give him the bad news.'

'What did the boss say?' Gulliver asked, as he and Jardine headed down to the car park.

'Apart from get your arses round to Lucas McIntyre's house before he does a bunk, you mean?'

'I'd worked that much out for myself.' Indicating the stairs they were descending as proof of that particular pudding.

'He didn't say a lot really. He takes it all in his stride. Anyone who can be celibate for ten years isn't going to get uptight about a political blog being taken down.'

Gulliver didn't follow her logic, nor did he have any intention of corrupting his own brain trying to make sense of it. He said something constructive, instead.

'At least it proves it's worth making the journey to talk to McIntyre.'

'If he's there.'

Gulliver was usually a glass-half-full sort of person, but even he couldn't accuse Jardine of being overly negative. They'd been told McIntyre took paranoia to new levels. It was likely he'd been warned by Fiona Baldwin. And he'd taken down the blog he ran with her dead ex-husband before his death. Neither of them thought he was currently in his kitchen, putting the kettle on in preparation for their arrival.

Their pessimism was proved justified ten minutes later when they hammered on the front door of a Victorian terraced house in Portswood and got no answer, however many times Jardine muttered *down a bloody rabbit hole* to herself.

She tried the property to the left, he took the one on the right, the one whose front door was adjacent to McIntyre's. A balding middle-aged man in jeans and a T-shirt opened the door to him. His reaction to Gulliver's warrant card was one of complete indifference.

'We're looking for Lucas McIntyre,' Gulliver started.

A small smile curled the man's lips. Gulliver knew exactly what he was thinking of saying.

You've got the wrong house, mate. He lives next door.

'Have you seen him recently?' Gulliver said, before the neighbour had a chance to deliver his line.

'I heard him go out earlier.' He pointed to where Gulliver's car was parked. 'That's where he normally parks his car.'

'You didn't speak to him?'

The neighbour shook his head.

'Nah. I don't have much to do with him. He's an oddball. Keeps himself to himself most of the time. And when he doesn't, it doesn't take long before you're wishing he would. He can bore for England when you get him going.'

'Odd in what way?'

The neighbour half laughed, half snorted.

'In every way. Mainly it's conspiracy theories. We're all being watched twenty-four hours a day, emails are being intercepted, that sort of bollocks. And he hates you lot.' The way he smiled said that particular trait was one thing he didn't blame McIntyre for, the one thing they had in common.

Gulliver had the feeling he wasn't going to get anything more than Jardine was—and the door she'd knocked on was still closed. He persevered, nonetheless.

'He didn't say anything about going away?'

'Not to me, he didn't.' He sniggered suddenly, a malicious glint in his eye. 'Maybe he checked himself into a clinic somewhere. He's been worse than normal recently. Like he thought they, whoever *they* are, had moved on from intercepting his emails and phone calls and were actually hiding in the street waiting for him.' He made a circular motion at his temple with his finger. 'I tell you, the guy's nuts.'

Gulliver had no problem guessing when McIntyre's paranoia spiked. He floated it past the neighbour.

'Did you read about a man being shot to death in the New Forest about a week ago?'

'Yeah, I saw it in the paper.'

Gulliver counted the seconds in his head before the neighbour jumped to the obvious wrong conclusion.

'That's not what you want him for, is it? He doesn't look like a cold-blooded murderer. Although a computer geek like him would know how to buy a gun on the dark web.'

'It's not why we want to talk to him, no.'

The neighbour looked a little crestfallen, as if he'd been looking forward to telling his drinking buddies how he'd lived next door to a killer and never even knew it.

'It was about that time when I noticed he'd got even more paranoid,' he said, feeling the need to justify why he'd jumped to the wrong conclusion. 'Like he thought he was next.'

Gulliver smiled politely with him, *if only you knew*.

A car went past on the street behind Gulliver and bibbed its horn. The neighbour raised a hand in greeting, the smile that had accompanied it immediately turning to contempt.

'My landlord,' he said, making it sound like *bloodsucker*.

'Acts like he's best mates with you, but it doesn't stop the bastard putting the rent up every two minutes.' He glanced behind him into the interior of the house. 'And don't bother trying to get hold of him when something needs to be fixed . . .'

It was clear the neighbour had got onto a favourite gripe. He'd have been happy to bend Gulliver's ear for as long as he stood there, rolling out complaints about broken boilers in the middle of winter and missing roof tiles not replaced for months on end while the heavens opened day after day.

Gulliver cut him off as a potential avenue of opportunity opened up in the midst of the griping.

'Does McIntyre own his house or rent?'

The question put another dirty look on the neighbour's face.

'Everybody rents around here. They're all buy-to-let properties. Rich bastards living up in London bought a lot of them, sent the prices through the roof. Ordinary working people can't afford them anymore.'

Gulliver was getting the impression that if he was McIntyre, he'd be the one avoiding his neighbour, not the other way around. He was ten seconds away from the neighbour telling him it was a disgrace the way the government gave all the houses to immigrants and asylum seekers.

'Have you got the same landlord?'

It seemed everything Gulliver said put the neighbour in a worse mood.

'Yeah. He owns half the bloody street. I think his brother owns the other half.'

'If I could take his name and number, sir.'

'Singh, like all the rest of them.' He pulled his phone out of the back pocket of his jeans, scrolled through his contacts all the way to the end, smiling to himself as he did so.

'Got him under *T* for *thieving bastard*,' he said, then reeled off the number. 'I wouldn't tell him you're police, if I was you. He'll disappear faster than McIntyre, scared you're going to arrest him for being a slum landlord.' He leaned in, lowered his voice. 'I heard he runs a brothel out of one of his houses . . .' His hand flew to his mouth, mock horror in his eyes. '*Oops!* Mustn't say that in front of you lot. You'll arrest me for a hate crime.'

Arrest you for being a moron, more like, Gulliver thought, leaving the neighbour to nurse his seething resentments alone.

29

'I DO BELIEVE YOU'RE ASHAMED OF ME, MAX,' SIOBHAN ANGEL declared, the harshness of her Belfast accent making the accusation sound even more heinous.

He pinched his finger and thumb together.

'Maybe a little.'

She swiped at his head, a blow he easily sidestepped.

'Cheeky monkey!'

'Where would you like to go?'

'Bingo?'

He knew she was getting her own back for his cheekiness, but he worked his little finger into his ear as if dislodging a lump of wax just the same.

'Did you say the pub?'

'You're as bad as himself.'

Her quintessentially Irish use of the pronoun *himself* in relation to his father in his role as the head of the household distracted him momentarily, diverted him from asking her how she knew the first thing about her estranged husband. He didn't want to think about how long she'd been staying with him, but she'd made no attempt to meet with his father in all that time, the alleged reason for her visit. At times, he worried she never would.

'That's settled then,' he said. 'I'll drop you at bingo, have a couple of beers myself, then pick you up again.'

'Did I say you're as bad as himself?'

He fed his cat, Leonard, while she went upstairs to change into something presentable. If it was up to his mother, the cat wouldn't get fed at all, left to fend for itself catching mice and shrews. Unlike himself, who she was fattening like a goose coming up to Christmas.

'Ever mindful of last orders,' he called up the stairs when she still wasn't down ten minutes later.

'I don't want you to be ashamed of me,' drifted back down.

'Here's a good tip,' he said, when at last she came down the stairs. 'If you're planning on nagging me to take you out when I get home from work, get ready in advance.'

This time her aim was better—or he was slower—catching him around the back of the head.

'Where would you like to go?' he asked her.

'The pub you always go to in order to put off coming home. I want to see what's so bloody great about it.'

He groaned to himself, already seeing where the conversation would go. It was where he'd been when Virgil Balan made his offer, where he'd met Stuart Beckford when he told him about it. He couldn't see a way how it wasn't going to crop up again tonight. The only thing he felt confident about was that they wouldn't sit at the same table, his mother refusing to sit outside like second-class citizens not allowed inside.

'This is nice,' she said, as they stepped inside The Jolly Sailor ten minutes later. 'I can see why you like it. How far was that? About four miles?'

'Something like that.'

She beamed at him.

'It'll only cost a couple of pounds in a taxi. I'll be able to meet you here on your way home from work now I know where it is.'

As often happened with Kincade, he couldn't have said whether she was serious or not to save his life. Nor did she break into a wide smile, *only kidding*, maybe give his cheek a motherly pinch.

'I'll have a glass of Guinness,' she said, sending him to the bar.

He was tempted to say he wasn't going to order it for her in a bucket or a paper bag. The phrase always made him smile, the way the Irish said *glass* when they meant *half pint*, as if pint glasses weren't also made of it.

'A bit older than the last one you brought in here,' the barman said with a smile and a glance at Siobhan as he pulled Angel's pint.

Angel wasn't surprised that he'd noticed. The last time was when he'd brought Kincade, and people tended to remember her.

'She's my mother, actually.'

'And there was me thinking she was your latest lady friend.'

Angel chose not to pass comment on the barman's eyesight, carried the drinks back to their table. He hadn't even got his arse properly on the chair before Siobhan started on him.

'What's on your mind, Max? And don't say nothing, or it's only work. I am your mother, remember.'

'Not according to the barman. He thinks you're my new girlfriend.'

Siobhan's head snapped around, caught the barman—who was about the same age—smiling back at her.

Please God, no, Angel prayed silently. *What have I done?*

'What a nice man,' Siobhan said, preening.

Angel wished they could get back to her giving him the third degree. Before that, he needed to discourage his mother, now touching her hair self-consciously.

'He's ex-Army.'

Siobhan looked again, longer this time before giving her verdict.

'He is not.'

'How do you know?'

'He hasn't got a ridiculous moustache like your father has, for one. God, how I hated that. It was like kissing a toilet brush.'

'I wouldn't know. I've never kissed a toilet brush.'

'Or a man with a moustache, I hope.'

'I'd kiss the toilet brush first.'

She nodded, satisfied, and he knew his reprieve was over.

'You were about to tell me what's on your mind, Max.' She wagged her finger at him, *you naughty boy, you*. 'Before you sidetracked me.'

He considered saying he didn't want to talk about it. That had the added benefit of being the truth. Except she'd wear him down in the end. Like if you're about to be waterboarded, you might as well tell them what they want to know, avoid all the unpleasantness.

'On the last major case I worked, I met an inspector in the Romanian Police called Virgil Balan.'

He paused, let the implications of the word *Romanian* sink in. Which they did, a too-late look of regret and horror colonising her face at what she'd pushed him into.

'Same nationality as the driver who killed Claire.'

'Yeah.' He leaned to the side, pointed towards the back door that led down to the River Hamble. 'I was sitting out there when he called me and offered to find him for me . . .'

He took her through the whole story, the way Balan had dug into his past, learned about Claire's death, and the ambiguous offer he'd made.

'You don't know whether it's official or not?' Siobhan said.

'No. And I was sitting at that same table when I told Stu Beckford about it a few days ago. He said he needed to think about it.'

'I'm not surprised.'

'He sent me a text today—'

'*A text?* I'd have expected better of him. *A text?* He should've called you at the very least.'

Angel shrugged, no room for recriminations in his mind or heart.

'Well, he didn't.'

'What did he say?' She went to take a sip of Guinness, not realising the glass was already empty. 'Get me another one of these, will you? I feel like I need a whiskey chaser to go with it.' He was halfway to the bar when she called after him. 'Forget the chaser.'

There were a number of bar staff waiting to serve customers as Angel approached the bar. The same barman who'd served him the first round elbowed the others out of the way in his haste to get to Angel first.

'Hope you don't mind me asking, but is your mother—'

'She's currently separated from my father.' Giving himself a mental pat on the back for the word *currently*, with its implications that the situation was up in the air. 'I don't know how long it's going to last.'

The barman nodded his understanding, repeated himself that he hoped Angel wasn't offended by him asking.

'Not at all,' Angel assured him, then carried the drinks back.

Siobhan glared at him.

'I said no chaser.'

'It's on the barman. He heard you yelling across the bar—'

'I was not *yelling*. And even if I was, I said *no* chaser.'

'Like I said, he's ex-Army. All those gunshots have made him deaf. Your accent doesn't help, either.'

Siobhan looked at him like she hoped for his sake there really wasn't a God, because he was going to pay dearly for his many sins if there was.

'I'm waiting, Max.'

Angel felt the same trepidation he'd felt when he'd read the text, the feeling of stepping blindly into something that led he knew not where.

'Stu said if the decision was his alone, he'd tell Balan to go ahead. Find Florescu. Then we decide what to do about it.'

She went to put her hand on his arm, thought better of it. Even so, she stayed leaning forward, not relinquishing all physical closeness.

'And what do *you* want to do?'

Do I look like a man who knows his own mind and heart?

'I'm going to tell Balan to go ahead.'

'You didn't answer the question.'

'I know I didn't. And if I ever have an answer myself, you'll be the first to know. We've got one abstention and one thumbs-up, so it's game on.'

'Stuart won't like it. He'll feel you've dumped the whole decision on him.'

'I know he will. That's why I'll tell him I'm with him all the way.' He pointed his finger at her. 'You asked me what I want to do. I answered that honestly. I'll tell Stu we're going ahead and he won't even think to ask me if that's what I want.'

'Because he's a man. And men only do what they want to do.'

It wasn't a road he wanted to go down, and certainly not with his mother.

'If you like.'

She leaned back in her chair, studied him a long time, this

child she'd brought into the world who'd turned into a man she only half understood.

He shook his head at her, a warning in his voice.

'Don't ask.'

'I wasn't going to.'

Now he wagged his finger at her.

'I used to be a priest, remember—'

'I wish you still were.'

'—so I'm qualified to tell you lying's a sin.'

It didn't matter whether she was lying or not. The question was in the air between them, words unnecessary.

What will you do if it's unofficial, and you have the fate of the man responsible for killing your wife in your hands?

30

Despite Lucas McIntyre's neighbour's advice, Gulliver informed the landlord, Mr Singh, of his status as a police detective. Mr Singh was happy to assist, clearly not nervous about being prosecuted for the slums and brothels and crack dens the neighbour accused him of owning. By the end of the short, productive call, Gulliver had the contact details for Lucas McIntyre's parents. They lived in Berwick-on-Tweed on the Scottish border, their details taken by Mr Singh as part of the vetting process when their son first became one of his tenants.

There was no guarantee McIntyre had scuttled back home to his parents, but Berwick sounded like a safe bet if you were worried about who might be looking for you three hundred and fifty miles away on the south coast of England.

'Don't even think about it,' Angel said, when Gulliver and Jardine floated the idea of a trip up North to interview him. 'Did you speak to his parents to find out if he's even there?'

'I did,' Jardine said.

'She thought they'd be more likely to open up to someone who sounds like they come from vaguely up that way,' Gulliver added. 'Or words to that effect.'

'Someone who isn't a posh Southern twat,' Jardine confirmed happily.

'And?' Angel said, wondering how the pair of them ever got any work done.

'I had a nice chat with his mam,' Jardine said. 'And she let it slip that Lucas was back home, but he'd told her not to tell anybody.'

Angel groaned to himself as he imagined the conversation, Jardine's Geordie accent competing with Mrs McIntyre's Scottish one.

'I don't even want to think about what you said to her.'

'Exactly,' Gulliver chipped in. 'She might sound like she's from that neck of the woods, but it doesn't stop her from being devious and tricking the poor old lady into shopping her son.'

Kincade had been listening to the three-way conversation with one ear, and couldn't help joining in.

'I've got a question.' Looking at Gulliver and Jardine. 'If the two of you bicker this much in a two-minute discussion, how on earth do you think you'd survive a seven-hundred-mile round-trip car journey without killing each other?'

It appeared Gulliver and Jardine had prepared for just such an objection.

'We'd fly,' Jardine said.

'Would you now?' Angel, of course. 'At your own expense?'

That put a dent in the two DCs' enthusiasm.

'What if we split the journey, stay with me mam?' Jardine said, hopefully.

Gulliver was right on it. Sounding as if she'd suggested spending the night in the toilets in a motorway service station somewhere in the Midlands.

'No way. I'm not staying in a house where everyone calls everyone else *Pet*.'

Angel held up his hand before Jardine responded.

'Nobody's going anywhere. Not by car, or plane.' He made shooing motions at them towards the door. 'I'll deal with it.'

They looked as if they wanted to stay. See how he planned to persuade paranoid Lucas McIntyre to speak to them, short of arranging for the locals to break down his parents' door at six in the morning. They were out of luck. He kept on shooing until they were gone.

Kincade was now giving him her full attention, also keen to see what he would do.

'I'm going to get Fiona Baldwin to do it for me,' he told her, pulling out his phone. Then, when Fiona answered, 'You sound surprised to hear from me, Ms Baldwin.'

'It is a bit of a surprise, yes.'

And not a pleasant one, he thought. Already, he heard the realisation creeping into her voice that she'd made a big mistake.

'I don't know why. You phoned Lucas McIntyre after we spoke to you, told him you'd given us his number. He immediately panicked, shut down his blog and buggered off back to his parents' house at the other end of the country. You know what he's like. You went to great lengths to stress how paranoid he is. You must have known what would happen if you told him we were looking for him. Surely you would expect me to call when it did happen.'

'Sorry, I wasn't thinking. It was a stupid thing to do.'

'Luckily for both of us, stupidity isn't yet a crime. But you have to ask yourself what happens next. Whoever killed your ex-husband will have kept an eye on the blog afterwards. To see if it was only your husband behind it, or whether there are any other potential threats. As you pointed out, Lucas has made very sure his name doesn't appear anywhere. If I was the killer, I'd be asking myself who else might be involved? *Is it the woman Harry Callaghan was stalking before I killed him?* And when he sees that the blog has been taken down, he'll be asking himself why. Maybe too many people are getting interested.' He paused to let the implications sink in, a harder edge entering his voice. 'I wouldn't want to be you when the madman who's already killed your ex-husband and Harry Callaghan starts asking himself those questions. Maybe you should go and stay with your own parents.'

'I wish I could. They're both dead.'

He was happy to let his silence answer for him.

Looks like you might be seeing them sooner than you thought.

He felt as if he'd laid it on heavily enough. Her continued silence suggested not.

'It was a big step forward when you mentioned Lucas, alerted us to the existence of the man most likely to know who your ex-husband was investigating. We're grateful for that. Then you did something that almost guaranteed we can't speak to him. We're back at square one. I'm thinking about putting out an appeal for witnesses. Get everybody talking about it. The killer's going to love that. He won't be able to clear those decks fast enough.'

He got the impression she had something unpleasant on her top lip when she replied.

'You've made your point, Inspector. I'll call Lucas again, ask him to call you.'

'*Ask?* If I was in your position, Ms Baldwin, I'd be *telling* him at the very least. *Pleading* with him. Better still, going up to Berwick myself and kicking his sorry arse all the way back here.'

'Leave it with me.'

'And if you have any trouble persuading him, ask him how long he thinks running home to mummy and daddy will keep him out of the hands of all those clandestine government agencies he's obsessed about. If half of what he believes is true, they already know what his mother cooked him for breakfast. His only chance is to help us. Otherwise, it's just a matter of time.' He paused, then gave her an added incentive. 'For both of you.'

Lucas McIntyre called back within the hour. He barely gave Angel a chance to say *hello* before an aggressive torrent came down the line.

'I can tell you before we start that if you come out with any of the threats you made to Fiona, I'll hang up.'

Facts, Mr McIntyre, not threats, Angel thought, and softened it.

'I'm sorry if my remarks came across like that. It wasn't my intention to threaten or scare her.'

He caught sight of Kincade at her desk, pulling a face at him.

Who are you kidding?

Seemed McIntyre felt the same way, spitting words down the line.

'Not fucking much you bloody didn't.'

'Let me get something straight with you, Mr McIntyre. If you continue to be aggressive and abusive, I'm the one who'll end this conversation. Then I'll call my colleagues in the Northumbria Police, have them arrest you and stick you in a cell until I find the time to come up there and interview you. And believe me, I'm a very busy man. Getting busier by the minute when people like you and Fiona Baldwin waste my time and make my job twice as difficult. Are we clear?'

An unintelligible grudging sound came down the line.

'Good. Now I want to give you some advice. I didn't threaten Ms Baldwin. All I did was present the facts in an uncompromising light. Which is exactly how you should view them. I'm aware of your attitudes towards the establishment and its agencies, but just because you think I'm throwing my weight around, scaring innocent citizens to get my own way, that doesn't mean what I said isn't true. You'll be the one who ends up dead if you ignore those facts, not me.'

Kincade had now stood up, giving a silent round of applause from behind her desk. He dipped his head at her, went back to McIntyre.

'I've only got one question for you. What was Russell Baldwin working on when he was killed?'

'You're admitting it? It wasn't an accident?'

'What was he working on, Mr McIntyre?'

'I don't know—'

'*Jesus Christ!* Are you stupid? Have you listened to a word I've said? There's a man out there who will kill you if he gets the chance.'

'And if you give me a chance to bloody finish, I'll tell you what I know.'

Angel bit down hard to stop himself from yelling at McIntyre that he shouldn't start a sentence with *I don't know* if he did know something.

'You can believe me or not and threaten to arrest me again,' McIntyre said, 'but I don't know all the details. I do know he met a young woman called Evie St. James—'

'The woman whose comments you removed from your blog?'

'Yes, her. Russell met her a couple of times, but he didn't tell me what it was about. She approached him because of the blog. Because he had a reputation for going after dirty politicians, refusing to be intimidated. But if he'd given me chapter and verse every time some nutter approached him, we'd never have got anything done.'

'The fact that he met her twice suggests she wasn't a garden-variety nutter.'

'Exactly. And he would've told me more about it after that second meeting if he'd got the chance.'

DS Ellis Hudson's words were immediately in Angel's mind. He'd told Angel that Harry Callaghan hadn't been drinking when he hit Russell Baldwin, but that Baldwin had alcohol in his blood.

'He had lunch with her on the day he was killed.'

'Yeah. Let's hope they'd already gone their separate ways and she didn't have to watch him get flattened.'

Amen to that, Angel thought. *We're going to have a hard enough job getting her to talk to us as it is.*

'Do you have contact details for her?'

McIntyre left a deliberate pause. Angel guessed it was to make a point.

I thought you had a dossier on everyone in the country.

Except he was wrong. It was embarrassment at what he was about to say, given his and Baldwin's obsession with invasions of privacy.

'Not as such, as in a phone number. But we'll have the email address she used to post comments.' He cleared his throat. 'And we have website analytics software that gives us visitor data. It includes the visitor's IP address.'

It wasn't necessary to know what other data the software provided, but Angel was sick of being viewed as a modern-day Nazi by people like McIntyre. He allowed himself a minute to enjoy making McIntyre squirm.

'What other data does it provide?'

'Is that relevant?'

'I won't know until you tell me.'

McIntyre cleared his throat again, then spoke at twice normal speed.

'The pages a visitor has looked at, the time spent on each page, links clicked—'

'If I could interrupt you there, Mr McIntyre? You're basically saying it tells you absolutely everything a visitor does from the moment they enter your site until they leave again?'

'That's right.'

Now Angel left a long pause, as if considering the implications for his investigation.

'That's very interesting. I understand now why you have such concerns about digital privacy. I'm assuming you need a licence to install it?'

'No.' His voice was so quiet Angel almost asked him to repeat it.

'I bet it's expensive.'

'No.'

'Don't tell me there's a free version?'

'Yeah. If you've only got one site.'

'And how many have you got?'

It took a long time for McIntyre to get out a single three-letter word.

'One.'

Angel left a shorter pause this time, just long enough for McIntyre to hear his unspoken words.

And we're the ones violating people's privacy?

'As far as our investigation goes, the email address and IP address will be sufficient to be going on with.'

It wasn't ideal, contributing an added delay—especially if it turned out to be a Gmail account—but it was better than nothing. Angel moved on, to things that were likely to result in precisely nothing.

'Do you have any idea what it was about?'

'I just told you I haven't. Politicians and all the rest of them get away with so much shit, it could be anything. It might be sex, given she's a woman, but equally, it might not.'

'Did he keep notes?' He immediately answered his own question. 'On the thumb drive on his keyring.'

'Yeah. He wouldn't keep details of contacts and meetings on his laptop. That'd be like painting a target on someone's back. You might think we're paranoid about invasion of privacy, but the view from your end—'

'It's not *my* end, Mr McIntyre.' A picture of Douglas Farebrother in his mind as he said it.

There was a pause that Angel had no problem deciphering.

You're all the same to me.

'The view of the establishment is that people like Russell who persist in trying to expose the truth are not entitled to any privacy,' McIntyre said, as if explaining Nazi ideology to an alien. 'Even if they're not monitoring everybody, they were sure as hell watching Russell like a hawk.'

He should've thought about that before he painted a target on his own back, Angel thought as he ended the call.

Lucas McIntyre texted Angel Evie St. James' email address and IP address within five minutes of ending the call. As Angel feared, Evie was one of the 1.8 billion people worldwide—more than twenty per cent of the world's population—who use Gmail as their email client. With almost fifty percent of Gmail users aged between eighteen and thirty-four, it had been even more likely, given that Evie's email address, *evie_st.james96*, suggested she was currently twenty-eight years old.

It wasn't an insurmountable problem, more of a royal pain in the arse. Google Ireland, responsible for user accounts across Europe, was happy to respond to official enquiries, both law enforcement and other government agencies. It required a warrant, which wasn't a problem. Google's sense of its own importance could be. They would review the request and then release limited information as they saw fit. The ISP was likely to be a better bet, but also involved a delay.

'Just send her an email,' Kincade said, when he told her.

'If she went to Baldwin with her concerns instead of coming to us, it suggests she thinks we're part of the problem. I don't want to spook her.'

'She's spooked already. From the moment she tried to get in touch with Baldwin again and discovered he'd been killed five minutes after he left her. If she has the ability to disappear, like Véronique Dubois did buggering off back to France, she'll be long gone already. Ordinary people don't have the ability to disappear off the grid. She's got her head down somewhere hoping it'll all go away. When she realises it won't, she'll face facts.'

He cocked his head at her.

'Where did all that come from?'

'Good question. But I don't think you'll spook her.'

That was when he had a mini-epiphany, a better way forward presenting itself.

'You're right, I won't spook her. Because I'm not going to email her—'

'I am?'

'Exactly. An email from another woman is even less likely to scare her off.'

'I was about to suggest it myself.'

'Of course you were.'

He left her to it, concentrated on getting the paperwork ready to apply for the physical address associated with Evie's IP address. Kincade interrupted him a couple of minutes later.

'You want to read it before I send it?'

That didn't take long, he thought, getting up, and going over to her desk, telling himself not to pick unnecessary holes in what she'd written.

We're investigating the death of Russell Baldwin. Fiona Baldwin gave us your name and details. We understand you met Russell for lunch on the day he died. We're keen to talk to you since you were one of the last people to speak to him before he died. Please call Southampton Central police station and ask for DS Catalina Kincade.

He mentally ticked off the points in its favour as he read.

No mention of Harry Callaghan's death and the escalating problem it implied.

Bending the truth saying that Fiona Baldwin was their source—another woman close to Baldwin, a name she would recognise.

Using Baldwin's first name on the second occasion.

The mention of the lunch with the implication that they knew most of it already.

'If she's spooked by that, we might as well give up on ever talking to her,' he said. 'Send it.'

She couldn't help laughing after she'd done so, a nervous sound, and at herself.

'I almost feel guilty. She's got a hell of a shock coming if she gets in touch. Thank God, it'll be your job to dump all of that on her.'

31

Liam Callaghan was going stir crazy.

He didn't like to admit it, but the second visit from the two detectives had put the wind up him. Made him feel as if he was walking around with a target on his back—one that he'd painted himself. He felt pretty stupid about that.

However, time is the great healer, in more ways than one. A soothing balm applied to the open wound of his grief. And a sedative to alleviate the rising panic that gripped him as the detectives spelled out the sequence of events that ended with three bullets in Harry's back.

He almost crapped himself when they showed him the video the crazy bitch female cop took when she chased a Range Rover down the street—the same vehicle Harry made his trip out to the New Forest in when he went to meet his maker.

He'd kept an eye out ever since, but he hadn't seen it again. And with every hour that passed without a man in a ski mask kicking down his door and pumping a full magazine of 9mm shells into him as he watched TV or made himself a cup of tea, the fear and panic receded further, the luminous target on his back dimming until it was no longer visible, a memory of something that hadn't been there in the first place.

And as the panic moved out, the restlessness moved in. He meant what he'd told the cops—he wasn't going to stick his nose into a psychopath's business anymore. He hadn't said it simply to keep them happy, get rid of them. Much as he'd like to make Harry's killer rue the day he was born, it wasn't going to happen.

That didn't mean he wanted to sit around the house doing nothing for the rest of his life. He was convinced if he cocked his ear towards the garden shed he could hear his bike calling to him.

Ride me.

Physical exercise, that's what he needed. The catharsis of physical exhaustion.

He took the stairs up two at a time, changed into his cycling gear. Then went to the bedroom window and peered out in case the Range Rover had returned in the time it took him to pull on his brightly-coloured Spandex top and shorts.

It hadn't.

Five minutes later, Liam was back in the saddle, working hard to get a burn going in his thighs, fill his lungs with oxygen all the way down to the bottom.

As Angel had said to Finch, Liam had swum a complete lap of the goldfish bowl. And the world was now a very different place.

THE MAN THEY CALLED MAGGOT STARTED THE BIG PICKUP'S ENGINE as soon as he saw Callaghan wheel his bike down the path and onto the street. He'd grown to like the vehicle as he sat watching Callaghan's house. It made him feel like a builder or a carpenter. Made him ask himself why he hadn't chosen a job like that himself. Something that left a man with a sense of achievement at the end of the day as he stood back and admired the result of his honest day's work.

Not a trail of ruined lives and worse of the sort Maggot left behind, a legacy of misery and pain. Something to be ashamed of, to make a man feel dirty.

Which is how he felt now.

How he'd felt ever since he first found himself under Seymour Grey's greasy thumb, a single stupid mistake that left him bound to him, his own liberty in the hands of that venal, self-serving parasite for as long as Grey required protection from himself, from the shitstorms his many vices spawned.

Because Maggot knew it wouldn't end with Liam Callaghan lying dead in a ditch with a tangle of twisted metal beneath him, blood staining the garish Spandex he wore so proudly like he'd just won the Tour de Bloody France.

No, there would be more unreasonable demands. More threats that Maggot would go down with him should Seymour Grey ever be called upon to account for his myriad sins.

Not for the first time, he cursed himself for his weakness. He should've accepted responsibility for his crimes at the time, suffered the consequences, moved on. Not grasped at the lifeline Grey threw him, then allowed the degenerate to draw him, little-by-little, ever deeper into his world of immorality and corruption.

It was too late now.

It had been too late for a long time.

He watched Callaghan swing his leg over his bike and adjust the helmet on his head, smiling grimly to himself. *How much protection do you think that's going to provide you?* Then he put the big truck into gear and pulled out into the road to follow the dead man cycling.

At least the guy liked a nice country ride, that was one thing Maggot could give him. If your bones have to break anywhere, your internal organs rupture and your blood spill warm and free, better that it's in the bucolic beauty of the English countryside than a filthy alley, the sounds of the birds in your ears as you slip away, not sub-human, misogynistic rap music that makes you glad you'll soon be dead pumping out of an inconsiderate prick's open window.

Maybe he'd wait until Callaghan was on the way home. Let him fill his lungs with the freshness of the country air a little longer, remind himself how good it was to be alive.

Until he wasn't.

It was the least Maggot could do.

Evie St. James wasn't getting a lot of sense out of her sister.

She'd come to Orla's grave as soon as she received the email out of the blue from DS Catalina Kincade. Her first reaction had been blind panic, her mind immediately blank before it was filled to overflowing with the last words Russell Baldwin had spoken to her.

These are dangerous people, Evie. Be very careful about who you talk to about what you've just told me.

At the time, she'd thought he was overreacting. Except that was why she'd gone to him in the first place. Because of his paranoia, the way he saw conspiracies everywhere. In a way, it was a compliment. Proof that he'd taken her story seriously.

She sagged at the knees as the memory of how she'd felt when he was proved right hit her. She'd been physically sick, as if she'd watched him turned into roadkill in front of her eyes.

And then the guilt had set in, the self-recrimination.

She couldn't believe how stupid, how naive she'd been—but that was with the benefit of hindsight, of course. The fact was, by going to Baldwin, she was responsible for his death. They must have been watching her ever since she accosted Seymour Grey in the street, accused him in public. Following her. Seeing who she talked to. And when she talked to Baldwin, a man who was already a thorn in the side of venal and immoral men like Seymour Grey, Baldwin's days were numbered.

Because this was a lot more serious than a few MPs fiddling expenses or making lewd suggestions to female colleagues at the Christmas party.

The fact that Baldwin's death wasn't quickly followed by her own only increased her guilt. They hadn't killed her precisely because she accosted Seymour Grey in the street, made a fuss in public. It would've been too suspicious if she'd had a supposed fatal accident shortly thereafter. They'd killed Baldwin instead. Killed two birds with one stone. Destroyed her chances of getting her story in front of a wider audience, if Baldwin's death hadn't already put the fear of God up her. Which it had.

And that's how it would've remained. Her scuttling back to her hidey-hole with her tail between her legs. Thankful to be alive, and certainly not about to put her head above the parapet ever again.

Then the email arrived from DS Catalina Kincade.

Shattered what little peace of mind she'd regained. Sentenced her to a night of relentless terror as every irrational fear she'd ever known waited its turn at the bottom of her bed to make its case, claim her for its own.

Nor was Orla any help in deciding what to do—however much Evie glared at the mound of still-fresh earth of her sister's grave.

It was easy enough to make a rational argument.

If they'd decided scaring her off wasn't sufficient, that it was necessary to permanently silence her, would they want her to contact a police station, ask to speak to a serving officer? The contact would be on record. Even poor dead Russell Baldwin hadn't thought every last police officer was corrupt, their noses deep in the trough.

But was she prepared to risk her life on a rational argument? What if there was an equally-rational counter argument?

She had her phone in her hand as she stood beside Orla's grave. It had been there for the past agonising half hour already, the jumbled collection of random thoughts that passed for her mind no closer to being made up.

Then it came to her in a sickening epiphany, a flash of uncompromising clarity.

If they were determined to kill her, it was only a matter of time before they were successful. As Russell Baldwin told her in his self-fulfilling warning, *these are dangerous people*. She wasn't so naive as to think his death was the first. Nor would it be the last.

She glanced around the cemetery, a winged angel made of weathered stone standing guard over one of the older graves catching her eye. That's what she needed. A guardian angel. Any kind of angel would do.

Who knows, maybe it was only a phone call away?

She'd already entered the number given for DS Catalina Kincade into her phone. Her finger hovered over the green *call* button for what felt like a lifetime, but still she couldn't bring herself to make the call as the counter arguments fought a desperate rearguard action. What if they were prepared to leave her alone unless she proved to them she was a threat? Responding to an email from a police officer, genuine or otherwise, might convince them that she was.

Her phone went back in her bag. She was angry at herself for being so weak, so indecisive. And as for dead Orla? She was no bloody use at all.

32

Angel had been suffering from a vague sense of trepidation ever since he interviewed Ralph Stone, the witness who'd seen the impact when Harry Callaghan's skip lorry sent Russell Baldwin to the big press room in the sky.

It wasn't anything Stone said, even if Angel felt the way he'd smacked his fist into his open palm as he described the moment of impact had been gratuitously graphic. It was what happened when he got back that worried him—Jack Bevan's immediate assumption that he'd returned from a clandestine meeting with Stuart Beckford. It was only a matter of time before an embellished version of the meeting that never happened started circulating.

In a similar vein, he felt increasingly disloyal to Kincade for not telling her about Beckford's willingness to give Virgil Balan the green light. A decision that would bring Beckford and himself closer together, although not necessarily in a good way.

For his own sanity, he needed to get out ahead of it.

'Stuart Beckford got back to me.'

His own determination to be honest with her was reflected

in her eyes when she looked his way. He wasn't expecting the way it manifested itself.

'I'm actually trying to pretend he doesn't exist.'

'I get the feeling that's not working too well for you.'

'You get the feeling right.'

'Are you interested in his decision?'

'Trying not to be. But I can't stop you telling me, if that's what you want to do.'

The conversation felt as if it could go round and round in circles for as long as they wanted to prolong it. For him, that was about thirty seconds ago.

'He wants to go ahead.'

'And what about you?'

'I'm going to go along with it.'

She glanced at the door, as if wishing they'd closed it before starting the conversation.

'Is that wise?'

He shrugged, the noncommittal gesture capturing his feelings perfectly.

'I'll let you know as soon as I know myself. But look on the bright side. If Balan's offer is unofficial, me and Stu could both end up sacked or in prison. Then you definitely won't have to worry about him because you'll be moving into my role.'

'Has it occurred to you I might not want your role?'

He scrunched his face at her, the confusion reflected in his voice.

'What happened to the woman who'd already been given the unofficial thumbs-up on DCI?'

The way she hesitated rang immediate alarm bells. Had recent events forced her to take a long, hard look at her life? Ask herself whether it was worth it? Maybe consider resigning, spending more time with her girls to compensate for the time she'd lost?

It wasn't a level of honesty he was prepared for. As it happened, he was wrong. And he certainly wasn't prepared for what she did say.

'You missed the point. Maybe I don't want it because I want you still in it. Maybe I like working with you.' She paused, then grinned self-consciously at him. 'However ridiculous that sounds.'

He didn't know what to say.

Humour felt inappropriate. Offer to recommend a good psychiatrist, or strong drugs. Instead, he took it as a challenge to go one better on the honesty front.

'Stu's decision to go ahead raises serious doubts in my mind about whether he's ready to come back, or is ever likely to be.' Now, he glanced at the open door, also wishing one of them had closed it. 'What I do know is if I'd told Finch or the Super about Balan's approach—'

'As you should've done.'

He gave a firm nod.

'As I should've done, and then told them what Stu said, he could forget any ideas about ever coming back.'

'Sounds like you've got the future of his career in your hands.'

He pointed at her own hands, currently clasped behind the back of her head.

'Yours too, now.'

'Except then you'd be out, as well.'

'And you'd get my job which you don't want.'

Again, they could've got into an endless loop. This time, she put an end to it.

'Thank you for telling me that.'

Her mouthed twitched as if she was about to say more, before she decided against it.

'Say it,' he said.

She hesitated again, then came out with it.

'What would you say if Finch said she thought it was time for Beckford to come back, then asked you what you think?'

'Let me think about it.'

'Is that what you'd say to her, or you're saying it to me now?'

'Both. And I've just had a great idea. You're the one who benefits from him not coming back. You can think of something for me to tell her.'

She chose not to reply, glancing at her watch instead. He knew what was coming, tried to head it off.

'Evie St. James still hasn't responded to your email?'

She gave him a look that was easy to interpret. She knew that he knew what she'd been about to say.

'*No*. I was going to ask if you fancied a quick beer.'

She didn't give him time to work a look of regret onto his face before shaking her head at him, her voice filled with resignation.

'I simply do not believe it. A prior engagement with Doctor Death? *Again*.'

'Actually, no.'

She narrowed her eyes at him as if she'd heard it all before. Like when her girls said they'd tidied their rooms.

'Really? Who's the lucky girl?'

'Her son.'

It took her a moment to process the unexpected information.

'Her son?'

'That's right. Oliver.'

'I bet he's a chip off the old sharpened wooden stake, eh?'

'I wouldn't know. I haven't met him before.'

So far, her mind had worked along its usual lines, concentrating on likening Durand to a vampire or one of the undead. It now clicked that they weren't talking about Durand herself.

'Why are you meeting him? Don't tell me he's thinking of becoming a priest? He wants to ask what it's like being celibate for years on end? Possibly until you die. If you play by the rules, of course.'

He made a rolling motion with his hand, *keep it coming*. Except she'd already grown bored with it. He raised an eyebrow at her, *finished now?* She nodded, *for the time being*.

'He's in his final year of medical school,' he said. 'He's thinking of becoming an Army surgeon.'

'Bet Doctor Death isn't happy about that.'

'She's not, no.'

'And she wants you to put him off?'

'She just wants me to talk to him.'

'What about his father?' Her face compacted as she saw an immediate problem. 'She doesn't want to wait until the full moon.'

He worked hard at keeping the smile off his face, but her creativity when insulting Durand was something to see.

'As far as Oliver's father is concerned, anything that pisses Isabel off is fine by him.'

'Even if their son ends up dead?'

'Think Elliot.'

Her estranged husband's name put the mandatory sour look on her face, but she couldn't disagree.

'You've got a point. Although I'm not sure even Elliot would see the girls harmed just to spite me. It's close, but not quite that bad. *Yet*. What are you planning on saying to Doctor Death Junior?'

He hadn't given it a lot of thought. In part, because he'd been too busy, but also because he knew the discussion was likely to be highly fluid. Time spent formulating what he would say in advance was most likely time wasted.

She didn't give him time to think about it now, before answering her own question.

'If it was me thinking of going into the Army, the first thing I'd ask is why you came out.'

'And if he asks, I'll tell him.'

'Really? What if he tells his mum?'

'She already knows.'

Kincade was struck dumb, as he'd known she would be. Her jaw dropped in an unflattering manner, her mouth flapping soundlessly, then an incredulous echo.

'She already knows?'

'Yep. She's the only person at work I've told.'

He was relieved when she shied away from making a facetious reference to pillow talk, as she would have done had the topic been anything less intensely personal.

'Not even . . .?'

He shook his head firmly.

'Not even Stu Beckford.'

They held each other's gaze for a long while. He, wondering if she'd ask. She, wondering if he'd volunteer. Which he did, before they both turned to stone.

'I'm happy to tell you. If you're interested, that is.' Sounding as if he'd offered to show her his holiday snaps.

She ran her eyes quickly over her desk. Trying to find something heavy with sharp corners to throw at his head as he looked expectantly at her. She glanced at her watch when she couldn't find anything suitable.

'I can spare you a few minutes . . .'

33

Liam Callaghan stayed out longer and later than he'd planned to. He'd taken the same route as on the previous occasion, planning to cycle to Romsey and back, a round trip of twenty miles.

Except two things happened when he got to Romsey. Two things that changed the course of his life. First, he felt as if he'd barely gone any further than the end of his road. He guessed it was the pent-up angst of the past days fuelling his legs and lungs. If he turned around and went directly home now, he'd be every bit as restless as when he set off.

Second, was the disappointing realisation that the catharsis of physical exertion wasn't such a cure-all for his worries as he'd hoped it would be. Luckily, the answer was obvious.

Add alcohol.

Decision made, he got back in the saddle and headed towards the village of West Wellow, four miles west of Romsey, and home to The Rockingham Arms.

Liam always felt self-conscious in his garish skin-tight Spandex and cycling cleats if he clip-clopped into a town-centre pub, but at a country pub where he could sit outside the roles were reversed. He felt superior, looking down on the flabby car drivers who hadn't worked up an honest sweat to earn their beer.

And although it was technically possible to lose your driving licence for being drunk on a bicycle, you'd have to do something exceptionally stupid or encounter a particularly miserable bastard of a traffic cop.

The first pint barely touched the sides. The second went down more slowly. By the end of it he was starting to relax, rolling the rhyme *mellow in West Wellow* around his mouth as he sat in the modest front garden, his pride and joy propped against the picket fence. The third pint he took slower still, savouring it, knowing it was the last one before he headed home.

Sadly, he also knew that as soon as he stepped through his front door, the catharsis the ride and alcohol had produced would melt away. His home was no longer a sanctuary, but a place where police detectives interviewed him, where his brother's van had been vandalised—unwelcome reminders that a callous killer had put three nine-millimetre rounds into Harry's back less than two miles as the crow flies from where Liam now sat.

The realisation of the proximity sent a shiver through him. Made him glance nervously around as if the killer were sitting watching him from a parked car, the black Range Rover or something he'd swapped it for.

He was worrying unduly. The lane was too small, as was the pub's car park, for anybody to sit and wait in a vehicle without attracting unwelcome attention.

Despite that, home suddenly felt like a long way away in the failing light. He'd seen enough cyclists come off second in a collision with a car or truck to suddenly feel very vulnerable.

. . .

Maggot was forced to take a gamble on the likely direction Liam Callaghan would set off in when he left The Rockingham Arms. The lane was too small for him to sit within sight of the pub, and as for the pub's own car park ... forget it.

Maggot had to choose.

Callaghan could go north up Canada Road, the direction from which he'd arrived. Or he could go south, dog-leg right and then left onto Canada Common and from there onto Black Hill Road. The latter was longer, but through prettier countryside. Going north meant joining the A36—the major road on which Callaghan would spend the majority of his journey home—after only half a mile.

Maggot hadn't been on a pushbike since he was at school, but his gut told him south, the more scenic route. He drove past the pub while Callaghan was inside ordering a drink, then parked on a dirt shoulder on Black Hill Road, a quarter mile beyond the junction where Callaghan would join it. Then he settled in to wait, confident nobody would pay him any attention. Just another pickup truck on a country lane. He felt more like a farm hand now, than a carpenter or builder. He'd happily swap places, spend his days riding a big green John Deere tractor up and down a field as the gulls and crows flocked behind him.

His phone rang while he was sitting with the windows open, the sound of birdsong competing with a dog barking somewhere in the distance, the faint smell of manure on the breeze. He knew who it was without looking, let it ring out. It rang again less than a minute later. He let that go to voicemail, too. Then the ping of an incoming text.

Maggot dug the phone out of his pocket, felt like throwing it out of the window.

He suddenly realised he was praying the Arrogant Prick had changed his mind, wanted him to abort. Calling and then texting to tell him Callaghan was no longer a threat before it was too late.

That wasn't the case, of course. The text was nothing more than a manifestation of the arsehole's petulant anger at an unresponsive hireling.

Answer the fucking phone when I call you.

Who can say when or why a man's patience finally gives way, the point at which the worm turns? When threats become hollow because a man has been pushed too far. Pushed to the point where he no longer cares about the consequences of his actions, so consumed is he by thoughts of taking the thing or person he hates most in the world down with him.

Often, it's the smallest thing. Something that pales into insignificance in the light of what has gone before.

For Maggot, it was those eight angry words on a small screen that summed up the pathetic man who tapped them out in his childish temper tantrum.

The epiphany was like a great weight being lifted. Catharsis concealed within the realisation that if he was prepared to accept and face the consequences of his past misdeeds, the Arrogant Prick's hold over him would fall away. He was filled with surprise—and not a little regret—that the answer had been within his reach the whole time, if only he'd known how to recognise it.

Today, Maggot would give the Arrogant Prick a lot more to complain about than insubordinate hired help who refuse to answer their phone.

Before he did, there was unfinished business to be concluded.

It seemed to him the air was cleaner, fresher, the smell of manure more wholesome, almost sweet, the birdsong more intense, as he glanced in his mirror at the junction from which he hoped Liam Callaghan would soon emerge.

. . .

LIAM'S PARANOIA GREW STRONGER AS THE TIME TO LEAVE DREW closer, the light seeming to fail faster, even though the sky was clear, no dark clouds hastening the onset of dusk.

He swung his leg over and stood astride his bike, looking left and right, trying to decide. He'd originally planned to go south, the longer, more scenic route. North onto the A36 would be faster, but would it be safer? He couldn't deny that even if he was unlikely to lose his driving licence, he might lose his life if the alcohol he'd consumed caused him to weave erratically. The lights on modern cars were far too bright. He knew himself how easy it was to be momentarily dazzled, even a brightly-attired cyclist with a flashing rear light disappearing into the gloom at the edge of the road.

He needed to pull himself together or he'd end up calling for a cab, asking for one with a bike rack on the back.

Get a grip, he told himself as he set off heading south. *Stick to the plan.*

He noticed the big pickup truck parked on the verge after he'd turned left onto Black Hill Road heading north, but it rang no alarm bells. The opposite, in fact. Thinking how he'd always fancied one. Maybe if Babs gave him Harry's van, he'd part-exchange it for a tricked-out Ford Ranger.

Not for the first time, he wished he were a rich man. He'd stop and knock on the pickup's window, make the farm hand or builder inside an offer he couldn't refuse. Then throw his bike in the back and drive himself home, maybe drop the guy off at his own home on the way.

Such were the thoughts going through Liam's mind as he cycled past the big vehicle, its motor already running. Seeing the exhaust smoke drifting on the evening breeze, the evidence of running the engine unnecessarily while it was parked, made him think about fuel consumption. And if he bought a tricked-out model with lots of chrome and big bull bars on the front like the vehicle he'd just passed, would it be a target for thieves? Maybe he'd stick with Harry's old van, after all.

In the quiet of the evening, he heard the crunch of the pickup's big tyres as it pulled off the verge and onto the road.

Almost as if it was waiting for me, he thought, and immediately felt stupid.

He glanced nervously over his shoulder just the same, his heart suddenly in his mouth, legs turning to water.

Jesus Christ! Will you look at the acceleration on that thing...

34

Angel had arranged to meet Oliver Durand at The Pig in the Wall, the same boutique hotel where his mother had asked the favour he was about to discharge. Not knowing how the evening would pan out—how much he'd end up self-medicating with alcohol as a result of re-living the darkest times of his life— he'd planned to walk to the hotel, a distance of approximately three quarters of a mile, and take a cab home if necessary.

Instead, Kincade drove them to Mayflower Park—the same waterside park where Liam Callaghan met Véronique Dubois and scared her all the way back to France. Angel gave Kincade a potted history of the background as they drove, details she was content to listen to with one ear as she concentrated on the traffic. More than that, it helped him ease himself into the narrative, get his mind and tongue moving, and hopefully in the same direction.

'It was in late two thousand and ten in the aftermath of Operation Moshtarak, also known as the Battle of Marjah . . .'

She listened without interrupting as he explained that Marjah, located fifteen miles from Helmand Province's capital, Lashkar Gah, was one of the region's chief Taliban strongholds.

It had also become Helmand's biggest drug centre—Helmand Province alone produces over half of the world's opium—providing the largest distribution markets for the region's major crop, raw opium, as well as hosting hundreds of heroin-processing laboratories. The toxic combination was in no way accidental. Drug traffickers paid the insurgents handsomely for protection on the same key routes used by the Taliban insurgents to transport reinforcements and supplies, a symbiotic partnership of evil that made Marjah a key target for coalition forces.

The initial offensive began in February 2010. The scope and size of the operation was compared to the 2004 Second Battle of Fallujah in Iraq, but by June, four months after the offensive on the Taliban stronghold, it was being viewed as a failure, described as a *bleeding ulcer* by one American general. Although Operation Moshtarak was declared officially over on December 7, 2010 with the city secured, fighting between coalition troops and the Taliban continued until 2013 as insurgents undermined a return to normal life.

Angel fell silent as they arrived at Mayflower Park and Kincade drove to the far edge of the car park, beyond the marked bays, the front wheels only inches away from the concrete ramp sloping down into the choppy water. They stayed sitting in the car, looking across the River Test to the historic Marchwood Military Port on the other side—built to support the D-Day assault on Normandy in 1944—as Angel embarked on his own uneasy voyage into the past.

'Our role was to create an environment where locals could live in peace. We were on a routine patrol one day—'

'Hang on.' Two sentences in, and already she interrupted him. 'I'm getting confused with your use of *our* and *we*.'

'By *our* role, I meant the coalition forces. When I said *we* were on patrol, I meant me personally and the other guys in the section.'

'You went out on patrol with them?'

'Uh-huh.'

'Did you have a gun?'

'Nope. We're not like medics. Padres don't carry guns. We also commit to not picking them up and using them in a firefight.'

She leaned away and contemplated him as if she'd let a dangerous escapee from a lunatic asylum into the car.

'Did you think I stayed behind in camp the whole time?' he said, smiling at her disbelief.

'I never really thought about it at all.'

'How do you think the men would've viewed me if I stayed in camp drinking tea and reading the bible all day, and then asked them when they got back, *how'd it go, lads?* You want to talk about killing a man today who you thought was armed but it was only his walking stick? Or tell me about your buddy who got both legs blown off by an IED and you don't know whether to feel relieved or guilty that he stepped on it and not you. You have to live it with them to understand.' He pointed at the car roof, the sky above. 'As a padre, they accept your direct line to him up there. You have to prove you've got a connection to their lives, as well. You might as well be on the end of a phone line back in England, otherwise.'

'I suppose. Didn't they view you as a liability?'

He made a V-sign with his first two fingers, pointed them at his eyes.

'I didn't carry a gun, but I've got eyes and ears like everybody else. I'm following in the footsteps of the man in front, watching for anything unusual, searching for explosives. The men know I'm not playing at it. If I screw up, I'm the one who gets blown to pieces. And if you want to be cynical, if I step on an IED, it means the man behind doesn't. The section hasn't lost any firepower as a result, either.'

He checked his watch, mindful of the time disappearing. She made a mental note not to interrupt again.

'You were on patrol . . .' she prompted, when he failed to restart his story, the reason for his hesitation obvious when he did, his chest visibly rising and falling, the remainder of his body still. He sounded as if he was reading from the instruction manual of a new washing machine he'd bought. A deliberate attempt to remove the emotion from his narrative—a similar survival mechanism to that used by soldiers engaged in combat, suppressing emotion in order to survive the battlefield.

She guessed it would become increasingly difficult for him to keep the facade up.

'It wasn't long before we came under fire from a bombed-out building. At least two AK-47s on full auto. Everybody took cover and the guys returned fire. I hit the ground, scrambled away. You've been pussy-footing along watching where you put your feet and suddenly everything goes out the window when you come under fire. You hit the ground and pray you don't get blown straight back in the air again in little pieces. I'm on my face in the dirt with rubble and plaster raining down. Clouds of dust make it impossible to see what's coming at you, rounds pinging over my head stitching lines in the wall behind me. And then somebody's screaming through the bedlam, *man down, man down*. One of the guys, Niall Elder, had taken a round in the gut. I got on the radio to organise a casualty evacuation while the section commander administered initial emergency treatment. Three men went into the building under covering fire, while we did what we could for the injured man.' He rested his hand on his stomach as if trying to ease trapped wind, fingers splayed. 'Bleeding in the abdominal cavity is almost impossible to control. We propped him against a wall with his knees pulled up against his chest to give some compression without restricting his breathing and settled in to wait. There'd been sporadic bursts of gunfire from inside the house the whole time, and then suddenly you realise it's gone deathly quiet.'

A similar quiet filled the car as he sat, eyes closed, feeling the burn of the unforgiving Afghan sun hot on his skin, the taste of grit in his mouth, his heart a heavy *thump, thump, thump*.

Because there's nothing comes close to saying the words that live in your mind out loud.

In that silence, the *ping* of his phone was like a hammer blow on the car roof. She startled, even if he didn't.

He pulled it out, read the brief text, pocketed the phone.

'That was Durand's son. He's already there.' He put his hand on the door handle. 'Better not keep him waiting.'

A fleeting surge of panic ripped through her before she saw the hint of a smile he was trying to hide.

'Better not open that door if you know what's good for you. *Sir*.'

He let go of the door handle, let the smile come.

'He's going to be fifteen minutes late.'

She wanted to tell him it wasn't fair to play games. She didn't. Not because of issues of rank, but because she knew what he was doing. A deliberate ploy to break the growing tension, allow him to make it all the way through the narrative.

That didn't mean she couldn't play games herself.

'Go, if you want to. You can tell me the rest of it another time.'

They sat looking into each other's eyes, faint smiles curling their lips, for what felt like forever. He was the first to give in.

'It's okay, I've got time. Anyway, I thought to myself, that was too close for comfort, I'm out.' He opened his hands wide—*and here I am.*

She shrugged indifferently. Like he'd told her how the movie he'd watched on TV the previous night ended.

'That's pretty much what I expected. If you can't stand the heat, get out of the kitchen.' Her brow creased suddenly as a potential problem presented itself. 'That's not much of a story if Durand's son asks you about it. You might have to make something more exciting up. You want to practice what you might say to him now?'

They did some more of the eyes locked, suppressed smiles routine, both of them enjoying the game.

Then it was over.

And she knew she wouldn't be the one to interrupt again.

'I was still with the section commander and Elder when one of the men who'd cleared the building came out and headed towards us, the other two still inside. I knew they were both okay or else all hell would've been breaking loose. The man who'd come out was still wired, but I could feel the sadness waiting behind it as he saw Elder. And the anger pushing ahead of him. I could've asked him what happened inside the building, but something didn't feel right. I wanted to take a look for myself. As soon as I headed towards the open doorway, he called after me, *there's nothing in there for you to do, Padre.* He didn't mean any dead or wounded Afghan Muslims wouldn't need or want me, a Christian padre. And I already knew we didn't have any more casualties inside the building. He was saying to me, *don't go inside.*'

Despite her determination to not interrupt, Kincade sucked the air in through her teeth.

'Not the right person to say that to.' She paused, the mischief glinting in her eye. 'Unless pig-headedness is a trait that's developed in later life, of course.'

'I entered the building,' he said, ignoring her. 'Found the two other guys in a room stinking of petrol and human excrement.

They don't deserve the anonymity, but I'm going to call them Smith and Jones. They were with two Taliban fighters. One was dead, face-down in a pool of blood, the other one wounded with a non-life-threatening leg wound. He was sitting on the floor with his back against the wall, wearing a dirty, blood-soaked kameez and worn-out Nike trainers. Smith and Jones were standing over him, arguing quietly and insistently. My ears were still ringing but I caught a lot of swearing and the word *traitor*. They didn't hear me at first, then Smith saw me and I heard him hiss, *not in front of the padre*. Being inside the building, their ears would've been ringing more than mine. Smith didn't realise how loudly it came out. The wounded insurgent heard it, too. He looked at me like Allah himself had appeared in front of him, said to me, *you're a priest, don't let them kill me*.'

She'd been staring straight ahead through the windscreen as he talked. Not seeing the water in front of them. Seeing instead images from countless TV news broadcasts. Of dust and smoke swirling around the ruined shells of buildings while heavily-armed men crept forward, taking cover behind burned-out vehicles in the deserted war-torn streets, orange-red flames lighting the sky in the distance.

Her head snapped towards him as he impersonated the wounded Afghan prisoner's plea, not sure if her ears were playing tricks.

'He had a Brummie accent?'

'Yep. He was British. Farid Ghulam. His father was an Afghan national, his mother British. He was born and brought up in UK, raised as a Muslim in Small Heath, Birmingham. When he was eighteen, he assaulted a police officer in the two thousand and five Birmingham race riots, got sentenced to two years. He was radicalised while he was in prison. As soon as he got out, he went to Afghanistan and joined the Taliban.'

'I'm not surprised they called him a traitor.'

'Nor me. So, Smith came over, put a hand on my elbow and started to usher me out. Doing it in a way that meant I'd have to physically resist him if I didn't want to go. Ghulam starts going crazy begging me. He's got his arms out towards me and he's crying and his accent's getting stronger as his nose fills with snot and he can't get the words out through his fear. *They're gonna kill me, man, they're gonna kill me.* I looked at Jones standing guard over him. He smiled and shook his head, said, *of course I'm not going to kill him.*'

'Sounds to me like they were going to kill him.'

The words were out before she could stop them. Too late, she realised she'd touched the root of the malaise that ended with him walking away forever. She gave him a guilty half-smile —*sorry*—then held her tongue as he explained why he turned his back on Farid Ghulam, closed his ears to his desperate cries for mercy.

'I allowed Smith to lead me towards the door. What was I supposed to do? Plant my heels and resist him? Say I believed Ghulam, a terrorist traitor, over them, the men I ate and slept and laughed and cried with, the men whose spiritual wellbeing I was sworn to protect? Then Ghulam screamed at me. *You are not a man of God.* Something hit my leg. He'd thrown something at me. At first I thought it was a lump of rubble.'

He dug in his pocket, pulled a set of crimson rosary beads from it. As if he needed spiritual support to get him through the remainder of his tale. Except that wasn't it at all, swinging them from his finger as he explained.

'This is what he threw at me. They belonged to his mother. She made him take them with him when he went off to join the Taliban. She refused to take them back when I tried to return them to her months later. Said they were stained red with her son's blood. She told me he only took them because he thought if he carried them, they'd protect him from the bullets of infidel Christian soldiers.'

He didn't need to say what hung in the air as thickly as any desert dust storm.

And he'd just thrown them away.

Angel pocketed the reproachful, incriminating memento, looked at his watch and cleared his throat.

'I wish Durand's son would text me now, say he's arrived.'

This time, she didn't tell him he was free to go. Nor was he serious. Having got this far, he couldn't have stopped if his life depended on it.

'I left the building with Smith, went back to where Elder was still propped against the wall. He was fading fast. I returned to camp with him when the medics arrived.' He stared right through her as he talked, the barren aridity of the desert reflected in his eyes. Then he reached out, took hold of her hand, squeezed it until she thought small bones would break, her lips a tight, sealed line. 'He was holding my hand like he thought I could save him when he died on the way back. There wasn't room in the transport for me, the injured Afghan and somebody to guard him. As soon as the medics arrived and saw Elder, they knew he was going to need me more than them on the way back.'

He let go of her hand, no residual awkwardness or embarrassment, even if she didn't feel comfortable massaging some life back into it.

She knew from talking to him on other occasions that Niall Elder wasn't the first person for whom his would be the last face a dying man saw before that of his maker. Elder's death was not the catalyst that made Angel turn his back on everything he thought he believed in. Nor was it the straw that broke the camel's back, one young man's pointless death too far.

'Jones killed him,' she said, when he didn't.

'Yep. Claimed Ghulam attacked him with a knife hidden under his dead comrade's body that had been missed when they searched both men.'

'Do you believe that?'

'I *want* to believe it. But nobody makes a stupid mistake like that. Certainly not experienced soldiers like they were. If I had to believe anything, I'd say they deliberately left it on the body, then waited for Ghulam to try to use it. That's not all.' He hooked his two middle fingers together like links in a chain, pulled until his fingertips turned pink. 'Jones and Elder were like that. Inseparable. Grew up together, joined up together, best man at each other's weddings, the works. Jones didn't know Elder was going to die when he went into that building, but he knew it would be touch and go. And I allowed him to stand guard over one of the men responsible. Another Brit, for Christ's sake. A man who not only shot his best friend, he did it while betraying the country Elder died for.'

He lapsed into silence. Staring out at the steady drizzle that had started coming down, the whole world outside the car an unending sea of different shades of grey—the water, the sky, the tarmac and the concrete buildings on the far side of the river, but none of it as black as his soul, his thoughts.

She knew that if she opened her mouth, a trite cliché would pop out. She kept it firmly closed, no easy task. Waited for him to continue. To tear himself apart in front of her to satisfy her idle curiosity.

She felt like grabbing his phone, texting Durand's son.

Forget The Pig in the Bloody Wall, get your arse into the back seat of this car. Then tell me you want to join the Army.

She stretched her arms out straight, fingers interlaced. Glanced surreptitiously at her watch as she did so, didn't fool anyone—least of all him.

'On the face of it,' he said, responding to her unsubtle

prompt, 'I made a monumental error of judgement. In my darkest moments, I ask myself whether I didn't know perfectly well what would happen when I allowed myself to be shown the door. Not only that, I went willingly, grateful to Smith, who I could blame for forcing me out. Tell myself I'd have stayed otherwise. Exerted my moral superiority over these young men hell-bent on revenge. Made sure Ghulam made it back to camp alive.'

Now, she was the one who prayed for the sound of Angel's mobile, summoning him to his appointment. He'd described the events that transpired. She knew him well enough by now to work out for herself what he'd put himself through in the aftermath. She didn't need chapter and verse. To have the subtle nuances of his guilt explained to her in excruciating detail. But nothing comes without a price. She understood that even if Durand's son texted him again, Angel would tell his tale to the bitter end, make the young man wait.

'I couldn't get Jones' face out of my mind. The way he smiled reassuringly at me. *Of course I'm not going to kill him.* Itching to do exactly that the minute I was out of the room. I asked myself then, and I still don't know now, was I face-to-face with pure evil? Or was Jones like everyone else? Basically, a good man pushed by circumstances out of his control beyond his personal line in the sand? Everybody's got one. And it's moving the whole time. I was forced to ask myself whether I was up to policing all those lines anymore.'

'Give me a murderer or a rapist any day.'

'Me too, Sergeant, me too. The thing is, I wasn't over there in the dust and heat and misery to be judgemental. That's the whole point. My role was to be the one person who listens to your darkest thoughts and doesn't judge you. It meant I had to treat Jones like anyone else, despite my own misgivings. That meant asking him if he was okay. If he wanted to talk about killing a wounded man in his custody. You know what he said to me?'

Kincade had no idea. Obviously. He was waiting for an answer, nonetheless. She threw out a couple of obvious ones, even though she knew the truth would be more complex, more insidious.

'Piss off? Mind your own business?'

His head started shaking before her mouth was open, proof that the truth was beyond guessing.

'You're the one who needs somebody to talk to, Padre. You're responsible for a man getting killed today.'

The words took a moment to register. When they did, her voice, her whole body, was filled with indignation.

'How could he blame you for Ghulam's death? Because you didn't insist on staying, and then Ghulam wouldn't have tried anything with two of you in the room?'

Angel squeezed out a bitter laugh as she jumped to the obvious and wrong conclusion.

'If only. I don't think he viewed Farid Ghulam as a man. He was a traitor. Sub-human pond life. He was talking about his best friend, Niall Elder.'

It was suddenly far too hot inside the car. The windows had steamed up, given the length of time they'd been inside talking, the coolness of the rain hitting the windscreen and windows. She let her window down, filled the car with a sudden burst of fresh sea air, not caring that the rain came pouring in. She was tempted to stick her whole head out, cool it down, even if it wouldn't do anything for the spinning on the inside.

'I can't even start to think about how he came to that conclusion.'

The look on his face said he had no such problem.

Worse, that he agreed with his accuser.

'Elder had come to me wanting to talk a couple of nights

earlier. A few weeks before that, he'd been on patrol and had to clear a house in a similar situation when they came under fire from it. The difference was, it was packed full of people and animals. Old, young, women, children, babies. Dogs, goats, you name it. Utter bedlam. Elder ended up killing an unarmed thirteen-year-old boy by mistake. His conscience drove him crazy for two weeks before he gave in and came to talk to me about it. It was then my job to convince him he wasn't a monster on his way to hell. Explain that people aren't either good or bad, you make your choice and you're stuck with it. We're complex creatures. We all have the capacity for both good and evil. Killing a man in wartime who will kill you if he gets the chance doesn't make you an evil person. Feeling exhilaration about being alive afterwards doesn't mean you're sick in the head. Feeling like your brain's going to explode because you don't know what to think doesn't make you an idiot. It was my job to convince him he was a good man doing a legally-sanctioned job to the best of his abilities and within the constraints of being human. And that he would continue to be a good man if he got back out there and carried on doing it . . .'

Kincade felt as if she'd seen the awful conclusion to Angel's story coming since the day she was born, only finally putting it into words now.

'He pulled himself together, got back out there and was killed the very next day.'

Two days later, he thought and didn't say.

'Yeah. And Jones blamed me. If it hadn't been for my pep talk, Elder would've been crying himself to sleep in his bunk or pumped full of sedatives in the camp sick bay instead of getting himself shot in the gut and bleeding out in a filthy street in a godforsaken hell-hole. He'd still be alive today.'

'*That's bullshit!* And you know it.'

The outburst came out as an insubordinate shout. She didn't care. Nor did he, his own voice equally raised.

'Of course, I do. You can trace flawed logic like that all the way back to the recruiting sergeant in the UK who did a great job when Elder first walked into the Army recruiting office. Jones was hurting, and he wanted to spread the pain around. I get that. But if someone accuses you of it, you see how easy it is to ignore, not let it eat away at you.' He jabbed his chest with an angry finger. 'Because deep down inside, you're worried it's true. Don't forget, it was less than twenty-four hours after Farid Ghulam shouted his last words before he was murdered at my back. *You are not a man of God.* And suddenly I'm thinking, you might be a confused, resentful Taliban terrorist with a stupid bloody Birmingham accent, but you're right, I'm not.'

His words had the ring of finality about them. The realisation that he wasn't cut out to be a priest. Except Kincade hadn't heard the name she'd been listening out for. *Cormac.* He was the reason Angel went into the military. She was convinced he was a part of why he came out again.

Angel proved her right a moment later.

'It made me question whether I was making things worse, not better. By helping them overcome their crisis of conscience, all I was doing was prolonging the very thing that was tearing them apart in the first place. Absolving them each little step along the way until they've come so far they don't know who they are anymore. I became an Army padre because I believed that if Cormac had someone like me to talk to, he wouldn't have done what he did.

'That all changed after Niall Elder and Farid Ghulam's deaths. What if Cormac had come to me before he was suicidal? Because all he wanted was for his big brother to tell him to walk away. To hell with whether our old man liked it or not, I'd back him up. Instead, I talked him around. Persuaded him to stick with it until in the end he's so sick of hearing my voice, he's asking himself, *what's the point of talking to Max? I've got a better way.*'

He made his hand into a pistol as he said it, put his index finger to his lips. Made a small explosive sound in his cheeks.

She didn't have it in her to tell him not to be so deliberately dismissive, trying to hide the depth of his pain behind a childish gesture. Again, she knew if she opened her mouth at all, something trite would slip out, something she'd be ashamed of later when she re-lived the conversation in her head. A loud fart would be no less inappropriate.

She fell back on the safety of logistics and arrangements. Things that knew their place, unlike unruly emotions.

'You better get going or you'll be late.'

If he'd been hoping for something more profound after eviscerating himself at the altar of her curiosity, he didn't let his disappointment show. She put her hand on his arm when he was halfway out of the car.

'I hope you don't have to go through all that again with Durand's son.'

He made light of it, as she knew he would.

'At least I'll have a drink in my hand if I do.'

She smiled with him, didn't say what was on her mind.

If only it was that easy.

35

'How'd it go with Doctor Death Junior?' Kincade asked, when Angel got in the next morning, alternating a thumbs-up, then a thumbs-down, a couple of times each.

A complete and utter disaster was in his mind, and thankfully not on his lips.

'We only had a quick drink, as it turns out.'

'You managed to spoil a student's appetite for dinner? That's some going. What about for joining the Army?'

He shrugged, *who knows?* Didn't answer.

'Did he ask why you came out?'

'Nope.'

'Really? What did he want to talk about?'

'Not a lot. He was only going through the motions to keep Isabel happy.'

After the honesty of the previous day, he felt a little slimy as the lie slipped out. He had no intention of telling her the real reason Durand's son had agreed to meet with him. The acrimonious exchange was still fresh in his mind, and would remain there for some time to come. It had started when they first met. Oliver had been as nervous as his mother had been when she asked Angel to meet with her son in the first place. Angel had tried to put Oliver at ease.

Call me Max. Or Padre.

No, I don't want to call you that.

Angel had smiled as he made a joke about it.

Makes you feel like you're in confession, eh?

Oliver had shaken his head, not saying anything. Looking at Angel as if he'd sentenced him to an eternity in the fires of hell. Forcing Angel to say something to keep the conversation alive.

You'll spend a lot of time with other padres if you do join up. Might as well get used to it.

That won't be a problem. But I can't call you Padre.

Why not?

Because that's what Mum calls you.

Durand had already told Angel her son didn't want to follow in her footsteps by becoming a pathologist, but this latest demonstration of his desire to be independent of her was a little extreme.

Except that wasn't it, as Oliver's next words made very clear.

And because you're part of the reason my parents got divorced.

Angel had expected to tell Oliver things that might have surprised and shocked him. He hadn't expected Oliver to do the same to him. Durand's son continued talking while Angel struggled to get anything coherent to come out of his mouth, the young man's voice growing more strident, more aggressive.

She never shuts up about you. Padre this, Padre bloody that. If I'd been my dad, I'd have divorced her. I'm sure there were other problems between them, but her obsession with you was the final straw. I don't give a flying shit about why you went into the Army or why you came out again. It's my life and I can make my own mind up without you or my mother sticking their oar in. But I wanted to meet you. See what all the fuss was about. And I wanted to ask you—

Without meaning to, Angel had taken a step towards Oliver.

And the young man had seen in Angel's eyes that he'd been on the verge of overstepping a dangerous mark. Because they both knew what he'd been about to say.

Did you sleep with my mother?

Angel couldn't have said what he'd have done if Oliver hadn't fallen silent in the face of the anger that even a glass eye in a duck's arse could see was a hair's breadth away from erupting out of him. He'd forced it back down, laid his hand on Oliver's shoulder and squeezed, not caring that the young man flinched thinking Angel was about to slap him. He gave him the only advice he could.

I won't tell your mother what was said tonight. If you care about her at all, you won't either. But, like your career, it's your choice.

He'd been sorely tempted to add a final line, akin to a verbal slap across the face in lieu of the physical one.

I hope you make a better one about your career than you did about what to say to me tonight.

He'd sat for a long while nursing his drink after Oliver left. Not knowing what to think. Isabel Durand's face in his mind, her voice in his ears. All those dry medical facts delivered in her oh-so-professional manner, trying so hard not to smile when he made inappropriate remarks or played his harmonica in the midst of her carving up a cadaver.

And him unaware of the turmoil going on behind the façade . . .

He was dragged from his reverie into the present by the mischief flashing in Kincade's eyes.

'You ended up having to tell me your darkest secret for nothing.'

'I was happy to tell you. You never asked, that's all.'

As on the previous day, she contemplated throwing something heavy and sharp at his head. Instead, she turned thoughtful.

'Are you okay?'

'What do you mean, *am I okay?*' Knowing exactly what she meant.

'I'm assuming you haven't talked to anyone about it for a long time?'

'No.' He pointed at the corner of the room. 'You don't have to worry you're going to find me over there curled into a ball, sobbing my heart out.'

They both knew he was deliberately making light of it, but only he knew to what extent. And she was right to ask. Durand's request and everything it led to had forced him to think about things that hadn't troubled him for a while, his mind too full of the complications Stuart Beckford and Virgil Balan brought into his life.

He'd woken in the small hours of the morning, long before the first grey dawn light seeped through the curtains to bathe the room in a creeping pale radiance. A cold sweat on his skin, the anguish in Cormac's voice turned to bitter accusation bridging the divide from fitful sleep to reluctant wakefulness.

I don't know what to do, Max.

Except when he'd looked again, it wasn't Cormac with the top of his head and most of his brains blown halfway back to England. It was Niall Elder, his hands busy buried deep in his own oozing abdomen, then wiping warm sticky blood onto Angel's face, spiteful words stolen from a murdering soldier on lips already turned blue.

You're the one who needs somebody to talk to, Padre. You got me killed today.

And suddenly murdered Farid Ghulam was there with them, two gaping holes in his chest and a crimson rosary swinging from his hands. Arms outstretched, but not to beg and plead for his traitor's life, looping the rosary around Angel's neck, pulling it tight.

You're a priest, I'm going to kill you.

Then a sharp crack, the sound of small-arms fire, followed by another.

He ducked his head, but it wasn't gunfire at all. It was only Kincade. Clapping her hands, two short sharp echoing reports her girls would surely know, her voice filled with concern.

'Are you sure you're okay?'

He recognised the look he saw in her eye, the intention to probe deeper as all women like to do. Stuart Beckford would *never* do that. He gave a dismissive wave, shut her down before she got started.

'I'm fine. Did you hear back from Evie St. James yet?'

The abruptness of the transition from personal issues to work-related matters did the trick. A visible change came over her as she put her concern and curiosity aside, geared up for the day ahead.

'Actually, yes. She replied to my email. She'll be here . . .' She consulted her watch. 'In about ten minutes. If she doesn't get cold feet, that is.'

'What did she sound like?'

'Nervous.'

'It's understandable. Meeting Baldwin and having his paranoia rub off on her, then learning he'd proved himself right. You want to interview her on your own?'

'I was thinking I might do it with Jardine.' She pointed an insubordinate finger at him. 'Don't say a word.'

He pinched his finger and thumb together, ran them over his lips like a zip. Words were unnecessary, but hung in the air nonetheless.

I thought the idea was to put her at ease, not in a locked room with two pit bulls.

. . .

Evie St. James made Kincade think of a bird that had flown into a plate glass window when she first saw her sitting in the reception area under Jack Bevan's watchful eye. Small and slight and somewhat dazed, her gaze never settling, as if watching for predators while vulnerable in an unfamiliar environment.

She stood up abruptly as they approached, as if she'd been told you could be arrested for bad manners. Kincade's welcoming smile did nothing to relax her, a hand not much more substantial than a sparrow's foot dwarfed in Kincade's firm grip when they shook.

The trepidation on her face as Kincade ushered her into an interview room suggested she'd mis-read the sign on the door as *Execution Room 1*. She took the seat Kincade offered, her hands resting in her lap as she picked the flesh at the side of her thumbnail.

'We understand you had lunch with Russell Baldwin on the day he was run over,' Kincade started, careful to avoid saying *died* or the more emotive *was killed*. 'What was the purpose of that meeting?' She smiled, offering Evie the chance to smile back. She didn't.

'I wanted to talk to him about Orla's death. She's my sister. And ask him to look into it.'

'Why? Was it suspicious?'

'*I* think so.'

All the emphasis was on the *I*, not *think*. Any doubt was in other people's minds, not hers.

'How did she die?'

After the speed of Evie's previous response—almost before the word *suspicious* was out of Kincade's mouth—the pause that followed was even more marked. She dropped her eyes to her lap, where her hands were still busy picking her flesh raw. An average-sized sparrow would have produced a louder response.

'Auto-erotic asphyxiation.'

Kincade was aware of the change that came over Jardine, knew that she sensed the same in her. This was very different fare to what Baldwin usually served up on his blog. A diet of politicians and other public figures lining their pockets at the taxpayers' expense.

'*Auto*-erotic asphyxiation implies a person is alone when they die,' Jardine pointed out. 'You think your sister wasn't?'

'I don't *think* it. I *know* it.' She took hold of the small crossbody bag she wore, about to pull out her phone.

'Let's back up,' Kincade said, her hand extended towards the bag. 'Who do you think was with your sister when she died?'

'Seymour Grey.' The venom and loathing she put into the name made Kincade recoil, but Evie had plenty more to spit out. 'I call him *See More Evil.*'

The comments Jardine found when trawling through Baldwin's blog were immediately front and centre in her mind.

Wherever you look, you See More Evil.

'I saw your comments on Baldwin's blog.'

Evie gave a fleeting, shy smile as if proud of her creativity.

'Yeah. I was afraid to spell out his name properly. He's a politician. I'm not sure exactly what he does. I know he's not a minister. Sort of one step down from that?'

'A parliamentary private secretary?' Jardine suggested, making it very clear which of them spent all day sitting next to Craig Gulliver. 'That's an MP who acts as an unpaid assistant to a government minister.'

Evie looked at her as if she'd been asked to run through their daily duties.

'Somebody important,' Kincade interrupted, dumbing things down. 'Do you know how old he is?'

'About fifty?' Making it sound like once you got past thirty, it might as well be a hundred and fifty.

There was a brief pause while everybody jumped to some

easy conclusions. They already knew Evie was twenty-eight. It was likely her sister was a year or two older or younger—either way, a damn sight younger than the Rt Hon Seymour Grey MP.

Evie herself saved Kincade and Jardine from having to ask the awkward question that begged to be asked.

'She wasn't a call girl, if that's what you're thinking. But she got invited to lots of parties. She dated some of the men. I mean, who wouldn't? And they were rich. They liked to buy her presents.'

Kincade and Jardine nodded their thanks for such a full explanation and made their own minds up.

'Had Orla been dating Seymour Grey for very long?' Jardine asked.

'About six months. The thing is, he never denied knowing her. His fingerprints were all over her apartment. But he said he wasn't there on the night she died.'

'What makes you think differently?'

'Orla called me that night. She told me he was there. He was in the bathroom.' Her mouth turned down, the scorn and dismissiveness of the young in her voice. 'Pretending to pee so he could take his Viagra.'

'Why did she call you?'

Evie looked at her like it was a trick question. The apparent stupidity put an aggressive note into her voice.

'Because she was scared, what do you think?' She looked back and forth between them. 'What would you feel like if some fat old bloke said he wanted to strangle you for fun to help him get some life into his limp dick? Then gets a rubber ball out of his briefcase and a roll of clingfilm.'

'I appreciate she was scared,' Jardine said patiently. 'What did she expect you to do about it?'

Evie had stopped picking at her thumb, her hands now constantly on the move, as if they might ease her growing frustration. She made no attempt to keep it out of her voice, a hint of hysteria bringing up the rear.

'*I don't know.* She wanted someone to talk to, that's all. Someone to tell her to get the fuck out of there and forget about the bonus he promised her or whatever.' She jabbed her scrawny breast with a chewed fingernail. 'That's what *I* should've done. But I didn't. I sat there like an idiot listening to her saying *I'm scared, Evie* over and over and over until all I wanted was to throw the phone out the window. Then she said to me, *I gotta go.* Those were the last words my own sister ever said to me.' She shook her head, anger and sadness and frustration at how she'd failed her sister, the first tear rolling down her cheek, bringing specks of mascara with it. She swiped angrily at it with her finger, sniffed a wad of snot back. 'Now whenever I hear somebody say *I gotta go,* I hear her voice.'

Everyone in the room heard it now. And it wasn't saying, *I gotta go.*

You let me down when I needed you most.

Kincade was very pleased Angel wasn't in the room. The parallels to his brother were too great. She wasn't exactly having the time of her life listening to Evie tear herself apart, but it wouldn't wake her in the middle of the night.

Evie took hold of her crossbody bag again. This time, Kincade didn't stop her. She pulled out her phone.

'I've got a record of her phone call that night.'

Kincade took a deep breath, saddened that everything she was about to say would shoot down Evie's hopes.

'That won't prove anything. A defence lawyer would say she called you because she was bored because she was on her own. Unless you recorded the call, you couldn't prove otherwise.'

Evie tried again, even less hope in her voice.

'She told me she took a picture of him without him knowing, but she didn't get a chance to send it to me. She must have been worried about the way things were going and wanted proof he was there in case anything happened. I don't mean in case she died. In case he hurt her.'

Neither Kincade nor Jardine wasted time looking hopeful. Instead, they waited. It wasn't long before Evie confirmed out loud what they all knew.

'Her phone was missing.' She glared at them as if they'd both been part of the team of lazy halfwits investigating her sister's death. 'That was suspicious. Orla was like any normal person. She never went anywhere without her phone, not even to the toilet.' She waved her own phone in their faces. 'The call I've got on this proved she had it on her that night. You should've looked into that.'

Kincade ignored the accusatory tone, the way Evie now viewed them as having been an actual part of the flawed investigation.

'What it *proves*'—all the emphasis on the word—'is that *somebody* called you from her phone, not necessarily your sister. A defence lawyer would say she'd lost it and somebody found it and it was unlocked so they called you as the emergency contact. Again, it would be your word against theirs.'

She didn't need to spell it out any further.

He's an MP, you're a call girl's sister.

Evie was back to looking like a dazed sparrow recovering from its collision with the plate glass.

'Is there anything I can say that you won't dismiss?'

Not a lot, Kincade thought, and suggested something.

'Did Grey have an alibi?'

'Yeah. He said he was with some other woman. Orla knew he saw other women.' She coughed out a sour laugh. 'She wouldn't have wanted to be the only one. Nobody would.'

She'd put up with it now, Jardine thought, and asked something more constructive.

'Did Orla see other men, as well?'

'Yeah, but nothing serious.'

'And where did this happen?'

'Up in London. But Grey has got a big house down here in the country somewhere. Like a mansion. Orla went to a party there one time. She said it was like an orgy. All these old men and young women . . .' She shuddered as she trailed off, their faces making it clear salacious details were unnecessary at this or any other point.

It was obvious Evie's story had got Russell Baldwin's muck-raking juices flowing, set him on the road that ended with his untimely violent death. How far he'd gone down that road was unclear. Given the seriousness of Evie's accusations, he would've made sure he was one hundred per cent certain about anything he published. The fact that he'd been killed suggested somebody was worried the incriminating evidence was there to be found by anyone who wanted to find it, as opposed to bury it.

It was clear to them both that Evie would not be the source of that information. They spent a few minutes establishing that fact beyond doubt, Evie confirming she knew nothing about Seymour Grey other than his name, and she didn't even know that of his alibi.

All that remained was for them to turn today into the worst day of her life. Put the fear of God—as well as dangerous men a lot closer to hand—into her. A very poor reward for finding the courage to come forward.

Kincade cleared her throat, that mandatory precursor to bad news.

'I'm afraid the situation has got a lot more serious. The driver of the skip lorry that hit Russell has also been killed in suspicious circumstances.'

Evie blinked rapidly a couple of times, the tears that had

dried up threatening to return. As did the accusation in her voice.

'You should've told me that first.'

'Would you still have come in?'

'Of course I fucking wouldn't. You tricked me.'

There was no point playing word games. Saying they hadn't tricked her, they'd simply been selective with the facts they put in the email. They could've justified their approach, saying they didn't want to scare her with too much bad news coming out of the blue in an email hiding in the middle of all the spam and messages from her friends. None of it would've made any difference. Evie felt deceived and manipulated. Nothing anybody said was going to change that.

'I'm sorry you feel like that,' Kincade said, in a way she hoped came across as it would from Angel. 'But you've provided us with the most promising lead we've had so far. Because of you coming in today, we've got a better chance of stopping these people from hurting anybody ever again.'

The look on Evie's face answered for her.

I'm not holding my breath.

KINCADE AND JARDINE TOOK THE STAIRS UP AFTER SHOWING EVIE out. Kincade took them slowly, trailing behind Jardine as she thought things through.

'Giving Grey a false alibi in the case of a suspicious death is a hell of a thing to do,' she said, pausing on the first landing.

Jardine had already gone a couple of steps up the next flight. She came back down, rather than look down on her superior.

'How much do you think she knows, given she's up in London? She thinks she's given him an alibi for what might be a genuine accident after all, just to keep his name out of the papers. Does she know two men are now dead as part of the cover up? If she does, she's either a monster herself—'

'Or she's very scared.'

A third option was as good as written on the stairwell wall.

Or she's already dead.

'We need to speak to her asap,' Kincade said, resuming her upwards journey.

This time, Jardine stayed put.

'Who is this guy, Grey, anyway? Your average sleazy politician hasn't got the connections to get rid of everybody who's a threat to him.'

Kincade didn't have an answer for her. But the way Jardine phrased the question, referring to connections and the ability to make problems disappear, struck her as very similar to Jardine's own situation.

She glanced down the empty stairwell, thinking, *no time like the present*.

'What's the latest with Frankie?'

The mention of her younger brother's name made Jardine look down the stairwell herself, except it was more a case of assessing whether she'd die instantly and painlessly if she threw herself down.

'Don't ask.'

It all started when Frankie was arrested and charged with assaulting his girlfriend Josie's ex-partner, Ryan Cox. The charges were subsequently dropped, but, two weeks later, Cox accused Frankie of interfering with his and Josie's four-year-old daughter, Rowan.

Frankie was arrested again and released on pre-charge bail. After twenty-eight days, he surrendered to custody and was released without charge.

Jardine was behind his release. She risked her career by accessing the PNC for personal reasons, looking into Cox's new girlfriend, Stacey Reynolds. Reynolds had a history of falsely accusing her partners, first of assault and then rape. Jardine had a quiet word with a friend in the Northumbria Police, suggesting that as a serial accuser, Reynolds was behind Cox coaching his daughter into making false accusations against Frankie.

So far so good.

Except Frankie couldn't understand why he'd been released. He badgered Jardine until she admitted what she'd done—warning him not to say a word to anyone.

Frankie immediately told Josie.

Josie went directly to Cox's house and assaulted Stacey Reynolds.

Cox ended up hitting Josie, either accidentally or deliberately.

Frankie didn't give a damn which, went to the house and beat seven shades of shit out of Cox—for the second time.

Frankie was arrested and charged with assault—making three arrests in all.

In the meantime, Stacey Reynolds approached a shyster solicitor with a track record of making complaints against the police. She suggested the only way the Northumbria Police knew to look into her background was because Jardine abused her role as a police officer when she investigated Reynolds' past herself.

The shyster solicitor immediately started digging the dirt...

Kincade knew all this, her own chequered past making Jardine feel comfortable confiding in her. She also wasn't about to be fobbed off.

'Has the situation got worse?'

Jardine's expression was easy to read.

When did you ever hear of a situation getting better?

Despite that, a small smile forced its way onto her face.

'Frankie's feeling guilty about potentially dropping me in the shit.'

'I should think so, too.'

'He wanted to do something to help.'

Kincade closed her eyes. She didn't want to think what shape the sort of help Frankie had in mind would take.

Jardine was nodding at her when she opened them again.

Yes, it's as bad as that.

'Frankie and one of his little gobshite mates broke into the solicitor's office and stole the files.'

Kincade put her hand over her face. Temporarily unable to speak complete words of the sort found in an English dictionary.

'Don't tell me they only took the files on you and him?'

Jardine shook her head, relief in the gesture that although the majority of the stupidity in the world appeared to be channelled through her little brother, things hadn't got quite that bad.

'No. They trashed the place, stole a load of other files as well. But the little twat he took with him got caught on CCTV. It's just a question of whether he gives up Frankie.' A nervous, stuttering laugh like she was late for her meds slipped out. 'I can't even hate him for it. Guess what he said when I asked him why he did it?'

It wasn't worth the breath expended saying it, but Kincade obliged, nonetheless.

'I was only trying to help.'

36

Angel wasn't in their shared office when Kincade got back after interviewing Evie St. James. That suited her just fine. It gave her an opportunity to research the Rt Hon Seymour Grey MP before updating Angel on exactly how bad a mess it was turning into.

Two minutes on the internet proved Lisa Jardine had been right, if a little out of date. For the past eight years Grey had been a garden-variety backbench MP, but before that he'd served as a Parliamentary Private Secretary—the eyes and ears of a minister in the House of Commons—first to the Secretary of State for Northern Ireland and then to the Home Secretary.

The feeling of excitement tinged with apprehension she'd felt in the interview room when Evie used the words *death, autoerotic asphyxiation* and *politician* in short succession intensified as she read.

Ever since the Profumo scandal more than sixty years earlier in 1961, the combination of attractive young women who made their living on the back of their looks, if not actually on their backs, engaged in inappropriate relationships with government ministers had caught the public's eye—and that of the agencies charged with protecting that public—like nothing else could.

Seymour Grey had never been a minister himself, but he'd been very close to the holder of one of the four Great Offices of State—the Home Secretary, with overall responsibility for law enforcement and the security services—as well as the minister with responsibility for the most troubled and contentious corner of the British Isles.

It meant a devious and ambitious man like Grey, actively looking to further his own interests both now and in the future, would have engineered opportunities to forge alliances, both official and otherwise, that he might later call upon and abuse. Men like Grey live by the principle *it's not what you know, it's who you know*. It went some way to answering Jardine's question about his ability to make inconvenient problems disappear quickly and permanently.

Other problems—those faced by the unfortunates tasked with persuading a sceptical public that the men and women governing them warranted the title *Right Honourable*—were made worse by the fact that hard facts are not required to start a shitstorm. Rumours, once started, are more than capable of sustaining themselves. And, if they flag, blogs like Russell Baldwin's *brinkmanship.com* are on hand to give them a fresh lease of life.

In the light of Grey's close links to ministers responsible for some of the most sensitive areas of government, the unwelcome interference-cum-censorship DS Ellis Hudson experienced when investigating Baldwin's death made a lot more sense.

'What are you smiling at?' Angel said, startling her as he came back into the room with a single cup of coffee in his hand.

'I'd call it a nervous grimace, more than a smile.'

'The sort of thing you'd see on the faces of the men in the trenches before they went over the top, you mean?'

'Exactly like that, yes.'

He offered the cup of coffee in his hand to her.

'You want this? I'll get another one.'

'Has it got anything in it? And I don't mean coffee, water and milk.'

He shook his head as he peered into the cup.

'Afraid not. I'm not sure there's any actual coffee in it, either. Or real milk. So? Let's hear it.'

He perched on the edge of his desk rather than sit behind it —as if he was giving himself the option of a quick exit should he feel the need—and sipped the increasingly-tasteless brown liquid as he listened to her confirm their worst fears.

'It makes sense,' he said, when she'd finished, thoughts of sanitised witness statements and 9mm semi-automatic pistols in his mind.

'Yeah, in the same way the spread of bubonic plague made sense when you put a lot of people together in cramped, unsanitary conditions with medieval healthcare.'

He smiled with her, feeling as if they were two of those soldiers in the trenches about to go over the top and run blindly into the German machine guns.

'What are you thinking?' he said, then held up a finger that proved he was ahead of her. 'Apart from wishing Evie St. James had got cold feet about coming in.'

She got up from behind her desk, went to stand at the window, although what inspiration she hoped to get from the view of the train station on the other side of Mountbatten Way was anybody's guess.

'It would be nice to know if we're dealing with something official, or whether we're looking at a rogue operation?'

'Fareprick turning up and sticking his nose into Ellis Hudson's investigation into Baldwin's death feels pretty official to me.'

'True. But what if killing him was unsanctioned, and that led to an official cover-up?'

The exact lengths to which secret service agents are authorised to go in carrying out their duties is a very grey area. There are no guidelines prescribed in law. A cynical person might argue that's the way the agencies like it. Self-regulation with the option to do exactly as they deem necessary when the situation arises. It makes them a popular target for civil rights activists who believe all government agencies should be subject to controls laid down in the statute books. In such an environment, the agencies are very keen not to wash their dirty linen in public, dealing with operatives who over-step the mark internally, rather than a messy public trial that only increases demands for regulation and transparency.

'It gets better and better, doesn't it?' he said. 'The logical next step is that killing Callaghan was unofficial, the hit carried out by the same man who pushed Baldwin, after he'd been disciplined or kicked out.'

'Like you say, it all makes sense. But if it's true, why is the killer still covering up for Seymour Grey, doing his dirty work for him?'

He ran his thumb over his first two fingers in the universal sign for money, but they both knew it was more complicated than that. What they also knew was as soon as they started digging deeper, red flags would be raised, and they should expect interference of the sort DS Ellis Hudson had been subjected to.

'Look on the bright side,' he said. 'You can go up to London, talk to the SIO on Orla St. James' death, and see your girls at the same time.'

. . .

Things didn't pan out quite as they'd predicted. Jardine was assigned the job of tracking down the SIO on the Orla St. James investigation, which proved straightforward enough. DI Tommy Elves had since retired, but was happy to meet to discuss the case, the weather, football, holidays, restaurants, cars, music, his first grandchild, films and anything else—apart from bloody politicians with their noses in the trough—they wanted to talk about, he didn't care, so long as it got him out of the house and away from the exhaustive list of chores his wife prepared for him at the breakfast table each morning. In fact, Jardine got the impression he'd have agreed to come down to Southampton at his own expense if she'd even hinted at the idea.

The hiccup occurred when Kincade tried to make the arrangement to see her girls. She went out of their office to do it, came back five minutes later looking like she'd been told her estranged husband had emigrated to Australia with them that morning, taking gold-digging, bunny-boiler Hannah Who-Gives-A-Shit-What-Her-Last-Name-Is with him.

'I don't bloody believe it.'

Angel did his best not to smile, knowing what was on its way.

'They want me to come, too?'

'That wasn't quite how it was put to me.'

'They don't want to see you *unless* I come too?'

The resignation in her weary headshake said he was bang on the money. Then a spiteful little smile broke out on her face.

'But you have to bring your mouth organ—'

'*Harmonica*.'

'—with you. And they've given me a list of songs they want you to learn.'

'They're a bit young for Bob Dylan and the Cowboy Junkies, but it shouldn't be a problem.' Patting his pocket where the offending article always lived. 'I was thinking of coming with you, anyway. There's no point applying for Grey's phone and bank records until we've spoken to DI Elves. Something tells me we're going to need a lot more than murdered call girl Orla St. James' sister pointing the finger at him.'

37

They agreed to meet ex-DI Tommy Elves on Hampstead Heath in North London. Not because any of them were paranoid or had watched too many spy movies, but it was only a mile from Highgate where Kincade lived before her family fell apart, and where they would later pick up her girls. It also suited Elves on two fronts. Firstly, because he brought along his dog, a springer spaniel called Dick, named after Dame Cressida Dick who'd served as the Metropolitan Police's commissioner from 2017 to 2022. And secondly, as he'd said to Kincade on the phone when they made the arrangement—*something tells me I'll need some fresh air after talking to you.*

The cab they'd taken from Waterloo Station dropped them at the entrance on Millfield Lane where Elves was waiting for them. The muddiness of Dick's coat suggested Elves had already walked off most of the dog's drooling exuberance in advance of their discussion.

They then started an anti-clockwise lap of the Highgate Men's Bathing Pond, the sign prompting the obvious question from Angel.

'Is it really men only?'

Kincade nodded as if she'd been the one responsible for the segregation.

'There's a women's pond, as well.'

Elves gave a dismissive snort that could equally have emanated from his dog.

'Don't forget about women identifying'—making it sound like *deluding themselves*—'as a man.'

'True.' She grinned at him suddenly, as if about to reveal another of her clever ideas. 'But they've removed all the internal partitions in the changing area, so there's no privacy.'

'What about people identifying as a duck or a seagull?' Angel asked, not wanting to be left out of the conversation he'd started.

'I think we should start talking about the Orla St. James case now,' Kincade said, surprising him that she should be the voice of reason for once.

'Or a fish,' Elves said, looking past Kincade between them to Angel.

'A pond snail?' Angel suggested.

Elves gave a thumbs up, continued with the game.

'A piece of duckweed.'

'*I've got it!*' Kincade yelled. 'Let's all three of us identify as police officers under intense pressure discussing a case.'

Neither of the men looked happy about that.

'I'm an *ex*-police officer,' Elves pointed out. 'Do you think if I identify as a still-serving police officer, I'd get my full salary instead of my pension?'

'It's worth asking,' Angel replied, 'although I'm not sure if it's a hate crime if they refuse.'

Both men looked at Kincade for an answer.

'I'd get more sense out of Dick,' she said, and meant it.

Dick, who was thinking of identifying as the meanest bull

mastiff that ever cocked its leg up one of the heath's trees, barked enthusiastically at hearing his name.

'Definitely more sense out of my girls,' Kincade muttered under her breath.

'Shall we discuss the case?' Angel said to Elves, as if the previous thirty seconds hadn't existed.

Elves looked as if he'd been about to suggest it himself.

'Good idea.'

They both looked at Kincade who was thinking of identifying as a person who'd had the will to live sucked out of them.

'Why not? I don't know why I didn't think of that.'

It had been a good way to start the discussion. Light-hearted banter to lift their spirits before discussing something that would make them plunge.

'Who found the body?' Angel asked, as good enough a place to start as any.

'Her sister, Evie,' Elves replied, the name not exactly putting a fond smile on his face.

'She didn't mention it when I interviewed her,' Kincade said.

'I don't suppose it's her favourite memory. She went to Orla's flat after she didn't get an answer when she tried to call her the next day. She had her own key. She found her hanging by a belt from a clothes rail in a wardrobe.' He laughed, a hollow sound devoid of humour. 'Like a very grown-up game of hide-and-seek. Except the wardrobe door was open making it easy.'

'What did the post mortem say?' Angel said.

'Death by asphyxiation. There's no question about that. She had alcohol in her bloodstream, but there was only one dirty glass beside an empty bottle of champagne that had magically been poured without leaving a single fingerprint behind. The toxicology tests also identified moderate recreational drug use. No surprises there. She was naked, so the erotic element makes sense, too. The question was whether the *auto* part was appropriate, or whether someone was with her at the time.'

'What made you look at Seymour Grey as the potential sexual partner? We know Orla saw other men as well.'

'Her sister did.' He laughed again, more amusement in it this time, although still tinged with bitterness. 'We can speed this discussion up a hell of a lot. Every time you've got a question, why did you do so-and-so, the answer is Evie. Every time the question is why didn't you do so-and-so . . .' He pointed at the sky. Not at the clouds above, but at the superior officers who would've been above if they'd been in a police station.

'She told us Orla called her on the night, told her Grey was there and she was scared,' Angel said.

'Exactly,' Elves confirmed. 'The thing is, he didn't try to hide their relationship. He'd have been stupid to. That's one thing Seymour Grey is not. His fingerprints were everywhere, we found his hairs on the pillow. At least we didn't find any crusty stains on the sheets. There was even one of his cufflinks under the bed. He was very grateful to us for finding it. His wife had bought them for him.' He shook his head angrily, his remembered frustration not diminished by the passage of time. 'But he maintained he wasn't there that night. He even admitted he'd been there two nights before that. And whilst he was happy to admit to screwing her every time he was up in London, he swore blind he wasn't into any kinky stuff.'

'Doesn't sound like any politician I've ever heard of,' Kincade said.

They all shared a smile, the amusement soured by the knowledge that they could joke about it as much as they liked, but they'd never stop what had happened to Orla St. James from happening again, not while young women continued to be drawn to power and money.

'Talk us through the scene,' Angel said, after Elves had

regained control of Dick who'd been straining at the leash when a young woman with a Chihuahua walked past in the opposite direction.

They'd walked three sides of the men's bathing pond. Now, they continued straight, towards Highgate No 1 Pond rather than complete the lap. Elves headed towards a bench overlooking the pond, clearly tired by having to fight against his dog the whole time as he talked.

'Let's sit over there.'

Angel let Elves and Kincade sit, happy to remain standing and not sit in a line like three wise monkeys. Elves tied the dog's leash around one of the bench's legs, then gave them all of his attention for the first time.

'As you know, Orla's phone was missing . . .'

'And she never even went to the toilet without it,' Kincade added, remembering the way Evie had described it as perfectly normal behaviour.

Elves, in his mid-fifties, scowled. *Tell me about it.*

'We got the call logs, of course. They showed the call from Orla to her sister. I explained to Evie that it proved nothing—'

'So did I.'

'—but there were no calls to or from Grey on the day she was killed. That also proves nothing.'

'Evie told us Orla took a photo of Grey,' Angel said.

'I know. And maybe she did, which would explain why the phone was taken. But her cloud storage was full so it didn't get backed up if she even took it. Nothing was conclusive.' A flash of remembered irritation passed across his face, left a scowl behind. 'I was reminded at every opportunity how important it was that things *were* conclusive. That I couldn't assume anything on the basis of things that were not there. Treating me like I'd only been in the job ten minutes.'

He lapsed into silence briefly, as if his doctor had told him he should re-live his irritations, the low points in his career, slowly, take a break between each one.

'CCTV?' Angel asked, moving away from Dick who'd smelled evidence of his cat, Leonard, on his trouser legs.

'They've got it,' Elves confirmed, 'but it hasn't been working for years. At least two of the neighbours, who, by the way, saw nothing, either on the night or ever, mentioned it to me. I think they were hoping I'd strong-arm the owner into fixing it. If I'd known Orla was going to be killed, I'd have been happy to.'

Angel didn't miss the way Elves said *killed*, and not *died*. It might have been a slip of the tongue, but he didn't think so. It was also another escalation. Being killed is very different to being present at an unfortunate accident. He kept his thoughts to himself as Elves continued.

'CCTV in the street caught a taxi dropping a man off fifty yards from Orla's block. It was dark and Grey lives up to his name . . .' He saw the confusion on their faces. 'Have you seen him?'

'A picture on the internet,' Kincade said.

'Same.' This from Angel.

'He's Mr Average. Average height, average build, average everything. A totally nondescript man in dark clothes and a hat. It could've been him or it could have been half the population of London.' He pointed back the way they'd come, towards the men's bathing pond. 'Including women identifying as men. We traced the cab driver and he couldn't remember a thing—'

'And he hasn't got around to having CCTV installed in his cab,' Kincade finished for him.

Elves gave her an approving look.

'I don't remember you being part of the investigation.'

'They all follow the same pattern.'

'What about cell-site data from Grey's phone?' Angel asked,

before the other two started rolling out anecdotes about how if it can go wrong, it will.

'Obviously, we applied for a warrant,' Elves confirmed, 'but it was refused.' He wagged his finger at them, worked a self-righteous note into his voice. '*How dare you ask, you impertinent little policeman! I'll have you flogged.*'

They both smiled with him, then Angel continued with the questions going nowhere.

'Any evidence of other people in her flat?'

'Drowning in it. She was a popular girl, if you know what I mean.' He stopped short of winking at them. Angel guessed it was only Kincade's presence stopping him. 'Evie gave us names, we identified and eliminated a lot of people and we were still left with a lot of unidentified prints and DNA. Nothing that was on the system, of course. By this time, I was starting to get nervous. I could hear some pompous twat of a defence counsellor asking me, exactly how many unidentified DNA samples do you have, Detective Elves? And yet you persist in hounding my client, the Rt Hon Seymour Grey, a pillar of the community and all that bollocks.'

'So why did you?' Kincade asked. 'You're getting pressure from above, you're operating in an evidence-free-zone...'

'Because I believed Evie. I believed her when she told me her sister called her and she was scared about what Grey wanted her to do. Why else would Evie go to her sister's place the next day? You don't immediately go to a person's house just because you can't get hold of them on the phone. Not unless you already suspect there's a problem.'

He looked around, checking there was nobody nearby to overhear what he was about to say, no mothers with young children or po-faced old maids ready to tut-tut.

'I spent a lot of time looking into auto-erotic asphyxiation and what they call breath play.' He gave them a guilty grin that said he'd never had so much fun while he was being paid. 'Got into a lot of trouble with the wife over it, too. Calling me a pervert, although I think she was more interested than she made out. Anyway, the idea is to restrict the flow of oxygen to the brain and induce hypoxia, which intensifies orgasm. You ask me, anybody who gets up to that shit has already demonstrated they're not getting enough oxygen to the brain. The thing is, most auto-erotic deaths are accidental.' He pinched his finger and thumb an inch apart. 'You're talking about a very narrow window of safety. The deaths occur when somebody tries to take it to the limit. Sensible, if that's a word that comes into it, people incorporate safety mechanisms to reduce the risk. Like a slipknot you can pull to release the pressure. They tie it around their wrist. But life happens. People screw up and make miscalculations or the slipknot doesn't work, they pass out and that's the end of it, never wake up again.' He paused, took a deep breath as if he was in need of oxygen himself, then ploughed on. 'Because of the dangers, breath play is usually done with a partner. If you're determined to go it alone, what you absolutely don't do is use a belt that hasn't got any safety mechanism built into it. Not unless you're even crazier than the rest of them. Talking to Evie tells me her sister wasn't.'

'What was the response when you pushed that argument?' Angel said.

Elves twirled his finger at his temple.

'Basically, I wasn't getting any oxygen to my own brain. It was pointed out to me that it was precisely because Orla spent her time with men old enough to be her father in what was basically a business arrangement, that she looked for such an extreme form of release in her own time.'

'Most auto-erotic asphyxiations are young men, aren't they?' Kincade cut in.

'That's right. And according to the studies that have been

conducted, it's more common than you'd think among couples. That reminds me of something else. The pathologist found bruising around Orla's neck.' Putting his fingers around his own neck as he said it. 'You might be able to put a ligature around your own neck, but you sure as hell can't manually strangle yourself and masturbate at the same time. The bruises were two to three days old—'

'Grey admitted he'd seen her two nights before she died,' Angel said, thinking out loud.

'My point exactly. What I'm thinking is that on that particular night he suggested some playful manual choking—'

'As all normal people do.' Kincade, of course.

'—and then, two nights later, he suggested something more extreme. That's when Orla panicked and called Evie, told her she was scared. Of course, the naysayers had an argument for that, too. She tried a bit of manual choking with somebody, not necessarily Grey, and liked it so much she decided she'd go the whole hog with a dangerous ligature around her neck—'

'Because responsible Seymour Grey had refused when she asked him to join in.'

Elves grinned at her.

'You're good at this.'

'Isn't she just,' Angel said, with more feeling than she wanted to hear.

Everything Elves had told them made sense—once you'd got past anyone wanting to deliberately starve their brain of oxygen. It had the feel of the truth to Angel, that impression bolstered by the fact that they now knew two men had been killed subsequently.

Even before that retrospective confirmation, the arguments back and forth had paled into insignificance in the face of Seymour Grey's trump card.

'Tell me about the alibi,' Angel said.

Elves had grown animated as he talked, the act of speaking his own theories out loud to people who accepted them reinforcing them in his mind. Now, the passion went out of him in a heartbeat.

'Astrid Persson. A Swedish national, but she's lived over here for the past five years. She—' His mouth clamped shut as if he'd been told his pension would disappear if he said another word. Then he pointed a knowing finger at Kincade. 'I think you could tell it.'

I think Dick the springer spaniel could tell it, she thought, taking up the challenge.

'Grey's fingerprints were all over her property.'

'They were.' He raised his hands, fingers splayed, then mimicked touching an imaginary vertical surface over and over. 'Almost as if he'd left them there deliberately.'

'His DNA was also found there.'

'Everywhere. Hairs in the bathroom, on the pillow—'

'We get the picture,' Angel interrupted, before Elves moved onto more intimate examples.

Kincade took a moment to think before her next answer.

'There was no evidence of anything kinky.'

'You'd have found more in the Pope's bedroom.'

Kincade made sure she didn't look at Angel. If they got dragged into a discussion about his background with someone like Tommy Elves, they'd never get away in time to see her girls.

'I'm thinking about CCTV,' she said. 'I'm going to say they've got it, it works, but there was a technical glitch on the night in question.'

Elves gave her an admiring look, turned to Angel.

'I don't suppose there's much unsolved crime down your way with this one on the team.'

'That's why we're up here solving yours.'

Elves let out a long *ooh* as if Angel had punched him in the gut.

'I'd be offended if I was still in the job.' He looked at Kincade expectantly again, much as his dog looked at him when he got the treats out. 'Anything else?'

She shook her head.

'I'm quitting while I'm ahead.'

Elves leaned forward and gave his dog's head a vigorous rub, some kind of subliminal transference going on, on account of it being inappropriate for him to do the same to Kincade for doing so well—certainly on the first occasion he'd met her.

'A wise choice. There's no way you would've guessed. His driver came forward and confirmed he'd dropped Grey at Persson's place and saw him go inside. He also claimed he waited outside in the car the whole time.'

The mention of Grey's driver registered in Angel's mind for reasons he couldn't identify. A feeling of something just out of reach, a memory that receded further into the depths of his subconscious the harder he tried to coax it out. Not only that, he got the impression that after everything Elves had told them, he was holding back now they'd arrived at the crucial point.

'What was the driver's name?'

Elves' face compacted, a mix of annoyance and frustration, as he proved Angel half-right. His hesitation wasn't indicative of wanting to conceal facts, more a reluctance to admit to his own failings.

'I knew you'd ask that. I've been trying to remember ever since we set up the meeting. But it won't come. And you know why? Because he had this stupid nickname. *Maggot*. The harder I try to remember, the more my mind's going *maggot, maggot, maggot*.'

'Who'd want the nickname Maggot?' Kincade said.

'Nobody, obviously. But you don't get to choose your own.

You're far too young to remember the film *The Dirty Dozen*. I'm too young, myself. But the character played by Telly Savalas was called Archer J Maggot. Grey's driver looked just like him.' He ran his hand over the top of his head. A simple gesture, but it made the feeling Angel had of missing something obvious spike. 'Bald as a coot. The character Maggot in the film was a nasty piece of work. I reckon Grey's driver was, too. I'd bet my pension he did a lot more than drive him around.'

It was all Angel could do to stop himself from making his hand into a pistol, jerking it up and backwards in recoil, once, twice, three times as he made small explosive sounds in his cheeks.

The graphic reminder of how Harry Callaghan had been executed made him almost miss what Elves said next.

'Evie was bloody lucky Maggot wasn't around when she accosted Grey in the street. She started yelling and swearing at him, accusing him of killing Orla. Grey's people defused the situation with the minimum of fuss. It would've been a very different story if Maggot had been there. It wouldn't have surprised me if he'd followed her and arranged for her to have a tearful reunion with her dead sister.'

No, Angel thought, *but did he follow her, see her with Russell Baldwin, and push him under a skip lorry, instead?*

38

AFTER TAKING THEIR LEAVE OF TOMMY ELVES AND HIS SPRINGER spaniel, Angel and Kincade headed north up Millfield Lane towards Highgate, the heath on their left. They'd learned a lot more from Elves than they'd been expecting. Angel had his phone clamped to his ear as they walked, deep in conversation with DCI Finch. Bringing her up to speed in advance of her making a formal request for the details of Seymour Grey's alibi, Astrid Persson, as well as those of Grey's driver-cum-minder, the man nicknamed Maggot. Kincade was equally deep in thought beside him as they approached what, in another lifetime, used to be her family home and her waiting girls.

'I thought I'd have to jog to keep up with you,' Angel said, after he finished the call and they continued trudging up the lane as if fighting through thick mud. 'It's as if the closer we get, the slower you're walking. At this rate we'll be standing still before we get to the end of the road.'

At which point she did exactly that. Stopped dead. Then sat on the low metal railing separating the pavement from the heath. He hesitated, decided that whatever was coming, it would be better if he wasn't standing over her when it arrived, then sat beside her on the cold railing.

'Being back is like a reality check,' she started, addressing the ground between her feet.

He didn't need to ask what she was talking about. The custody arrangements for the girls. Walking through leafy Highgate towards the big house where her estranged husband lived with them only reinforced what she was up against.

She took hold of her little finger ready to count off points.

'Let's start with what Elliot has got going for him . . .'

He was tempted to hold his own hands beside hers, allow her to move seamlessly from her fingers onto his when she got into double figures. A lot of the time, humour makes unpalatable facts easier to swallow. In these circumstances, he wasn't sure. His hands stayed firmly on his knees as she started making Elliot's case for him.

'He has a stable, well-paid job with excellent prospects. He's already got places for them in the best schools. Their friends are all here. He's got an excellent support network. His family are nearby and have known the girls all their lives.' She'd forgotten to move from finger to finger as she talked, still holding her little finger, perhaps because moving so easily and rapidly from one to the next reinforced the depressing inevitability of her words. Now, she gave up altogether, her hands taking on a more animated role, gesticulating in the air as she continued. 'My own bloody mother is on his side, for Christ's sake, available to help out at the drop of a hat. And so is Hannah The Angel.'

He gave her a curious look.

'Who?'

'Exactly. Just because I know she's a gold-digging bunny boiler, it appears nobody else can see it. What everybody else sees is Hannah the devoted new partner who supports dad-of-the-year Elliot in his relentless battle against his psychopathic cop bitch wife—'

'Let me know if you need any more adjectives.'

She elbowed him hard in the upper arm, the unexpected blow almost toppling him off the low railing.

'Anyway, Hannah The Angel, who is also devoted to—'

'The psychopathic cop bitch wife's children?'

'Exactly. This vision from heaven only works part-time—'

'Helping old ladies cross the road?'

'Probably. When she's not working in a soup kitchen for the homeless. It means she's available to do all of the chores Elliot can't do because he's too busy earning millions. She drops them at school and picks them up, ensuring there's never a moment in their day when they're not being looked after by a caring ...' She shook her head in frustration as words failed her.

'Gold-digging bunny boiler that only you can see?'

'Precisely. And certainly no judge would ever be able to see.'

'What about her employing a private investigator behind Elliot's back to dig into my dad's background?'

It had happened a few months back. Carl Angel found a man nosing around his property, who then asked a lot of personal questions. Kincade responded quickly and decisively when Carl phoned her as she was on her way home from work. At the time, she'd been encouraged, hoping Hannah's underhand meddling would drive a wedge between her and Elliot. Reflecting on the situation, she recognised the problem lay in her swift response.

'I can hear the judge now. *How many times did you say you banged the PI's face into a brick wall, Ms Kincade? When all he was doing was investigating Hannah The Angel's legitimate concerns for her partner's children? Children she loves as dearly as if they were her own?*'

She took a deep breath that he felt he let out, as if it had passed through the railing between them. He wasn't sure exactly how humour had made inroads into the conversation, but it had, and now he continued with it.

He curled his thumb and first three fingers into his palm, his little finger the only one left sticking straight out, then offered his hand to her.

'Use mine. I assume you were about to list what you've got going for you.'

'It's very kind, but I was about to run through what I've got *against* me. If you still want to be helpful, you better take your shoes off, as well.

Needless to say, he kept them on as she started to damn herself with her own shortcomings.

'I'd be taking them away from all of the above. School, their friends, Elliot's family, their grandmother, all the rest of it. What I'm offering in its place is an unsettled living arrangement, currently with the sweetest old man—'

'My father? *Sweet?*'

'Unless you prefer *adorable*?' She raised a questioning eyebrow at him, carried on when his face said he'd prefer not to think about it at all. 'Whatever description I use, it won't trump his criminal record for murder and eleven years in prison. On top of that, he has potential serious health issues. Love him as I do, Hannah The Angel has got Carl Angel beat hands down. Then there's the job. Long hours and shifts, all of which can change at a moment's notice—'

'Because of your nightmare of a boss?'

'I'd almost forgotten that. On a more serious note, there's the possibility of repercussions from when I was working undercover and that cover was blown. All the crazies know who I am. And I'm not even going to mention Elliot's accusations about what I got up to with those crazies in order to get them to accept me. Needless to say, I won't be putting myself forward for mum-of-the-year.'

'Anything else?'

She showed him her eye teeth.

'Grievous bodily harm against my nightmare of a boss?'

The obvious rejoinder—*a spell at His Majesty's pleasure would sort out the unsettled nature of your accommodation*—wasn't even close to being spoken, but she saw it in his eyes, nonetheless.

After the semi-joking way in which she'd sung Elliot's praises and then denigrated herself, the resignation in her voice when she summed the situation up was all the more poignant.

'The bottom line is always what's best for the children. And I can't put my hand on my heart and say that having the girls come to live with me at your dad's house would be best for them. I've got a simple choice. I accept that fact and make the most of it, or I go to court and have a judge tell it to me, and then live with the festering resentment.'

'And what does making the most of it entail?'

'Sucking up to Elliot.'

He smiled with her, continued in the same vein.

'And if you suck hard enough?'

She shrugged as if she hadn't really given it any thought. Throwing out suggestions now about what she would settle for.

'A child arrangement order where they live with him, but which gives me access at weekends and during holidays. And a parental responsibility order that gives us equal responsibility for their welfare and education and all the rest of it.'

'Will he accept that?'

She scrunched her face. The doubt in her voice proof that however much you think you know somebody, you can never be sure. Particularly in new and different, aka difficult, circumstances.

'I think so. I want to believe he isn't such a complete bastard he'd argue I'm unfit to have joint responsibility for their welfare.'

'Unless Hannah reverts to gold-digging, bunny-boiler mode and poisons his mind.'

'Poisons it *more*.'

Neither of them said it, but a look passed between them.

There are times when a man like Seymour Grey's factotum, Maggot, comes in very useful.

They got up together, his knees protesting more than hers, and continued their journey up Millfield Lane in a thoughtful silence. She stopped again when they got to the corner of what she still thought of as *her road*.

He knew what was coming.

'Ashamed of me?'

'Not at all. The opposite—thinking of you. Do you want to run the risk of meeting Elliot, Hannah or my mother? Potentially all three?'

'I don't have a problem with it. Do you want to run the risk of the girls refusing to come out if I'm not with you?'

She pointed at him, to give herself something to do with her hand that might otherwise hit him. Then addressed him like a disobedient dog.

'Stay there.'

'Aren't you going to tie me to the lamp post?'

I wish drifted back over her shoulder as she set off to where the man she viewed as *the winner* lived with their daughters.

He took a call from Tommy Elves while he was waiting for her to get back.

'I forgot to mention that Grey's alibi, Astrid Persson, has got a criminal record. Nothing serious, but you'll find her on the PNC. I don't know what your plans are, but you might be able to save yourselves another trip.'

Angel had been about to call Craig Gulliver, get him to run

Ms Persson's name through the PNC for that very reason. The fact that the same thought had gone through Elves' mind, proving he'd been thinking about it after the meeting ended, his memory responding, told Angel something about the man.

'This case sounds to me like the one that got away. The one that's going to haunt you forever.'

He was expecting Elves to laugh with him at the old cliché. Say something along the lines of not being a proper copper if you didn't take your own personal demons with you when you retired. Instead, a sour note entered his voice.

'Not exactly. The whole thing left a bad taste in my mouth. Everybody knows there's always been one rule for people like Seymour Grey, another one for ordinary people. It's different when you actually come face-to-face with it yourself. Have your nose rubbed in it. You learn something about yourself. About how important your principles are to you. And the closer you get to your pension, the less they seem to matter. I'm not saying we deliberately looked the other way, but we didn't go after Seymour Grey as hard as I would've liked to. It's half the reason I decided to retire. I'd put in my thirty years, and I thought to myself, if you don't have to shave every day, you don't have to look yourself in the eye in the mirror every morning.' He paused, considering whether to justify himself further, decided against it. 'Let me know how it all pans out.'

Angel called Gulliver the minute Elves was off the line, gave him the name and waited as Gulliver tapped away at his keyboard in the background.

'Tax evasion,' Gulliver said a minute later. 'She managed to keep out of prison, but paid a five-thousand-pound fine. Sounds to me like some of her boyfriend's bad habits rubbed off on her. Apart from his ability to wriggle out of things.'

Angel tut-tutted at him down the line.

'I don't know how you got to be so cynical, Craig.'

'Between you and Lisa Jardine I haven't got much chance of avoiding it, have I? *Sir.* I'll text you the details.'

They came through immediately, and Angel lost no time calling the phone number Gulliver supplied. It went to voicemail—no surprises there—but at least it was a personalised message left by a woman with a discernible foreign accent.

He'd barely finished leaving a message asking Ms Persson to call him back when a fast-moving object with four legs making a lot of squealing noises from both its mouths slammed into his legs and separated into two distinct girls.

He hoisted Daisy onto his shoulders as Isla did her best to look as if she was too old for such childish things. Their mother joined them at a more sedate pace, a resigned look not doing anything to cover the pleasure underneath.

'He can't carry you and play his mouth organ at the same time, Daisy,' Kincade said, as her youngest voiced her unreasonable demands. 'He has to hold your legs so you don't fall off.'

Two small but surprisingly powerful legs clamped tightly around his neck put paid to that objection, but her mother was ahead of her.

'Now he can't breathe.'

He gave a hoarse wheeze to prove the point, managed to squeeze out a few words.

'I've been teaching your mum to play. She's really good.' Then to Isla, 'The mouth organ is in my inside jacket pocket.'

A moment later, it wasn't, thrust eagerly towards Kincade with a rousing chorus of *pleeeeease, Mummy* from both girls.

'Maybe after we've found a church so that Angel can go to confession and confess to the sin of lying.'

Daisy slapped the top of Angel's head in delight.

'*Yay!* I love confession.'

'Why don't you girls tell me what sins you've been up to lately?' he said, as they headed off. 'Then I'll make some suggestions about how to improve them.'

Maybe that child arrangement order doesn't sound so bad after all, Kincade thought, as her daughters took up the challenge trying to out-do one another.

39

Angel tried calling Astrid Persson every time he got a break from entertaining Kincade's girls. It went to voicemail the first three times. After that, the phone was switched off. Experience told him if he called another hundred times, from London or when they were back in Southampton or on the dark side of the moon, the result would be the same.

Ms Persson was avoiding them.

He tried one final time as he waited on the corner of Kincade's road while she dropped her daughters back home, got the *currently unavailable* message again.

Two minutes and a quick search on the internet later, and a local taxi was on its way, its arrival coinciding with Kincade's return.

'Let's see if Ms Persson has just switched her phone off or gone to ground altogether,' he said, as they settled back into their seats.

'We'll miss our train.'

'There'll be another one.'

She didn't bother pointing out there would be another

Christmas, but it might not be a good idea waiting for that, either.

'Maybe the tax evasion is what Grey is holding over her,' she said, instead. 'It might be a lot worse than whatever the Inland Revenue found out. You can get seven years for it.'

'It's possible. Good old-fashioned intimidation by Grey's man, Maggot, feels more likely.'

They discussed it back and forth, no further forward by the time the cab dropped them outside Astrid Persson's mansion block in South Kensington. Kincade made a pithy, pertinent remark as they climbed out of the cab.

'You'd need to evade your taxes to live here.'

'Unless the nice man she gave an alibi helps out with the rent.'

'I bet he charges it to his parliamentary expenses if he does.'

He shook his head in dismay. To think that Craig Gulliver had accused him of being cynical.

There was no response when they rang Ms Persson's bell. Not on the first, second, third or fourth time. They picked a different bell, tried that, and were inside the block before Kincade got the second syllable of *police* out, her ID held towards the camera.

Two flights of stairs and a short corridor later and they were in front of Astrid Persson's very closed door. Angel put his ear to it and listened. The faint sound of a TV came from behind it. On a whim, he tried calling again. Seymour Grey liked his women young, and young people get withdrawal symptoms if separated from their life support systems for more than a minute or two. His theory was validated when he got voicemail again rather than the unavailable message. Her phone was back on. He left a very different message this time.

We're outside your door, Ms Persson. We're not leaving until you open it.

He pocketed the phone, showed Kincade his hand, fingers splayed.

'Five minutes.'

'Three.'

It was four. The door opened on the chain, and a blond woman peered suspiciously through the gap, as if she'd had problems with fraudsters posing as detectives before.

'Let me see some ID.'

They both thrust their warrant cards into the opening. Astrid made a point of looking from card to face and back again for each of them until she was satisfied. The door closed briefly, then swung fully and reluctantly open.

Shame you weren't so concerned for your personal safety when you gave Seymour Grey an alibi, Angel thought following Kincade in.

'I plan on making a complaint about harassment,' Astrid said, leading with her chin as she swept down the hall and into a sitting room with the highest ceiling Angel had ever seen.

'That's your choice, Ms Persson. If you want my advice, don't channel that complaint through Seymour Grey. He might not be available to help you for much longer.'

He gave Kincade a small nod—*over to you*—a gesture that always felt like letting an attack dog off the leash.

'I'm going to run through a sequence of events with you, Ms Persson. It starts with the death of a young woman called Orla St. James, allegedly as a result of auto-erotic asphyxiation. You provided Seymour Grey with an alibi for the time of her death. That alibi was accepted at the time, but is now subject to review.'

She paused, made a point of looking around the spacious living room with its high ceiling and large sash windows, the parquet flooring almost completely covered by a thick Persian rug, an ornate marble fireplace on the chimney breast.

Angel heard the unspoken subtext, even if Astrid didn't.

Nice place for an alibi.

'You told the investigating officer Mr Grey was here with you at the time,' Kincade continued. 'Do you still stand by that statement?'

'Of course. It is the truth.'

Angel didn't miss the way Astrid's sing-song accent grew stronger, a sure sign of nervousness. Kincade smiled at her like she'd never doubted it.

'Let's continue with the sequence of events...'

Angel paced the room as Kincade laid them out. A deliberate policy to further unsettle Astrid as Kincade hit her with the points like nails hammered into a coffin containing the earthly remains of her previous, safe life.

Orla's sister Evie refused to accept the coroner's verdict of accidental death.

She approached Russell Baldwin and shared her suspicions with him.

Unknown to either of them, she was followed by Grey's minder-cum-driver, a man nicknamed Maggot.

Baldwin was pushed in front of a skip lorry immediately after meeting Evie and died from his injuries.

Baldwin's girlfriend approached the skip lorry driver, Harry Callaghan, believing Baldwin had been pushed.

Callaghan started to re-trace Baldwin's steps himself.

His fingers were smashed with a hammer as a brutal warning.

After ignoring the warning, he was driven out to the New Forest where he was executed.

That killer was still on the loose, continuing to clear the decks. The surveillance of Liam Callaghan was proof of his thoroughness in identifying potential threats to his master.

Kincade paused to let her words sink in.

Astrid sagged listlessly on the chaise longue she was

perched on, as if Angel had been hitting her over the head with a sandbag, not pacing the room behind her.

'Let's go back to the beginning of the sequence,' Kincade said, when it looked as if Astrid might slide onto the floor. 'To your alibi. Tell me, what do you think is the best sort of alibi?'

Astrid stared uncomprehendingly at her, her mouth slightly open, no sound leaking out.

Kincade helped her out.

'I don't mean being at a charity dinner with a hundred other people or anything like that. I'm talking in general terms.'

Astrid was shaking her head, but still no words from her, English with her cute sing-song accent, or even unintelligible Swedish. This time, Angel joined in.

'An alibi that can't ever be retracted?'

Kincade beamed at him, her star pupil.

'Exactly.' Then to Astrid, 'And what's the best way of ensuring an alibi can never be retracted?' Angel went to answer, but Kincade stopped him with a raised finger. 'Give her a chance, sir. And here's a clue, Ms Persson. I don't mean an alibi that's carved into a stone tablet.'

Angel couldn't hold it in any longer. He blurted it out before Kincade stopped him again.

'An alibi given by a person who is now dead.' He held up his own finger, a point of clarification necessary. 'When I say *person*, I don't mean you, Ms Persson. I mean somebody, anybody.'

'Although it could be you,' Kincade pointed out.

'Probably will be, soon enough,' Angel agreed, and drew a baleful glare from Astrid.

If Astrid thought Angel's remark was uncalled for, Kincade really gave her something to stick in her smörgåsbord.

'If you'd told the truth at the time, hadn't provided Seymour Grey with an alibi, your life wouldn't currently be at risk. And Russell Baldwin and Harry Callaghan wouldn't already be dead.

I wasn't going to mention that Baldwin's girlfriend is pregnant, but I think I will. She's pregnant. And because of your lies, Ms Persson, the kid's never going to know its father.' She looked away from Astrid, her face twisted in disgust as she addressed Angel. 'What's the penalty for perverting the course of justice, sir? And I don't mean a lifetime of guilt for all the harm you've caused.'

'A maximum sentence of life imprisonment, subject to mitigating circumstances. It strengthens the accused's case if they help prevent the fucking bloodbath from carrying on until everybody including the accused themselves is dead.'

Both women recoiled at the tone and volume of his voice, the unexpected profanity of his words.

He came around to stand in front of Astrid. Looking down on her as she cowered under the weight of his contempt.

'Do you know a man nicknamed Maggot?'

Astrid flinched as if he'd spat in her face, then nodded, even if words still wouldn't come.

'Did he threaten you if you didn't give Grey an alibi?'

Another nod.

Angel hunkered down as the moment of truth approached. Put his face in front of hers instead of his groin.

'Do you know his real name?'

And another.

Later, Kincade would say it was Angel's own fault. If he hadn't crouched down like he was talking to a child, he wouldn't have fallen flat on his back when Astrid finally found her voice.

40

Liam Callaghan jerked awake, the roar of a pickup truck's engine in his ears as the nightmare refused to release its grip. Feeling again the sickening jolt as the pickup's bull bars nudged his rear wheel, the red-raw grazes on his knees and elbows and palms stinging in sympathy, the world swimming in and out of focus as it had when his plastic-helmeted head hit the unforgiving tarmac.

His immediate thought: *I'm in hospital, tubes and wires poking out of my flesh and orifices, connecting me to humming machines that keep my broken body alive.*

He shook his head to clear it, ground his knuckles into his eye sockets, the sprinting of his heart slowing as the familiar room took shape around him.

Thank God!

He was in his own bed.

He threw off the sweat-soaked covers, threw on shorts and an unwashed T-shirt, headed downstairs to make himself a cup of tea—three-thirty in the morning or not.

He still couldn't believe what had happened.

His whole life hadn't passed before his eyes as the bike

beneath him bucked and weaved before tipping him onto the rough, hard country road, but the folly of the past days since Harry's death did. In that moment, he was convinced he was seconds away from being reunited with his brother, two hapless nosy idiots together on the other side of the grave.

He'd hit the ground hard. Skin and flesh came a poor second as he slid and bounced down the road on all those angular, projecting joints, hips and elbows and knees, before coming to a stop in the gutter. Expecting to hear the eager whine of the pickup's engine as it reversed back over him, finished a job long overdue.

Instead, the driver's door flew open. A man jumped down, the approaching crunch of his boots on the gritty road loud in Liam's ringing ears.

His mind went into panic-fuelled overdrive.

The killer had no intention of reversing over his head. Risk blood and skin and hair getting caught in the tyre treads. Much cleaner to put three 9mm rounds in him, as he'd done to Harry. Pick up his brass and drive away with nothing more than a scuff of rubber on the bull bars.

He'd tried to get to his feet, although God only knows what he thought he'd do. Stagger off across the fields in his dazed and bruised state? Hope the killer's gun jammed?

It was already too late. The killer was standing over him before Liam was even on his knees. Strangely, his hands were empty, no 9mm semi-automatic pistol resting casually in his executioner's grip.

Liam raised his eyes to the face staring down at him, not knowing what to expect. Anger? Pity? Contempt? Cold determination? Or nothing at all, the indifference of a professional with no more remorse than if he squashed a cockroach under his heel.

Liam's eyes went to the killer's empty hands once more, hope blossoming inside him.

Was this a final warning? Break Harry's fingers, knock him off his bike. Variety is the spice of life, even if you're a homicidal maniac.

Liam bit his tongue. Determined not to beg or make wild promises, maintain as much dignity as a man in ripped and muddy Spandex on his bruised arse in the gutter can.

The killer squatted down, their faces a foot apart. Liam prayed this would not be the last face he ever saw, but he took in every detail, nonetheless. It wasn't the face that existed in his mind of the cold-blooded killer who'd shot Harry to death. There were no horns, for a start. Despite that, it was the face of a man some hard-wired, primeval instinct warns you to be wary of, to keep within sight. Except something wasn't right. It wasn't that the lips were too full or the nose too dainty. Then it came to him, a nervous giggle threatening to slip out at the absurdity of it.

He was wearing a toupée. A cold-blooded killer in a toupée.

The guy caught him staring, made Liam very glad he'd stifled the laugh. Liam held his breath, prayed the guy's vanity didn't get the better of him, compel him to teach Liam a lesson for his mocking thoughts. To Liam's surprise, he took hold of it, ripped it off. Threw it into the field behind where Liam lay.

'Stupid bloody thing.' He ran his hand over the shiny bald dome of his head as if surprised at what he felt. 'Didn't stop the bastards from calling me Maggot my whole life.'

Liam kept his mouth tightly shut, his face expressionless, at the admission.

Then Maggot cleared his throat, and Liam knew the reason he was on his arse in the dirt at the side of a country road had finally arrived.

'You probably worked this out for yourself, but I . . .' He

cleared his throat again, struggling to say the words that had been so easy in his head. 'I killed your brother.'

Liam never thought he would hear those words spoken to him. What man would? Was this why he was still alive? Not because he was being given one last chance. Because the killer called Maggot wanted to gloat before killing him? More of the variety that spices a cold-blooded killer's humdrum life?

He made a sudden lunge to get up, but Maggot anticipated the move. Liam might never have heard those words before, but Maggot had clearly spoken them, knew what to expect when he did.

He punched Liam, a hard, straight right to the jaw. Sent him sprawling onto his back once more.

'I'm not going to hurt you.'

'It's a bit fucking late for that,' Liam yelled through his throbbing jaw, biting back the final word. *Arsehole.*

Too late or not, he didn't try to rise again as Maggot continued his fruitless search for absolution.

'If I could turn back the clock, I'd do it in a heartbeat—'

'That makes two of us, mate.'

'—and I know I can't ever make things right, but I promise you I *will* make them better. The man who wanted your brother dead is going to pay. If anyone deserves to die, it's him. Don't ask me his name because I won't tell you. I don't want you calling the police—'

'Are you fucking insane? I want to come with you.'

Maggot gave him a sad smile, shook his head.

'You wouldn't like the way it's going to end.' He pushed himself upright, laid his hand on Liam's shoulder. 'Once again, I'm sorry . . .'

It looked to Liam as if he wanted to say more. Explain himself. Tell Liam about the hold the anonymous monster he worked for had over him. In the end, he bit it back. Liam understood that. Making excuses only demeans you.

He watched Maggot walk back to his pickup, then drive away. The vehicle was barely out of sight when another, much muddier pickup came driving down the road. Old Farmer Giles behind the wheel pulled off the road when he saw Liam and his bike in a tangled mess. Liam made up a story about hitting a pothole. The farmer smiled good-naturedly, clearly not believing a word of it, then put Liam's bike into the back of his truck, helped Liam into the cab and drove him home.

Liam learned a lot about sheep that evening.

Now, in his kitchen at three-thirty in the morning, he sipped at the hot tea and debated whether to call the police. In general, he didn't have a good word to say about them, but the two detectives who'd interviewed him struck him as different to the rest of the lazy bastards who were only interested in handing out speeding fines. There was a chance they knew the identity of Maggot's employer, and were desperate for any new information.

But did Liam want to see the man who ordered Harry's execution go to jail? Maybe wriggle out of it or walk away with nothing more than a slapped wrist. Or did he want Maggot to do what Liam had fantasised he might do himself to avenge his brother's death? Gun in the mouth and pull the trigger until the magazine clicked empty, and bollocks to the mess on the carpet.

Liam was only surprised the decision wasn't as easy as he thought it would be.

41

'You already interviewed him?'

Angel knew DCI Olivia Finch wasn't deliberately working the accusation and disappointment into her voice and onto her face, but she needed to spend time in front of the mirror practicing, especially if she had her heart set on continuing up the greasy pole.

'Uh-huh. Ralph Stone. DS Ellis Hudson also interviewed him when Baldwin was killed. Stone came forward, said he'd been driving towards Callaghan's lorry when it hit Baldwin...'

'To tell Hudson he didn't see anyone push him?'

'Yep. He's clever, too. He mentioned seeing Lacy Cooper's kid running towards the road. That then fitted with what Cooper told Gulliver and Jardine—'

'For Christ's sake, Padre...'

The exclamation hit him where it hurt. He'd been giving himself a hard time ever since Astrid Persson knocked him onto his arse with the name Ralph Stone. Until that point, all they'd got was the nickname Maggot, so called because of his bald head and resemblance to Telly Savalas. Angel noticed Stone's toupée when he interviewed him. He was annoyed at himself for not putting it together, however much of a stretch that would've been. What he didn't need was Finch also giving him a hard time. He was about to say something insubordinate, ask her what it was like reviewing everybody else's work and decisions with the benefit of hindsight, when the exasperation in her voice told him he'd reacted too fast.

'Will you stop looking at my bloody coffee machine and just pour yourself a cup.'

Whoosh!

Angel didn't wait to be told twice, even managed to remember to pour her one—although her outstretched hand and fingers flicking at him, *gimme here*, was an unmissable aide memoire.

'What did Agnetha have to say about him?' Finch asked, making it sound like, *do I want to hear this?*

He wasn't sure if her saying Agnetha was a rare Finch joke referring to the Abba singer or genuine confusion over the two similar Swedish women's names. He didn't bother to ask.

'*Astrid* thinks he's ex-MI5. Seymour Grey was a parliamentary private secretary to the Home Secretary at one point. As such, he would've been privy to some of the dealings the Home Secretary had with the security service. Astrid thinks Stone screwed up at some point and Grey covered for him. Ms Persson and details are not natural bedfellows, unless you're talking about the detailing on a Gucci handbag or shoes. Whatever it was, Stone ended up in Grey's pocket.'

'Doesn't sound like a good place to be.'

'It isn't. Astrid reckons they hate each other. She might not be big on detail, but she can read people well enough.'

'Do I take it Stone was kicked out for over-stepping the mark with something he did for Grey?'

The question took Angel straight back to Astrid Persson's luxury apartment. He'd asked her the same question. Which is when he'd got the impression she wasn't as stupid as she liked to make out. She claimed Stone threatened her, forced her into giving Grey an alibi. She also claimed she'd agreed to do so because she believed Grey was innocent. He'd had no part in Orla St. James' death, but his life would be ruined nonetheless if it became known he was there. As far as Astrid was concerned, Grey's only crime was in not reporting the tragic accident to the police himself. She was adamant she knew nothing of the subsequent deaths of Russell Baldwin and Harry Callaghan. As such, she was unable to comment on what Stone might or might not have done for Grey and been kicked out of MI5 for.

'Probably,' Angel said, then explained.

Finch let out a sigh when he'd finished, a rising tide of weary resignation.

'We'll never know.'

'Nope. My guess is that Stone's superiors knew he was in Grey's pocket and weren't happy about it. They were actively looking for an opportunity to get rid of him. They knew he was involved in Baldwin's death in some way but couldn't prove it, and quietly kicked him out anyway. He didn't complain because he knew things would get worse for him if he pushed them into a full investigation. That's also consistent with the different modus operandi. Stone pushed Baldwin in front of a lorry—something that could be and was viewed as an accident—while he was still employed and had to be circumspect about what he did for Grey. He was off the books by the time he took Harry Callaghan out to the New Forest and executed him, and didn't give a shit what it looked like to anyone.'

Finch's brow creased in confusion, as Angel's had when the same question she now asked had crossed his mind.

'If Stone's already out on his ear, why did he continue to do Grey's dirty work?'

'Presumably whatever Grey had on him was sufficiently

damning that even the security service couldn't sweep it under the carpet. As you said, we'll never know.'

It wasn't a problem. Not knowing why Stone had done what he did wouldn't take the shine off the satisfaction of matching his DNA to the blood sample taken from Callaghan's forehead, and having Lacy Cooper identify him as the man she saw push Baldwin. With a suspect in custody and premises and vehicles to be searched, further evidence was almost guaranteed to be found.

That wasn't all.

Stone had nowhere to turn. The security service would act like they'd never heard of him. With no other options available, they were hoping he would give up Seymour Grey as part of a plea bargain.

They had to catch him first, of course.

Easier said than done. He wasn't your average man in the street. He would be well aware of the methods used to trace and track people, adept at sidestepping them himself. The phone number Angel had called to arrange to meet with him was now out of service. No doubt it had been that way five minutes after Angel finished interviewing him. As for the address he'd given, nobody at the premises had ever heard of a bald-headed man called either Stone or Maggot. His ex-employer would have details of every aspect of his life—and in far greater depth than any normal employer was entitled to hold—but getting access to that information presented a different set of problems altogether. Problems that would not be resolved by anyone holding the ranks currently drinking coffee in Finch's office.

There was also the possibility that Astrid Persson would tell Grey about their visit. Dire warnings from Angel not to do so paled into insignificance beside the threat of a late-night visit from a man as ruthless as Ralph Stone. Grey would then alert Stone, who would be doubly cautious.

The final unknown was whether Stone's killing spree was over, whether the decks were sufficiently clear for his master to call him off. Specifically, whether Liam Callaghan was still at risk.

It was why Gulliver and Jardine were currently en route to Liam's house as Angel and Finch contemplated the enormity of the task ahead.

42

Sitting in the stolen pickup backed into a field entrance a quarter mile from the stone gate posts that marked the entrance to Seymour Grey's country residence, *Woodlands,* Ralph Stone felt more at peace with himself, more in control of his own destiny, than he had since his wife left him all those years ago.

Apologising to Liam Callaghan had been cathartic. It made him feel how he guessed an alcoholic must feel as they embark on the ninth step—making amends to those you've harmed.

Except what he would do in the hours ahead made a mockery of the second part of that commitment.

Make amends to those we have harmed, except when doing so would injure them or others.

People don't get any more injured than Seymour Grey would today.

He wished he could have granted Liam Callaghan his wish and brought him along, given him the chance to personally avenge his brother. His refusal wasn't only because of what he'd told Liam, that he wouldn't like the way the day would end. Ralph Stone knew all too well, had the scars on his conscience to prove just how hard it is to pull something as small as a gun's trigger when the man on his knees before you, already drowning in the viscous slime of his own snot, begs for his life, hot piss unchecked by muscle or shame streaming down his trouser leg.

Liam Callaghan would have come away disgusted with himself that he'd failed his brother, tears of shame in his own eyes that when push came to shove, he wasn't man enough. He'd still have his humanity intact, but what does a man who can't look himself in the mirror care about that?

From thoughts of Liam Callaghan, Stone's mind, his tormentor par excellence, took him deeper into his personal shame, a picture of Russell Baldwin's girlfriend, pregnant Véronique Dubois with her big swollen belly, in his mind. Stone hoped that even if Grey had got the cancerous idea into the open sewer of his mind that Véronique posed a threat and should be dealt with as Baldwin had been, he, Stone, the man they all laughed at and called Maggot, would have drawn a line. Told Seymour Evil to go fuck himself in his arrogant, self-serving arse.

He was very grateful he would never have to find out.

An older pickup than the one he was sitting in drove past as Stone sat and nursed his morbid thoughts. Flat cap on his head and cheeks red raw from a lifetime in the wind and rain, Stone would've swapped places with the driver in an instant, rejoiced in a life of shovelling horse shit and milking cows as they farted in his face.

A weaker man might weep at the unfairness of life. How one mistake led to another down a road that permits no turning back, sacrificing his humanity in the faithful service of a man who caused the grass to wither beneath his feet. And does the Almighty give a flying shit whether it was unwilling service or not?

Because Ralph Stone had blood on his hands just the same. And there would be more of the same before the day was out.

'Looks like he's still alive,' Lisa Jardine said, seeing a shadowy figure approach through the opaque glass in Liam Callaghan's front door. 'Hang on. He's stopped. He must know it's us.' She hammered on the door again, yelled through the glass like a fishwife in the docks. 'We can see you, Mr Callaghan. Might as well let us in.'

'How could he resist an offer like that?' Gulliver asked himself under his breath, as Callaghan resumed his journey towards them on the other side of the door.

The front door opened a moment later. The man who opened it didn't look anything like they'd been led to expect. They'd been told Liam Callaghan looked a lot like his brother. The man in front of them fitted that description perfectly—given that Harry Callaghan had been dead and in a refrigerated drawer in the morgue for the best part of two weeks. Liam looked haunted, and not by his dead brother. Being informed that the man who'd killed his brother had been watching his house would've taken the edge off his day, but even so.

Jardine checked it was actually the right man.

'Liam Callaghan?'

'Yeah.'

'We need to have a word.' Already moving past him into the house, Gulliver bringing up the rear.

Jardine went straight down the hall and into the kitchen. A bicycle was sitting upside down on a towel on the kitchen table, its rear wheel removed. She couldn't help smiling to herself, thinking they'd mistaken the expression on Liam's face.

'Now I know why you look so guilty, servicing your bike on the kitchen table while your wife's out.'

'I'm not married.'

The denial put a small dent in Jardine's flow, but not much.

'Then let me give you some womanly advice. You're likely to stay that way if you bring anyone home and they see that on the kitchen table. Makes them worry about what you might keep hidden under your bed.'

Gulliver had been inspecting the bike as Jardine delivered her unasked-for advice. Now, he pointed at the rear forks.

'How did they end up bent like that?'

It was obvious what Liam wanted to say. *Like what?* Given he was in the middle of working on the bike, even he could see it wasn't going to wash.

'I had an accident.'

If he'd wanted to be evasive, he should've chosen a different word. A tumble. A mishap. Not accident. His brother killing Russell Baldwin had been passed off as an accident until very recently. And look where that led.

Gulliver took a closer look at the damaged forks, gave his considered opinion.

'You don't get damage like that going down a pot hole. Did somebody hit you?'

Jardine had been looking closely at Liam himself while Gulliver concentrated on the bike. It seemed to her he was keeping his hands very close to his sides.

'Show me your hands, Mr Callaghan.'

Liam hesitated momentarily, but her tone—*don't make me ask twice*—clinched it. He held them towards her, palms down, as if it was his fingernails she was interested in.

'Now turn them over.'

He did so, as reluctantly as if he'd got a bag of cocaine taped to each palm.

Jardine winced.

'That looks painful. You need to buy yourself a better pair of gloves.'

Gulliver re-phrased her earlier question as Liam ignored her.

'Who hit you, Mr Callaghan?'

'Some old pickup.'

'Not a black Range Rover?'

Liam gave a scornful laugh.

'What? Like the one your lunatic sergeant chased down the road? I do know the difference between a Range Rover and a pickup truck.'

'Maybe so,' Jardine said. 'But I'd put money on the fact that you don't know the difference between acting like a normal, sensible person and being a complete twat who wants to get himself killed like his big brother did.'

'Tell us what happened,' Gulliver interrupted before Liam had a chance to object to Jardine's tone and remark. 'You've obviously been knocked off your bike. The fact that you're here means you had a very lucky escape. You might not be so lucky next time.'

Liam stared back at them both. They could see his brain turning like the gears on his bike. What they couldn't see was why he didn't want to say anything. As far as Jardine was concerned, there was only one possible explanation.

'You've just been knocked off your bike, and yet you're still clinging to some stupid idea about getting even with your brother's killer, avenging his death yourself. Let me tell you something about this man. He's ex-MI5. You might be great in a pub brawl, but you haven't got a chance against somebody like him. I have no idea why you're not already dead.'

Liam stared hard at her for a long moment, the gears still turning.

'Because . . .' He paused, making the brief lack of words sound like *shit for brains*, 'he's not interested in killing me. He knocked me off my bike because he wanted to apologise for killing Harry.'

Jardine looked at him as if she suspected he'd landed on his head, not his hands.

'*Apologise?*'

'Yeah. You know, say sorry. He said he wished he could turn back the clock.'

Gulliver and Jardine shared a look as Liam waited for one of them to say something.

'What else did he say?' Gulliver asked.

'Nothing.'

The reply came back so fast Gulliver recoiled.

Then Jardine was in Liam's face.

'*Jesus Christ*, Callaghan. You're determined to go the complete twat route, aren't you? Don't you realise if you say *no* that fast, we hear *yes*? Tell us what else he said.'

'He's going after his own boss, isn't he?' Gulliver said from behind Jardine's aggression. 'Nobody knocks a man off his bike just to say sorry. All you'll do is annoy them more. But sorry, I'm going to get the bastard for you? You didn't mind getting a few scrapes and bruises to be told that, did you?'

'Which is why you don't want to tell us,' Jardine added. 'Because you're scared we'll stop him.'

Liam didn't need to answer. His face said it all.

I hope you're too late.

43

If I was in charge of vehicle acquisition in the security service, I'd get rid of all the black Range Rovers, Ralph Stone thought, *and buy a fleet of pickup trucks.* Black Range Rovers with tinted windows never said anything good about the occupants. Spooks or drug dealers or stupid pricks who wanted other people to think that's what they were.

If he'd been in an ostentatious Range Rover today, Seymour Grey's driver would have been wary of it pulling out from a field entrance as he drove past, then sitting on his tail. But a muddy pickup? What else would you expect to see coming out of a field entrance? Sitting on his tail because Old Farmer Giles driving it was in a hurry, all that horse shit to shovel and sheep to shear.

He hung back as they got closer to the gates, his brain subconsciously interpreting speed and time and distance, allowing for the electric gates to swing open, but not to close again. Grey's driver hit the remote button early, only slowing momentarily. Stone stamped on the accelerator as soon as Grey's Bentley Mulsanne swung in, the same surge of power that ejected Liam Callaghan effortlessly from his bike's saddle kicking in, off the gas and a hard right throwing the pickup through the gates starting to close. Right foot to the floor again, rear end fishtailing out of the turn on the loose gravel, swinging around the Bentley, left hand down into its front wing, the pickup's engine screaming, wheels spinning spitting gravel, the Bentley off the drive and onto the grass now, a massive copper beech immediately ahead. The driver hit the brakes too hard, traction a distant memory, the big car slewing silently on the wet grass, an inexorable slide into the ancient tree.

Stone was out of the pickup by the time the Bentley's bumper hit tree bark. Door wrenched open, Glock 17 thrust into the driver's startled face as he fumbled with his seatbelt.

'*Out!* On your face on the ground.'

Stone dropped to his knees on the driver's back as soon as he was down, punched the breath out of him like it wasn't ever coming back. Twisting his arms behind him, the *zzzzip* of heavy-duty cable ties cinching around his wrists, then dragging him up to his feet again. Leaning into the Bentley to pop the boot, teeth bared at Seymour Grey squealing like a stuck pig in the back seat.

Stone manhandled the driver into the boot, banged the lid shut on his too-slow head, then back into the car for Grey, dragging him bodily out of the back seat, his soft women's hands fluttering, trying to get a grip on his fear, on his phone, his lifeline to help that wasn't ever going to arrive, not in this life. Stone ripped the phone out of Grey's fingers, ground it into the dirt under his heel. Frog-marched the sweaty shaking excuse for a man to the pickup, squatting down, arms around Grey's trembling legs and up, tipping him into the pickup bed where he belonged. A piece of human excrement indistinguishable from the horse shit already there. Except at least horse shit is useful for something.

He thought about moving the Bentley, using it to block the gates. If he parked sideways across the drive immediately inside them, the gates wouldn't be able to open even if the police had the remote control.

On any other day, in any other circumstances, it's what he would've done.

Just not today.

Instead, he climbed into the leathery opulence of the Bentley, backed it away from the tree and onto the drive, then opened the gates as he approached them. As soon as they were fully open, he rammed the left-hand one, jamming it open, plenty of room for the police vehicles to get past. The whine of the electric motor trying to close the gate against the Bentley's weight followed him all the way back to the pickup.

He was aware of sounds coming out of Grey's mouth, an ever-changing litany of imperious commands, hollow threats and pathetic pleading, all melding into a single irritating white noise that he would soon silence forever.

At the house, he let the pickup's tailgate down, dragged Grey bodily from the truck bed, manhandled him to the front door and then inside, down the long hallway lined with the heads of endangered species Grey's ancestors had shot for their own amusement or Grey himself had bought from a film prop supply company. Past the staircase curving off on the left and then into Grey's inner sanctum, his study, the den of iniquity where all of Grey's schemes to enrich himself at other people's expense were spawned.

Stone pushed him roughly into the big chair behind the even-bigger desk with its carefully-antiqued red leather inlay, then pulled a folded document from his pocket, laid it in front of the man who'd made his life a misery for more years than he cared to remember.

'Sign that.'

Grey stopped his incessant whining long enough to read the first line.

Last Will and Testament.

He didn't bother reading any further.

'Have you gone crazy?'

A stupid question. They both knew he had. A long time ago.

Stone picked up a gold fountain pen shaped like a dildo as Grey sat frozen in stunned silence. Thrust it between Grey's unresisting fingers.

'*Sign it!*'

Still Grey seemed incapable of causing his limbs to respond. Stone pulled the Glock from his pocket, screwed the barrel into the side of Grey's neck where it overflowed his collar.

Grey came alive with a violent jerk, gripped the pen between his shaking fingers. Put the pen to paper—

'Not there, you fucking idiot,' Stone screamed, grabbing hold of Grey's hand and moving it. '*There!*'

'You're insane,' Grey hissed, but he signed on the line just the same as Stone pushed his whole upper body sideways with the gun.

'You'll pay for this,' Grey spat, his usual arrogance returning as Stone re-folded the document. 'You'll spend the rest of your life in prison sucking child molesters' cocks.'

Stone flicked his wrist, a blur of movement too fast to see. Grey's cheek split apart as the Glock's sight ripped through his flesh as easily as any surgeon's knife, an oozing red pus welling up and spilling down his face like tears of blood, a savage reminder that his words were as welcome as a Tabasco suppository.

'*Shut it!* If I want to hear an arsehole speak, I'll fart.'

Grey shut it. Naively convincing himself that if he acquiesced to this maniac who used to be at his beck and call, there was still some way out for him.

He was so wrong.

Stone had thought long and hard about what came next

while he sat waiting in the pickup. His initial thoughts about making Grey's death long-drawn-out and painful had quickly been dismissed in a moment of clarity. By doing so, he would only demean himself. It made no difference to Orla St. James, Russell Baldwin or Harry Callaghan.

Because Ralph Stone knew there was no such thing as God, or the ever after. That they, the slaughtered innocents, were not sitting white-robed at His feet. Looking down on him, hearts filled with a spiteful satisfaction that would banish them to the eternal fires of hell, as he avenged the wrongs he'd perpetrated against them on Grey's behalf.

And above all else, he was a professional, not a sick crazy fuck.

He took hold of the back of Grey's chair, swivelled it so that the immoral, venal monster was facing him, pressed the barrel of the Glock against his forehead and blew his poisoned brains all over the red flock wallpaper.

Ralph Stone wasn't sure he'd ever derived such satisfaction from a job long-overdue, now successfully accomplished.

It was a pity it would be so short-lived.

He put the Glock's barrel into his mouth, the taste of metal he'd always wondered about on his tongue ...

44

'Is this what being a professional is all about?' Kincade asked, left hand braced on the dashboard as Angel threw the car around a curve. 'Not hoping we get stuck behind a tractor and we're too late to save Grey before Stone gets to him.'

Angel glanced in his rearview mirror at Finch in the back seat, her phone to one ear, finger in the other to cut down the road noise. He lowered his voice nonetheless.

'I think that's called not being human.'

'That implies you can't be both.'

'Not at the same time, no.'

The philosophy was running high as they sped towards Seymour Grey's country residence, Gulliver's car so close on Angel's rear bumper their eyes met every time Angel glanced in the mirror, Armed Response Vehicles from the Tactical Firearms Unit also on the way.

Both ends of the lane on which Grey's property was located had been closed off, uniformed officers re-directing irritated, inconvenienced motorists. A police helicopter circled noisily above.

'I don't think they're going to be necessary,' Angel said,

raising his voice as the pulsating *whop whop whop* of the helicopter's rotor wash resonated in the car. 'Not if they're watching for Stone escaping on foot across the fields.'

'You think he'll have topped himself after killing Grey?'

'It fits with him apologising to Liam Callaghan.'

As was often the case when the adrenaline was flowing, humour and insubordinate ridicule found a way in. Angel knew what Kincade was going to say even before she opened her mouth.

'A bit like going to confession, you mean? Admit your sins, say you're sorry, then straight into the front row in heaven, no questions asked.'

The sight of two Armed Response Vehicles waiting outside the gates to Grey's property up ahead gave him an excuse to not answer. She wasn't looking for one, anyway. The fun's in the asking.

'What's going on there?' she said, as they pulled to a halt in front of the gates, one of them jammed open by an abandoned Bentley Mulsanne.

The answer was obvious. Angel said it nonetheless, his pulse quickening.

'Looks like an invitation to me.'

She glanced up at the helicopter circling overhead.

'I'm not sure about Stone killing himself, but I don't think he'd be stupid enough to make a run for it.'

Neither of them needed to say out loud the only option that left.

A sergeant from the Tactical Firearms Unit met them as they got out, looking like something out of a *Terminator* movie, dressed all in black. Balaclava tucked under his chin and goggles pushed up over his helmet, his Heckler & Koch HK416 carbine cradled loosely in his hands.

He waited for Finch to finish her call, then brought them up to speed.

'Grey's driver was in the boot of the Bentley. Stone's armed with a Glock 17. The driver can't be sure, but he thinks he heard a single gunshot.' His tone of voice reflected his scepticism. Grey's driver had been inside the boot of the car, disorientated in the dark, expecting to hear the sound of the Glock 17 that had been stuck in his face being fired. The sound he actually heard might have been a bird scarer in a neighbouring field or a farmer with a shotgun. 'We have to assume Stone is alive and armed. The driver told us Grey keeps shotguns and deer-hunting rifles in the house. We also have to recognise that Grey might still be alive.'

Stone wants to go down in a blaze of glory, Angel thought, and didn't share.

'You want to go in?' Finch said.

The black-clad sergeant with his evil-looking black carbine glanced down the driveway towards the house.

'We don't have any option, ma'am. I don't think he plans on coming out voluntarily.'

Everyone in earshot did the translation from *voluntarily* to *not in a body bag*.

Ordinarily, the function of strategic firearms commander or tactical firearms commander must not be undertaken by the SIO responsible for the investigation, or by any other person connected to it.

The exception is during a kidnap operation, prior to the safe recovery of the hostage and where the operational priority is the preservation of life.

Given the possibility of Seymour Grey still being alive, that put the ball firmly in Finch's court. She nodded once, effectively signing Ralph Stone's death warrant.

'Go ahead.'

The two ARVs led the way, four officers in each, followed by Angel, with Gulliver bringing up the rear, the detectives all now wearing ballistic vests. The ARVs separated at the end of the drive, Angel and Gulliver's cars coming to a halt between them, the four vehicles in a curved line facing the front of the house. Everybody was out before the echoes of tyres crunching on gravel had died away.

Which is when the Tactical Firearms Unit's sergeant was proved wrong.

The front door opened and Ralph Stone stepped out, a double-barrelled shotgun held at his side.

There was a flurry of activity as the firearms officers scrambled into position, eight Heckler & Koch HK416s trained on Stone seconds later, the air filled with the sound of men wired to the eyeballs on adrenaline shouting over and over.

Armed police! Put the gun down!

Stone stared back at them, a bemused expression on his face as if he'd come out to shoot a few rabbits that had been causing havoc in the vegetable patch and was surprised to see them on his front drive.

Angel yelled at the firearms officers to stop yelling, glanced at Finch and got a nod of authorisation, then addressed Stone when the clamour died down.

'Put the gun down, Stone.'

Stone kept hold of it.

'Isn't this where you say we can work something out?' He cocked his head at Angel when he didn't reply. 'What exactly could we work out, Inspector? A reduced sentence down from fifty years to forty, on account of me doing the country a service killing Seymour Grey? Or were you thinking of my eternal soul? You'll put in a good word with the man upstairs for me? Don't look so surprised. I made some calls after we met. You're an interesting man. I've heard they call you *Padre*. I'd have liked to see your face across an interview table trying to tell me killing a degenerate like Seymour Grey was a sin.' He touched his throat with his free hand, the movement causing a ripple of tension through the men facing him from behind their cars. 'I bet those words would've stuck in your craw, Padre. Because you know as well as I do nothing's black and white. It's all grey, heaven help us.' He smiled, tipped his head backwards at the house behind him. 'Although it's a little bit less grey than it was when I got here.'

'Don't do this, Stone.'

Stone looked along the line of armed men facing him.

'Don't do what, Padre? And aren't you meant to call me Ralph? Try to build a rapport between us so that I lay down the gun—notice how I didn't raise it as I referred to it—and your trigger-happy friends here don't get a chance to use their toys.'

Again, he looked along the line of men who only saw him as *the target*, his voice mocking.

'How many kills have you got, boys? Anyone into double figures yet? No? Shame on you!'

Angel screamed at him, the voice of desperation, of a man pissing into the wind. A futile attempt to stop events that had been ordained long before he'd ever heard the name Ralph Stone, a relentless advance towards the inevitable.

'*Stone! Don't!*'

But Ralph Stone did.

The last words he would ever utter were filled with the insane glee of a man pushed beyond the limits of his sanity, trapped in a war of attrition waged against his humanity.

'Here's a free kill on me, boys!'

With that, he raised the shotgun and charged at Angel. Eyes wild and a scream from the bottom of his blackened soul, spit-flecked lips pulled back over teeth bared like a rabid dog's.

A bullet ripped through his throat before any of them even

heard the shot. Then another, and another. Small explosions erupting on the surface of his body, little puffs of blood exiting his back. No movie-style boneyard foxtrot jerking like an epileptic marionette, just a slow, graceful sagging to his knees, then toppling silently face-first into the gravel, *whoomph*, an impact Angel felt in every bone in his body.

'Are we supposed to feel like we failed?' Kincade asked, as they stood in the doorway to Seymour Grey's study and contemplated his corpse slumped forward across his desk, the back of his head a bloody mess, more of the same spattered across the wall behind him.

'Failed who?' Angel replied, his voice a low growl of warning that set Kincade's teeth on edge.

She didn't even think about going there.

Instead, she stepped into the room, went over to the desk.

'There's a note.'

A squeak of incredulous laughter slipped past Angel's teeth.

'Don't tell me Stone forced him to write a confession. From what we've been led to believe, there'd be a stack of paper an inch thick if he did.'

Kincade picked the single, folded sheet up with a blue-gloved hand, opened it, instinctively reading the first line.

'Last will and testament...'

'Not much point forcing Grey to leave him everything if he was about to play at being a target for the armed response guys. Unless—' His mouth clamped shut when he saw Kincade's face, an expression on it he couldn't read. 'What?'

'It's not Seymour Grey's will.'

She offered him the document rather than say more, then watched him as he read aloud.

'I, Ralph Edward Stone, being of sound mind, declare this to be my last will and testament . . .' He trailed off, reading the remainder silently, then looked up at her smiling at him. 'He left it all to Véronique Dubois. Seymour Grey witnessed it before Stone shot him.'

'Yep. Stone might not have much to leave, but it's better than a poke in the eye with a sharp stick.'

Angel flicked his fingers dismissively at Grey's still-warm corpse.

'Don't be so sure. Grey will have paid him well for doing his dirty work. That way Stone couldn't ever claim he had no choice.'

A shudder rippled through Kincade at the suggestion.

'I don't know how I'd feel about receiving money paid to the man who killed my unborn baby's father.'

'Then you better not tell her where it came from.'

'We'll tell her it came from heaven, shall we?'

'She can always refuse it. Or she can take it and use it to do something good with it. Continue Baldwin's work exposing corrupt politicians, maybe? That's got a nice poetic justice feel about it.'

'I suppose. Let's hope she doesn't call her child Luca.'

'I think what you're referring to is spelled *l-u-c-r-e*.'

'How do you know that's not how I was spelling it?'

The somewhat pointless conversation continued as they made their way out of the house to wait for the forensic pathologist to arrive and perform an equally pointless procedure—pronouncing the blindingly obvious, that both Stone and Grey were indeed good and dead.

They joined Durand beside Ralph Stone's body when she turned up half an hour later.

'Careful when you cut this one open, Doctor,' Kincade said, mock concern in her voice. 'You're going to find a big soft heart inside.'

45

'It's like a caravan,' Angel said, 'just not as big and with a pointy end.'

Vanessa Corrigan did well not to laugh at his assessment.

'I'd recommend you don't apply for a job as a salesman at a yacht broker should you ever decide to leave the police.'

They were in the saloon of her yacht, a 1972 Nicholson 32 offshore cruiser, which, being a Mark 10, was actually thirty-three feet long. She was giving him the grand tour, although he would've questioned the use of the word *grand*, had *Desiderata* not been her pride and joy, her means of escape from the bedlam and relentless pressure of her job as Deputy Governor of HMP Isle of Wight.

He'd smiled to himself when he saw the boat's name, and then again when he noticed the full poem framed on the wall in the saloon. His father liked to quote Kipling's *If* as if it charted the one true path through all of life's problems and uncertainties. For him, it was the words of *Desiderata* that epitomised his approach to life in an increasingly frenetic and indifferent world, its first line in particular.

Go placidly amid the noise and the haste, and remember what peace there may be in silence.

Vanessa didn't miss the expression on his face as he read the first few lines, but chose to say nothing, comfortable, as was he, that words were not required to acknowledge the presence of a kindred spirit.

'Which way up do you sleep?' he asked, now standing in the doorway to the forward cabin—what he'd called the pointy end —the single berths on either side converging ahead of him. 'Heads this end so you can play footsie, or heads together at the pointy end?'

She worked a look of blissful rapture onto her face that didn't sit well with the mischief in her voice.

'You make it sound so romantic.'

He glanced at the sea toilet as he came back into the saloon, thinking its proximity to the berths dictated which way he'd choose to sleep.

'There's nothing romantic about that.'

'I don't suppose the facilities in Iraq and Afghanistan were any better. And didn't you live in a bare cell as a priest?'

'You're confusing priests with monks. I didn't wear a hair shirt, either.'

He slid onto the bench behind the galley table on what he was learning to call the port side of the boat, bounced up and down a couple of times.

'I think I'd rather sleep here.'

She nodded like it was a fair point.

'It converts into a double berth.'

He looked at the distance between the bench and the table, a frown appearing on his brow.

'Looks more like a one-and-a-half-person berth to me. Maybe even one and a quarter.'

She raised an eyebrow at him, words unnecessary. Then changed the subject as a faint flush climbed up her neck.

'Unless you want to take a look at the engine—'

'Let's save that for later.'

'—we'll get going.'

Despite the discussion around sleeping arrangements, they hadn't planned an overnight stay. Although the famous yachtswoman Claire Francis had single-handedly crossed the Atlantic in a Nicholson 32 Mark IV named *Gulliver G* in 1973, Vanessa had planned something a little less adventurous for Angel's maiden voyage.

From Southsea Marina where *Desiderata* was berthed, they would sail a more modest fifteen miles to the Folly Inn on the Medina River, a couple of miles south of East Cowes on the Isle of Wight. The pub where they would have lunch was less than two miles as the cormorant flies from where Vanessa worked, but it was far enough removed in every other way for it not to be a problem.

A small problem occurred when Angel was delegated the vitally important task of untying the bow and stern lines and asked if she meant what he called *these ropes*.

She explained that *rope* usually refers to a material. *Lines* are made of rope. What a particular line is called is then dictated by its purpose—halyards for hoisting sails, sheets for trimming sails, docking lines to stop the boat from drifting unattended out to sea.

'I'll just untie these ropes,' he muttered under his breath, as her border collie, Jasper, supervised and barked advice from the foredeck.

Except his phone rang before he got a chance to do so.

He knew exactly who it was calling.

He'd tried calling Virgil Balan a couple of times, but it had gone to voicemail on both occasions. He'd left a message asking

Balan to return his call both times. Afterwards, he'd spent a long time navel-gazing, unsure if he wasn't secretly relieved he'd been unable to make contact with Balan, give him the green light on what might lead to dark places.

The respite, the delay in actually saying the words that might forever damn him and Stuart Beckford, had been nice while it lasted.

And now it was over.

He pulled out his phone, saw that he was right. He called to Captain Corrigan that he needed to take the call, then wandered back along the pontoon.

'I was starting to think you were avoiding me, Virgil.'

The good-natured chuckle Angel guessed hid so much came down the line at him.

'*Never, Padre!* I've been busy, that's all. You know how it is.'

Angel knew how, but not what. Balan may have been referring to the work he performed for the Poliția Română who paid his salary, or he might have meant busy undermining the efforts of that police force on behalf of the people-trafficking gang his half-brother had worked for.

'Have you talked to your friend, Stuart Beckford?' Balan asked, when the words Angel wanted to say stuck in his throat.

'Uh-huh. We'd like you to go ahead.' It struck him Finch had used the exact same phrase, *go ahead*, to authorise the Tactical Firearms Unit to enter Seymour Grey's house. Two words that resulted in Ralph Stone's death. Would those same two words spoken by him now result in the death of Bogdan Florescu? At his own and Stuart Beckford's hands, or those of Virgil Balan, disgusted that the two British policemen didn't have it in them to beat a man to death in cold blood.

'Go ahead?' Balan repeated, as if there was an echo on the line.

Angel almost laughed out loud. Wanted to ask Balan if the call was being recorded.

'Yes, Virgil. We'd like you to locate Bogdan Florescu's whereabouts. I will, of course, make enquiries on my end about extraditing him back to the UK. You might be better versed in that than me. I'd appreciate any assistance you can give in that respect.'

He wouldn't have been surprised to hear the sounds on the other end of the line mute as Balan wedged his phone between his shoulder and ear in order for him to applaud.

'Excellent, Padre.'

As with everything Balan said, Angel had no idea whether he was expressing his enthusiastic agreement with Angel's decision or complimenting him on covering his arse so well.

'And should I contact you on this number to keep you updated, or is there anyone in your team who will be dealing with it?'

Stop playing games with me, Balan, Angel thought and was a hair's breadth away from saying.

'Use this number for now, Virgil.'

'Perfect, Padre. I hope to have good news for you very soon.'

Is Florescu already in a cell? Angel thought as Balan ended the call. An unofficial one nobody ever returns from because nobody ever knew they were there in the first place.

'Everything okay?' Vanessa said, after Angel had untied the lines and hopped into the cockpit beside her, where Jasper immediately started nuzzling his leg. 'It doesn't look like it from your face.'

He gave the dog's head a brisk rub, thought about making a joke of it. Saying he was worried because he'd heard lady boat skippers were as bad as lady drivers on the roads. He wasn't sure whether what he did say was serious or not.

'How about a change of route? Go around the Isle of Wight and keep on going.'

'As bad as that, eh?'

She was aware of the circumstances of his wife's death, but not Balan's offer. Their relationship was still in its infancy. She needed to see the good in him before he admitted to entering into a pact that might result in him sacrificing a part of his humanity in the name of revenge.

His hesitation told her the call hadn't been a simple case of his job allowing him no respite. Momentarily, she looked as if she was going to press him, then she decided against it, moved them on. He wasn't sure he liked the way she did it, stepping away from the tiller.

'Here, you take it.' She waited until he'd done as he was told, then gave some advice that shouldn't have been necessary. 'Remember, move it in the opposite direction to the way you want to go.'

The simple instruction put more of a crease in his brow than it should have in a man entrusted with running complex investigations that had a direct impact on the public's safety.

Except that wasn't it at all.

'I never realised steering a boat was a metaphor for life itself.'

She snuggled up close beside him, a guiding hand on top of his on the tiller when he got too close to another boat, then looped her arm around his waist when she deemed it safe to do so, only open sea ahead of them.

He got the hang of it soon enough, even if everything was arse about face. He still had a question for her.

'Should we go to the left of the Isle of Wight or the right to get around it?'

'You decide. You're the skipper.'

'Better hope that's not another metaphor for life, or I'll end up steering us straight into the path of an oil tanker...'

A finger pressed to his lips told him enough was enough.

'Just breathe in all that fresh sea air and shut up.'

'You can't talk to the skipper like that. I'll have you flogged.'

'Is that a promise...?'

Maybe this sailing lark isn't so bad after all, he thought, as they fought over the tiller, the open sea and the endless horizon beckoning, had the Isle of Bloody Wight not been in the way.

ALSO BY THE AUTHOR

The Angel & Kincade Murder Mysteries

THE REVENANT

After ex-drug dealer Roy Lynch is found hanged in his garage, a supposed routine suicide soon becomes more insidious. As the body count rises, DI Max Angel and DS Catalina Kincade are forced to look to the past, cutting through thirty years of deceit and betrayal and lies to reveal the family secrets buried below. The tragedy they unearth makes it horrifically clear that in a world filled with hatred and pain, nothing comes close to what families do to one another.

OLD EVIL

When private investigator Charlie Slater is found shot dead in his car on historic Lepe beach, DI Max Angel and his team find themselves torn between the present and the past. Did Slater's own chequered past lead to his death at the hands of the family he wronged? Or was it the forgotten secrets from a lifetime ago he unearthed, old evil spawned in Lager Sylt on Alderney, the only Nazi concentration camp ever to sit on British soil?

FORSAKEN

When DI Max Angel and DS Catalina Kincade are called to a hijacked lorry, what they find inside makes them think its destination was a slaughterhouse, not a warehouse. The discovery of a woman's hairs on a blanket makes it clear that cheap Romanian refrigerators weren't the only goods the murdered driver was transporting. After the human cargo is set free by the killers, Angel and Kincade find themselves caught up in a race to locate the girl before the people traffickers catch her and condemn her to a life of sexual slavery.

JUSTICE LIES BLEEDING

When Angel and Kincade are called to Southampton Old Cemetery, not all of the dead bodies they encounter are ancient relics buried six feet underground. In the untamed wilderness of the cemetery's darkest corner a woman sits propped against one of the old gravestones, her hands bound together as if in prayer. As Angel and his team piece together the final days of her life and it becomes apparent she went voluntarily to her death, two questions vex the team - who did she arrange to meet in a graveyard at night and why?

THE UNQUIET DEAD

When a man is found dead in the New Forest, cold-bloodedly shot in the back as he crawled away from his killer, DI Max Angel and DS Catalina Kincade soon learn the victim was more than the out-of-work truck driver and part-time drug smuggler he appeared to be. He's been sticking his nose into the business of a man whose ruthlessness is matched only by his greed and moral corruption, trying to get to the bottom of the tragic accident that left his life in ruins and a muck-raking journalist dead.

The Evan Buckley Thrillers

BAD TO THE BONES

When Evan Buckley's latest client ends up swinging on a rope, he's ready to call it a day. But he's an awkward cuss with a soft spot for a sad story and he takes on one last job—a child and husband who disappeared ten years ago. It's a long-dead investigation that everybody wants to stay that way, but he vows to uncover the truth—and in the process, kick into touch the demons who come to torment him every night.

KENTUCKY VICE

Maverick private investigator Evan Buckley is no stranger to self-induced mayhem—but even he's mystified by the jam college buddy Jesse Springer has got himself into. When Jesse shows up with a wad of explicit photographs that arrived in the mail, Evan finds himself caught up in the most bizarre case of blackmail he's ever encountered—Jesse swears blind he can't remember a thing about it.

SINS OF THE FATHER

Fifty years ago, Frank Hanna made a mistake. He's never forgiven himself. Nor has anybody else for that matter. Now the time has come to atone for his sins, and he hires maverick PI Evan Buckley to peel back fifty years of lies and deceit to uncover the tragic story hidden underneath. Trouble is, not everybody likes a happy ending and some very nasty people are out to make sure he doesn't succeed.

NO REST FOR THE WICKED

When an armed gang on the run from a botched robbery that left a man dead invade an exclusive luxury hotel buried in the mountains of upstate New York, maverick P.I. Evan Buckley has got his work cut out. He just won a trip for two and was hoping for a well-earned rest. But when the gang takes Evan's partner Gina hostage along with the other guests and their spirited seven-year-old daughter, he can forget any kind of rest.

RESURRECTION BLUES

After Levi Stone shows private-eye Evan Buckley a picture of his wife Lauren in the arms of another man, Evan quickly finds himself caught up in Lauren's shadowy past. The things he unearths force Levi to face the bitter truth—that he never knew his wife at all—or any of the dark secrets that surround her mother's death and the disappearance of her father, and soon Evan's caught in the middle of a lethal vendetta.

HUNTING DIXIE

Haunted by the unsolved disappearance of his wife Sarah, PI Evan Buckley loses himself in other people's problems. But when Sarah's scheming and treacherous friend Carly shows up promising new information, the past and present collide violently for Evan. He knows he can't trust her, but he hasn't got a choice when she confesses what she's done, leaving Sarah prey to a vicious gang with Old Testament ideas about crime and punishment.

THE ROAD TO DELIVERANCE

Evan Buckley's wife Sarah went to work one day and didn't come home. He's been looking for her ever since. As he digs deeper into the unsolved death of a man killed by the side of the road, the last known person to see Sarah alive, he's forced to re-trace the footsteps of her torturous journey, unearthing a dark secret from her past that drove her desperate attempts to make amends for the guilt she can never leave behind.

SACRIFICE

When PI Evan Buckley's mentor asks him to check up on an old friend, neither of them are prepared for the litany of death and destruction that he unearths down in the Florida Keys. Meanwhile Kate Guillory battles with her own demons in her search for salvation and sanity. As their paths converge, each of them must make an impossible choice that stretches conscience and tests courage, and in the end demands sacrifice—what would you give to get what you want?

ROUGH JUSTICE

After a woman last seen alive twenty years ago turns up dead, PI Evan Buckley heads off to a small town on the Maine coast where he unearths a series of brutal unsolved murders. The more he digs, lifting the lid on old grievances and buried injustices that have festered for half a lifetime, the more the evidence points to a far worse crime, leaving him facing an impossible dilemma – disclose the terrible secrets he's uncovered or assume the role of hanging judge and dispense a rough justice of his own.

TOUCHING DARKNESS

When PI Evan Buckley stops for a young girl huddled at the side of the road on a deserted stretch of highway, it's clear she's running away from someone or something—however vehemently she denies it. At times angry and hostile, at others scared and vulnerable, he's almost relieved when she runs out on him in the middle of the night. Except he has a nasty premonition that he hasn't heard the last of her. Nor does it take long before he's proved horribly right, the consequences dire for himself and Detective Kate Guillory.

A LONG TIME COMING

Five years ago, PI Evan Buckley's wife Sarah committed suicide in a mental asylum. Or so they told him. Now there's a different woman in her grave and he's got a stolen psychiatric report in his hand and a tormented scream running through his head. Someone is lying to him. With his own sanity at stake, he joins forces with a disgraced ex-CIA agent on a journey to confront the past that leads him to the jungles of Central America and the aftermath of a forgotten war, where memories are long and grievances still raw.

LEGACY OF LIES

Twenty years ago, Detective Kate Guillory's father committed suicide. Nobody has ever told her why. Now a man is stalking her. When PI Evan Buckley takes on the case, his search takes him to the coal mining mountains of West Virginia and the hostile aftermath of a malignant cult abandoned decades earlier. As he digs deeper into the unsolved crimes committed there and discovers the stalker's bitter grudge against Kate, one thing becomes horrifyingly clear – what started back then isn't over yet.

DIG TWO GRAVES

Boston heiress Arabella Carlson has been in hiding for thirty years. Now she's trying to make it back home. But after PI Evan Buckley saves her from being stabbed to death, she disappears again. Hired by her dying father to find her and bring her home safe before the killers hunting her get lucky, he finds there's more than money at stake as he opens up old wounds, peeling back a lifetime of lies and deceit. Someone's about to learn a painful lesson the hard way: Before you embark on a journey of revenge, dig two graves.

ATONEMENT

When PI Evan Buckley delves into an unsolved bank robbery from forty years ago that everyone wants to forget, he soon learns it's anything but what it seems to be. From the otherworldly beauty of Caddo Lake and the East Texas swamps to the bright lights and cheap thrills of Rehoboth Beach, he follows the trail of a nameless killer. Always one step behind, he discovers that there are no limits to the horrific crimes men's greed drives them to commit, not constrained by law or human decency.

THE JUDAS GATE

When a young boy's remains are found in a shallow grave on land belonging to PI Evan Buckley's avowed enemy, the monster Carl Hendricks, the police are desperate for Evan's help in solving a case that's been dead in the water for the past thirteen years. Hendricks is dying, and Evan is the only person he'll share his deathbed confession with. Except Evan knows Hendricks of old. Did he really kill the boy? And if so, why does he want to confess to Evan?

OLD SCORES

When upcoming country music star Taylor Harris hires a private investigator to catch her cheating husband, she gets a lot more than she bargained for. He's found a secret in her past that even she's not aware of - a curse on her life, a blood feud hanging over her for thirty years. But when he disappears, it's down to PI Evan Buckley to pick up the pieces. Was the threat real? And if so, did it disappear along with the crooked investigator? Or did it just get worse?

ONCE BITTEN

When PI Evan Buckley's mentor, Elwood Crow, asks a simple favor of him – to review a twenty-year-old autopsy report – there's only one thing Evan can be sure of: simple is the one thing it won't be. As he heads off to Cape Ann on the Massachusetts coast Evan soon finds himself on the trail of a female serial killer, and the more he digs, the more two questions align themselves. Why has the connection not been made before? And is Crow's interest in finding the truth or in saving his own skin?

NEVER GO BACK

When the heir to a billion-dollar business empire goes missing in the medieval city of Cambridge in England, PI Evan Buckley heads across the Atlantic on what promises to be a routine assignment. But as Evan tracks Barrett Bradlee from the narrow cobbled streets of the city to the windswept watery expanses of the East Anglian fens, it soon becomes clear that the secretive family who hired him to find the missing heir haven't told him the whole truth.

SEE NO EVIL

When Ava Hart's boyfriend, Daryl Pierce, is shot to death in his home on the same night he witnessed a man being abducted, the police are quick to write it off as a case of wrong place, wrong time. Ava disagrees. She's convinced they killed him. And she's hired PI Evan Buckley to unearth the truth. Trouble is, as Evan discovers all too soon, Ava wouldn't recognize the truth if it jumped up and bit her on the ass.

DO UNTO OTHERS

Five years ago, a light aircraft owned by Mexican drug baron and people trafficker Esteban Aguilar went down in the middle of the Louisiana swamps. The pilot and another man were found dead inside, both shot to death. The prisoner who'd been handcuffed in the back was nowhere to be found. And now it's down to PI Evan Buckley to find crime boss Stan Fraser's son Arlo who's gone missing trying to get to the bottom of what the hell happened.

Printed in Dunstable, United Kingdom